Greg Bills

Consider This Home

A Novel

Simon & Schuster
New York London Toronto Sydney Tokyo Singapore

SIMON & SCHUSTER
Rockefeller Center
1230 Avenue of the Americas
New York, New York 10020

SIMON & SCHUSTER and colophon are registered trademarks of Simon & Schuster Inc.

Designed by Deirdre C. Amthor
Manufactured in the United States of America

10   9   8   7   6   5   4   3   2   1

Library of Congress Cataloging-in-Publication Data

Bills, Greg, date.
        Consider this home : a novel / Greg Bills.
             p.   cm.
           1. Young women—United States—Fiction. 2. Mothers and sons—United States—Fiction. 3. Gay fathers—United States—Fiction. 4. Utah—Fiction. 5. Las Vegas (Nev.)—Fiction. I. Title.
PS3552.I473C66   1994
813'.54—dc20   93-38753
                                                                                        CIP

ISBN 0-671-79873-1

For My Parents

Acknowledgments

I wish to thank everyone who has helped my novel move from inside my head onto the pages of this book: my editors, George Hodgman and Gary Luke, unsung hero and copy editor, Gilda Abramowitz, and everyone at Simon & Schuster; my agent, the remarkable and indefatigable Mary Evans; friends and family, who read the novel for me at various times; and most especially, Jeff Solomon, who provided insight and support at every stage of my work on this book.

In memory of MacDonald Harris

Acknowledgments

Home
Is where I want to be
But I guess I'm already there
　　　　—Talking Heads

Summer

Daron: Mom

Daron loves his mom, but he doesn't really know her. When he tries to wrap his mind around his mother and consider her objectively, she ceases to inhabit her physical body. He can observe the woman who lives with him in an apartment in Las Vegas and pays for his clothes and food, but his mom also surrounds him with a vast, invisible field of force, in which love, anger, and need cluster and vibrate. She tingles in his fingertips when he refolds the bath towel after drying his hands rather than leaving it squished and twisted on the rack. She lurks in his T-shirt drawer—in the shirts she has selected, purchased, carried home, unpacked, washed, ironed, folded, and stowed away. Her code is nestled deep inside his understanding of the world; in the ways he interacts with people; in the beliefs he holds about places, colors, and foods; in the ways he performs small tasks such as hanging a new roll of toilet paper with the sheets rolling down against the wall. Her way of seeing meshes as inextricably with his mind as her code for the body twines in the spirals of his DNA.

She is a natural force, and he is her natural product. Yet, unlike other manmade objects—unlike a comic book, whose ink and paper can be traced to a certain printing press, a paper mill, a factory—his origin in the unseen assembly plant of her body seems increasingly unlikely to him as he grows. Despite the evidence, he finds it difficult to imagine that his ten-year-old body ever fit inside her, that his birth could have occurred.

His teachers have told Daron that he is gifted, and he believes he is old enough to figure out the world. He knows that his mom has raised him on her own and that she loves him, but he needs to learn more if he is going to understand. When he wrote a research paper on witchcraft in the spring, his teacher emphasized the importance of applying a scientific method to his research; Mrs. Carlson baffled his fourth-grade class with her insistence on primary and secondary sources, warranted information, and source credibility. Unfortunately, his mom is his sole primary source; no other woman in the world is *his* mother.

His mom is always turning over a receipt or tearing a scrap from the newspaper in order to jot down a column of groceries to buy, chores to do, or questions to ask at parent-teacher conference. She claims it puts her mind in order and makes her thoughts concrete. Daron decides to follow her example and find out what he knows. He spreads his red notebook open against his knees, then stares at the stretch of white ceiling above his bed to compose his catalogue.

MAGAZINE MOTHERS: His mom's magazines are full of articles about mothers with unruly children. His favorites are the problem columns: "I Stole My Daughter's Boyfriend," "I Found My Son Wearing My Clothes." Her magazines are stuffed with glowing advertisements of working mothers with briefcases on the table and sponge mops in their hands. Their children peer into the kitchen with faces as clean and shiny bright as mannequins.

FAIRY-TALE MOTHERS: Most of them are dead before the stories begin. A plague of stepmothers has taken their place. They are vain, avaricious, and evil. They believe their stepchildren eat too much food, their stepdaughters are too beautiful, their stepsons are too fond of their husbands' first wives. The stepmothers have the same problems as the women in the magazine columns, but they act more directly: Lock them in a tower! Banish them to the woods! Cut out their hearts! The truth Daron finds in fairy tales is that there is no love outside the bond of blood; if a child loses his mother, his throat will be exposed to the claws of every witch in the kingdom. He doesn't like to think about this.

TV MOTHERS: Marge Simpson. Carol Brady. Roseanne Connor. Claire Huxtable. Laura Petrie. Harriet Nelson. Donna Reed (he can't remember her last name in the series). Samantha. June Lockhart—who plays Mrs. Robinson on *Lost in Space* and Lassie's mother (well, Lassie's owner's mother). The woman who marries the father toward the end of *My Three Sons*. The woman who marries the man on *Eight Is Enough*. The woman who lives with her mother and her male housekeeper who used to play a driver on *Taxi*. He doesn't believe that there are really mothers like these loose in the world.

MOVIE MOTHERS: He has rented *Aliens* three times so far from the store in the shopping center. His mom won't stay in the room when he watches it. When she passes through to get a drink from the kitchen or carry clothes out to the laundry, she shakes her head and says, It amazes me how many times they get that woman to strip to her underwear. He ignores his mom and watches the mother monster, a black leather praying mantis with a dripping Erector set tower protruding from her throat. She detaches from her distended egg-laying sac with a squelch to skitter after Ripley, the heroine. She stalks and hunts and kills, but the movie never explains her motives. Does she love her children (are they all girls, like ants and bees?), with their horny spouts and slimy inner-tube heads? Does she cry over her dead and vow revenge? Or is her protective instinct built into her biology? He imagines another movie from the Alien Mother's perspective as she fights for the survival of her brood against a hostile universe.

COMIC BOOK MOTHERS: In *Steel King*—his favorite comic—the hero, a man of metal, visits his mother periodically. She is never seen. He sheepishly approaches a vast black hole rimmed with gray steel, like the vent of a colossal furnace. Her voice rises out of the hole in tiny letters; they are not sealed in word balloons like those of the other characters; they seep like mist from the ground. Don't disappoint me, she tells him.

KATHLEEN MILLER: His mom is—Daron forgets how old—under thirty. Until recently he has never considered that his mother might be young, but when she talks to her friend Carole about going back to school or going on dates, he is forced to view her as a young woman free to make choices, free to change her life. This unsettles him.

Because she is intimately familiar, he must struggle to describe her. If someone asked, he would say she was pretty, but he would never think about it otherwise. She is of regular size and shape. He and his mom have the same color hair, a plain, lusterless brown—mousy, she says, disheartened, when she works it over in front of the bathroom mirror. She takes pages torn from her fashion magazines to the hair salon, but the results look the same: short and falling close to her head. She wears makeup and a light perfume. Her clothes are the kind mothers wear: jeans and sweats, and her uniform at the hotel.

His mom tells him everything, even things he doesn't need to know, things that bore him. She tells him how she haggled with the operator over a phone bill, how her friend Carole and the boss had an argument in the staff lounge. She tells him stories about her childhood, about his grandparents, his uncle and aunt, his great-aunts and great-uncles and second cousins, and other people in Sterling, Utah, where she grew up and where he lived when he was little, although he has no clear memories of it.

She tells him everything but one thing. He has asked her one question about his origins many times—directly and innocently when he was younger, and now with increasing guile, alternating bluntness and subtlety—but her answer is an evasion, bordered by silence. Daron is left guessing with half an equation—his mother—of which he is the sum.

Kath: 1

Near the start of KathLeen's shift in the casino at the Bellefleur Hotel, the light flickers on the phone at her cashier window. She lifts the receiver and cradles it against her shoulder
while she continues to count out crisp twenties. "Window four,"
she says and waits to hear what the problem is. They call her
with minor questions; with anything more important, anything
that they could blame her for, the supervisor would come down
on the floor to find her.

"KathLeen, it's Trudi in the office. I'm holding a call from
your father. Should I transfer?"

"No," she says curtly. "I'll come up." She shuts her eyes and
breathes for an instant, then finishes her transaction and pulls
the WINDOW CLOSED bar across the counter. Kath leans against
the waist-high partition to speak with Jane at the next window.
"I need to take a call in the office." Jane smiles and nods, and
Kath hopes that she has understood. While Jane wears the same
plain cream blouse and pleated blue skirt as Kath, Jane is a fossil, a veteran of forty years as a cashier, and she is losing her
hearing.

Kath slips out the back door of the booth and skirts around
the edge of the casino floor. The light in the vast room is subdued, the ceiling painted black, the walls and partitions mir-
rored. In front of the EMPLOYEES ONLY door, a woman in a
pailletted evening gown fringed with feathers sits at a slot machine surrounded by the scum-rimmed glasses of several mixed
drinks, cradling a styrofoam cup of quarters in her lap. Kath suspects that the woman has been playing since the night before;
she doesn't realize that time has passed, that it is already afternoon in the world outside.

Automatically, Kath stops in the staff washroom to rinse the
dirt of money from her hands. Normally, she wouldn't take the
time when a call is waiting, but she is in shock. Her father hates

the telephone; he does not make phone calls. There is only one possible answer: her mother is in the hospital. Or dead.

When she emerges from the bathroom, her friend Carole is slouched on the staff-room sofa in her cocktail waitress minidress. "Hey, Kath. Are you on break already? I just snuck in for a cig." She pats the sofa cushion beside her. "You look kinda upset. Come sit down and tell me about it."

"There's a call waiting." She points in the direction of the office, then leaves without waiting for Carole to respond. Upstairs, Trudi hands her the phone, and she pulls it around the corner into the hall. "Hello, Dad?"

"This is Don Miller. Your father." He speaks with stiff formality, and Kath holds her breath, awaiting the horrific details: the drunk driver, the failed brakes, the scream of crunching metal, the crash of broken glass.

She doesn't expect to hear that her mother has moved out of the house.

Her father tells her that Ardeth packed and left the house while he was out irrigating the vegetable garden. Kath pictures her mother filling the small bag with the blue cloth sides; her mother had always complained that the white plastic Samsonite was too heavy for a woman. Her mother has taken the car; she refuses to drive the truck. Her mother told Kath's younger sister, JuLee, that she was leaving—but not where she was going or why.

"You've got to settle this, Kath." Her father is adamant. She is the only one to fix the situation. Her brother, Carl, is on his mission in Panama. And, at eighteen, JuLee is too young, just a girl; she doesn't understand about man and wife. "I'll need you home," he says, sternly but hopefully.

She doesn't see how she can help after six years away. She and her mother don't get along that well. They talk on the phone from time to time, and her parents have come to visit in Las Vegas, but her connection to her family seems part of a different, earlier life. She doesn't want to go home; she can't return to Sterling. "Dad, I can't up and leave for Utah just like that. I have a job. I'm at work. I'm sorry."

"I understand, Kath. You've chosen your own path in life." Her father retreats into a hollow silence. "Um. Good-bye." He hangs up the phone noisily, as if anxious to push the unfamiliar plastic instrument from his hand.

Kath sighs, expelling the tension that has built inside her. She thanks Trudi and hands the receiver over the desk. As she leaves the office, the phone rings again, and Trudi calls her back in from the hall. "KathLeen!" Trudi says, laughing. "It's your aunt this time!"

Kath guesses that her father's sister, PearLeen Miller Pratt, was listening at her father's side, leaning on the green tile counter to the left of the sink with her arms folded. Her aunt speaks in a hush when Kath takes the phone. "This is Aunt PearLeen. I'm calling from the bedroom." She imagines PearLeen kneeling with her elbows propped on the quilted comforter of Kath's parents' bed. "Oh, Kath, please come. He's got the gun out."

She cannot count the times the gun has come out since her childhood. Her father never explains himself, but when he is depressed, whenever there is a reversal or a crisis, he takes his rifle from the closet and leans it by the back door. After an hour or two, he will go hunting—in season or out. The gun's appearance always terrified her mother; she must have guessed from some intimation, from his body language, that it stood for something darker, something else. All the women in the family grow frantic when the gun comes out.

But Kath doesn't feel the panic now. In the six years away from Sterling, she has lost her awe of men and their weapons. She knows the acts her father is capable of. But she understands that there will be no rest for her, that somehow she will be pressed into service. She recognizes that she has not changed so much that she is prepared to disobey her father. "All right," she tells her aunt. "I'll see what I can do."

She asks Trudi if Mr. Warren, the manager, is still in his office. She finds him hunched at his desk, working on the payroll. "Excuse me, Mr. Warren," she begins, and forces her voice not to waver. "I've got to get off work for a few days. I've got to leave now."

"Not possible. You can't leave now." He doesn't look up from his pile of papers.

"I have to." She tells him the story, the truth; it is the first time she hasn't made up an excuse to miss work.

"You can wait a few days, surely. You can't just skip out like this. Who am I supposed to get to sub for you?" He looks up at her and brushes his thinning hair from his forehead.

She doesn't know who's available. He can get Bart or one of the utility people to fill in. She doesn't care. "My dad's got his gun out," she says, and stares Mr. Warren down.

Kath lifts another suitcase from the closet in the hall, and unsettled dust motes flash in the low red light bleeding through the venetian blinds. She carries the cases into the bedroom and sets them on the bed.

Her son, Daron, kneels by the bed and helps her clear out the junk from the cosmetics case. He pulls out a bundle of old birthday cards, instruction booklets, and curling iron warranties. At the bottom he finds a framed photograph: the only picture of Merrill she kept. In the photo they pose on horses in the mouth of a canyon, green leaf and red rock furred out of focus behind them. Her husband, Merrill "Skunk" Nelson, rides a black mare, and Kath sits on a smaller chestnut with Daron's tiny three-year-old body clutched close to her on the saddle.

Daron looks up at her carefully, and she jolts with apprehension. She shouldn't be intimidated by her own child, a ten-year-old boy, but his green eyes flicker in his quiet face with unsettling calculation. Kath does not reach for the pile of clean laundry until Daron returns his attention to the photo. "Is this him?" he asks.

"No," she states emphatically. She understands his question. "Skunk isn't your father."

Daron positions the frame upright on the bedspread and flicks at the glass front with his finger until the picture topples onto its back. "Then why were we with him?"

"He took care of us. He's my husband." Kath folds gray sweatpants over her thin forearm, then folds them again into a neat square bundle. She has never hidden her marriage from Daron, but she hasn't discussed it, either. "We needed him."

"Oh."

One, two, three, four . . . She counts to five and hopes that her son won't ask the next logical question. She has never lied to Daron—perhaps she tells him too much—but she doesn't like to talk about Merrill with him. Or about his father.

"That's a dumb hat, Mom." She sighs with relief at the change of subject. In the picture she wears the blue cowboy hat, cocked so the front of the brim points up beneath a bright peacock-feather band.

"Skunk bought that hat for me in Yellowstone." She drops a folded pile of Daron's shirts and sweats into one side of the suitcase and stuffs sock balls around the perimeter.

"I went there, didn't I?"

"Sure did." She bought him a felt pennant with a picture of Old Faithful. It hangs over his bed next to a banner of the Mormon Thirteen Articles of Faith. Daron has been as many places, as far from home, as she has: Yellowstone and Las Vegas. But where is home to him? They have lived in the apartment for six years, more than half his life. Daron couldn't possibly sense how impermanent and unreal their whole life in Las Vegas seems to her; he doesn't taste the queasy soup of comfort and unease that rises in her throat when she thinks of going home to Sterling.

She steps into the bathroom, stares into the mirror at her hopeless hair, and scoops handfuls of scattered cosmetics into a zippered pouch. She calls out to Daron, "You can learn to ride a horse while we're home."

"Yeah, right."

"Come on, it's fun. Have I told you the story—"

"About how you rode off on the pony and got lost. Yes, Mom."

"You'll have a good time."

She wants their trip to seem like a vacation for Daron. She wishes he could have rich childhood days in Sterling like her own, full of summer light and the green scent of weeds. She wants him to ride a horse, collect lizards, and play hide-and-seek in the orchards. She doesn't want their visit to make him miserable.

She takes a shower; then she and Daron load the car. They drive silently through darkening neighborhoods. She doesn't know what to say to Daron about the reason for their trip. She can't explain why, after years of avoiding even the suggestion of a return to Sterling, she has decided to go home and take him with her. She can't explain the fear her mother's flight has filled her with, how it has shaken places inside her that she had thought stood on solid ground. And she wonders if she hesitates to speak because Daron, with eyes steadied under shaggy bangs, will understand more than she intends and will look deeper than she herself has dared. For now, she tells him nothing.

She turns onto the Strip, driving past Saharas of parking lots dotted with cars and between towering marquees illuminated like miniature cathedrals or pagodas of plastic and neon, then drives north and east on I-15 out of the city. For a time, in the rear-view mirror, the sky is dust-coated cantaloupe. But even Vegas lacks the wattage to consume the desert dark, and the city glow fades. Her headlights pull at the black pavement. She hallucinates that the desert is piling up against the sides of the road like fabric bunching behind a sewing machine needle. Kath drives through Nevada desert and the corner of Arizona stitched onto the freeway, then enters her home state.

Willard's Truckstop Café sits beyond the limits of St. George in the direction of Sterling and of Salt Lake far to the north. Its sign ascends and ascends to call people from the freeway. Its picture windows gleam across the vast parking lot with twenty-four-hour brightness. She slips through the gap in a dark ring of semi rigs at the perimeter of the lot and parks near the entrance. She nudges Daron awake and leads him around the low brick wall bordering the walk. Inside, it is too light and too warm. She feels out of her element, still wet with the night, tracking midnight chill onto the beige industrial carpet. She squeezes, then releases Daron's shoulder and locks her other fingers around the strap of her purse. They stand by the cash register, and she watches Daron lean against the curved glass of the dessert display. Cream pies, frosted cakes, and Jell-O squares with whipped cream revolve endlessly inside the transparent cylinder on silver racks.

"Two?"

She looks up, jerks out of drowsiness, and the hostess smiles at her indulgently, as if she recognizes Kath's dangerous lack of attention. You've been on the road too long, the smile says, you'd better have a cup of coffee. Living in Vegas, Kath has developed a fondness for coffee. But this is Utah, and there is always a pause before a waitress offers to fill the cup—the Word of Wisdom cautions against coffee. Kath won't order it here.

There is no slack anywhere in the woman's peach shirtwaist uniform; she fills every shining inch. Before Kath answers, she notices the woman's highly teased reddish hair and thick plastic nametag: HI. MY NAME IS EUBA. "Excuse me, is Rhonda in tonight?"

"I'll put you at one of her tables. Would the boy like a cushion to sit on?"

"No thanks." She winces for Daron's sake; he suffered all year as the smallest boy in fourth grade. The woman leads them to a booth.

Daron slides along the bench opposite her and immediately begins flipping the metal flap over the opening of the sugar container. He leans on his elbow, his cheek heavily scrunched into his palm. "Are you hungry, baby?"

"Can I get pancakes?"

"Sure." She opens the menu. An exclamation point of dried gravy lines the crease in the center. "We'll get you a short stack, okay?"

"KathLeen, it's been like forever!"

Her cousin Rhonda jogs down the aisle to their table. She has lost her baby fat and grown her hair. A dusky blond braid twists, fixed with bobby pins, at the back of her head behind the waitress cap. Definite hollows have appeared in her once chubby cheeks. Her mouth remains small, and pert, and pink. Rhonda is twenty-one; when Kath was her age, Daron was already three. She gets up and hugs her cousin.

"I heard. My mom called. I'm sorry."

Aunt PearLeen must have dialed Rhonda from her parents' house; she had probably called as many people as she dared before Kath's father noticed. In Sterling, Don and Ardeth Miller's failing marriage would be a major event. Guilt rises in Kath as a slight buzzing headache; she shouldn't stop to relax when there is an emergency at home. Rhonda must think it is strange to find her so sleepy and slow, but she had hoped to find Rhonda working. She needs to ask something.

"My mom said Uncle Don put the camper on the truck and went hunting."

"Then my mom hasn't called him?"

"No. Sorry." Rhonda turns to Daron and smiles as broadly as her tiny mouth can manage. "I'll just go tell Euba and we can talk. I'm supposed to go off in half an hour, and it's not like we're busy. Can I get you something?"

"Yeah. Daron would like a short stack of pancakes. And me . . . just a little . . . what's good?"

"Cliff just made bear claws and apple fritters for tomorrow. Warm. Sticky. I'll bring us some."

Rhonda slips through the door at the far end of the counter. "That's your cousin Rhonda," Kath explains. But Daron watches a semi twisting out of the parking lot onto the ramp of the interstate. He doesn't appear to listen.

When Rhonda returns, she lays out silverware and pancakes

for Daron and offers Kath a plate of Danish. She scoots in next to Daron on the opposite bench and tugs off the cloth-wrapped cardboard of her waitress cap. She frees her blond braid, and the neatly twisted end slithers out of sight down her back. She brushes the anchoring bobby pins into a pile and wipes them into her palm, then into her pocket. She doesn't speak until the ritual is over. "People our parents' age just don't break up. I don't understand it, Kath. I saw them together at Sacrament Meeting last Sunday. Do you know what it's about?"

Kath shakes her head. She unfolds a napkin and pulls an apple fritter onto the impromptu placemat.

"I mean, you don't need to tell me. I just wondered if it was something you knew about."

"No. I don't think anyone knew. Except my mom, I guess." She watches Daron unwrap the foil from a pat of butter and drop it on the pancakes. Creamy rivulets melt and flow to the outer circumference and drip. He soaks the stack in maple syrup and digs a rough path toward the center as he eats. He never looks across the table at her, and she wonders if he is angry that she didn't tell him about his grandparents and he had to hear it first from Rhonda. She hates herself for not knowing which truths to protect him from and which truths to disclose.

"Mom said your dad is sure you can get Aunt Ardeth to go home. I wonder how he thinks you can do it." Rhonda lifts a packet of cigarettes and a lighter from a pocket at her waist. "This must really upset you, though."

"Yeah, I guess so."

"You guess so? Jeez, Kath, you've gotten tough in your old age." Kath can't decide whether Rhonda's assessment stems from shock or admiration, but she accepts it as a compliment. For Daron's sake and her own, she wants to be tough and solid during their stay in Sterling, like tempered steel. Rhonda reaches around Kath's purse for the ashtray. "Do you mind?"

"Do your parents know you smoke?"

"There are a *whole lot* of things my parents don't know about me."

Kath vaguely disapproves of the gray cloud Rhonda blows carefully out of the booth, although, given her own record, she really has no right. She smoked at Rhonda's age, and she didn't stop because the Word of Wisdom warned against tobacco, but because she was pregnant. She sees the mistakes that Rhonda will make; she has made them all and knows their consequences. But it would do no good to tell her.

Rhonda rips the tip from a bear claw and holds it gingerly to nibble at with her small, squared teeth. She asks Kath what life is like in Vegas, what her job is like. They compare the life of cashiers and waitresses. "You can't get a good job, if you're a woman, unless you've got a doctorate or something," Rhonda says. "Look at us. We're just the housewives of the public sector. Feeding people and cleaning up after people and giving out their allowances." Rhonda was the valedictorian speaker at the high school. She takes classes at the college in Alma. Rhonda is too smart for Southern Utah; she should have gone up north to school—although not to Brigham Young University, where girls only go to find a husband. When Kath was a senior she had the application materials for BYU in a large white envelope on her dresser, but she got pregnant and never filled out the forms.

Daron's pace slows as he reaches the last pie-wedge of pancakes. He combs the tines of his fork through the pool of syrup on the plate and drains his glass of water. Kath asks Rhonda about home, and the news is that nothing has changed.

They both grew up in Sterling. Rhonda, Kath, and Kath's sister, JuLee, were friends, although Kath was much older than the other two. They were the only girls in the family. When people talked about "The Miller Boys," it required further clarification—there were many male Millers in town—but "The Miller Girls" always meant the three of them. Only JuLee remains a Miller. Rhonda has always been a Pratt, and Kath is an estranged Nelson. But she suspects that the gossips of the town still whisper "That Miller Girl" when they mention her; she has given the tongue-waggers the most scandal to talk about.

Rhonda has a boyfriend. "He's from Arizona. His name is Manuel."

"What?"

"Like the kinds of cars: Automatic and Manual. Manuel."

"He's Mexican?"

"Manuel Ortiz."

Daron slumps low in his seat, plants the toes of his shoes on her bench, and shuts his eyes. She slides over to give his legs space. Rhonda lights her third or fourth cigarette, and there is a lull in the conversation. Kath is certain that Manuel is another item on the list of things Rhonda's parents do not know about. Rhonda is being outrageous. She deliberately wriggles against her constraints. Kath was outrageous, too—back then.

She and her boyfriend, Tom, would buy beer and drive up one of the canyons. They would hop naked from rock to rock in the creek. She would sneak in through the bathroom window at four in the morning. Yet even in her wildest days Kath believed that no one should live life dangerously, without guidance. Her Primary teacher at church had explained that the rules—Heavenly Father's laws, brought home by the father and supported by the mother—were a coloring book with pictures to follow. Kath had strayed outside the borders, but she never forgot where the lines were. If she chose wild colors, she never forgot what shape the colors were meant to fill. Tom's outrageousness had been of a different order. It warped him; he refused to acknowledge the lines. She would have married him anyhow—her shoulders jerk at the padded bench thinking of it—but he left the book entirely. He disappeared outside the margins. He thought he could be happy beyond the lighted boundaries, among unprinted pages.

She looks at her watch and pulls out her wallet. She can't do anything for her family until morning, and she has no plan for how she might act and what might be accomplished. But she feels an urgency to get to Sterling and turn off the road down her parents' driveway, if only to put Daron to bed. She needs to ask Rhonda her question. "Do you have the check?"

"Never mind that." Rhonda raps her fingers lightly on the table for emphasis.

"You're sure?" She tucks her wallet into her purse. "Before I go, there's one other thing. It's . . . This is hard." She touches her lip to stop trembling. "Maybe you've heard what Merrill's up to."

"Same as ever, I guess. He's still driving the truck for his dad. You're still married, right? Haven't you and him talked or whatever? Since you left?"

"No." Kath nudges Daron's legs under the table to wake him. "We're not in touch."

Daron: Car Trips

His mom's fingers grip the steering wheel in bloodless rings, and her shoulders hunch forward in tight alert. She is nervous, and it isn't just the headlights smearing with speed in the opposite lane that make her wary. Her eyes focus on the road ahead, but they are tracking something else besides the dark. Daron would ask her what she sees there, but he knows she wouldn't give a satisfactory answer. He sinks back, bored but uneasy, into the passenger seat.

He might try to sleep. It would be comfortable with his head against the ledge of the window if he hadn't forgotten his pillow. When he was a little kid the car would lullaby him. When he cried at night his mom would drive him around the city, with the engine throbbing, his car seat quivering, her voice singing and her hand against his cheek. He looked up through the windows at night sky and the tops of buildings brightly banded with neon. They slipped down the glittering streets, and light poured down into the car. Sounds—laughter, car horns, the *binkabinkabink-abink* of coins pumped from streetside slot machines—softened and drifted. And the luminous casino cowboy smiled down into the windshield and waved and waved, hello, hello, welcome, welcome, until Daron shut his eyes. But it isn't as easy to fall asleep any longer.

The trip might be better in the daytime. He can't read his books or comics in the dark, and the batteries are dead in his video game. It would be futile to ask to turn on the overhead light. The night presses blank-faced against the side window. Only sometimes, in the light of the stars and the exposed piece of moon, large silhouettes rise into the sky, dinosaur landscapes, stalking the car at the horizon. His mom's face clouds with light from the dashboard instruments—greenish yellow at her nose fading into the black shadow tangled in the hair pushed behind her ears.

It might be better if he had someone to play with. If he had a sister or a brother, he would be able to play car games, word games, sing field-trip songs—do your ears hang low, ninety-nine bottles of beer, the wheels on the bus, John Jacob Jingleheimer Schmidt *TRA-LA-LA-LA-LA-LA-LA*. But alone with his mom in the sealed chamber of the car, he is afraid to make a sound. If he had a brother or a sister, he would always have someone to talk to. He could exchange information, speculate. Maybe his sister would have overheard his mother's phone call. Maybe she would know more than what Rhonda said.

If they were going somewhere fun, the trip might be more bearable. If he were going to Disneyland, he could ask every ten minutes—like the kids in TV shows—how much longer? How many miles have we gone? While the car pulled the pavement under its wheels and spit it out the back, his excitement could build like a twisted rubber band. At the crest of each hill he could search the new perspective for his destination.

But they are going to Sterling, and after the first hour of novelty he will feel nothing but boredom. And a slight, persistent itch of apprehension. His grandparents live there, and his cousins, and aunts, and Mr. DeSoto, the man who taught his mom to ride a horse in the story she always tells. He lived there once. If he remembers anything at all—and he can't say with certainty that these sensations belong to Sterling, that they originate from those days when he was three or four—he remembers a small house behind another house and something (inside the small yellow house?) cold and wet against his bare back. He can't remember anything else, after that cold and that wet.

When his mom talks about Sterling it sounds tiny, uninteresting, like a town from a TV comedy. He pictures Sterling as a brown cardboard box, unfilled, and he yawns.

His mom fiddles with the radio, but the stations do not hold. If he could see the radio, the whooshing of static around the edges of the music would look like whipped cream, creeping from behind to stuff the mouths and ears of the unsuspecting singers. He would not be surprised to hear the roar of static coming from the air if he rolled down the window. It's what the night sounds like.

When a clear signal appears, his mom flips it anyway. She will not settle into any song. She fights them with her fingers ever ready at the knob. She cuts them down at the chorus. Out here, she will never choose a song he enjoys. When she does pause, it will be on a slow, country-western tune, a woman singing like tears falling. "Don't leave me here . . . in a world . . . filled with dreams that might have been . . . hurt me now . . . get it over . . . I may learn to love again." He doesn't like the music, and it doesn't make sense. Why do people want to listen to songs that make them sad?

Kath: 2

Bones scatter across the black lawn, milked from their hiding spots in the grass by the bright moon. As she carries a suitcase to the porch, Kath looks for Madame in the dark corner where her chain is staked into the ground. She must be sleeping inside. When Kath was six, their dog Cookie punctured her esophagus with chicken bones. She had seen Cookie coughing, her head slung over a pool of red saliva on the broad white slab of the back stoop. Her father shot Cookie himself, by the stable under the oak where he buried her. With each dog who followed—Sparks and Panda and Champion—her father continued to scrape the plates after dinner and slide the bones and cartilage into the dog's dish. Kath would slip outside after her father headed for the television and pick out all the bones from the hard pellets of food in the bowl. Kath is glad that Madame doesn't eat bones; she totes them around the yard, arranging them in endless patterns on the grass until they turn white and flinty from exposure.

Kath tries the knob. The door is locked, and all the windows are dark. Before she wakes Daron, she piles their luggage next to the fern stand on the porch. She looks out to the open hatch of the car and the glowing interior to see him sleeping, his head nestled close against the glass.

She doesn't want to wake JuLee up. She finds the key stuck to the magnet under the milk box on the back stoop and lets herself in. Madame's toenails click across the kitchen linoleum, and she whines quietly but excitedly as she nudges her cold nose into Kath's palm. Kath scratches Madame's ears as the dog licks into the nooks between the fingers of her other hand. "Hi, girl. How's my girl?"

Without finding the lights, she senses the kitchen's familiar order. The cutting board on its nail by the sink. The wooden dish-drying rack on the drainboard. The pig-shaped brass hook-board hung with pale dish towels. The kitchen witch—a Mother's Day gift from JuLee, made with fabric and a soda bottle—standing on top of the refrigerator. The washer and dryer squatting in the utility-room alcove on the right. She leaves the open door and crosses the kitchen into the hall. Madame accompanies her, half seen at her knee. At the end of the hall, moonlight seeps through her parents' empty bedroom. The door to Carl's room is shut. She eases gently into the room she shared with JuLee and hunts for the rise of her sister in the dark. Both beds lie flat under neatly draped spreads. She checks Carl's room. No one is home.

Leaning into the car, she nudges Daron awake and walks next to him along the sidewalk, up the steps, into the kitchen, down the hall, into her brother's room. He doesn't speak; he won't remember the journey from car to bed. He kicks off his shoes but can't manage to shrug off his jeans until she helps him tug the narrow legs over his feet. The mouth of the sheets breathes the fresh scent of laundry soap as he slides his legs under the covers; while Carl is on his mission, her mother has continued to wash his sheets. Kath folds the top sheet over his stomach and opens the window above the bed.

"Mom?"

"What, hon?" She turns on her way to the door, but he doesn't continue. Sleep eats his question.

She locks up the car, pours orange juice, and sits on the back steps in the magnificent cool. She sees the yellow square of the kitchen window of the nearest neighbors, the Mortensens, beyond the stable, across the drainage ditch and the flattened weeds and dirt of the field where the Mortensen boys ride their dirt bikes. The moon is nearly down, and there is no other light. Madame stands in the center of the yard. Her back is broad and flat, curving only at the legs, like an ottoman. Kath blows kisses until Madame rushes to her outstretched hand. Kath scratches her fingers into the patch of white bursting from black at the dog's throat. When she fails to move her fingers for a moment, Madame steps away. Kath finds her hand catching at air.

She retreats into her mind again, to a room with a simple table and chairs in white-painted pine. She furnishes the room like a dollhouse, setting down the four-legged table and the two slat-back chairs into the expectant space. She sits and looks across to the other, vacant chair. She relaxes without taking pleasure in the slackening of muscles and the deepening of breath; what she seeks to feel is nothing.

Kath uses the room less often since leaving Sterling. Although sometimes at work she will slip from her stall with its protective Plexiglas and sweaty old-money smell and open the door in her mind, she has stayed away more and more. She had almost forgotten her fear and the need to escape; Las Vegas had given her real distance. But now, back in her parents' house, she feels the world constricting, and her need for refuge is renewed.

Once, when she was watching the April Latter-day Saints Conference on television (she tries to watch Conference with Daron, to give him some religion since they don't go to church), one of the General Authorities explained the nature of her room. The man stood behind the podium in his dark suit with the Tabernacle Choir arrayed in wings of blue and white robes behind him. He turned his gray wrinkled head from side to side, speaking in the slow unearthly inflections used by all the leaders—the Prophet, the President of the Ladies' Relief Society, the bishop at sacrament meeting—to speak of the Lord and His works. He said that the members were "in the world but not of the world." They ate and worked and slept and loved on the earth, but theirs was a greater mission. They were like a clear plastic template laid across the map of the world. On this earthly plane, they would carry out the ordinances of the church; they would be baptized, hold the priesthood, marry and be sealed, do the work of the temple, redeem the dead by baptism. But their seeming presence on earth was in some way illusory, preparatory. Although the lines on the template corresponded to the lines of the terrestrial map, the members would one day be lifted off. Their lines would be revealed as celestial and eternal, their essence separate from the essence of the world.

Kath feels the separation. She feels apart. Although she is sealed for time and all eternity to her family, she knows that someday she will withdraw alone into a room where no bond will stick.

The other chair in her room is for Daron. If she could open the door wide enough but not too wide, she would pull him in.

Each time she looks at his chair across the tabletop, she vows one day to risk it. To rescue him again, to rescue him better and forever.

Her left shoe lies buried in bones. She hears them clatter when she shifts her sore butt. Madame has brought presents. The dog returns from around the corner of the house with a rib bone clamped in her jaws. She drops it onto the others and looks up at Kath. Pay attention, Madame says, pay attention to me.

"You're right, girl. You're right." She presses the damp, cool side of her orange juice glass to her forehead for a moment, then stands. She kicks the bones from the sidewalk to prevent anyone from tripping. "Let's go to bed."

She drags her suitcase into the hall bathroom and finds a T-shirt to sleep in. Madame sits outside the door. In her old bedroom, she peels down the sheets of her bed, but she will never fall asleep in it. She lies instead on JuLee's bed and twists her legs to the side to leave a place for the dog at the bottom. She does her times tables and counts back from two hundred with no effect, no drowsiness.

She jumps up and brushes her fingers along the wall to her parents' room. She curls in a corner of the empty king-size mattress and buries her head under the sheet to block the house from her sight. Madame flops next to her. Move it, dog, she thinks. You're on my feet. Move it. She shifts under the dog's bulk but doesn't speak. In the tomb of her mind, she pushes at the door. She sleeps.

A hand grips her upper arm, rocking her gently. She wakes into the thought that, if she concentrated, she could discern the individual placement of each finger on her flesh. "Ardeth?"

"Dad?" She opens her eyes. He releases her and rises to lean against the dresser in the dawn light.

"Kath." He lifts off his tractor-store cap, and she sees the mold the cap has made of his hair. "I didn't see your car."

"It's out front." She sits up and pulls her knees toward her chest. Her dad sinks at the end of the bed. "So how are you, Dad? Are you okay?"

"No. I'm fine." He stares at the cap in his hands. She watches for his face as it lifts to look out the window. His eyes are narrowed and dry. Her father never cries.

Daron: Dogs

Daron wakes up in an unfamiliar bed in an unfamiliar room to the sound of a strange dog barking. He stands on his pillow and leans against the wagon-wheel headboard to peer out the narrow rectangular window. The yard outside is a square of grass bordered by flowers and vegetables, and just beyond by fields and stands of trees bathed in a white, early-morning light. The dog has stopped barking, but Daron hears a chain rattling below the window like a noisy ghost.

His grandparents' dog appears on the lawn with her head bent to snuffle in the grass. The dog is neither small nor large and has an indefinite shape to match her unremarkable size. With her tail down and her head lowered below her shoulders, she looks like a tortoise wearing a black fuzzy bath rug. He knows her name is Madame. His mom talks about the family dogs all the time: Harpo, who disappeared; Cookie, who choked on a bone; Sparks and Panda, who were hit by cars; and Champion, who died while Kath was home alone. His mom apologizes to him that they can't have a puppy in the apartment, but he doesn't feel deprived. He knows that he shouldn't be afraid of dogs, but he finds most animals larger than cats alternately threatening and boring.

Daron scratches his index finger on the open screen, and Madame pauses to glare up at him from the corners of her eyes. He will need to get along with her unless he stays in the house all day.

He pulls his notebook out of his bag and sits Indian-style on the bed with his back against the headboard. At the top of a fresh page, he writes down the two bits of doglore he knows: (1) Never approach a crouching dog. This is canine language for "Stay the hell away from me!" and (2) Dogs can smell fear. If love smells like flowers, then fear smells like hot tar. Dogs cannot stand human fear. People must be firm, not fakey. Dogs can tell the difference.

Daron isn't ready to go out and be friendly to whoever else is up in the house, so he lists the other dogs he knows.

Lassie, Snoopy, Toto, Clifford, Benji, Santa's Little Helper, Astro, Dino (sort of), Droopy, Scooby, Pluto, Marmaduke, Odie.

Bashful: Mrs. Killian, the neighbor who sometimes watches him in the peeling lime-painted house between their apartment complex and the convenience store, has a Pomeranian. It sits in the palm of her left hand, and she strokes around its nose with her right index finger. Bashful never moves on his own. She carries him everywhere—into places, such as the supermarket, denied to dogs. Because he can't believe that anything so weak and immobile can live on its own, Daron suspects that an artery curls out of Mrs. Killian's palm and through Bashful's ribs to pump fresh blood into the butterfly wings of his heart. Before Bashful, Mrs. Killian had mothered five other Pomeranians: Happy, Sleepy, Grumpy, Hoppy, and Doc. She started with her first dog just after Snow White came out. Bashful will be the last of the line because, as Mrs. Killian explained, she will not name one of her loveydears Dopey. His mom will not let him tell Mrs. Killian that there is no dwarf named Hoppy.

Foxie: On the way to the sitter's house, his mom would sometimes stop to pick up her friend Carole, who was a cocktail waitress at the same hotel. Carole lived with her boyfriend John and John's dog, a black Afghan with a long, long face, huge feet, and a tail like a feather duster. One afternoon when he and his mom arrived, John was tossing all his stuff into the open side door of his van. Carole stood on the porch, and the Afghan stood next to her with her head cocked under long black ears and tresses. The dog watched the boyfriend intently, but with serene disinterest, like the princess on the cover of Daron's *Arabian Nights*.

Carole shouted at her boyfriend. Go! Fine! But what about Foxie? What about your fucking dog? Who's gonna take the time to get the stickers out of her feet? Who's gonna comb her hair? Carole still has the dog.

Tiny: For two or three weeks in the shopping center pet store where Daron went for crickets to feed Jerry the Lizard (until he died), there was a chihuahua in the smallest dog cage, on the top row, nearest the warm orange heating lamps in the ceiling. The dog would appear from out of its nest of shredded newpaper, raising its downy, shivering, baby-mouse body onto its minuscule piston legs. Its ears pointed up, but the rest of it was round, and the roundest were its black, terrible eyes. It would turn and turn itself around between its water bowl and the newspaper. And sometimes it would look out at him and snap its triangular mouth, rolling its head up and down each time. The tiny jaws pumped open, open, open, voicelessly behind the thick glass.

Daron hears a toilet flush through the wall, and Madame barks again. He stands at the window to find Madame balanced on her hind legs against the gate at the end of the yard. He prepares himself to go outside and pick up one of the bones he sees on the sidewalk. He will throw it as far as he can across the grass and wait to see if Madame will fetch it and bring it back to him. He will repeat the experiment until they become friends.

Kath: 3

Kath's father cracks the eggs on the lip of the skillet, and they slide down the slope into the sputtering bacon grease. He folds the eggs loosely to preserve pockets of liquid yolk in the center. Nothing fancy. He cooks nothing that wouldn't be easy to prepare at a campsite. Eggs, bacon, toast, and orange juice. She sees him from behind, from the counter bar which divides the kitchen from the dinner table. He looks different, older, than she remembers, although she doesn't know if the images held in her mind are from last summer, when he visited, from the year she left, or from some point deep within her childhood. His shoulders have rounded, and the muscles of his arms have slumped toward gravity like water-filled balloons. His pant legs bunch on the tops of his scuffed thick-soled work boots. The worn seat of his overalls droops, and she wonders at what age men lose their butts. When he turns to deliver her plate of two eggs and three crisp strips of bacon, he is solemn. His head squares off along the line of his ears and at the jaw and forehead. All his other features—the length of his brow, his narrow eyes, the set of his mouth—follow the same horizontal. His face holds no flux or mobility.

She asks him questions as they eat together, perched on stools at the counter, elbow to elbow, the knee of his overalls brushing the fray-rimmed hole at the knee of her jeans. "Where is she?" "Do you think she'll be in touch?" "Why did she leave, do you think?" "What is it?" "What's happening?" "What's going on?" His voice comes slowly, deliberately; his fork pauses before his mouth with half-congealed egg perched on the back side of the tines; his answers are considered at some length, though they are identical. "It's a mystery to me, Kath. I just can't see into it."

"Do you want me to call around?" She dreads the idea. She longs to slip in and out of Sterling unannounced.

"It'll work itself out, God willing. Your mother's a good woman. She knows marriage is eternal." His eyes find hers for the briefest instant, then move on beyond her shoulder. Daron steps up sleepily behind them. "But I'm glad you're here, honey."

"Come sit." She gives up her stool for Daron and clears away her plate. He climbs onto the seat and rests his chest against the bar; he is slow to get going in the morning.

Kath's father leans toward Daron across the counter, squints his eyes, and smiles. "Want me to fix you up some eggs, skunk?"

"He doesn't like eggs," she answers sharply. It isn't the eggs; it's the nickname. Dad used to call her "skunk" when she was a girl. She liked the name until her husband, Merrill, changed its association. *Skunk* jabs at the hollow of her throat; the two *k*s catch like fishhooks in the soft tunnels of her ears.

"All right then, Kath. We've got cereal." Her father, nonplussed, takes the plastic milk jug from the fridge and sets it before her as an offering, to mollify her. She wonders if he makes the connection—if, in his world of simple truths, without nuance, he recognizes the reason for her burst of anger. Her father is opaque. She has never been able to see into his emotions, not even as a child, not even as a toddler who tripped on the garden hose and went looking, crying, hoping for a hug.

She finds Daron a bowl and Frosted Flakes. A banana. And a spoon. No one speaks, and not one of the three of them can speak until something upsets the tense wordless weight that anchors them in place. Her father stares into the sink in desultory contemplation of the greasy pan and dirty dishes. Daron pours his milk, wielding the full, squared jug cautiously with both hands. She watches him with her arms crossed, her ear against the hanging cabinets above the bar, pining for a cup of coffee she knows she will not have.

Her sister appears through the door to the hall. JuLee pauses to tie the belt of her robe, and they turn to her eagerly. The paralysis breaks; the circulation returns. JuLee looks up. "Hiya, Daron." Her hair is mussed on one side. "Hiya, Kath. It's good to see you guys."

"Hi."

JuLee pauses very close to her, and the arms of her robe spread as if she will hug Kath. But she doesn't. She turns and opens the refrigerator, releases a Dr Pepper from its plastic collar, and pops the tab on the top. "I'm sorry I slept through breakfast. I would've cooked waffles for you."

"I think we should pray as a family." Her father shuts off the faucet at the sink and takes a dish towel from the piggy hookboard. He carefully dries his hands. "It will help us in this time of tribulation."

JuLee finds a free space on the counter for her soda and lowers herself to her knees. Kath follows. Daron, with an open incredulous mouth, looks down at them and at her father standing over them. A dot of milk lingers at the crease of his lips. "Come here, hon." She hopes that he will follow her directions without question before her father notices how alien and awkward her son seems at prayer. Daron slips from the stool and comes around into the kitchen. She pulls him down to kneel beside her and squeezes him tightly into the crook of her arm. She brushes a hand over his hair and whispers in his ear, "Shut your eyes."

From behind, her father's hand descends to roost firmly on the top of her skull. The tip of his longest finger lies at her brow. Blinking her eyes open, she finds his other hand seated on JuLee's head. With her arm firmly braced around Daron, they are all connected by bonds of flesh. They are a family.

"Dear children, in the name of Jesus Christ and by the authority of the priesthood I hold, I bless you. Though we are passing through a time of trial, I know that ours is a true and eternal family and a path will be shown to us. Heavenly Father, I ask of you today to help us to heal the wounds that have separated us. Show us the way that we might bind this family more closely together. Whatever struggles and dangers may come our way today, let us be strong and wise. And I would like to convey a special blessing upon you, my daughter KathLeen, today that all your insights and special talents will serve you well in the task"—the phone rings— "of bringing our family together . . ." After several rings, Kath looks up. Neither her father nor JuLee makes any move to acknowledge the sound.

"Amen," she says. "Excuse me." She ducks from beneath her father's hand and stands. The phone is mounted on the wall; a Rapunzel tangle of yellow cord hangs almost to the floor. As she touches the receiver, she considers her father's blessing. She wonders again if he understands where her pain lies and what balm is needed to soothe it. His blessings have always been vital to her. In blessing her, he touches her, his hand leaves its warm imprint in her hair, and the concern he cannot speak to her he speaks to God. She brings the phone to her ear. "Hello?"

"I'm sorry. Is this the Miller residence?"

"Mom?" The voice is silent, and through the phone lines to the room where her mother sits—no doubt in a comfortable chair, with a tablet and a pencil in her lap—Kath hears a television, far off, down an invisible hallway. Her father closes his prayer in the name of Jesus Christ. She relaxes into her old phone position, with her back against the threshold and her big toe curled into the crack of the open door, above the hinge.

"KathLeen? Did he make you come up?"

"It's okay, Mom. Really."

"No, it's not okay. I'm sorry you had to bother."

"It's no bother."

Her mother says, Hmmmmm, to undercut her with doubt. Her mother must find it difficult to believe that Kath would trouble herself over the state of her parents' marriage.

"So where are you, Mom?"

"Cousin Berma's." Berma is her mother's second cousin; she lives with her mother, Ina. Berma is Merrill's aunt. "As long as you're here, why don't you come to lunch."

"I don't . . ." She can't go there—the house is next door to Merrill's parents—but she has no choice. Her father waits behind her, sucking his tongue in scrutiny at every word Kath speaks.

"Merrill's not home, if that's what you're worried about. No chance you'll run into your rightful husband."

"Mom . . ."

"I'm sorry. It would be nice to see you, dear. Did you bring Daron?"

"He's here."

"Then there's no question. I'd love to see my grandson. How about two?"

"Two." Kath imagines her mother jotting a neat note on her tablet.

"I'd better speak to your father a minute. Bye for now."

Kath extends the receiver toward her father. "It's Mom."

At first he studies the molded plastic cupped in her palm, the holes vented in the top and bottom, the rows of buttons in between. He navigates between her and the end of the counter without lifting his eyes from the phone. "I'll get it in the front room."

As her father leaves the kitchen, she rests the receiver on its back on the counter. She and JuLee stare at it; they would like to eavesdrop, but neither would forgive the other for making the suggestion. The screen door bangs, and she turns to see Daron on the back stoop, his hands in his pockets, watching Madame sniffing at the edge of the vegetable garden.

"When did you get here?" JuLee sips at her Dr Pepper while holding up a piece of toast between two fingers for consideration. Like their mother, she has an extra pad of fat at the knuckles, which smoothes the back of her hand and makes her fingers seem stubby.

"Late last night. How about you?"

"You didn't ask Dad where I was or anything, did you?"

"No."

"Thanks." JuLee opens a package of Hostess Snowballs from the cookie jar. "I slipped through the front door while you two were eating. Wiped my face with a washcloth, put my robe on. Pretty swift, huh?"

"Pretty stupid." She starts to ask who it is—it must be a man to keep her sister awake and away from home—but her father returns. He blinks twice at the linoleum and raises his eyes along the length of the kitchen. "Dad? What did she say?"

"There's chili in Tupperware in the freezer."

Kath: 4

Berma Kimball Mortensen lost her husband in the Philippines in World War II. After they graduated from high school and married, her father, Eldon, gave them some acreage along the back end of the property, on the post office road. Henry built her a house there on the rise above the gully and the clump of cedar trees. The house was small, tight, and neat, with its clapboards painted a bright yellow and its windows—from a catalogue— identical and perfect: like a playhouse for two quiet children. Then came Pearl Harbor. Then the draft board and sad good-byes at the bus stop. And Berma sat in the little house above the cedars and the curve in the post office road and waited for night-fall, when the radio signals were better and she could pick up KSL News from Salt Lake City. She helped out with all the Ladies' Relief Society activities, sent postcards to orphaned sailors, and taught the youngest class of Primary at the ward-house. Berma waited for his letters, and sometimes they looked like Swiss cheese with all the words cut out of the paper by the Navy. Henry had vowed to use his time on board the ship as an opportunity for missionary work. In every letter he reaffirmed his testimony that theirs was the one and only true church. Then the sergeant came to the yellow house with the sealed envelope.

Among Henry's personal effects, which Berma shut in a box with the folded triangle of flag, were a booklet of dirty limer-icks on cheap paper and a postcard of a soldier pointing to de-capitated heads on a fencepost—signs of Jap butchery. On cold mornings she stuffed socks and dish towels in the whistling chinks in the wall, and she waited after a rare snow for her fa-ther to come dig a path from her door to the slushy ruts of the post office road. After the War, things were looking up for the Kimball family feed store, and the newly incorporated town of Sterling, Utah, erected its first public monument to the fallen men of the town—a brass plaque on the face of a brick column with a citation to Henry L. Mortensen in one of the two neat rows of raised type. Joe Nelson, another boy in Berma's class, re-turned from the service and proposed to Berma's sister, Clovis. They married and, with help from her father, built a nice big house next door to her parents' on the front road.

Berma waited, and Joe, with a good heart toward his sister-in-law—with a good heart, in fact, toward all the widowed, struggling Sisters of the Church—offered to repaint the little house and plane the bottom of the door so it would shut properly, and perform any other task she might have for him to do after work at the feed store. But she felt it was wrong: he was her sister's husband, and she had no right to monopolize his time. Besides, Clovis was too quick to offer his services, to demonstrate how much abundance her man could provide—enough for two women or more. Berma didn't cotton to her sister's flavor of charity.

Berma waited, and the prefabricated windows opened nicely in the summer, and the coal stove heated adequately in the winter if the bed was pushed near and no heed was paid to the greasy smokiness that lingered through the day. Clovis and Joe had three girls in quick succession; they spent the rest of the fifties and sixties working on one boy and three more girls. Then Berma's father had a heart attack hoisting a gunnysack of rabbit pellets. She touched his cheek at the viewing and rubbed at the orange foundation smeared on her fingertips during the long service afterward. Berma waited for the end of summer, then moved into her old room to be a comfort to her mother. Joe took over at the feed store and hired Peter Mortensen, Henry's cousin, to remodel the kitchen for Berma and her mother, Ina, the two widows, as a Christmas present. Berma's yellow house endured the seasons untended and forgotten on the hill.

Whenever Kath's mother chose to remind Kath of the peril she was ignoring, she would illustrate her point with the fate of her second cousin's home. Kath never understood the parallels between her life and Berma's, but Ardeth would adopt any example to prove her conviction that life without a husband and home was pitiless. "Any sensible woman would have found another husband to live there with her," she would say. Kath can't imagine what conclusion her mother would draw from the house now that she has set herself adrift. For Kath, the house has offered different lessons.

Merrill Nelson proposed to Kath for the first time in Berma's abandoned kitchen. He took her along the post office road, two parallel ruts coiling in the dirt, and parked next to the largest cedar tree at the base of the hill. They climbed up and slipped into the house. The two tiny rooms were used for storage sometimes, but they were too far from the Nelsons' to be very useful. Merrill's father, Joe, had taken out the stove and the stovepipe, and a pile of tar shingles and sticks and dust grew beneath the hole. Kath looked up at the opening, and a red eye of sunset blared down at her. Merrill opened the dusty window, and they sat on crates in the glow. Merrill found her hand and held it with both his own, gently but firmly, as if it were a frightened thing with its own racing heart. On the end of Merrill's crate, a black porter with white goggling eyes proffered a platter with a pyramid of perfect oranges. She looked at the picture instead of Merrill.

"I believe you have true repentance in your heart, Kathy," he said. "You have acknowledged your transgressions. And you're strong enough to overcome them. I'm sure of that about you, at least. You're strong enough.

"Why I called you this morning is that I had a dream last night. And I know it was a special dream. It felt solid, you know, real. I was in a white place, in our premortal life, and the young Elders of the Church were gathered as for a meeting. The other young men and I were greeted there by the patriarchs, who brought the premortal daughters unto us to pair us for marriage in this world. Each girl was more comely than the last, but I wasn't happy with any of them. Then I saw you, Kathy. And truly, you were the most beautiful girl of all. I placed your hand on my heart and said, I want you for my wife, would you take me? You smiled and said yes. And there was just time for us to kiss before we were taken away to be born. As they led me off—and this was the end of the dream—I turned back and called to you, don't forget your vow. And you shouted out from that white place as I woke up. I will remember, you shouted, I will remember!"

Merrill's hands began to sweat, but she didn't mind. She

looked at his face now that it was safely doused in the dark. She
lost her fear of him and wished that they had pushed the crates
together.

"I don't think you remember your vow, Katie. Or the darkness
of the world has obscured it from your eyes. But I testify to you
that it's true. I do want to marry you. I do love you, Katie. But it
isn't just for the sake of romance between a man and a woman.
I want to be a father to your son. The two of you can't live forever in your parents' house, cause he won't be little forever, and
I can give you a home. Oh, Katie, I love the Church so much, and
to be able to bring you and Daron to safety under my priesthood,
that would be great."

Merrill had just returned from his mission, and he was fresh
with zeal for the Church and for life. She found that more reas-
suring than his blue eyes and tall, lanky frame. She craved his
guidance; what kept her apart from him that night was her
shame. She had a fatherless child and an ugly history. She wasn't
the pure spirit she thought Merrill deserved. She turned him
down gently, and they left the broken rooms in silence.

The derelict house, canting sideways and peeling yellow, stands
above the gully Kath and Daron follow on the way to meet her
mother for lunch. She decided that they would walk the scenic
way along the post office road, which threaded the hills at the
back of town. She had forgotten that the path along the hilltops
from Berma's old house leads directly to the Nelsons' back door
and not to Aunt Ina's. She would do anything rather than meet
Skunk again in the hills, so she leads Daron down into the dry
wash that skirts the Nelson property. While Daron stares down
distractedly at his sneakers as they pound the flakes of dried
mud into powder, she chatters cheerfully—but quietly—to distract herself. "So when Gus and Amantha DeSoto started renting out ponies to ride, Grandpa took me over. I couldn't have
been more than six." The shade of the intermittent cedar trees
above does not reach into the gully, and the sun is whitely mer-

ciless. Kath sweeps her short hair up in the back and pulls a hand along her damp neck. "I remember his name was Honey. I'm sure he was completely tame, but I thought he was this huge, wild beast. In fact, I'm sure he was very tame, because Grandpa and the DeSotos left me on his back and went onto the porch. One of their sons was supposed to be watching me from the barn somewhere."

Daron bends to lift a curl of sediment, but it crumbles before he can put it in his pocket.

"I don't know how I got the pony out the back gate, but somehow we ended up on the trail. Behind the ranch buildings the ground really drops off. If the pony had lost his footing we'd have been at the bottom of a ravine. I guess Heavenly Father was looking out for me." Kath rolls her dry lips and feels the gritty, uneven surface of her lipstick. Her mother will deride her for looking sloppy and hot. "Grandpa and the DeSotos got very worried about me. They called the sheriff's office and everyone in the church ward and were out on horseback hunting for me. But I wasn't scared at all. I rode Honey all the way to the post office road, then into the hills here." Between breaks in the bushes, she looks toward the Nelsons'. Skunk Nelson found Kath sitting on the grass behind a shed, holding tight to the pony's reins. He was thirteen, spotted with pimples, and infamous among the kids in town for his body odor. Kath had been more frightened of him than of being lost and wouldn't tell him her name. But he had seen her visiting his Aunt Berma next door and ran to get his father. Kath clung to the horse and cried until her mother arrived to take her home. She avoided Skunk for the next thirteen years, until she married him.

Kath doesn't want to tell Daron this part of the story. She finishes quickly and brightly. "When they found me, the DeSotos were so glad to see I'd taken good care of the pony, they let me come and ride for free whenever I wanted."

"So you want to make me go there?" Daron drags along a tumbleweed, stewing up a small dust cloud behind him.

"No," she says, too harshly. "We'll probably ride somewhere

else." She doesn't want the DeSotos to see her back in Sterling.

"Mom? Why did Grandma leave?"

"I don't know. I guess we'll find out. But don't worry. I'm sure things will be fine." She turns to smile at him, but she isn't sure at all.

"Did they fight when you were growing up?"

Although she could honestly answer no, the question makes her uncomfortable. "We were a happy family," she says.

Kath sees the green tar-shingled roof of Aunt Ina's house and leads Daron up the chalky slope of the gully. A manmade irrigation ditch slices straight across the flat land before the shrubs at the back of the yard. The ditch turns at the corner of the hedge and flows along the boundary between Aunt Ina's yard and her daughter and son-in-law's. "Think you can jump this?" Kath asks.

Daron searches along the banks of the green-brown water. "Looks like there's a bridge over there."

He points to the weathered planks spanning the water between the neighboring lawns, but she won't risk straying that close to Merrill's house. "We don't need it. Come on." She runs a few steps, then leaps. She lands neatly on both feet and waits while Daron hurls himself over. He lands more uncertainly, on one knee, and his comic book flies from his back pocket. He shakes the dirt from its fluttering pages and follows her through the bushes. She guides him around the far side of the house to the front door.

Across the main road, Merrill's semi sits parked on the gravel shoulder. "Let's hurry in." With her palm to the small of his back, she marches Daron along a path lined with well-watered petunias.

"Why?" Daron brushes the knees of his jeans.

"Because we're late." She finds Daron observing the glances she makes at the truck and quickly rings, then knocks at the front door.

Her mother answers, in a gray tracksuit with the zippered

jacket open to a pressed pink T-shirt. Her silver-white hair sweeps into an immaculate pouf; she has spent the morning at the beauty shop. Her mother is always carefully put together. "Kath." She smiles but furrows her forehead. "You've cut your hair so short. It looks pasted to your head."

"Good to see you too, Mom. Can we come in?" She pushes past while her mother catches the screen door for Daron behind her.

"What's the rush?"

"You said he wasn't here."

"He wasn't, this morning. I'm not a party to his schedule, honey."

"Have you told him I was home?"

"Your husband has been cucumber cool to your father and me for years. And I can't say as I blame him. To this day, I can't see why you up and left like you did."

Cousin Berma stands outside the door to the kitchen, waiting for the family friction to subside before she intrudes. She has put on one of her summer Sunday dresses, with a patterned profusion of orange and pink daisies. Her hair, dyed a deep butterscotch, rises above her head in a Utah beehive. "KathLeen. It's been so long."

"Hello." She hunts around her for Daron and finds him lingering behind her, touching the screen door and clutching his comic. "Daron, say hello to Cousin Berma."

"Hi." Daron twitches as Cousin Berma studies him through her round, honey-colored glasses.

"Well, young man, do you like brownies?"

"I guess so."

"Then let's go get one, why don't we." Cousin Berma turns toward the kitchen. She looks back to smile at Daron and swings a cupped palm at her waist as if coaxing a puppy to follow her. Daron looks up at Kath, but she keeps a blank face, and he wanders through the swinging door after Cousin Berma.

"Isn't that just typical of Berma. She just doesn't consider I

might want to see my grandson." Her mother touches Kath's elbow and turns her away from the kitchen, in confidence. "He's
still so small. What does the doctor say?"

"Mom." She had almost forgotten her mother's blunt, tactless
approach to conversation. "He's not sick. It's not that unusual."

"If I was you, I would see about exercises or something. You
don't want him to grow up stunted."

"He's not stunted!" Her voice comes out too loud; she covers
her mouth with her fingertips and looks to the kitchen door.

"I'd like to talk to him for a bit." Her mother brushes a dot of
lipstick from her tooth before the hall mirror. "If that's okay
with you," she adds pointedly.

"Of course, Mom." She tries to hide her irritation under con-
ciliation; if she gets furious, she will never survive the ordeal of
the afternoon. "I'll go get him." In the kitchen, she finds Daron
at the pullout counter slurping the last of his milk through a
bent-neck straw. Cousin Berma grates a block of cheddar cheese
at the sink. "Hon, your grandma would like to see you for a
minute." They both look over at Kath, surprised, as if they can't,
at first glance, recall her face.

Daron slides from the tall stool and pauses in the middle of
the worn blue-sparkle linoleum. Cousin Berma wipes cheese
from the back of the grater. "You better run along, dear."

"I think Grandma's in the front room," Kath says. Daron starts
forward, then returns for his comic before pushing through the
flapping door. In a few minutes an easy intimacy has grown between Daron and Berma, and Kath feels a twinge of jealousy. She
has to work so much harder to be close to her son. She did not
have an intimate family. As she grew up, her mother and father
withdrew their hugs, their pats on the cheek, their caresses, as
they took away the bottle, the diapers, the crib, and the night
light. She was raised into adulthood with an awkward awareness
of her hands when they reached for another body. She has
promised herself that her son will not grow up that way.

"I shouldn't have done it, Kath, I know," Berma says. "I don't
want to spoil his appetite. But I like to make children happy."

"It's fine. I'm sure Daron will be your fan for life now. Can I help you with something?"

"You don't have to, Kath."

"I'd like to. It would be nice to stay and talk with you." She has two topics to broach with Berma, both awful.

"Well, you could cut up some veggies for the salad." Cousin Berma carries the grated cheese, pouched in a paper towel, to the oven. She opens the door and sprinkles the cheese on the contents of a baking dish inside.

"What are we having?" Kath opens the refrigerator.

"I'm trying a new chicken casserole. With a chow mein noodle crust."

"Sounds good." She looks in the crisper drawers at the bottom. She takes a cucumber, a carrot, a tomato, and the lettuce head to the counter.

Cousin Berma sits on the stool she set out for Daron, engulfing the seat with her broad-hipped floral dress. Her silence stills the air.

Kath looks over from her place at the cutting board. "Is something the matter?"

"Oh, Kath. It's silly." Berma breathes heavily.

"No, go on. What is it?"

"Could I ask you something, Kath?"

"Sure. Go ahead." She washes the lettuce.

"I've never talked to anyone about . . . but you're a single woman. I feel okay with you." Cousin Berma slips off her glasses and wipes at them absently with the uncheesed paper towel. "Do you listen to the radio ever, Kath?"

"Yeah. Quite a bit." She tears the lettuce leaves into pieces.

"There's a call-in program I've heard. For seniors. Once I heard this therapist, and she talked about single seniors and . . . " Her voice vanishes, and Kath turns. "And what's missing from our lives. What . . . pleasures we think we need to give up."

"It wasn't one of those terrible sex shows, I hope." She hunts in a drawer for the peeler. She remembers how tiring talking to Berma can be.

"I still feel things, Kath." Cousin Berma reaches out to brush the back of Kath's blouse, for understanding, for support. Kath pretends she doesn't notice her touch and steps sideways to the next drawer. "I'm lonely sometimes, Kath. Of course, I would never do anything . . . how ridiculous! But I feel wrong, I guess, about just wanting to."

"Maybe you should talk to the bishop about this." Kath stares intently at the cutting board.

"It's just that, with Mother how she is, I really don't get to church much anymore."

"I think you're thinking too much. You're not really unhappy. These psychologists get everybody riled up." She is inexplicably irritated.

"An old woman like me. It's silly." Cousin Berma stands and looks to the window ledge over the sink, at the African violet and the herbs in little brown pots. "I guess I thought you could help me, Kath. That maybe you would know. Because of what's happened with you, I suppose."

Kath resents the conclusion that Cousin Berma has drawn. She assumes that Kath is like her, that she has fallen away and become a Jack Mormon, no longer connected to the Church and its precepts with her heart. She sees Kath as the black sheep of the family—as everyone in Sterling must—and Kath wants to cry out. Why can't they be made to realize that she didn't have any choice? She scrapes chopped carrot onto the lettuce in the bowl. "No. I don't think I can help."

They both stare ahead, tight-lipped, until the silence becomes painful. Kath can't abandon the salad and leave the room. And she can't tolerate the acrimonious quiet, with Berma trembling, her spotted hands on the drainboard. Kath examines the thoughts at the top of her mind: Merrill and her mother. They are improbable topics, but she decides to try them to deflect her anger. "Does Merrill still stay with his parents?"

"Well, what with being on the road all the time, he doesn't really need a place of his own." Cousin Berma seems revived; her syllables rise sharpened and firm. "You are in the doghouse in the Nelson family. That's for darn tootin'."

Cousin Berma's soft voice fills with wounded malice directed at Kath, and Kath cringes. She has forced a sweet woman into cruelty. She wants to disavow the hurt she has caused, the betrayal of trust. Berma is right: they are both single women—the years don't divide them. And she can't afford to hurt the one person who might find her worthy of friendship. She drops the peeler and cucumber into the sink. "I'm sorry, Berma. I'm sorry." She squeezes her eyes to fight tears.

Cousin Berma puts her hands on Kath's shoulders. "What is it?"

"I'm sorry. I'm just scared."

"Of what, dear?" Cousin Berma pulls Kath to her, holding her tight.

"I'm not sure. And that's what scares me."

Daron: Isaac and Abraham

Daron considers himself a connoisseur of comics. Some of the other kids he knows will buy comics haphazardly— a special issue of *Spider-Man,* three or four *Steel Kings* in a row, an occasional *Batman*—but Daron is more dedicated. He loves the ability of comics to create a world from panel to panel, from issue to issue, from title to title. He pores like an archaeologist over the data of the books which slowly reveal the DC Comics Universe, the Zenith Universe, the Marvel Universe. They are as byzantine as life, but unlike life's random twists and turns, the comics cosmos is carefully supervised. No detail is overlooked by its creators.

Daron grows quickly annoyed with people who insist that comics are a waste of his time. He always finishes his homework, does his chores when he needs to, and he reads plenty of "real" books; these objections are irrational. His grandmother's complaint when she greeted him in the front room of the old house was a sanitary one. *You don't read those dirty old things, do you?* she asked. *You be sure to wash your hands before lunch.*

She brushed his bangs from his face and eyed him speculatively, as if he might not measure up to some unspoken standard. Then she led him out onto the front porch.

While his grandmother nervously shifts and rearranges the slatted redwood deck chairs, Daron sits rolling his comic in the palms of his hands. She crosses the porch to stand next to a post and stare out over the drainage canal and the border of flowers at the opposite house. In comic books, he thinks, empty moments never happen; they would never show panel after panel, page after page, of the same front porch and the same sunfaded sky.

When something does happen, Daron feels it as a charge crackling in the motionless air. His grandmother waves her small, pudgy hand, and a shape slips from the shadows along the side of the other house. In the sunlight, the figure becomes a man. He approaches the ditch and, without looking down, strides the planks over the water. He is the tall blond man from the horse-riding photograph. The man doesn't follow the stones set down for a walkway but plows a straight line across the lawn to the porch, crushing the bloom of a petunia under his cowboy boot as he breaches the row of flowers. He hesitates at the bottom of the steps, rubbing his palms over his dark blue jeans and the slight paunch under his T-shirt. He has the unnatural clean-cut look of a fresh-clipped dog. Unruly waves remain in his short yellow hair.

Daron's grandmother motions the man up, and as he hoists himself heavily from step to step, she looks at Daron and nervously strokes the hair behind her ear. *Daron,* she says, *this is your father.* She points at the man as if there is some question whom she means. *I'll knock on the window,* she tells the man. *Then you'll need to go.*

Hiya, Daron, he says. *It's me, Skunk.*

Skunk stretches out his hand, and Daron rises halfway from the chair to shake it, then sinks back. Skunk grins, and Daron tries to look cold and bored. He turns his head to the window, hoping that his grandmother will soon knock on the glass.

Whatcha got there? Skunk asks.

They both look down at the cover of the comic in his lap. It says *X-Men* in large letters; Daron doesn't bother to respond.

Your mom let you have those things? he asks. Skunk sits in the chair that Daron's grandmother spent so much time arranging. You like superheroes, huh? Do you know about the Holy Superheroes? You should read their books. They're called the Bible and the Book of Mormon.

Skunk waits, smiling, as if he expects Daron to laugh, but when Daron doesn't, he looks down at his water-stained boots and twists a blue-stone high school ring around his finger. Your mother sees to it you read the Bible, doesn't she? Skunk asks.

Daron sees the pale whiskers shining like tiny flecks of ice on Skunk's chin. He doesn't answer, because they don't have a Bible in the house.

You get to church regular, right? Right? Skunk curls his hand around Daron's arm. Now look here, Daron, you should show just a little respect and answer me, son.

You're not my father, Daron says. He twists his arm to set it free, but Skunk cinches his fingers tighter.

That's not for me or you to say. It's up to God to decide who's really family and who isn't. But I know we got a bond, son, and that's what's important here. Skunk releases Daron and leans back with his hands behind his neck. So tell me, he asks, you don't get to church much, do you, Daron?

No, Daron says, and looks to the door and the window.

Then I guess I better tell you one of the important stories so you can learn from it and grow up righteous.

You see, a man is judged by what he does on this earth, Skunk begins. Heavenly Father has tests for every man to see if they'll measure up. Like you, Daron. If He tested you now, you wouldn't be ready and you'd fail bad, so you better listen up. You see, for some men He has special tests, harder tests, because He needs to find soldiers and prophets to fight the fight and lead the people.

Skunk leans forward with his elbows crooked on his thighs and his face near Daron. He speaks slowly and carefully, fixing Daron's eyes with his own, as if he were calming Daron after a bad scare, as if he were telling a bedtime story.

There's a story in the Bible, Skunk says, about what a good man might be asked to do to show his worthiness before God.

In this story, there was an old man named Abraham. He was a hundred, and his wife, Sarah, was ninety. They had no children but they wanted some, so they prayed and prayed until Heavenly Father granted them a son.

The boy they had was named Isaac, and he was a fine kid. They raised him to be quick and strong. He helped the ranch hands, washed the trucks, and did the chores around the house. He was always obedient to his father and mother. He was their only child, and they loved him very much.

But Heavenly Father had special plans for Abraham. He was meant to do great things to spread the gospel of Jesus.

Although Skunk doesn't seem to notice, Daron allows a skeptical scowl to cross his face. He doesn't know that much about the Bible, but he knows that Jesus wasn't alive in the Old Testament. Skunk tells the story as if it just happened yesterday, and Daron is a little frightened by the urgency beneath his calm voice.

Heavenly Father wanted to test Abraham, Skunk says, so He came down from heaven as a sunbeam through a crack in the clouds. He called out, "Abraham."

Abraham said, "I'm here, Father-in-Heaven."

"Abraham," Heavenly Father said, "take thy only son, Isaac, and go unto the mountains. When thou gets to the spot I will show thou, I want thou to offer him unto the Lord as a sacrifice."

Abraham was real sad about this because he loved his son dearly. It sounded wrong; it sounded bad. But if the Hand of God points you out for a task or He asks something from you, you must never question it.

So Abraham got up early the next morning and put the camper on his truck. He loaded it up with supplies and woke up two of the young ranch hands to go with him. Then he crept into Isaac's room and said, "Come on. Get up, son. Let's go hunting."

They all climbed into the camper and truck. Abraham slid his gun into the gun rack in the back window of the cab and drove up the road into the mountains until they came to their usual campsite. Abraham waited for the Word of God to tell him what to do next. But it didn't come, so he took the little chain saw from the cupboard in the camper and walked out into the forest to cut firewood. He was working at dividing a tree trunk into logs when everything grew quiet. A darkness wrapped around him, and Abraham dropped to his knees to pray. A ray of pure white light dropped down from heaven, and riding on that beam was the Angel Moroni. You've seen him on top of the temple, haven't you, Daron? The angel is like the most beautiful person you can imagine, only he's giant and walks in the air.

The angel pointed up the mountain and told Abraham, "This is the place."

So Abraham went back to the camp and put his skinning knife, lighter fluid, and matches in the pockets of his hunting vest. "You wait here at camp," he told the young men. "Isaac and I will go check things out up above and then come back." He filled a backpack with wood and handed it to his son. "You can carry the kindling."

They climbed the zigzagging trail up the mountain, with Abraham leading the way toward the place the angel had shown him. Isaac followed after him. As they trudged the steep and rugged path, Isaac's pack grew heavy on his back, and he wondered why he needed to carry so much. He shouted to his father, who was scrambling up the rocks, "We got wood to start a fire, but what are we going to cook on it?"

All Abraham said was "The Lord will provide." Because

sometimes a man must keep his silence. But Isaac was a good boy and didn't ask any more questions.

They continued up the path until they reached the level clearing Angel Moroni had shown Abraham in the vision. Abraham set down his pack and dug a broad, shallow bowl in the earth with his camp shovel. He ringed the pit with rough black stones. He stood over Isaac, who was sitting on the ground. "Why don't you set up the wood for a fire?"

Isaac took the scraps of kindling and small logs from his pack to build a pyramid in the center of the pit like he'd been taught to do in Boy Scouts. When Isaac bent down to his chore, Abraham crept behind him, and stretched his arm around Isaac's middle to hold his son, and tied off the boy's arms and legs behind him like a calf with some laundry line. Isaac was scared and shouted, "Dad! What are you doing?"

Abraham said, "Heavenly Father spoke to me and told me to give Him my son. I must obey Heavenly Father, just as you must obey me, your own father."

"I understand, Dad," Isaac said. "You must do God's work for the family." After that, Isaac was quiet and well behaved, and Abraham didn't need to use the balled-up sock he had brought to stuff in Isaac's mouth to stifle him.

Abraham lay his son on the firewood in the pit and squeezed the can of lighter fluid into the kindling. He drew his skinning knife from its leather case. He blessed the knife with consecrated oil and asked for it to serve Heavenly Father's purpose well. He held the point of the knife to the soft spot at the base of his son's throat and prepared to thrust in and up to cut Isaac open.

The Angel Moroni appeared again, in garments of gleaming white, and swept the knife from Abraham's hand. "Abraham!" the angel shouted. "Lay not a hand unto the lad. Do not do anything unto him. Thou hast proved thy loyalty unto the Lord because thou was willing to surrender up thy son."

Abraham heard this low moaning behind him and looked back to a find a huge eighteen-point deer with his rack caught between the trunks of two leaning trees. He had never seen such a beautiful animal. Abraham unstrapped his gun from his pack. It was a thirty-aught-six, and he aimed and shot the deer cleanly through its breast into its heart. Sometime when you come again, Daron, I'll show you what the gun was like. If you're real good, I might even let you fire it.

Skunk sat back and capped his knees with his large hands. Now, I don't want you to get the wrong idea here. In the Bible, Heavenly Father gives Abraham the animal as a replacement sacrifice. But that was the old days. We don't believe in animal sacrifices and idols and incense and all that stuff anymore. No, I like to think God gave Abraham such a fine animal as a gift for his loyalty.

So after the deer fell over with one clean shot, Heavenly Father appeared, and He and Moroni stood before Abraham with their bare feet floating off the ground. He said, "Thou hast proven thyself worthy, Abraham, and I will make a covenant with thou. I bless thou and promise that the true Church will be restored on earth and thou and thy family will multiply and fill the land with beautiful children to worship unto Me. There will be as many children as there are stars in the sky or grains of sand upon the beach, and thy children will all be the chosen of God and will come unto Me at last in the celestial kingdom."

Heavenly Father laid his mighty hand upon Abraham's head, and Abraham laid his hand upon Isaac, and so the blessing was passed on to his son.

Daron's grandmother knocks on the window, and both Daron and Skunk squirm in their chairs. She holds out the fingers of her hand and mouths the words *Five minutes* through the glass.

So, Skunk continues, the end of the story is Abraham unties Isaac, and Isaac helps his father skin and clean the deer. They return to camp and eat venison stew for lunch. And Isaac is so hungry he eats as much as the men.

But the important thing is the lesson, son. We must obey Heavenly Father's words in all the things He says and through all the vessels He uses to speak to us. We must obey His Prophet here on earth, who is the President of the Church, and also his Counselors. And we must obey the Council of the Twelve, and the Quorum of the Seventy, and our Stake President, and the bishop of our ward. And each family must obey without question the word of the father who brings the priesthood of Heavenly Father into the home. If we obey, then we will be blessed many times over.

Okay, Skunks says, so I'm gonna bless you now. He jumps up and shuffles around behind Daron's chair.

Daron doesn't try to keep him in sight; he stares straight ahead at the ditch, where the flowers seem pummeled to limp, ragged shreds by the summer heat. He feels Skunk's fingers descend hot and thick on his skull.

Like you say, I may not be your dad in blood, but I do know you're under the protection of my priesthood, and I'm gonna make it my solemn duty to look out for you.

As Skunk mumbles a blessing, his hand growing sweaty in Daron's hair, Daron knows that he will not tell his mom about Skunk. Not because Skunk has said that a man must keep his silence, but because it helps him to imagine that he is dreaming, and telling his mom would make it real.

Kath: 5

Kath's mother calls Daron in from outside, and they start lunch. They sit in the shadowed dining room, a lightless cubicle accessible from the front sitting room through a rounded arch. Although each piece of heavy furniture has been polished free of dust and the panes in the china hutch sparkle along their cut-glass edges, the air sleeps mustily around them. Kath and Cousin Berma sit quietly at opposite ends of the rectangular table. Her mother and Daron sit across from each other. Her mother asks Daron an endless series of questions about school and sports and hobbies and little girlfriends while she neatly parcels and consumes her lunch with a quick-moving knife and fork. Daron is bored, and her mother displays an interest in his answers sufficient only to allow her to frame the next question.

The casserole is eerie in its blandness—soft and white, with even the chow mein noodles creamed into its homogeneous texture; it alters the temperature of Kath's mouth but provides nothing else. She dumps more dressing on the salad, intending for the brace of vinegar to rescue her from her disconnected grogginess.

"And what do you do with your afternoons after school?" Her mother tucks a lettuce leaf between her lips.

"Stuff. Mostly." After one smallish forkful, Daron has made no attempt to eat the beige mound on his plate. He sits with his chair pulled slightly away from the table, looking glumly into his lap. "Watch TV. Or play games. Write stuff."

"Are you on any teams?"

He shakes his head.

"Do you go to Cub Scouts?" He shakes his head again. "Your ward does have Cub Scouts?"

A long quiet breath circles the table, and Kath realizes that the question was directed at her. She looks from Daron and the rim of his water glass to her mother. "Um, I'm not sure. I guess so."

"It wouldn't be too hard, some Sunday, to ask, would it, Kath?"

"No." She and Daron have no interest in uniforms or den mothers or merit badges. But there is little point in making this clear to her mother.

"What do you write about?"

"Stories." Daron drinks from his glass; his voice rises from its dulled slump. "And scientific observations." Kath hasn't heard about these; he writes in a series of red-cover spiral notebooks, but he never shows them to her.

"That's interesting for a little boy. Are you a budding scientist?"

Daron shrugs. His eyes fall to his lap again.

"So what have you observed, for example?"

He looks up again. "That people are really bigger than they look. Everything is wound up real tight inside us. Intestines and veins and everything. If we were worms, with our digestive system stretched out, we would be a hundred feet long or more."

"Daron," Kath scolds him. Cousin Berma smiles. Her mother says nothing but lines up her knife and fork along the edge of her plate.

Cousin Berma curls her napkin in her fist and drops it on the table. "Anyone like more chicken? Salad?"

"This might be a *good* time to take Daron into the kitchen for dessert," her mother announces sharply, implying to Cousin Berma that their earlier trip to the kitchen was inexcusable.

"All right," Cousin Berma speaks flatly. "Come on, dear." Daron stands to follow her, and catches the comic that was spread open in his lap before it slips to the ground.

When they are gone, her mother folds her napkin over a finger and dabs at her pinched lips. "Spoils his appetite. That woman has no sense. Women who don't raise their own seldom do have that sense of what's good for children."

"She's fine. She's been nice to him."

"That's fine. But that's not the most important thing about child raising. You've got to know what they need. Not what they want. What Daron needs, and it's so clear that I don't know where your mind is, he needs guidance. I won't say he needs a father because you never would listen to me about this. After you made the first one become . . . okay, perhaps he wasn't your mistake. But then you ran away from the second one, who could do so much for you—which, I might remind you, is something you still haven't explained to me. I can't honestly say if a third one would do you any good. But if you won't come to your senses and come home, at least there must be some group in your ward or in the stake or somewhere in Vegas that gives young boys a father figure to look up to. And he's ten, Kath. He should have been baptized two years ago, and how will it ever happen without a father?"

She listens to her mother ramble and recriminate; she slides the back of the spoon across the polished wood with her thumb in its bowl. "I didn't come here for you to advise me on Daron."

"I know. Your father sent you." Her mother pauses, as if she expects Kath to take the initiative, ask a question. When Kath doesn't respond, when she bites at her lip, her mother continues. "I don't want to hurt him, you know. I just want to keep things quiet till I think it through."

"Aunt PearLeen was at the house when you called yesterday."

"His sister." Kath hears her mother's recognition that nothing can be kept quiet now and her disgust at the lengths to which Kath's aunt will go to spread the news. "Your dad has made his own bed then."

"I wish you would tell me what this is all about. I realize we don't get along and—"

"Yes we do. I'm your mother."

"I don't really see what Dad thinks I can do, but for his sake I've got to try to—"

"It's no mystery that he called you. You are the oldest. Carl is gone. He would be the hardest to tell. I don't think I could. Perhaps I wouldn't have left if he was home." Her mother turns distractedly to look through the archway and out the front window. "JuLee is still my baby. Of course it had to be you."

"It had to be me what?"

"For your father."

"For him what? Why can't you and Dad get together and talk this out?"

"He could never, you know. It's simply not in him to do that." Ardeth shakes her head, and Kath wipes at the wet corners of her eyes, upset.

Her mother reaches into the pocket of her tracksuit jacket and pulls out a zip-top Baggie, which she unfolds and places next to Kath's plate. Inside is a carefully smoothed-out condom wrapper—blue with white lettering on the outside, ripped at one end, shiny silver within. Merrill had used the same brand with her the first and second times, before he told her that they were a sinister invention of the zero-population people, satanists who wanted to stop men from multiplying. "I was sweeping out the bed of his truck. I found this wadded up in a corner."

She slid the exhibit back toward her mother's placemat. "But it doesn't mean anything. Did you talk to him about it? Someone could have just thrown it in."

"There's a new girl at the Food King in Alma, where JuLee works. Woman, I should say. The new floor manager. He's given her rides home when he drops JuLee off. She's not your father's type of girl at all. But there it is."

"Mom."

"It's not enough to go on. I said the same to myself. But why does it bother me so? I prayed about it, Kath. I prayed that it was nothing, and I think God answered me. I felt the difference between this thing that I thought he was guilty of and the anger it gave me. It wasn't just what he did. If you took that away, if I'd never found this thing, I would still have this knot in my heart. I didn't want to think that Heavenly Father would say this to a wife and mother. I prayed it every day, but it was the same. I think I may not love your father anymore."

"Mom." Kath can't think it. Her parents are married eternally; it is the source of her life. She feels that if her parents separate the world will lose its meaning; nothing solid will remain to grab hold of. She can't even take comfort in rejecting her mother's hypocrisy over marriage. First Cousin Berma and now her mother have opened up to her like oysters, and she sees them now as puny things clinging helplessly inside the shells they have presented to the world. If she could think, it might make her pity them, love them more, but she can't think and fight the dizziness. She walks the slow steps toward the room in her mind, breathing deeply.

"I won't . . . " Her mother begins to stack the plates and silverware together. "I was about to say I wouldn't leave him, because that would be wrong. But I can't say that yet. I'm not sure what I'll do."

"So, what should I . . . what do I tell him?"

"Nothing yet. I need time." Her mother stands and sets her hand gently on Kath's forearm. Kath stares at it, stunned. Her mother never touches her, and the sensation feels too odd to give her comfort. "Thanks for coming, Kath. Your father and I really need you here right now."

"Oh, Kath." Cousin Berma sticks her head in the room from the kitchen door. "Would you say hello to Mother before you go?"
"Sure."

Kath gathers Daron from his comfortable spot reading in the padded chairswing on the back patio, and they follow Cousin Berma and Kath's mother up the stairs. Aunt Ina has been moved into the tiny room Berma and Clovis shared as girls because it is close to the bathroom, installed years after the house was built, in a closet at the top of the stairs. Aunt Ina lies in one of the single beds. A television sits in the center of the other mattress with its screen angled for Ina to watch; a remote control waits on the nightstand between the headboards. In the corner behind the door, at the foot of the empty bed, is a metal-frame table with plastic shelves and drawers—a baby's changing table—filled with Aunt Ina's clean linen and diapers and bottles of oil rub and vapor rub and talc for bedsores. The walls are papered for a children's room: a print of yellow roses tied with blue ribbon, faded into abstraction. There is not enough room for four to fit, and her mother waits in the hall while the three of them line up in the aisle between the beds.

Aunt Ina lies under a pink sheet on a large piece of lamb's wool. Her straight long hair spreads on the pillow. Her seraphic bones stretch up through liquid skin at the brow, at the elbow, at the cords of her knuckles. She is the same color everywhere— hair, lips, eyeballs, fingernails, tongue—gray lint. Cousin Berma slips her mother's hand between her own, without pressing it, without seeming to touch it, as if it were a curlicue of smoke. "KathLeen Miller and her son are here to say hello. KathLeen is Ardeth Miller's daughter."

"I don't . . ." Aunt Ina's voice is shockingly strong. Kath can't imagine any muscles left to push air out of her body and generate the sound. The voice seems to rise from somewhere else, some other part of the room. "I don't know her."

"Ardeth Miller is Trenton and Della Campwell's daughter. Della Taylor. Your cousin Della who moved to Salt Lake." Kath wonders how far into the past they will need to go before Aunt Ina finds something to snatch with her memory. Aunt Ina's milky blue irises shift from her face to Daron's and back, maybe seeing them, maybe not. "Della was Uncle Grover's daughter. A beautiful blond, you always said."

"He didn't have one red cent when she married him." Aunt Ina remembers Della, Kath's grandmother, beautiful and blond on her wedding day. But with all the connections left to be made, all the arduous transfers from face to face, name to name, Aunt Ina will never make it into the present and join up Daron with his great-grandmother through the file of blood. She will never understand where to fit the unknown boy at her bedside.

Kath takes Aunt Ina's hand from Berma. It moves her deeply, touching Aunt Ina's silky fingers and feeling the frail pulse of life beating out from the shrinking room inside where she will always sit, unstooped and ready to dance, or pull beets, or open the blooms of her hands against her husband's back. Surprising herself, Kath kisses Aunt Ina's forehead—sweet rosepetal, lightly oiled. "Good to see you, Aunt Ina." She stretches her mind to accommodate the vast scope of Ina's life. Aunt Ina has lived through the ages of every person in the house—Daron, Kath, Ardeth, Berma—and lived beyond them. She has absorbed more afternoons in scarlet wing chairs and more sunsets on padded porch swings than she can recount, and as she forgets the days and hours, as her memories become innumerable, her final testament is her own failing but persistent body. It serves as proof that the present—joyous, unendurable, or strange—will not hold and must melt forever into the future. For an instant Kath feels the weight of Aunt Ina's experience falling through time with a glacier's slow force. The feeling fades, but the memory of its enduring heaviness comforts her.

She won't make Daron touch Aunt Ina. Kath once went on a

round of visits with her father and a group of Elders who laid hands on the sick and the old, and she remembers how frightening it can be. But she does want Daron to see Aunt Ina and know. Kath would like him to see and learn—learn much sooner and younger than she did whatever it is she has just learned from Aunt Ina herself, whatever it is that already grows dim and cool as she stands behind her son with her hands on his shoulders. "Aunt Ina, this is my son, Daron. Daron is ten years old."

Daron: In the Bible

After standing in bare feet and pajamas in the kitchen to tell his mother and grandfather good night, Daron creeps into the front room and tugs the huge, leatherbound Family Bible from the bookshelf. He drops the heavy volume on his bed and spreads it open. In the early pages, in Genesis, chapter 22, he finds Skunk's story.

Skunk changed the details a lot. In the Bible the story is both starker—sparser—and less certain. In the Bible Isaac does not agree with his father's plan. The Bible doesn't say what Isaac thought. It is not interested in what people think. It is not interested in the concerns of children. It heaves forward down the steps of each verse like the irreversible march of a comic book's panels.

After reading the story again in the Bible, Daron feels gravity lose its hold, leaving him to float in space. He lies on the bedcover, not sleeping, and waits for his mother to make her bedtime noises in the bathroom next door.

He wonders what Isaac's mother thought. He wonders if Sarah knew before it happened, and if she had agreed to it. In the Bible Sarah dies at the beginning of chapter 23, when she is a hundred and twenty-seven. She dies in a place called Kirjath-arba, and Abraham travels there to mourn for her. It frustrates Daron that the Bible does not say when Sarah moved away from Abraham. It does not say why she moved. It does not say whether she took Isaac with her when she left.

Kath: 6

As Kath looks at her father across the table with his midnight snack of milk and a plate of coconut macaroons, she sees a man who has never kissed with any comfort or with the desire to shape another mouth into softness under his own wet lips. His jaws work evenly as his tongue shifts the wad of cookie to the other side of his mouth for further chewing. His thumbnail on the side of the milk glass is split, and his knuckles are knobbed, perhaps swollen by arthritis she hasn't noticed or been informed about. His eyes are cast down on the empty bud vase in the center of the lazy Susan. His body is crusted and stolid, and if there ever was passion inside him, it was liquid metal in a thick mold, looking for cracks to spurt from, but finding none and cooling, hardening into a gray bar of duty that would never flash or bend or throb with a wild keening ring for the sheer hunger and want of love.

Kath cannot reconcile this man and his wife with the lively people in the two family stories she knows about their courtship. She has heard them—The Apple Story and The Outhouse Story—many times, from many people, in a multitude of variations. She used to compose the stories in her head as paintings or movie scenes or, most often, as faithfully reenacted rituals. In her heart, she has celebrated her parents' marriage as a holy eternal fact, and the events that preceded it seemed impossible and wondrous, like shells from a lost sea unearthed in desert sand. As she sits in the half shade of the overhead lamp, she wonders if she has misread their significance, if they are the fossil record of creatures who have ceased to exist.

. . .

The Apple Story invariably begins with the Depression. The Miller family survived the Depression somehow, but they lost their ranch. They moved into a too-small house at the edge of Sterling, and Kath's grandfather hired himself out to other ranchers and farmers. He filled whatever odd-job positions he could find. Often, her grandfather was far from home in some other corner of the county, and her grandmother raised the children on her own: five boys and two girls. The people in the ward watched out for her as much as possible, but no one had enough to be overgenerous.

The children worked when they could: after school, and during the two weeks off for harvest, and full time during the summer. They planted, weeded, pulled beets, baled hay, cleaned cowsheds, ran errands for elderly Sisters, did yardwork, were stockboys and delivery boys, tended the horses of farmers without motor tractors, and milked cows at the dairy until the new pump machines arrived and Mr. Madsen and his son could do all the cows, twice a day, by themselves. Kath's father, Don, the youngest boy, usually worked in other people's yards after school to earn pennies. MargaLee, the oldest, had the best and steadiest job in the beauty shop.

Her first summer in Sterling, Ardeth Campwell went to the beauty shop on Saturday mornings with her mother. She sat in the sill of the front window and kicked the scuffed heels of her sandals against the wall while her mother had herself done up by Mrs. Bright with curls tight enough for the week to come. Sometimes, if she didn't have a customer, MargaLee would invite Ardeth to sit in the other chair. She would twist Ardeth's hair into complex braids. On one of these occasions, while Ardeth watched blond pigtails take shape in the mirror and imagined she was Shirley Temple as Heidi, her mother asked Mrs. Bright if she knew of someone who could help out in their yard; Mr. Campwell spent such long hours at the shop that certain chores did not get done. "MargaLee, doll"—when Kath's mother told the story she slipped into a brassy singsong for Mrs.

Bright's voice—"what about that brother of yours?"

Ardeth's mother asked how old the boy was, and Ardeth twisted her head excitedly when she heard that MargaLee's brother was her age. Because school hadn't started yet and Primary was divided into boys and girls, she hadn't met many boys. The pigtail flipped out of MargaLee's hand and began to unravel. She couldn't take the time to braid it again because another customer had come in. "I walked through town with one pigtail, and I didn't even notice," Kath's mother always noted.

MargaLee agreed to ask her brother Don to stop by the Campwell house on Friday afternoons. Two days a week, Don would knock quietly at the back door, and Ardeth's mother would stand on the stoop and point out which flowerbeds needed weeding or where a pesky patch of dandelions had sprung up in the grass. Ardeth would watch Don in his plaid shirt and dungarees through the bay window in the dining room. Once or twice she knocked on the glass and waved, but she was too shy to go out and introduce herself. (Although, according to Kath's father, Ardeth was a flirt. She would knock until he looked up, then duck to the side and roll herself up in the curtains.)

The Campwell ladies, Ardeth and her mother, worked extra hard that summer to fit in. Her father had come down from Salt Lake in the winter to start up his tractor franchise. She and her mother had lived with her grandmother until the house was built, and arrived in Sterling at the end of June. Ardeth's mother involved herself in every project she could. She hosted a Ladies' Relief Society luncheon—"they thought she was showing off her new house"—and she tried to be included in every visit that the Relief Society made to the sick and needy in the ward. In August of that first summer, their visit was to Don's sister PearLeen.

PearLeen was the only Miller child who didn't work for money outside the house. She was pale and thin—"frail" was the agreed-on label for her condition. She was susceptible to colds and fevers. She had anemia. And she had asthma. At the end of July PearLeen had fallen off a tire swing in the tree behind the house.

It had knocked the wind out of her; unlike a healthy child, she didn't recover her breath in a few minutes. She lay on her back in the dust until her mother carried her inside. After she had spent a week in bed, the Relief Society ladies decided to visit her. Ardeth's mother drove the car into St. George one day to do some shopping and bought a fancy fruit basket wrapped in crinkling green cellophane to take to PearLeen. She wouldn't allow Ardeth to unwrap it to see inside.

When the other women saw her mother carrying the basket toward them down the street to the Miller house, they weren't pleased. Ardeth had run ahead of her mother, and she heard one of them. "Isn't that typical. Such a production." Ardeth's mother did things with flair—overdid things, some thought. Some of her gifts looked less like helping out and more like charity. And no one in Sterling, no matter how needy, took charity.

Ardeth went inside the hot, cramped house with the ladies, but she was shut out of the sickroom. "It might be catching, you never know. And children are so prone," they said. Mrs. Miller led the ladies in and closed the door. Ardeth was left alone in the dark passage between the kitchen and the back bedroom, where PearLeen had been settled to sleep alone. "For the first time in my life," Aunt PearLeen would interject whenever she overheard the story being told.

Through the torn screen door she watched two of Don's brothers playing catch in the dried grass. She heard the click of the latch of PearLeen's door behind her, and Mrs. Miller emerged with the fruit basket in one hand and a ceramic bowl of Mrs. Tanner's chicken noodle soup in the other. Ardeth followed her to the door of the kitchen. "Come on in"—Kath's mother melted her voice into sweetness to imitate her husband's mother. Mrs. Miller set the soup and fruit by the sink and opened a cupboard. "Oh. I don't have a cookie for you, honey." The woman stepped toward her and unexpectedly took her hand. "Let's take a look at that dress." She walked Ardeth down the hall that cut the house in two and opened the front door. She led Ardeth into the bright square of sun on the plain wood floor and stepped back to look at her pink dress. "That is a fine thing. You're like a candy princess."

Ardeth spun so that Mrs. Miller wouldn't miss out on admiring the gathers in the back. "How's PearLeen?"

"Not so poorly today. I expect it's just a bit too much heat for her. She'll go back to her own bed tomorrow or the next day."

"Could I see her?"

"I don't see why not, honey. I'll go see how she's fairing."

Mrs. Miller left her, and she wandered down into the kitchen again. She noticed the fruit basket on the counter. It was wrong—Kath's mother would lower her eyes at this point in the telling—but she knew it was her last chance to look inside. She delicately peeled a corner of the cellophane and spied oranges and gleaming nutshells, a cardboard tray of powdered figs and a small tin of coconut candies. At the top of the heap was an apple, larger than her two fists, shining and red, with faint lines of dots trailing down from the well of the stem. Without considering her misbehavior, she took the apple before refolding the package. She slipped it below her stiff underskirt and held it in the band of her white stockings. She thought she might give it to PearLeen when the ladies weren't looking.

But she didn't get to see her. The ladies emerged in an elaborate and unsuccessful pantomime of quiet tiptoeing. "She's napping, honey," Mrs. Miller said. "But you come back again. She'd like that."

She and her mother returned home across town. The apple bulge tightened the waist of her stockings uncomfortably as she walked, and her mother noticed her fidgeting. "You better stay away from PearLeen Miller for now. I don't want you sick." When they came to the arched gate at the side of their house, Ardeth saw Don watering one of the rosebushes. Her mother told him that they had been to see his sister. He mumbled something, and her mother went inside the house. Ardeth remained behind in the checkerboard shadow of the lattice arch. She said, "Hi."

"Hi," he said back, and edged furtively to the other side of the arch.

"I've got something for you," she said. "Wait here." She ran until the corner of the house blocked her from his sight and reached under her dress. She rushed back and held out the red fruit to him. "You deserve a treat," she said as he took the apple and grinned at her. After that, they spoke to each other almost every day all through summer, and the school year, and into high school, when they started to date.

The Apple Story was Ardeth's favorite. She was convinced that her little theft had transformed her into Florence Nightingale, but she would tell the story casually, concealing all but the faintest hint of her satisfaction.

When he was in the mood to tease his wife, Kath's father would tell the Outhouse Story, beginning with the pledge. At a cookout during the summer before their senior year, Don and Ardeth had made a pact to attend every school and church dance together. The vow made Don uncomfortable. He didn't have nice clothes to wear or time to learn how to dance properly. He worked at Ardeth's father's tractor store all the hours he wasn't in school. The Miller family continued to struggle—"treading in quicksand," her father called it. Don had lost his second-oldest brother, James, in the War, his father had gone blind with cataracts, and if things kept going as they were, it looked as if Don would be sent to Korea, and not on a Church mission, when he graduated. He was reluctant to celebrate, to allow himself to be too happy; but Ardeth was insistent, and that was enough for him to agree to the plan.

The next dance after Homecoming was on Halloween—the first dance in the new gymnasium. It was a costume ball, and that posed another problem for Don. Going as a ghost would be the easiest, but his mother would box his ears if he wasted a sheet. Ardeth would have given him one, but he didn't like taking things from her, and besides, he wanted his costume to be a surprise. On the afternoon of the dance, he and his best buddy, Doug Pratt, bought black and white paper and string at the drug-store; they decided to be pirates. They made eyepatches and skull-and-crossbone armbands. They wore white shirts and dark pants, tucking the legs jauntily into their cowboy boots. They tied red calico kerchiefs over their hair. Don unscrewed the wood handle of a baling hook and scrunched his hand up inside the sleeve of his shirt to hold the hook dangling out of the but-toned cuff. They climbed into Doug's rusty car and roared off, yohohoing, to get their girls.

They swashbuckled up to Una Mae Thompson's front porch and kidnapped the masked Cinderella who stepped out to greet them. Doug lifted her over his shoulder and carried her to the car. "Don't muss my dress," Kath's father would squeak in Una Mae's voice.

The next stop was Ardeth's house. Doug and Una Mae waited in the car, holding hands over the gearshift. Don shouted, "Avast ye, mateys!" when Ardeth's mother opened the door. She jumped back in mock-shock and led him in to eat a sticky can-died apple in the front room while Ardeth finished getting ready. He and Ardeth's mother and father gathered at the bot-tom of the stairs when she descended. "Their jaws all dropped," her mother would gloat. She wore a floor-length gown of shim-mering green with a tightly cinched waist and a huge bustle be-hind. Her face was heavily powdered, with a beauty mark on her cheek, and her head was crowned by a towering wig of white cotton bunting.

"You look pretty," Don said, and waved his hook in admiration.

"Oh Don, you'll put an eye out," she said. "Or, more likely, snag my dress." She shifted with difficulty back up the stairs, then down again with a piece of cork from her sewing kit. She twisted it onto the end of his hook. "That's better." She said good night to her parents, and they told her to be careful and call them when she got to Uncle Eldon and Aunt Ina's, where she was stay-ing for the night with various cousins and girlfriends under the gaze of Cousin Berma as a chaperone. Ardeth took his arm, and they went off to the dance.

They danced the slow numbers close but not touching at the waist; he flinched whenever his hand strayed onto the bare flesh of her shoulder or neck; he fetched her glasses of orange punch with licorice swizzle sticks; they realized that she would need to stand all night because of the bustle. The evening proceeded in a courtly manner, almost like Homecoming, until they decided to enter the Spook Tunnel.

The Drama Club and Spirit Leaders had decorated the hallway behind the gym by blocking all the windows and building a maze with blanket walls. Simon Tervalion, one of the Catholic boys bussed in from Pinevale, was in charge of the scary noises, and the girl Spirit Leaders were dressed in filmy gowns as wraiths. Ardeth squeezed the fingers of both hands into his arm in an attempt to show fear—"but we all know your mom is afraid of nothing"—while he bought two nickel tickets. Amy Johnson parted the black curtains for them and smiled hard at Don.

Inside it was pitch-black, and Ardeth gripped him tightly while he felt his way along the swaying walls. The path weaved from one side of the hall to other. A record played the sounds of a raging storm, there were bells and whistles, and Simon blew ominous "Catholic music" on his oboe. From time to time a ghostgirl would approach with a candle to say "Boo!" or to ask them to put their hands in a bowl she carried—"Feel the witch's brains!"—"These are deadman's eyes-Ha-Ha-Ha!" When they were somewhere in the center, they heard a crash, and the record and the oboe stopped. The beam of a flashlight played over them. "Hiya, Ardie! Hi, Don!" A ghostgirl, Teresa Somebody, stood near them. "Would you stay here a minute, please?" She vanished through a part in the blankets.

They waited in the darkness, and he wrapped his arm, slightly more tightly than usual, around her shoulders. The dance, even the other people in the Spook Tunnel, seemed far off. They heard voices muffled by the blankets, but no one nearby. "Are you scared?" he asked.

"Kind of. Maybe. Yeah, I am," she replied without great conviction.

He felt for her chin and turned her face to him. Slowly, he lowered his lips to hers, and they had their first serious kiss (and Kath always wonders what her father considered serious, whether lips were open, whether tongues were involved). The overhead lights came on, and several voices went "Awww!" in disappointment. "Sorry, everybody!" Simon Tervalion shouted from a corner. "You can all go through again in a minute!"

They wound their way out of the disenchanted Spook Tunnel with the static crackle of the kiss on their lips. They danced a few more times, and Ardeth decided that she absolutely had to get rid of the bustle and sit down for a while. She disappeared into the girl's room, and by the time they found each other again, the dance was over.

He and Doug drove Ardeth and Una Mae to the Kimball house for the sleepover party. Cousin Berma was out on the porch to collect the girls when the car pulled up, which prevented any good-night snuggling. They drove down the street toward home, but Halloween was too fresh on their minds to forget about. At the corner of Main and Roosevelt, near the center of town, a group of boys had gathered under the streetlight. Two of Don's brothers and Doug's cousin DeLyle were among them.

He and Doug joined forces with them, and they roared around the streets of Sterling in Doug's jalopy, seeing what tricks they could play. They soaped windows on one street and stacked trash cans in a pyramid in the center of another. They talked about the all-girl party the entire time and soon were pulled toward the house by an irresistible force. Don's brother Frank had mentioned the outhouse-tipping they used to do before the War, and Eldon and Ina Kimball were the only people anyone could think of who still had an outhouse.

They parked the car halfway up the turnoff road and crept quietly along the hedge in front of Joe Nelson's house. They sent out survey parties to the lighted windows in the Kimball house, and he and Doug found most of the girls in the kitchen, making popcorn balls. They sat at the kitchen table or stood around drinking lemonade from tall frosted glasses in their pajamas and nightgowns and robes, all flowery and childish. Una Mae was measuring the Karo syrup, and Cousin Berma stood by the refrigerator with a candy thermometer, bemused. Don couldn't find Ardeth but assumed she was in another room where there were records playing and laughter.

The boys gathered again at the edge of the vegetable garden, then made a rush on the outhouse, down the path behind the corn. They lined up against one wall of the tiny shack, one of them counted "One—two—three," and they heaved their shoulders into the wood. Beyond all the dramatic grunting and groaning, they didn't notice—or didn't pause to reflect on—the squealing within. The outhouse landed with a thud on its side in the dirt. The door fell open, in fact broke off its hinges and landed separately on the ground. The boys were laughing, panicked, exhilarated, ready to run, when a girl crawled out from inside in her nightgown. The boys froze with guilt in a circle around her, anticipating the shame they would feel when her gaze passed over them, but Ardeth, as she climbed to her feet and pulled her robe from the dark interior, only studied the other boys long enough to find Don's face in the crowd. She glared at him voicelessly. She hunted for the armholes of her robe as she crossed the lawn to the back door of the house.

Kath's father claimed that the outhouse-tipping infuriated her mother and she didn't forgive him for three years. Her mother denied any grudge. What had angered her that night, she said, was that Don had danced the last three dances of the Halloween ball with Amy Johnson while she was occupied in the ladies' room.

Kath uncovered the true source of her father's fascination with the story one day in the lumberyard office. Douglas Pratt had married PearLeen, and before he left to start a construction business, he and Kath's father had worked together as partners in a lumberyard next door to Mr. Campwell's tractor store. On slow days he and Uncle Doug would sit around the office splitting cartons of beer neither of their wives would ever know about—although Kath had been aware of the empty bottles in the trash cans out back for as long as she could remember. They had drunk a few each on an afternoon in Halloween week when her mother dropped Carl and Kath off at the office to be watched for a few hours while she went shopping. Her father and Doug sat behind the opaque glass door of her father's inner office and must have thought that Kath was out of hearing as she played with her dolls on the floor of the storefront. Or else that she was too young and wouldn't make the necessary connections. Or else they were too drunk, and their judgment had vanished.

They reminisced about the dance, her mother's conceited rich-girl's costume, their wild night of pranks. Kath scooted on her butt across the floor until she was next to the door. When they spoke of that Halloween's highlight—the outhouse-tipping—her father grew quiet, as if he were still embarrassed by his actions. But Uncle Doug chuckled. "No panties on her. That's what I remember." His father shushed Doug, slamming his fist, Kath guessed, for quiet, on the blotterpad of the desk. "Then you reached inside and found them, right? And where did you keep them?" Her father didn't speak. "Where did you say you put them when you went in the service?"

"In the toe of my dress shoes."

"In your dress shoes halfway around the world."

In any event, the kiss in the Spook Tunnel was the last one her father got from her mother until after the Korean War.

Kath wonders when the kisses stopped again: whether, in the later years, there were secret bedroom smooches or quick pecks on the cheek, or whether their lips had dried long ago. Her father's face betrays nothing. There is no mark on its graying, weathered surface that reveals any anguish at the loss of his wife's affection or any satisfaction from the presumed caresses of the woman at the Food King.

Kath wonders how Daron will look at his mother in twenty

years. A woman who has shut herself off like a lightswitch. Acrid smoke sealed in a dark bottle. Or as a living memento of his childhood, like a comic whose pages have faded but whose contents are known by heart so that he need never look inside her again to see if her story has changed. She wonders how she would be reflected in a stranger's eyes, what hardness might be found, what sorrows. But she has lived too much inside herself, untold to the world, and every eye that looks on her now is a stranger's.

"She didn't say anything to you?" Her father's head bobs nervously out of the light from the hanging lamp, and the striations of brown and gray in his hair dissolve into undifferentiated black.

"She needs time," Kath says. She knows her father won't press her further; she counts on his wordless discomfort to save her from elaboration. His lips clench stoically; he shuts his eyes and opens them slowly. He plucks invisible crumbs from the tabletop and returns them to the macaroon plate. Perhaps there is a thimbleful of liquid metal left inside him, like mercury—real hurt—squeezing from its reservoir under pressure to twitch his fingertips. She wants to comfort him. "I'm sure she'll call soon."

She hears the key turn in the front lock and the door creak with deliberate stealth. Her back is turned to the sound. From his chair her father could see to the front of the house, but he doesn't hear, doesn't look. She listens for the small sounds JuLee makes as she slips unobserved through the length of dark hall and shuts the door to her room; Kath hasn't seen her sister since breakfast.

"There's the twenty-fourth," he says.

On the twenty-fourth of July, Pioneer Day, for as long as Kath can remember, the whole Miller family has gathered on the lawn behind the house for a barbecue. Her mother has organized the whole affair since its inception, delegating food assignments, borrowing grills from the neighbors, renting the needed additional chairs and tables. Her mother's talents have always developed best from complex plans and meticulous preparation. She would see to it that the charcoal was the proper temperature, she would check on the ice cream makers grumbling away full of ice and salt in a shaded corner of the patio, she would ensure that the children all had paper pioneer hats and bonnets to wear, and she would reassure herself that one of the older children had properly prepared a talk on Brigham Young and Utah's heritage by requesting a private audition in the bedroom before the dinner began. She would fret over any element that might be out of her control and would call almost everyone that day to remind them of their appointed tasks—who was buying the sparklers, who was taking the photos or bringing a video camera, who would transport the ice blocks to the park for the children's tradition of sliding the steeply sloping grass down to the pond.

With his fingers lined along the rim of his glass, her father contemplates all of these exigencies; they must terrify him.

Kath is annoyed that her father has already considered this problem. But her father is a practical man. He will worry about who will do the grocery shopping and pay the utility bills before he worries about who will be left to love him.

"She'll be back by then. That's over two weeks away. You'll see."

"Should we cancel it? Or what should we do? I don't know what." He carries the cookie plate and the empty glass to the sink. When he returns to the light, his shoulders have stiffened, resolved. "I think I'll go to bed now."

"Me too. Good night."

He walks by her, distracted, and she sits for a few minutes staring across the room at the kitchen witch in the shadows above the fridge. She switches off the lamp over the table and moves hesistantly through the hall toward the bathroom, not trusting her familiarity with the house to serve her any longer. Outside her old bedroom she hears JuLee sobbing. She opens the door and finds her sister face down on the bed snuffing her tears into a pillow. Kath leans against the doorjamb. "Are you okay? What's wrong?"

"Nothing," JuLee says. "Nothing. Nothing. Nothing."

Each "nothing" is a key used to lock another door to keep Kath out. She could remind JuLee how they used to confide in each other as girls and dissect every tremor and shock of life together until it made sense or they lost interest in the subject. But she remembers the last times JuLee tried to comfort her. After Tom, and after Merrill, JuLee had asked what was wrong and what she could do to help, but Kath wouldn't answer. Since Tom, Kath has kept her thoughts in an empty room, and she knows that JuLee won't forgive her for that silence.

Daron: Sterling

On Friday morning Daron buys a new lined notebook in the gas station convenience store to begin his study of Sterling. He sits in the front room during the long afternoon with his notebook, a fresh pen, a road map, and a sheaf of typing paper from his grandfather's desk.

After studying the map, he practices on the loose sheets to teach himself to draw a diagram for the front cover:

First, sketch in an outline of Utah. States in the West are easy to draw: they look like children's building blocks—unlike those farther east, which become small, squiggly, and river-bounded. Take a sheet of eight-and-a-half-by-eleven-inch white paper and draw a substantial rectangle lying lengthwise across the upper right-hand corner. Fill in the rectangle with crosshatches, and what remains is Utah.

Next, sketch in another rectangle of approximately half the size of the first, standing in the lower left-hand corner. Do this very lightly in pencil, because you will want to erase it later. Within this imaginary pencil box, you should draw a slender upright rectangle, rather small, in the upper right corner. You can erase the pencil marks now, if you want.

Transform the new rectangle into another Utah. Label the

baby Utah DESOTO RANCH and color it purple, because the signs on the freeway for DeSoto Touring and DeSoto Horses are painted royal purple and lavender.

The tiny rectangle you have chipped out of the DeSoto Ranch is Sterling.

If you wish to be fancy, you might try to add the I-15 freeway, which starts in the lower left corner of the state and shoots in a red artery through Utah somewhat left of center into the block at the top where the Great Salt Lake and Salt Lake City are waiting for the blood supply. There should be a little space between the freeway line and the square called Sterling. To hook them together, you should draw a capital U in black. Touch the ears of the U to the freeway and the rectangle of Sterling to the U's hanging belly. Sterling hangs from the freeway on its access road like the pendant of a forgotten necklace. The old highway ran through Sterling and became Main Street; people had to pass through Sterling to get anywhere. But not anymore, which explains the abandoned hotels and empty campgrounds. The flaking signs at the ends of town say WELCOME and COME BACK SOON, but no one sees them.

On the top line of the first page Daron writes: HISTORY.

He found *A Visitor's Guide to Southern Utah* in the glovebox of his grandfather's truck (along with a vehicle registration card; a knotted blue dress sock stuffed with various sizes of washers and nuts; a Phillips-head screwdriver; a blob of gray doughy substance coated with crumbs, gravel, and sunflower seed shells, which, when Daron held it up, his grandfather identified as plumber's clay; a wax paper tube half filled with Necco wafers; and a copy of *Raise the Titanic!* by Clive Cussler, missing its front cover). In the guide, the history of Sterling is encapsulated in six sentences, which Daron transcribes into his notebook:

The community of Sterling (7 mi. southeast of I-15: exit on the Sterling Valley Road) began life around 1853 as

Solomon's Spring, a shady watering stop between Fillmore, at that time the territorial capital, and St. George, Las Vegas, and other Mormon settlements farther to the south and west. The town was named after Micah Moroni Sterling, who arrived in the valley in 1887 with ambitions for establishing mining ventures in the surrounding hills. Although his explorations for gold, copper, and phosphates yielded few results, Sterling garnered his reputation, as well as his wealth, from the general store, restaurant, and other services which were provided by his "Traveler's Haven." Many of the original buildings are still viewable in the southern end of town, including the original post office, which operated until a new structure was erected in 1973. While the Sterling family and their "Traveler's Haven" can no longer be found, the town of Sterling continues to thrive as a modest community with its primary activities of farming, ranching, light industry, and tourism. The town is also notable for its attractive municipal park and its annual Autumn Flower Show.

When Daron asked his grandfather about Sterling, his answer was more concise: "This town used to be a good place to raise kids. I don't know anymore."

Kath: 7

Kath's father finished the frozen chili at lunch on Friday with a toasted cheese sandwich and a sliced banana with sugar. Late Friday afternoon, her father left to check up on the lumberyard in his semiretired position as the owner and executive manager, and a few Sisters from the ward, prodded by Aunt PearLeen, appeared with pyrex dishes of dinner to help out during the time of crisis. RaNae Wilcox and Carolinda Montgomery spoke to

Kath in flustered half-whispers, but she couldn't tell if their halting voices were due to the shock of her mother's departure or their surprise at seeing her in Sterling again. Dutifully, Kath put the pans in the oven at the times and temperatures printed neatly on the included recipe card. When her father finished a few chores in the yard, she brought them to the table. There was a potato dish in a round tureen, made with Tater Tots, peas, and a cheese sauce. There were frozen green beans transformed into a side dish with the addition of a crunchy layer of bread crumbs. The entree was another interpretation of the chicken casserole Aunt Berma had prepared. This time, it had the consistency of glue, and the chunks of canned chicken were chewy, with the faint, acrid taste of burnt rubber. Daron stared at the casserole disconsolately, as if resigning himself to the idea that its creamed whiteness was the sole, official dish of Sterling. The plate of butterscotch oatmeal cookies was the dinner's salvation, and everyone, including her sullen, hollow-eyed sister, remained at the table until even the crumbs were gone. As much as she dreaded the event, Kath began to look forward to the food at the Saturday barbecue with Uncle Douglas and Aunt PearLeen.

After shopping to buy ice cream to take with them, Kath, Daron, JuLee, and her father squeeze into the cramped cab of the truck. Kath resists the impulse to scrunch her body down below the level of the windows as they pass through town. It would be tempting to hide if she weren't wedged between Daron and the passenger door, and if she didn't know that Daron would not forget an act of childishness from his mother. Instead, she stares down at the silver handle of the toolbox on the floor.

"Here's a bit of history for you, Daron," her father says brightly. He gestures out the side window with his thumb. "That corner there is where your mom got hit by the ice cream truck."

"Dad," she says. "He doesn't need to hear this story." She looks down again, conscious of her bare legs beneath the hem of her light cotton summer dress. There are bruises on both shins from banging into open drawers at work, and without nylons to cover them, her legs seem battered and pale.

"Your mom was running down the street from home to catch up with the truck. They only came from Alma on Saturday afternoons. And she slipped on the wet sidewalk out in front of Brother Hyrum's place and a whole handful of quarters rolled out into the street. She went right on after them, the idiot, and the driver slammed his brakes. But the front tire still popped over her leg. Not much more than a sprain, but it was the stupidest thing she did as a child."

"Yeah, but she was really proud of it," JuLee says. It is the first time she has spoken voluntarily in two days, and Kath notices that they have all shifted to listen with unusual attention. "Whenever anybody had stitches or a cast Kath would top them. Remember when I dislocated my shoulder? Soon as I got home from the doctor she said, 'That's nothing. I got run over by an ice cream truck.' " JuLee smiles, but, as Kath meets her eyes, her expression freezes, then melts back into blank distraction. Years before, she and her sister had been the best of friends, but now, after a few initial attempts at cheeriness between them, JuLee regards her with the cool, wary gaze of a stranger.

Kath turns her attention outside the cab again in time to see the glossy nose of the semi rig still parked across from the Nelson house.

She presses her back against the bench and hopes that the combined screen of her father at the wheel, her sister with her legs curled sideways to avoid the gearshift, and her son with a tall grocery sack on his lap will be sufficient to block her from view. She looks out the opposite window, and when she believes it is safe again she glances quickly forward.

Merrill stands by his rig stripped to the undershirt of his church garments, spraying window cleaner on the rear-view mirror. Her father taps his horn and waves. Both JuLee and Daron shift uneasily on the bench. Merrill looks up, and Kath twists the knob of the window crank in her fist.

"I'm sorry," her father says after a moment. To her. Or to no one in particular. "I forgot."

They pass one end of the post office road, which winds through the hills at the border of the DeSoto Ranch in a broad arc to emerge at the side of the old Sterling post office, now converted to a daycare center. The truck bounces over the bars of a cattle gate set in the road, and Kath sees the entrance to the Ranch marked by a small wooden placard: DES with the brandmark burnt into the wood below. Mr. DeSoto relies on hiring out horses for sight-seeing tours and organizing rafting expeditions on the Colorado, but he has hung on to the property, which surrounds Sterling on two sides. Although the ranch buildings are not visible from the road, Kath feels the impulse to hide again. Every turn in the street reveals another monument to the past, which has not subsided since she fled from it. She had promised Mr. DeSoto she wouldn't return. When she and Daron came down the hill to him on that twenty-fourth of July, she had told him everything that happened. Everything but one thing. He had taken them in to Mrs. DeSoto, who worked with tweezers on the stickers in Daron's bare feet. Mr. DeSoto wanted to call the police, but Kath said no. She couldn't explain but made him vow to tell no one. He insisted on the condition that she put as many miles between herself and Sterling as she could. She had promised, and she wonders what he will do when he hears that she has returned.

The one thing she hadn't told Mr. DeSoto was that she had seen it herself. She hadn't heard it speak, but she had seen it. The angel in the branches of the tree. With her worry for her parents, she forgot, until now, to feel afraid.

At the point where the road curves at the end of town to rejoin the freeway, a row of newer houses rises on a hill looking back at Sterling, all of them owned by a Pratt son or Pratt son-in-law. Douglas and PearLeen Pratt's house, the house Uncle Douglas inherited from his parents, sits below the newer houses in a hollow on the other side of the road. Her father turns down the sloping drive to the house, and Kath watches two chestnut horses running opposing circles in a corral on her side of the road. "Bet you'll get your chance to ride a bucking bronco today, skunk." Her father leans into the steering wheel to look past JuLee and grin at Daron.

He parks in the dirt behind a boat trailer next to the three-car garage. Before Kath has climbed out of the cab Aunt PearLeen rushes from the front door, where she must have been waiting to pounce. "Kath! Hello! Why, you look just fine!" she announces. "And here's little Daron! Hello, young man! And JuLee, good to see you!" Aunt PearLeen hugs each of them lightly while her head lifts to speak to the next in line. As she hugs JuLee, Kath notices how she squeezes with the heels of her palms, stretching her shell-colored fingernails away for safety.

"Hi, Don." She waves at him across the bed of the truck. "Doug's out at the corral."

"I'll take Daron to see the horses." Her father tugs off his baseball cap and lifts his Stetson from its hook on the gunrack. "Maybe we'll turn up some of your cousins to play with."

Kath takes the grocery sack from Daron, but he lingers in the same spot with awkward, empty hands; she didn't allow him to bring comics or a videogame. "Go on," she says. He stuffs his fists in the pockets of his jeans and follows his grandfather along the drive to the distant, galloping horses, whose flanks shine flashing in the sun.

"Rhonda's in the kitchen. Shall we?" Aunt PearLeen wheels around in her white suede boots, assuming they will follow her into the house. JuLee looks at Kath blankly, then shuffles behind her aunt like a zombie along the gravel path to the door. JuLee has acted all morning as if she has no volition. She got herself ready and climbed dutifully into the truck with the slow, heavy motion of tragedy. She wouldn't talk to Kath or allow the slightest light to enter and illuminate her pain. Kath sees that everyone in her family has retreated to an inner room, and while each room may be in the same house, the connecting doors are gone.

She trails JuLee and Aunt Pearleen into the long, open front room. They weave around clusters of calico easy chairs, curio cabinets, and end tables dotted with figurines. Thatched baskets of dried flowers line the walls. A family of stuffed geese made from blue-and-white-checked gingham squat in a corner. Over a mantelpiece shelf stacked with tole-painted boxes hangs a large needlepoint picture of three kittens—black, orange, and brown—tumbling together atop a ball of pink yarn. PearLeen pauses at each table to show Kath the results of her latest projects. Her hands sweep around the room, pointing out and explaining, and JuLee steals away to the kitchen. PearLeen delicately touches her fingernails to the shoulder seam of her cream sweatshirt—another project. She has appliquéd irises to the left side and edged the appliqués with a line of purple glitter.

While PearLeen discusses the kind of backing material she used and how the pattern was cut, Kath's eyes fix on the white patch in her aunt's black hair. The white maple leaf rises from above her right eyebrow to float loose on a teased black lake. Her aunt is a small woman, and the blaze of white combines with her large breasts to create a sense of top-heavy prodigiousness; her lower extremities slim down into nothing like a genie from a bottle. She has small perfect features and small slender hands. With the sequined strap of a guitar slung over her shoulder, she could be Miss Pearleen strutting onstage at the Grand Ole Opry. No residue of the frail girl from the Apple Story remains except for the endless needlework, which, Kath knows, represents the long nights PearLeen sits up with a respirator for her asthma.

"So what do we do about your father?"

Kath concentrates on her aunt's lips, tucked together like petals of Austrian Copper. "Do?"

"He'd better meet with his lawyer is what I think." PearLeen fingers her strand of pearls ("*real* pearls from the *South Seas*"). "And none too soon."

Kath tilts her head and shrugs, noncommittal. There is no point in refutation; her mother will never receive a fair analysis from Aunt PearLeen. Kath shifts casually around her aunt into the kitchen.

JuLee sits at the kitchen table with an orange soda and pores through a copy of *Seventeen*; she surrounds herself in its cocoon of glossy pages. Their cousin Rhonda stands over the sink, intently plucking flecks of shell from a hard-boiled egg.

"Now what do you have there?" PearLeen takes the sack from Kath and looks inside. "Mmmmm. Snelgrove's Premium. For special! What a treat!"

"Hi, Kath." Rhonda flashes her miniature smile from the sink. "Sit. Sit. Let me just tuck this into the freezer. There we go." PearLeen shuts the freezer and walks to the sink. She tidies as she goes: she shifts the canisters into a perfect row of descending sizes; she gathers empty butter papers, plastic wrap, an egg carton, and stuffs them in the trash under the sink. Rhonda moves aside for her mother to wash her hands. "I need a pick-me-up," PearLeen shouts. "I *need* a pick-me-up." She lifts a pitcher from the fridge. "Would you like a lemonade, Kath? Fresh lemons?" Kath nods—why not—and PearLeen brings a brimming plastic tumbler to the table for her. She sits. "So what do you think about it, Kath? You talked to your mother. You must have some opinion."

Rhonda smiles behind her mother's back. Her shrug and her eyes assure Kath: I'm sorry, she's impossible—ignore her if you can.

"Honestly, I just think they need to talk and they'll be fine."

"Well, that doesn't work for some, dear." PearLeen, careful of her lipstick, sips at her drink through an infinitesimal opening between her pursed lips, with her mouth barely contacting the glass, like a hummingbird imbibing nectar. "Doesn't seem to have worked for you, for instance."

Rhonda stops her fierce dicing of the eggs on the cutting board. "Mom! I don't think Kath needs this right now."

"You're right. You're right, Rhon. You are so right. I'm extra sorry, Kath. I know it must be hard for you. Children are the real victims in these deals." PearLeen bounds up and twirls around the kitchen in her high-heeled boots, searching for some task, some detail to attend to. "How's that salad coming, Rhonda-hon? Put in tons of black pepper. I love fresh-ground pepper in potato salad."

Escape. Escape, Kath thinks. I just want to escape. She looks at the clock by the stove, a Swiss cuckoo clock, and counts the hours.

"I think it's a female thing, though." PearLeen returns to her chair and her lemonade. JuLee sighs and switches from *Seventeen* to *Sports Illustrated* without lifting her head. "I saw this program. Was it Sally or Oprah or one of those horrible things. Anyway, the doctor said that sooner or later all women are going to go through it. Like a man sowing his wild oats, as they used to say. But with women it comes later on. These yearnings. This dissatisfaction. Anyway, I don't believe it. You can certainly resist. Heavenly Father gave us free will so we could choose not to follow these impulses."

Kath thinks of Berma's yearning and speaks her name aloud: "Cousin Berma . . . " She catches at the words as they leave her lips. She doesn't want to parade Berma's secrets, and speaking her name feels like another betrayal.

"Oh, Berma. She *does* take these shows too seriously. There's a lady that thinking a lot does no good for. She listens to that talk radio and wants to argue all these absurd things with you." PearLeen hooks her hands together, then flutters her fingers up and down like a butterfly breathing on a rock. "You know, she wanted to give us the ERA. We spent a whole summer with that. Whenever I'd see her, at the grocery store or what-have-you, she'd say there's nothing wrong with equality. But, PearLeen, she'd say, the Church isn't against equality. And I'd tell her back that if she'd come to Relief Society when we talked about it, she'd know the truth. If they force us to have ERA, I'd say to her, the next thing we'll be getting is unisex bathrooms. They don't want us to have any protections at all, these women, these women who were pushing this thing through. And you know the kind of women they were, Kath, I'm sure. They wanted to take the Bible and change it to 'Our Mother in Heaven,' and make all the 'he's into 'she's and so on. And then, sooner than not, they'd be putting it in the water."

Kath gulps her lemonade until the ice clicks at her teeth. Her aunt seems wired and manic, like the crackheads she has seen on the streets of Vegas. PearLeen's energy exhausts the air in the kitchen as if to fill her life with chatter and activity so there won't be time to think.

Rhonda rolls her eyes and moves behind PearLeen's chair. "What is it they'd be putting in the water, Mother?"

"To stop the babies, you know. To leave Americans barren of seed."

"Oh, Mom. Barren of seed?"

"It's no joke. And you younger women still need to watch out. These women—they're not really women in my book—are still around. Even in Utah. If they can't stop babies being made, they're going to kill our babies in the womb. You must be ever-vigilant. All of you. I hope you've been listening too, JuLee. It's time for you to know these things."

"Potato salad's ready, Mother."

"But we don't have to be gloomy. We don't have to be gloomy. When Berma would argue this or that, I would look her right in the eyes and smile and say, but, Berma, I'm perfectly happy. We've got things set up the way Heavenly Father wants them, and that's better than any law could ever be. They can't force me to go out and work. I'm very very happy at home taking care of my family."

"Do shut up, Mother. Since when have things been so fucking happy around here?"

"Rhonda!"

"Come on, Mom. JuLee and Kath don't want to listen to any more of this crap. Only they're too polite to say it."

"Rhonda . . . you are . . . you are . . . not a nice girl." PearLeen stands, shaking all over. The white leaf flutters above her brow. Then, quickly, her clenched jaw slackens, and Kath can sense her aunt's brain shifting into retreat. PearLeen smiles. "I'll find the boys. And Uncle Doug will set to getting the charcoal lighted." She strides past the dining table into the front room. "And things will be fine. They'll be fine."

Rhonda slides the salad bowl onto a shelf in the fridge. "I can't take her anymore. I can't."

"She's probably worried about you. Being protective." Kath can't bring much conviction to her aunt's defense. She doesn't know why she bothers, unless it is an instinct to hold every family together against all adversity.

"Protective, yeah. She's a strangler. And Dad's worse."

"What's this I hear about me?" Uncle Douglas barrels into the kitchen from the back door. "Are you girls gossiping about your handsome uncle again?" Kath can't tell whether he heard anything Rhonda said, but she doubts it. He has always teased the three of them about their long whispered conclaves, pretending that he was their constant, unavoidable subject.

"What else would we have to talk about?" Kath says. "Hello, Uncle Doug."

"Long time no see, Katie-Kate." Her uncle's large hand swings through space to land with a soft blow between her shoulderblades. She used to believe his hands were the size of the squared-off paddles used in pizza ovens. They are flat and broad, spreading out from his cuffs. He always keeps the three pearl-topped snap buttons of his cowboy shirt tightly cinched around his wrists. Other than his face, his hands are the only region of her uncle's flesh she has ever seen. He has never rolled up his sleeves or taken off his shirt or boots and socks. He wears the blue plaid shirt buttoned up to the neck without even a hint of his silvery white temple garments showing underneath at the throat. Kath's mother told her that after Uncle Douglas was set apart for his mission and received his garments, he was in a house fire started by a too-dry Christmas tree. He had been horrendously, seepingly burned on his arms and feet and legs—the extremities his garments did not cover. But beneath the loose white one-piece suit of his garments, his flesh had been entirely spared—pinkened but unburnt. He was living testament to the admonition that one should dress in the garments of the Lord at all times.

Years ago Kath and Rhonda had watched Aunt PearLeen hang clean garments on the line to dry. They shivered in the breeze like empty scarecrow skins. Kath had asked Rhonda the story about the fire, but she had never heard it. When Kath married Merrill, they were required to wait before receiving their temple endowments and garments—because Kath needed to rise from her fallen state. She never got them. They didn't save her from peril.

"Why don't you come on down, Kath, and see my discovery with the boys." He slaps her lightly again and opens the door to the basement staircase. Daron enters the house in front of her father. He looks across the room at her, persistently but unreadably, then disappears down the stairs with the two men.

"What discovery?" Kath asks Rhonda as she gets up to follow them.

"Don't say anything to him about it. I tried. It doesn't do any good with him." Rhonda shakes her hair out of a loose French twist. "After dinner, let's go out, okay?" Kath nods. "Okay with you, JuLee?"

Kath looks at her sister, who slides her palm across the face of the magazine to turn the page. "I can't tonight. Sorry," she answers dully.

Rhonda bites her lip and shrugs. "We'll go to Boonies."

Kath takes the basement steps two at time, as she did when they would run down to play. She thinks about Boonies—a dump—and Tom taking her there, and wonders if Rhonda has started frequenting bars, along with smoking and improper boyfriends and swearing at her mother. She crosses the cluttered recreation room toward the light in the unfinished half of the basement.

She wanders through corridors and enclosures sketched in with two-by-four frames and partitioned, here and there, with drywall. Most of the rooms are stuffed. Beneath the smeared windows sunk in wells in the backyard are months and months of household supplies suggested by the Church for times of disaster. Aunt PearLeen has overstocked the Pratt emergency larder possibly ten or twenty times above the requirements. Rows and rows of food cartons rise to the ceiling. A translucent wall of water in rectangular plastic bricks shimmers at the end of one corridor. She shifts carefully around a pillar of dehydrated fruit boxes toward the voices in Uncle Douglas's workshop.

Her father assists her uncle with the lid of a crate. They lift the plywood sheet up and off and lean it against the table saw. The inside of the crate seems to be stuffed with black plastic garbage bags. Uncle Douglas waves her in from the doorway. "Hey, Katie-Kate. Let me recap the story for you."

Daron stands far apart within the sphere of one of the three harsh bulbs dangling from the upstairs floor joists. He watches her enter the room, then looks skeptically at the box, with his hands balled into fists at his side.

Uncle Douglas chooses a blade from his pocket knife and starts cutting the strips of electricians' tape sealing the seams of the plastic. "So I was up in that box canyon . . . remember, we used to take the horses to that ridge, the Devil's Whip?" She has no memory of the Devil's Whip, but she can imagine it—the burnt-red rock curving upward like the fuselage of a jumbo jet, only vaster, marked with boulders at its crest like the bumpy hide along an alligator's spine. "So I was puttering around up there with my Winchester. Thought I might do a little shooting at the birds or just hike around to see where the wash drains from. And I notice there's this lip along the bottom of the sandstone wall. Sort of like a tube had been cut into the rock, then part of one side had been peeled open. I thought something might be living under there, so I knelt down to look. Idiotic thing to do, of course, since if there's a coyote in there or something, I hardly want my face at ground level to it."

He peels off plastic in all directions. Bulging beneath it are fist-sized balls of wadded newspaper. "I poke a stick in and sort of drag it out along the ground, and out come these little triangle pieces of red clay. I'm no expert, so I think maybe they're just rocks. But they look like pottery. Then I pull out a bigger piece that's got a curve to it. And for sure that's pottery. Here." He reaches into a tomato juice can on the work counter and lifts out a red shard, broken into a point at both ends, with a distinct bend in the center. He hands it to her, and she rests the smooth, cool clay in her palm. "So I clamber all the way down to the horse and get the flashlight out of the saddlepack. I shine it inside along the wall, and I see this thing, this dark shape toward the back."

He tosses the paper balls from the crate, and they bounce around the cement floor and settle at their feet. From the monochrome newsprint, something, yellow-brown, rounded like the bottom of a jug, begins to emerge. It looks as dry and brittle as the fragment in her hand; she closes her fist. Daron steps forward. His face drains of the light from one bulb but doesn't yet enter the glow of the next, where the crate rests. "Here she is." A few more wads of paper slip, and she sees two openings, two parallel punctures or crevices. The jugshape contorts, no longer smoothly rounded. Below the two punctures, which open onto black from inside the sphere, there is another, triangular hole. And beneath that, in two rows, a rictus of yellow teeth. She stares at the visage of a dry, fleshless skull.

"I'll eat my hat if she's not a Lamanite princess." Uncle Douglas rolls the rest of the newspaper free. "Come closer. Have a look. Come see the old girl, Daron. You know the story about the lost tribe of Israel? They sailed right on over here from the Old World. The whole Book of Mormon tells us what they got up to. You could probably find the old girl's name in there somewhere."

She thinks that it can't be . . . but it is, a body dumped unceremoniously into a crate, folded over on itself. Huddled, without flesh, the bones will never again be anything but cold. The skull rests its chin, broken-necked, on an apex of tattered cloth, presumably covering bent knees. One arm wraps forward around the ankle to mingle tapered yellow fingerbones with tapered toes. The other arm bends back, snapped loose and lolling along the spine. A sheath of brown fabric covers the ribcage and the legs. Kath wonders if the dress is the only evidence Uncle Douglas has used to determine that this was a woman's body.

Other than the skirt—pulled apart at the bottom to reveal a loose fibrous mesh but appearing brittle, like cornhusk—the bone-bared skeleton is unsexed.

Kath bends in, almost unwillingly. On the rear slope of the skull she notices fragments of scalp—like bits of burnt paper, already ash-powder but holding together tenaciously in their former shape. And on these dry dermal islands, willfully unfallen, are isolated obsidian threads of hair. She can't stop looking at these patches. She remembers slipping out onto the covered front porch after her father had skinned and gutted his kill to examine the deer's fresh-cut antlers. When she saw the ends, wet with pink porous marrow holes, she would forget the horns' weird forking beauty and shudder at their amputation. But, as the skin animates the skull, she doesn't feel shock but sorrow. She—this body—is a woman; in some past moment beaded on the string of time, the woman is alive; there are veins under the flesh where the blood beats against the touch of the woman's fingers as she raises a hand to clasp her throat, clenched and sore from thirst. She is alive; then—Kath feels it—now, she is dead.

"The feds aren't going to let you keep this. They aren't going to be too happy with you, Doug." Her father withdraws from the light and stares too intently at an elaborate socket set on the workbench.

"What they don't know can't hurt me. It's not like I would be showing her off to eveybody. It's just a little piece of history for the grandkids to see. History's important for kids."

She is alive and now she isn't. She waits on the other side of the line Aunt Ina is approaching. Her body may be lost to time, but she is not far away. She could still be helped. Kath sees how she might ease into her uncle's house one night, unannounced and unheard, and carry the woman away with her. She might be surprised by the lightness of the body. Or its heaviness. She could learn the path to the Devil's Whip and return the woman to her rest.

When she looks over at Daron, he glares at her, full of tears and disgust, then scrambles from the room, pushing the black air out ahead of him with his hands. Kath knows not to follow; he won't see that she has been dreaming of rescue, and he will not allow her to comfort him.

Daron: Horses

When he sleeps tonight, Daron knows that he will dream of her. She will trail the desert dust into all the rooms of the house. She will hold her hand to his sleeping mouth until his breath whistles loud through her fingerbones.

But he is not afraid of the dark.

To be honest, as he sits in the basement with the lights out, everyone gone, the pilot flame in the water heater hissing through the quiet from another room, he feels slightly nervous. But he is too old for this fear. He knows it. There are no mysteries beyond the reach of the light; the rooms have simply disappeared from sight, as if squid ink has stained every particle of air. At night he bravely touches his way down his grandfather's hall to the bathroom. He pours himself water in the kitchen without finding the switch. He acts with ease in the domain of the lightless.

But in this basement, in this dark, he may have reason for fear. The boxes loom in rows, gravid with hidden contents. The cartons are stamped on the outside with labels for condensed milk, fruit cocktail, sloppy joe sauce, bean salad. But these familiar trademarks may give a false sense of comfort; they may be a ruse to disguise fearsome contents. He has seen into one of the crates and has reason to doubt.

Daron lingers in the basement, uneasy, by the wall of water jugs, where the last light from the windows has collected on the plastic surface in a fishscale rainbow, because what waits for him upstairs seems worse than the inexplicable, worse than ghosts.

He is avoiding his cousins, Jared and Jason. Jared is fifteen and Jason two years younger, but they are the same height—Jason's taken a growth spurt, Uncle Douglas explained. They have eyes, but they are barely visible beneath folds of thick eyelid. The two squint perpetually as if emerging from a movie theater.

When his grandfather led him out to see the horses, Jason and Jared sat on the corral fence with the heels of their boots hooked on the lower rail. The chest pockets of their white T-shirts bulged with sunflower seeds. They reached in and drew the black ovals one at a time to their mouths. Jared dropped the whole seed onto his tongue, chomped, and twisted his shoulder to spit the husk into the weeds behind him. Jason held each seed between his thumbs and sheared them open with his front teeth. His tongue would flick out, pink and wet, to suck the kernel from the open shell.

His grandfather pointed Daron out to them and explained who he was. Jared smiled; the squint consumed his eyes. He jumped down into the corral and reached over to shake Daron's hand. You ever rid a horse before? Jared kicked the pointed toe of his boot absently at the nearest post.

His grandfather puffed out a single deprecating laugh. Your cousin's a city boy.

We'll teach you, Jason said, and shifted on the rail.

Jared crossed the packed earth to grab for the reins of the horse. It ran alone in a circle paralleling the border of the corral, riding an invisible merry-go-round. Jared caught up the reins, slowed the horse, and turned it, brushing his hand along the shining neck. He walked it over.

He had seen horses before—in pictures and sometimes along the road when he is in the car—but never this close. The size of a horse was a surprise. And the alien shape of their heads was disconcerting: the wide flat plane between wet eyes and the long protruding tunnel from the eyes to the nose and mouth. Tabitha pressed her burnt-butter breast against the top rail and leaned her head out. She snorted rhythmically through looming nostrils and curled her lips from her huge flat teeth at the prospect of food in his grandfather's hands. Jared filled a trough with a garden hose. We'll get you a saddle and show you what's what. The horse reversed herself and dove her head toward the water. We'll try you on Camelot, he said. She's more gentler than Tabitha here.

His grandfather left to search for Uncle Douglas behind the barn, and the cousins took him to the low shed where the horses were stabled. They had cigarettes hidden in a Havoline can behind several jars of leather polish. You ever smoked? Jason asked. Want one?

He's a kid, Jared interrupted. Jason shrugged, and Daron turned in the door of the shed to watch Tabitha pace along the near length of the corral. Hey, Daron, shut the door. Jared struck a match on his boot and held the flaming head out for his brother. With the cigarette clenched in his teeth, Jared took real drags deep into his lungs while he messed around with the straps and stirrups on a battered saddle slung over a sawhorse. Jason took shallow sucks of smoke into his mouth and blew them out again, holding the cigarette cautiously between his thumb and forefinger.

They shouted over each other in their eagerness to ask him about Las Vegas.—Do you know any high rollers?—Shit, Jason, you don't even know what a high roller is.—What about the showgirls?—Do they walk around with their tits out in the casinos?—Course they don't, fuckhead. That's against the law.—Who you calling fuckhead, asswipe?—Watch it.—*You* watch it, motherfucker.—Had me a girlfriend from Nevada, from Mesquite.—Yeah, Jared told all his friends he got laid, but he didn't.—None of your business anyway, is it, shit-for-brains.—Fuck *you*.

Daron grunted and mumbled when they absolutely expected a response but kept quiet. He wanted them to realize he was bored with them. He might have preferred cruelty from them; he knew how to deflect the sting of taunts, to draw a circle inside himself and sit within it.

Jared and Jason wanted to impart their years of teenage wisdom. From their perspective, Daron should have been eager to observe them as they decoded the cipher of adulthood. The cigarettes and swear words, the naughtiness of sex—their rebellion was meant to be a privilege for him to discover. But he had already rejected this stage of growing up and imagined that he might somehow skip forward to avoid the messy teenage years.

Mostly, Jared and Jason wanted to get Daron to ride. They cajoled him aggressively: Don't want us to think you're chickenshit, do you?—Fuck, even your mama can ride a horse.—Come sit on this saddle, shrimp, and I'll show you all you got to do.

They pressed the point as if it were important. They wouldn't let go of it. And he ran out and stood behind an oak at the edge of the lawn until his grandfather and Uncle Douglas strode by on their way into the house.

At least in the basement dark they have left him alone. There's no way he is going to ride a fucking horse.

Kath: 8

Boonies sits just far enough outside the town proper to be reasonably removed from the respectable commerce of Sterling. By day the building bakes in the center of its gravel parking lot, looking, with its cinderblock shell of pale industrial green, like a bomb shelter or an outbuilding where toxic wastes are manipulated. At night it is an island of light, separate from the bright clustered windows of town, and jewel-like on the road fronting the freeway. The corroded sheet metal sign above the door states that the establishment is called Hathaway's Tavern and Café, but Kath has never heard anyone call it that.

Luminous green glass lamps hang over the three diner-style booths in the front window. They are, by decades, the newest fixtures in the room and provide the most light. Farther in, toward the bar at the rear, things grow dim, as if doom has settled in along with thick stagnant smoke over the greasy vinyl chairs. For Kath, the oddest aspect of the decor is the shag carpeting of sculpted seafoam green swirled around with white. Wherever shoes have trod on it, the pile has been stomped into a flat gray mat. She is baffled by the impulse that would lead someone to carpet a saloon.

The decorating theme of Boonies, so far as Kath can determine, is fishing. Along the walls at eye level and above are numerous examples of stuffed fish. Large trout flip about in frozen paroxysms with tails and fins curled, mouths gaping, glass eyes glinting. A rack by the cash register holds an assortment of fish flies in small plastic packets. Annabeth, the owner, tends the register and ties the flies during lulls in the day with the hooks held in the clamp of a pair of pliers. Kath remembers when Annabeth bought the bar and her mother and RaNae Wilcox brought out a Book of Mormon and a plate of peach cobbler cookie squares under the auspices of the Relief Society. Her mother returned with the assessment that Annabeth was hopeless. The woman had taped up newspaper in the south-facing windows of her house and wiped her nose on the cuff of her shirt—a man's shirt. Her mother had noticed the buttons lined up on the wrong side.

Annabeth paces the back of the room in a denim shirt with rolled-up sleeves and a white apron, serving food and drinks across the bar. A few "off-duty" truckers put back beers at the bar, and the Saturday-night regulars from town have congregated around the pool table. Kath and Rhonda sit at a table in the half-light closer to the entrance. Kath had planned to buy one beer and nurse it as long as she could, but she hasn't managed to administer her sips as slowly as she intended. She has ordered another, then another. Her ears have begun to tingle with heat, and her vision tilts gently sideways. Although she has gone out with her friend Carole in Vegas a few times, she has grown unaccustomed to alcohol. Drinking reminds her of Tom, and thoughts of Tom knock her off balance.

"So anyway, after you guys left I told them. That's why I was a little late picking you up." Rhonda's bangs fall across her eyes. Her loose hair looks dry and electric. She started the evening with two rum and Cokes, then switched over on the last round to beer with a tequila chaser. Her small features ease into mobility like softened wax. "I said, look, I want to bring a friend to meet you. My dad says, fine—so who is this boy? I say, I want him to meet everybody. I thought he could come on the twenty-fourth. And Dad says, so who is he? And I say, his name's Manuel. And he says, what? And I say, Manuel Ortiz. And Dad says, I don't believe it. And he was taking off his boots at the kitchen table and slams one really hard on the linoleum." Rhonda tilts the shotglass of clear fluid into her throat and follows it with a gulp of beer. "Hold your horses, princess, he says. You're not bringing no spic to any family party. While you're under my roof, and you listen here, he says, you're not going to go around town with a wetback." Rhonda empties her mug.

"I'm sorry," Kath says. She is sympathetic, although she can't believe Rhonda was surprised by her father's reaction. One of her chief pleasures in seeing Tom was that he remained a necessary secret.

"The whole time he's going on about it, my mom is standing with her arms crossed, looking worried. Or whatever those little tightass shakes of her head are supposed to mean. I say nothing. With my dad it's better, you know, if I shut up. So when he goes, my mom comes close and tells me she's going to explain what my father meant. Like it's not perfectly clear what he meant. We just don't want you to make yourself miserable, she says. We, your father and I, have got nothing against those people. They're good customers, and they're all very nice. We just want you to find somebody you can be happy with. Yeah, right."

"That's too bad." The growing crowd or the beer has made the room swelter, and Kath shrugs off the linen jacket she borrowed from Rhonda to wear over her dress.

"I hate them."

Kath finishes her beer in a large swallow and watches a stripe of residual foam skid down to the bottom of the mug. The song changes on the radio, and one of the regulars reaches up to the shelf over the pool cue rack to crank up the volume: "Momma, Don't Let Your Babies Grow Up to Be Cowboys." "Maybe they'd change their mind if they met him. Is he Mormon?"

"Shit, Kath. Not you too."

"Maybe that would impress them." Skunk's religious devotion had impressed Kath's parents. It remains the asset her mother never fails to mention.

"Right. That's why the Church has a special separate ward for Mexicans. Because they love the Lamanite people so much."

Kath can't say anything to deny it. In third grade, she met Rita Montoya playing jumprope and spent every recess with her for two months, until she brought her home to do a school project. Her mother expressed her disapproval cryptically—"When you start piano lessons next week," she had said, "you won't have much time for new friends"—but Kath understood. She had known from some unspoken injunction that she and her friends shouldn't become too involved with Catholic girls like the Lopez sisters. But Rita was Mormon, and Kath had thought this made her acceptable. She learned from her mother that even Rita's baptism couldn't purify the tincture from their friendship. She gave Rita up. "I'd like to meet Manuel." She smiles into Rhonda's eyes.

"Thanks." Rhonda stares out the front window, her head tilted to listen for the knock of the pool balls. "Another round?"

Kath scans the field of empty glasses on the glossy table. "Okay."

When Rhonda returns from the bar with beer and chasers for them, Kath decides to ask her about JuLee. "What's up with her? Who's her boyfriend?"

"Boyfriend?"

"Do you guys still talk about stuff? Like we used to?"

"We talk. Yeah." Rhonda slugs down her tequila. "So what makes you think she has a boyfriend?"

"I'm pretty sure about it. She hasn't said anything to me. She wouldn't, I don't think. But she's been staying out all night."

"If she does, she hasn't told me about him."

"Do you think . . . ?" Kath swirls her tequila, clear as water, but perceptibly thicker as it rolls against the walls of the shot-glass.

"What?"

"Do you think it could be something bad? She came home crying one night."

"JuLee's tough."

"Yeah. I guess I just don't know her very well anymore."

"We're all tough, we Miller Girls." Rhonda chipmunks her cheeks full of air, then blows out in a violent burst. "Whew, I'm drunk."

"I'll drive you home."

"I didn't say I was done drinking."

"You're done." She grabs for Rhonda's purse before her cousin can react and fishes the car keys from the center pocket.

"How'll you get home?"

"I'll drive it back in the morning."

"I've got work early."

"That's okay. We're going to church. Come on." She takes Rhonda's elbow and tugs her to her feet.

Kath deposits Rhonda as quietly as possible at the back door of the Pratt house and drives home along the flat black streets of Sterling. She parks Rhonda's Toyota in the space behind her car in the driveway. Without Rhonda's jacket, the desert night chills her skin, and she folds her arms over her chest.

She hears a heavy truck door slam on the back road. She looks to the end of the drive and beyond the house to the road but sees nothing. She is nearly to the kitchen door when she notices him with the steel plates of his boots scuttling close on the concrete. He has a baseball cap screwed tightly over his blond hair. "Merrill." She bites down on her fear, leaving her voice a pinched, flat exhalation.

"I waited for you."

"Please." He continues his approach. She darts onto the porch, scooping the house key from her purse. He follows her into the light. "No, stay there, please. Don't come any closer."

"I've been more than patient, you know. You skip out on me and I don't bother you a bit. But we've got something to talk about now."

"No."

"Come off it, Katie. Be a reasonable girl. Chances are you'll like what I've got to say. Here." He holds out a yellow rose with its stem clipped off below the tight bud. "Picked this in my dad's yard for you. For peace, okay?" He gestures for her hand, but she presses her arms together again, with the house key crushed between her palm and her bicep. "Remember when He sat in the tree calling to us across the yard? Then afterwards, you said His tears were the yellow roses?" She shakes her head. She shakes her head until Merrill looks slightly disgusted and drops the rosehead at her feet. "When can we talk?"

"Why?"

"Why? Come off it. If I told you all about why, then we'd be talking about it now, wouldn't we? And I don't want to be having a serious talk with you when you've gone out and gotten yourself drunk."

"I'm not drunk."

"Oh no. Course not." He grins and digs his thumbs into the pockets of his jeans. "What kind of mother are you, Kath?"

She doesn't answer; he knows what kind of mother she is. "I can't do it tomorrow. Monday." She searches frantically for a place they could meet where she would feel safe. She fights against retreating to the room in her mind and escaping the question. "Noon at the café."

"I'll be there. Don't be late. Don't flake on me, Katie." He points his finger and fires it like a gun. "Pow." She waits as he follows the drive into the backyard, crosses the lawn, and climbs into his truck. She waits until she sees the headlights, and hears the gears grind, and he pulls away. She waits until the sound of the engine disperses into the creak of crickets and the shuffling of the chickens. She will not unlock the door before he is safely in the distance, because, somehow, an open door would be as good as an invitation for him to come inside with her.

Daron: Palmyra

Q: *In what year did Joseph Smith have his first vision in the grove?*
Q: *What are the names of the "seer" stones that allowed Joseph Smith to translate the golden plates?*
Q: *With whom did Joseph Smith receive the vision of revelation of the Aaronic Priesthood?*

Daron cannot answer any of these questions, but this does not prevent Sister Sillitoe from calling on him again and again. Her Primary class of ten unruly boys fidgets on the metal folding chairs in the cramped, hot circle of the classroom—a cubicle, once a book storage closet, next to the gymnasium in the wardhouse. The boys make faces, jab elbows, twist to look out the high window where a segment of the aluminum flagpole is visible, and kick at the legs of the chairs. Daron appears to be a model student. With his itching white shirt pulled taut against the chairback and his hands knotted together in his lap, his slow-burning resentment is easily mistaken for good behavior.

From his vantage on Sister Sillitoe's immediate right, he can see the lesson plan in her lap, neatly inscribed in blue ballpoint ink on a yellow legal pad. There are, unfortunately, no answers to crib. When Daron fails, the other boys answer as if the questions are as worn and familiar as their own names. *Eighteen* twenty. *The Urim and Thummin. Oliver Cowdery.* While it shames him to appear stupid, it angers him more that he has been inserted into the class against his will. His mom roused him early on Sunday morning and dumped him at the door of the church gymnasium for Primary. He imagines how he will be sullen and nasty to her all day in revenge. Although his mom has been so vague and distracted since they arrived in Sterling that she might not notice.

After all the impossible questions are dispensed and answered, Sister Sillitoe uncovers the pictures she has placed on an easel frame in the corner. She drags the easel over to the circle of chairs with loud squeaks of its wooden feet on the linoleum. The pictures are color illustrations glued to rectangles of stiff cardboard. As she tells her story, she stands as straight and jointless as an old-fashioned clothespin and points aggressively at the appropriate scene with her pen.

THE FIRST VISION

The first picture is a painting of tall trees with narrow straight trunks. The leaves are green fainting into yellow in the sun. A man in brown pants and a white shirt kneels at the left end of a meadow. His hands are raised to the sky, and streaks of pale pink paint descend in rays through the trees toward him.

Pioneer Day is coming up soon, Sister Sillitoe announces. And we all know that this is the day we set aside each year to celebrate the coming of those intrepid pioneers who suffered many hardships as they crossed the Great Plains to start our state. It's important to know why Heavenly Father led them to come here. And to find out we need to find out where the Church began.

Our story begins when Joseph was ten years old and moved with his family to Palmyra and a few years later to Manchester. Could you tell us what state these towns are in, Daron?—he winces and shakes his head—They're in the state of New York. Joseph's family was quite poor, and he had to work at whatever odd jobs he could find to make some money. Our Prophet never had an idle or an easy life. Look at the clothes he is wearing in this picture. They are not expensive clothes, are they? They are not designer jeans and two-hundred-dollar sneakers.

At this time, in this part of the country, there was a great excitement among the people and in all the churches. People were trying to decide which church was true, which one Jesus loved the most, and which one they should join. There were eleven people in Joseph's family, and some of them joined the Presbyterian church. Joseph went to the Presbyterians to hear them out. He also went to hear the Methodists and the Baptists. There was lots of talking and fighting among these churches, and they made Joseph very confused. So he decided that the smartest thing to do would be to ask God which church was the right one to join.

Early one morning he walked out into the forest until he came to a meadow among the tall trees. He knelt on the grass and clasped his hands in prayer. He asked Heavenly Father which church he should join to worship Him the best. All of a sudden, the forest grew dark around him. Joseph found that he couldn't move or talk, and he trembled in fear. Silently, he prayed and prayed, and suddenly a pillar of blinding light appeared over his head. He saw two men inside the beam. The Elder pointed to the Younger and said, "Listen to my Son." Joseph asked the Son his question, and the Son answered him so that there wasn't a doubt in Joseph's mind about what he should do. In *Joseph Smith,* chapter two, verse—Sister Sillitoe flips the pages of her notepad—nineteen, he says, "I was answered that I must join none of them, for they were all wrong; and the Personage who addressed me said that all their creeds were an abomination in his sight." Does anyone know what the word *abomination* means?—Daron thinks he can answer this; he hopes he is right. It means it's a terrible thing, he says—Yes, she says, the Son wanted Joseph to know that all the other churches were bad and wrong and he should stay far away from them.

Let me tell you, Joseph suffered greatly from this vision, because when he told anyone about it, they all laughed at him. They gave him grief because of it. But Joseph never gave up. He always believed in his vision.

THE SECOND VISION
Sister Sillitoe has drawn an illustration for this scene herself. In black felt marker she has drawn a square. Inside the square are a table and two chairs. A stick-figure man sits in one of the chairs with his round paddle hands pressed together. A series of thick lines radiates from one of the upper corners of the box.

About three years after he had his first vision, Joseph was sitting in his bedroom, praying to God. He looked up and noticed a great light growing in the room. Soon, the light became brighter than day, and standing in the center of all this white light was an angel. He was wearing white clothes, and his bare feet hung in the air above the floor. Do you remember the angel's name?—Moroni, Daron says. Sister Sillitoe smiles, nodding—The Angel Moroni told Joseph that he was God's messenger. He had come to see Joseph to tell him about a very special book written on gold plates that told all about the early people of America, how they had come to this country from Israel, and how they had been delivered by our Savior. The angel told Joseph that God wanted him to translate this book so that the people of the world could have the true gospel once more. Along with the plates were two stones named Urim and Thummin, which were attached to a breastplate, and these stones would allow Joseph to understand the writing on the plates and turn it into English. Moroni showed Joseph a vision of the place the plates were buried. After the angel left, Joseph prepared to go to sleep, but the Angel Moroni came back and told Joseph the same thing two more times that night and once more the next day so that he wouldn't forget any of it. Look how beautiful the angel is . . .

Sister Sillitoe flips over her drawing to reveal another picture on the reverse. A brilliant orange forest surrounds two young men. One man, a blond angel in a white robe with a golden sash, gestures toward the other man, who kneels on the ground with what looks like a thick three-ring binder resting on his raised knee. The kneeling man is draped in a long brown cape, like what Dr. Frankenstein would wear to walk around his castle. At the angel's feet is a hole in the ground and an overturned stone. Soon Joseph walked to the hill he had seen in his vision. The hill is called Cumorah. And he lifted up a rock at the top and found the plates buried in a stone vault underneath. Joseph was excited, and he was going to take the plates with him. But the angel returned and told him he must wait. He visited the hill every year for four more years, until in 1827 the angel allowed him to take the plates and the stones and breastplate away with him. With the help of friends like Martin Harris and Oliver Cowdery, Joseph was able to translate the golden plates and restore another testament of Jesus Christ to the world.

THE PRIESTHOOD VISION

In the picture, two men in plain white shirts and brown pants kneel in the grass at the edge of a stream. Between them—burning the detail of the forest surrounding them into a blazing blank—is an old, bearded man in snowy robes who rests his hands on their bowed heads.

One day, while Oliver Cowdery was recording Joseph's translation of the plates as he recited them, they found a passage about baptism. They decided to take a walk in the woods and pray to Heavenly Father for guidance. John the Baptist, who baptized Jesus, came down to them in a cloud of light and laid his hands upon them. He told them that he was following the orders of the apostles Peter, James, and John to bless the two of them and bestow on them the Priesthood of Aaron. They were instructed to baptize each other by immersion in water. Joseph baptized Oliver and blessed him by laying on his hands. Then Oliver baptized Joseph and blessed him. This was the Aaronic Priesthood, which each of you may be blessed to receive when you are twelve. What is the name of the other Priesthood worthy men shall receive?—Sister Sillitoe looks at Daron. He shifts his eyes to the window and feigns distraction. Melchezidek! Dwight shouts, and she nods—And when Joseph and the others received this Priesthood everything was in place to restore the True Church on earth once more.

She peers at the watchface on the inside of her wrist. Yes, so next week we'll talk about the gospel truths that were restored along with the one and only True Church.

Now it's time for our test. Did everyone study? Who would like to start?

Sister Sillitoe removes a small paper sack from her purse and slips her fingers into it in preparation. No one volunteers. Daron wouldn't even if he knew what was expected. He feels manipulated. She has smiled at him and called on him to win him over. He has been overeager to please her; he won't fall for it again.

She calls on the boy on the left to recite the Eighth Article of Faith. He stands and stumbles through it; she prompts him several times. When he finishes, she lifts a plastic decal from the sack and sets it in his hand. She moves on to the next boy. By the time she arrives at the end of the circle, Daron has memorized the passage completely. He stands and recites it without stumbling: We believe the Bible to be the word of God as far as it is translated correctly; we also believe the Book of Mormon to be the word of God.

Very good, she says. She gives him a decal. Do you have a chart at home to put it on? We'll get you a chart.

Next week we will do number nine. Sister Sillitoe walks to a copy of the Articles of Faith tacked to the back of the door, the same poster he has in his bedroom. Let's practice it together: We believe all that God has revealed, all that he does now reveal, and we believe that He will yet reveal many great and important things pertaining to the Kingdom of God.

Remember that the Church has a living Prophet, our President. And Heavenly Father reveals new things to him all the time. Let's try reading it again.

Again.

And again.

He moves his lips to the shape of the words without adding his voice to the chorus.

Kath: 9

When the Frosty Mug drive-in closed after a grease fire, the café became the only restaurant on Main Street. A sizable crowd swarms in for lunch at noon, and Kath has to wait for a booth on the slatted park bench by the cash register. She twists the strap of her purse around her hand and looks at the people chomping rapid lunches along the counter. Their faces set off a vague series of recollections, of shoe salesmen who have measured her feet, of tellers who have cashed her checks, and of women who have helped her mother arrange flowers or the dishes at a potluck. They are not fresh memories, and she can't give them names.

The waitress, a vaguely familiar blond woman in her late forties, smiles and motions Kath to a booth in the corner. She slides onto the bench and watches up the street in the direction from which Merrill should be coming. She left Daron at Cousin Berma's for the afternoon, and she was tempted to find Merrill across the ditch at the Nelsons' and get it over with. She doesn't want to leave Daron near his house for long, although she trusts Cousin Berma to keep him in sight. She didn't cross over because she is afraid of Merrill on his own ground, and she refuses to offer him her fear.

It wasn't her first opportunity to see him. At Sacrament Meeting on Sunday, he was sitting in the third row with his parents and two younger sisters. From her position, between her father and Daron in the fifth row, she could see his thick neck and wavy hair, his prominent cheek, and some of his large nose. His shoulders bulged above the pew, racked in an undersized green sportcoat. She was angry that he could appear in daylight, no different from any other man in the church. She wonders if it was her fault that he could still come out of the shadows.

She watched his back, unnoticed, through the first half of the meeting, but as the congregation rose for a hymn, Merrill turned and stared directly at them. His gaze seemed to focus on Daron as he flashed a thumbs-up. Kath looked over at her son. Daron's face revealed nothing. For some reason he had decided not to speak to her that morning, and she never found out what he knew or suspected or felt. To avoid Merrill and his family after the service, she led Daron out a side door to the car while her father stayed behind for another meeting.

Kath orders coffee and anticipates Merrill's disappointment at the black pool in her cup. He had been the man to show her it was possible to be good again. But she has backslid. The bitterness of the coffee is her bitterness that only in his house could she be a proper person. But his house was the one place she couldn't stay.

She rips into a packet of Sweet-N-Low and shakes the powder into her cup. She supposes her story is the story of all Mormon girls, like Rhonda's story, like JuLee's. They run wild in their teens, then settle into marriage and motherhood and Relief Society luncheons. Her story was the same. Up to a point. And she couldn't help the difference when it came. It has left her ashamed. She starts crying, but they are tears that she refuses to show, not to Daron, not to her family, and certainly not to Merrill. She wipes her eyes with a napkin dipped in ice water and sits back to wait.

· · ·

Sometimes, when Kath held Tom, in the bed of his truck with their backs to the cab, he would cry and cry. She would try to comfort him and succor his pain. She would ask him why and why: why he cried, and why he wouldn't let her close enough to smooth out the ache that bent him forward with his hands on his ankles, his head between his knees. She loved him. She thought that she could help him if only she knew. She would have denied, if she had been confronted with the fact, that she—her love—prolonged his anguish.

She couldn't have known then—and she has continued to argue this assertion with herself—that his hurt, his sickness, would inevitably clabber their love into the sour and wrong. If there were signs of the truth, she did not understand that they were intended to alert her. And they were intended. Whether or not Tom acknowledged his wish to tell her, he wanted her to notice and know. He loved her enough, she recognizes to want to make himself known to her. But he didn't speak it; he had expected her to be observant and clever. He imagined her to be a different girl. And she had learned that she loved a different man.

She and Tom Anderson dated occasionally in high school. Six times—seven if you count their first pizza together with friends after a football game. They enjoyed each other's company, but Tom was two years ahead in school, which kept them apart in the classroom; their circles of friends seldom overlapped; and, finally, they clashed over their desires. Tom would ask to slip off and be alone with her, but she always protested in favor of staying with friends and being sociable. She wasn't attached to these other people, but she couldn't find the means to break her inhibitions and leave with him eagerly. She was slow to learn transgression.

She did want him. Tom was on the track and field team, and she went to practice, before she knew him and after, to watch him run the hurdles, his long tan legs scissoring open over each obstacle. She leaned against the bleacher railing, rubbing the steel crossbar low against her waist until it warmed from her touch. When Tom finished his laps, she watched his stomach as he bent over, pumping in and out under the sweat-stuck film of his tanktop. She knew the reason behind her trips to the stadium, although she had never wanted a boy this way before. What she had never guessed was that these tugs at her body would become unendurably strong.

She had no one to talk to about Tom. She was hungry, she was starving for him, but this craving went unvoiced. She was dimly aware of girls her age who talked about boys this way—girls who glibly requested tampons and pads from their friends in the locker room and caught them in a midair toss; girls who joked about diaphragms, and knew how to apply them, and might, in fact, have used them; girls who ditched class at lunchtime and sped into town in their parents' cars with their cigarettes held out the window to dampen any lingering scent of smoke inside. These girls went to church with Kath and her friends; they went to seminary and Mutual and church dances; but with the crucial difference that they did not believe and Kath and her friends did. These girls had their religion, accepting all the teachings tacitly, but they did not let it interfere with their fun. Kath couldn't separate her life that neatly—although she might have if she had discovered how.

Her closest friends were her sister and her cousin Rhonda, and she recognized that they were too young to understand. Their schemata of boys possessed only two paths. On one track, boys—boyfriends— were rarefied concepts, to be discussed and debated in notes folded and folded and folded into tiny triangles for ease of passing at the back of math class. On the other track, boys in actuality were snotty-nosed, with dirty fingernails—utterly crude and gross. There was no room for craving, for heat and aching; it would frighten them. When Kath started to date Tom, she told them she had a boyfriend, and they saw it as an acquisition, like a hair crimper or a new cassette. They thought she was lucky. They were jealous, giggling, full of abstractly knowing questions.

She had no one to give her advice, and she couldn't bring herself to tell Tom of her longing. She didn't want to ease her way into an uncertain place. Consequently, nothing happened. Tom never complained; he never asked for more. He simply wished that they could find time to be alone together and talk. But she didn't believe—then—that he sought conversation.

They had one serious kiss. It was early in the summer before Tom left on his mission. They had gone to a movie, then come home; her parents and brother and sister were in bed. She made toasted cheese sandwiches and lemonade. They sat in lawn chairs across the yard from the house, laughing quietly, throwing a Frisbee for Champion in the soft dark. She tilted her head to drain her lemonade and found Tom kissing the stretch of her throat. He knelt in the grass between her legs and rested his hands on her thighs, below her shorts. He touched his lips to hers and, without breaking the bond, stood up over her, pressing down with his mouth. She wanted to slither away into the liquid of the kiss but kept thinking of her parents and their Halloween dance. She considered Tom's actions from a distance: this was a serious kiss. Tom made a brief, wet exploration with his tongue. "Wait," she said, and pushed him off.

"I'm sorry," he said. "I'm sorry." He apologized and apologized, until her brief hesitation became his breach of faith and she couldn't ask him to kiss her again. He said good-bye and left her awkwardly alone with one empty chair and two empty plates.

They managed not to see each other for the rest of the summer. Tom lived outside of Sterling in the barely discernible town of Clearidge, and he spent the summer helping at his father's gas station. She avoided places like the movie house and the Frosty Mug drive-in, where Tom's friends might be likely to congregate. Her family attended his missionary farewell, but she stayed home—sick with a late-summer cold, she told them. In the fall she went back to school, and Tom's parents drove him north to the Missionary Training Center in Provo to learn Spanish.

He mailed her one letter from Mexico City. The text was so generic that she imagined he had copied it from a training manual. His partner at that time was Elder Bartsch, a "nice guy," a redhead from Pennsylvania. They were working with a family and fully expected to have two baptisms, husband and wife, by the end of the month. "I am grateful," he wrote, "to be able to serve the Lord in such an important task. I hope that you will write to me. Your friend, Elder Thomas E. Anderson."

She knew that the mission leaders scrutinized every letter a missionary wrote, and Tom might have been forced to be impersonal. She scoured the letter for hints of hidden meaning, then satisfied herself with having a sample of his scrawling handwriting to tuck into the corner of her dresser drawer.

In the last months of her senior year Kath almost lost her virginity to Derek Mortensen, a varsity debater and student coach of the tennis team. That year she had grown accustomed to men's tongues in her mouth. She had done almost everything with boys that could be done short of anything that really mattered. She and Derek were at the drive-in in St. George watching the second feature, *Alien,* for the umpteenth time, and she let him slip his hand into her panties. He rummaged around under the cotton crotch for a while—they were sitting in bucket seats, at a bad angle—then he groped first one, then two of his fingers inside her. She envisioned Tom's narrow hands on her stomach, then his thumb sliding firmly into her. She broadcast her thoughts out of Utah, over Arizona and Chihuahua State, deep into Mexico. She wanted to leave her wetness on an LDS Elder's fingers; the idea of waking Tom telepathically with the slickness of her love, of getting him hard in his cot in the mission home, seemed vaguely blasphemous and excited her. She would have taken anything from Derek then. She unbuttoned his jeans, but he was too drunk—or too frightened by her aggression—to get an erection.

Tom returned from his two-year mission after less than a year. A lot of idle speculation drifted around the high school, but none of the proposed reasons for his dismissal were persuasive. Kath assumed that Tom must have hated it, that he made himself a nuisance and they kicked him out of the program.

Tom found Kath again at Boonies. She and three girlfriends were ostensibly having lunch in the café, but Annabeth kept slipping them shots of Wild Turkey along with their Coca-Colas—as a graduation present, a celebration, although the ceremony was three weeks away. For Kath, drinking Coke was virtually on the same level of misbehavior as hard liquor; cola and coffee and liquor and cigarettes all blurred in significance under the aegis of the Word of Wisdom. She blended her alcohol into her drink with her straw rather than taking it straight like Cynthia.

If Tom didn't recognize her when he stomped in, it may have been the henna in her hair, the carnival-gypsy makeup, or the tunnels of banging brass bracelets on her wrists. He walked past their booth to the bar and ordered a beer. He was underage but acted with no doubt that he would be served. He left a wake of galvanized silence behind him. Her friends smiled—Kath with them—and their eyes darted around to see him. He wore torn jeans and a muscle shirt, with his hair already grown far out of the regulation short-short missionary cut. Cynthia whispered in admiration, "What happened to *him*?"

Tom took the beer, a sweating can of Coors, and leaned on a post by the door. He watched something—the road perhaps, or a drifting hawk—in the distance out the window. "Excuse me, you're Tom Anderson right?" Cynthia turned to him, her legs jetting diagonally along the outside of the bench.

He looked over as he swigged from the beer can. "Hey, Cynthia. Lookin' good." He scanned the other faces and found Kath's. "Hi, Kath." He grinned. Kath felt her friends stiffen at the realization that they had become a backdrop for her reappearance in his consciousness. In a musical, he would have taken her hand and lifted her from the table to dance a carioca over the shag carpeting. They were suddenly a couple, they were lovers, awaiting a few formalities.

Kath and Tom reigned in their kingdom of two for the length

of the Wild Summer. Kath never spent a night in her parents' house if she could help it. She learned how to lift the screen from its track and slide in and out of the bathroom unheard. They went all over together, day and night, pushing his Toyota pickup hard and fast up dirt roads into the canyons and sometimes farther into the red rock country and the National Parks to the east. They went camping—"It's with the girls," she told her mother—in Zion and Bryce and Arches.

Tom never pushed her sexually; he was content to let her decide how far and to what degree. They stood one night on a scenic overlook above the Goosenecks of the San Juan. The river had carved a coiling, swirling canyon deep in the earth. The twists seemed new-made, as if a worm had been dropped in the sand and the grains stuck to the mucus of his segments as he squirmed away, leaving the path of his dance behind. The sun headed down, and the red rays curved along the vistas, then into their eyes. She felt energy there, restrained. Isometric tension. Tom stood behind her with his arms sashed around her waist. Tom never wore a shirt outdoors that summer; he lived in his torn jeans and a pair of faded madras shorts. His toasted gold skin persisted in her vision as an afterglow. When she touched him, he was cold—his compact chest and stomach were cool against her back. When she tasted him, he was salty. She tasted the stale beer she had sucked from his tongue a moment before. "Fuck me," she said. "Please, Tom. Fuck me." It thrilled her to say the word, how the final consonant snapped the saliva at the back of her throat. Saying it, she already flowed for him. "Fuck me."

He did. They set up the tent in the campground and built a fire. They each drank a plastic cupful of Jim Bean. Tom had another. Then he pulled her into the dark of the tent and took off his clothes. He slid off her shorts and panties, left on her Zion's Park T-shirt.

It was fast, intense; it was good; it was always like that. Tom was tender, he was graceful in his choreography of seduction: kisses, tugs, strokes, pinches, hugs in a mellifluous recipe of syrups and liqueurs, tarts and sours, which she slurped down with delight, accepting and absorbing, flexing and stretching, partnering the dance he shaped. Before he slipped into her, he would have brought her up to a peak, regulated her breath into rhythmic puffs. Inside, he was swift, a piston, with his hands planted beside her shoulders, his eyes closed, his teeth clenched, with a feral intensity, a look almost of pain. Coming, he often lifted off to curl at her side in a cashew and squeeze himself into completion. With Tom, she never doubted that love was accomplished quickly, finished alone.

Afterward, he often cried. Until their final time, she cherished his tears. She had been raised in a touchless house by a stoic father. She hadn't learned that men could weep and seek the solace of another's touch. From the Church and her family, she was taught the ideal of toughness and restraint in men; rebellion pushed her to seek something sweeter, something yielding. She discounted any danger in Tom's sobbing. His tears prompted her to be strong. She bolstered him securely in her arms and felt assured that her support would further enmesh them.

Tom never volunteered his reasons for weeping, and she was never bold enough to ask. She did not draw any conclusions from the intensity of his sadness; she denied any consideration that it might be serious or that it might connect with her. Because if she were ever to acknowledge that his sorrow was more than an aspect of his lovemaking, if she couldn't posit tears as a natural epilogue to sighs and penetration—and this was the deeper truth that her ignorance of his feelings could not conceal from her— she knew their love would end.

As the Wild Summer exhausted its supply of days and August heaved, hot and heavy, toward Labor Day and longer shadows, Kath found her own crisis. They hadn't taken precautions. It was not that she hadn't thought about it long before there had been any need. Cynthia was on birth control; she carried the plastic pill dispenser, round like a phone dial, in an inside zipper pocket of her purse. Janet carried condoms and a tube of spermicide in her blue nylon backpack, although she never seemed to have a reason to use them. Kath might have done something similar—she supposes—despite the obstacle of her family, but she feared that Tom would balk at even a glimmer of readiness, a modicum of preparation. While she was, after all, the one to make proposals for the acceleration and expansion of their repertoire, spontaneity was always a necessary ingredient. She sensed that if she took time between Tom's requisite shots of whiskey and his moment of action to make a suggestion or, more directly, to remove a rubber from its packet, the thread he followed from the drink to the sex would break and he would become unmoored, unable to find his way anywhere but to tears.

When two cycles had wheeled around without her period, she rode quietly to St. George in Cynthia's coffee-colored Buick to visit her friend's ob-gyn. Cynthia referred to him by these initials, and Kath imagined her body being audited by an officious bureaucrat in a subterranean office. Instead, the building was a pale yellow stucco, and the nurse and doctor spoke with her in sweet, careful tones. They appeared to view her situation as hopelessly delicate, even terminal. Later, when the doctor called Cynthia's house with confirmation, Kath sensed that her summer had indeed reached its termination. She was a full seven weeks strong and healthy; the months would swell her. She rubbed her hand on her stomach—Was it visible? Could she see it in profile in the bathroom mirror?—and she felt the cold ebb of autumn under the skin.

Her family took the camper to the Grand Canyon for Labor Day weekend; she stayed home. She spents hours on Saturday planning and shopping for an elaborate dinner for Tom. She sketched out the appetizers, the salad, the entree and its accompaniments, the crowning dessert. She dismantled the recipes into lists of raw materials and drove into Alma to buy them. As she hauled the sacks from the hatchback to the kitchen counter, she bent over aching on the back steps. The spasm subsided and didn't return, but she continued to sit. She watched Champion behind the rosebushes as he dug his way under the fence, forgetting that the chain would snap him back before he reached the other side. She hunted down the dark hole, the thumbprint in her mind, where thinking failed. And, finding it, she stayed there. The chocolate ice cream in the sack at her hip dissolved into a thick froth while awaiting inclusion in the unborn puff pastries. The milk on the counter, the vegetables and meat in the car, warmed to a tepid heat and essayed the first steps of the feverish dance of rot. And she sat, opening the dark space around her like a wide umbrella—wide enough to shut out and to keep in to the proper degree.

Tom arrived at the appointed time and found her building her empty interior room, his dinner uncooked and ensacked in three places: the car, the porch, and the kitchen. She failed to notice him until he stroked her shoulders, her neck and face. "Tom." She said his name as if she were coining a new word; she had forgotten the most basic things.

"Come inside." He crushed her to his side and led her in through the kitchen, down the hall to her parents' room. He lifted her onto the bed and climbed up beside her. They were laid out side-to-side on the slithery shell of a polyester bedspread marked with seahorses in green and orange pastel. She took his hand. He seemed to know enough about what she wanted from him to wait before he spoke. They stretched out, unmoving, and watched the square of window reflected in the mirror across the room. When the light sighed red and tired into the sheer curtains, he brushed her cheek with his free fingers. "What's wrong?"

She had exited the darkened room inside her and felt overly alert in the act of living once more at the surface of her body. Sensations stabbed with a precision not unlike pain. "Just. Just . . ." What she needed from him was too encompassing to express. "Just hold me . . . love me."

Tom rolled over her; he hugged her shoulders, with his knee between her thighs. He buried his face against her neck, and she felt the moist susurration of his breath in her hair. She gripped the seat of his jeans and pulled him fully onto her. She moved her hands to his bare back, then down again under the waistband of his shorts. "I want this. I want it."

They pulled at each other's clothes. She found him naked in his white socks before she had time to consider. One palm pressed at his spine, the other wrapped his stiffening dick. Tom knelt slightly over her, dipping his head for brief kisses with his tongue sharpened like the stamen of a pink flower. "Will you tell me what's the matter?"

She clutched his shoulderblades and arched up to him, brushing belly to belly. He followed her body down when she relaxed, and entered her. "I will," she said. "I will," she said, after each fast thrust. "Only don't stop." He dragged his tongue across her lips. "I will. Only don't stop."

He closed his eyes and pumped fiercely. He was lost in it; she felt brave. "I'm pregnant," she said. "Don't stop." If she could keep him inside, nothing would change; love would never end. He continued for a few strokes as her words fell down the blazing tunnel to his mind; then he pulled out. She reached for him to put him back. "Please." He softened rapidly in her hand—she grasped desperately at a damp, dwindling sponge. Tom squeezed tears from his eyes. He twisted his face away. With conscientious effort, she had allowed herself no expectations, but she had assumed, dimly, that Tom would show them both the joy of the moment, that he would propose, that their lives would twine more intimately together. She smothered these dreams, comprehensively, before Tom could uncover them and kill them for her.

She put on her clothes, wordlessly, in a nonexpectant hush reinforced by the dousing of the sun. "I'll cook something for us." Before the mirror, she brushed her hair back with her fingers. Tom lay naked on the bed, his face buried in a pillow, knees still bent, buttocks in the air. He sobbed audibly as she held her breath to listen. A slight irritation crept in bitter lines along the edges of her tongue. "Get dressed. I'll fix dinner."

Kath finished unloading the car, stored away the salvageable groceries, and fed the dog. Tom did not appear. She looked into the bedroom from the hall and heard the stream of the shower beating against the tile in her parents' bath. She fixed omelettes and link sausages with the thought that preparing one of her father's simple meals might be comforting. It wasn't. She looked up from folding the eggs when Tom entered the kitchen. His wet dark hair loped back from the square cage of his forehead. His fingertips were translucent and malleably soft. His eyes were beads of oiled glass. "How do you think I feel, Tom?" She eased the spatula under the omelette and transferred it from pan to plate. "I need you. I need you *now*. And when you cry like that . . ."

He stood with his eyes to the green checkerboard linoleum; she observed his control eroding, as if he were melting. "My God, Kath. It's worse than you know." He stared at her, begging for relief. She held off, monitoring the progress of a grease streak in the tilted pan. But she had cared for him for too long to stop, and where else could she hope to find comfort for herself? She hugged him hard, shutting her eyes and tensing every muscle. With her eyes open, she saw the pearls of water posed on the curls of his hair. She let him go, and after a moment he released her and left to sit at the table. "You know when we dated in high school?" he started. "And I always said I wanted to go somewhere private and talk? Because I thought I knew I could talk to you. I thought I could see that you would *understand*. That's how long it's been since I've been going to tell you."

As they ate omelettes and sausage, and later, over empty plates as the night turned black and desert cool through the screen door, he told her what he had wanted to tell her. Tom didn't ask if she wanted to hear it, but, if he had, she would not have been able to answer. The telling was inevitable, like melted ice cream, like nightfall.

When Tom was eleven years old, he received a blue-and-yellow box kite for his birthday, along with a spool of gleaming white string. He lashed the kite to his back with firm, meticulous care and pedaled his bike along the dirt shoulder of the old highway from Clearidge to the park on the outskirts of Sterling. At one end of the park a flat field of grass was divided from the lawn of the town cemetery by a low chainlink fence. The backstop of a baseball diamond nestled in each corner, but enough open ground remained between them for Tom to get a good running start for his kite without worrying about stumbling into the rutted pits that served as bases. The kite caught the wind easily, and he played out the string, easing slowly back along the edge of the shallow pond. He reversed up the steep slope of the hill until he could walk along the ridge above the pond and reel the kite out to the end of its string. From this vantage, he could scan the entire park to see if any of his friends from school were around, but he saw no one on the two tennis courts, at the basketball hoops on the blacktop, or moving around the jogging track that circled the pond. If none of his friends showed up before he was done flying, he was going to visit his grandmother on Main Street.

A length of string stretched from the spool in one hand to the fingers of the other, and he tugged gently to feel how solidly the kite was held in the sky by the breeze from the south. When he was convinced that the kite was stabilized, he twisted to look down the opposite face of the hill, which descended to a dry wash at the park's rear perimeter where his friends sometimes played. Two men lay in the patchy grass under one of the trees on the wash's bank. Their faces were turned from him to face the wash; they did not look up to see him. At eleven, Tom had little precision in guessing ages, and the men might have been eighteen or twenty-eight. The men were curled in toward each other, their feet tangled together, studying each other. The dark-haired one had raked his fingers through the shock of reddish-blond hair above the other man's brow. At first Tom thought the reddish-blond one had eased his hand into a pocket of the other's khaki trousers, but he realized that the hand disappeared into the center of the pants, where the zipper would be. While he looked at them, the men never moved.

The string slackened in his hands, and he searched the deep

blue and bright white of the sky. He followed the string as it unspooled down the hill and into the pond. He ran down the hill,
winding the string crudely onto the spool. Eventually, the frayed
end slid up out of the water onto the shore at his feet. The string
had snapped in the sky. He searched on his bike along the path
of the wind but never knew where his kite had gone.

Tom thought about the men afterward, and recognized that he
had seen the real thing. He knew the names. His friend Danny
Myers preferred spelling bees and math contests to sports and,
consequently, had been called too many of the names in Tom's
presence. He had beaten boys up for saying them. To Danny. To
him. Fem. Fairy. Pansy. Sissy. Prissy. Girl. Mommy's boy. Queer.
Fag.

By the time he was in junior high he knew more of them.
Cocksucker. Asslicker. Buttfucker. Cornholer.

But that day in the park was the only time in all the years before and for many years after that he had been given a picture of
the truth. The Hand Through the Zipper. The image floated toward him years later, magical and tangible, when he throbbed
under the sheet at night. He suffered a kind of wanting that
pricked him deep into the skin but left no trace of its source, like
the barb of a cholla cactus attaching itself to his flesh at the suggestion of a touch. He knew only the soreness, not the source of
his longing. When he rubbed himself, dreaming of the Hand
Through the Zipper, he never held the image up to scrutiny, to
see what it might tell him. He couldn't understand—and didn't
want to.

Long after his friend Danny Myers had moved to Atlanta and
they had stopped exchanging letters, Tom learned the full meaning of the names they had tossed around in elementary school:
crudely from his buddies in the locker room, and clinically from
television and *Time* magazine. In a news photo, men marched,
arms embracing, through the streets of San Francisco, like am-
bassadors from an alien world. They offered no connection to
him; the photo was exotica, like the peaked temples in Kuala
Lumpur and the droning forests of the Amazon. He wondered,

briefly, if the men of the Hand Through the Zipper were emissaries of the same planet, but they had become familiar to him through use, like the faces of Aunt Jemima, Betty Crocker, and the Quaker on the breakfast table. He didn't consider the connection for long.

Tom made the track team in his freshman year at Mesa Vista. He loved to run, to extend, to surge, to eat the ground with the soles of his shoes. He loved to push his body up toward exhaustion—where his lungs were swollen crab claws snatching air—and beyond, to a blurred land of furious speed where the pain was lost and his body melted to plasma. Waiting for the coach's call, he would study his teammates as they put in laps, shot the discus, rolled over the bar, skidded into the broad-jump pit. They heaved oxygen into their chests, they furled and unfurled their legs in warm-ups, they pushed their hands toward the sky, uncovering the hairy damp of their armpits. His observation thrilled and worried him. His body had developed late, hair still sprouted with noticeable speed, and he assured himself that he examined the other guys' bodies to make certain he looked normal. When he undressed on the long wooden bench between the lockers, he kept his eyes from the slapping and shouting in front of the showers. He stood under the violent showerhead buried deepest in the murky steam of the shower room and prayed to the Lord that he would not get hard.

Mrs. Cankerborg taught his fourth-period honors English class and dealt unflinchingly with literary matters that every other teacher would delicately avoid. She was a Catholic. The students knew it was only a matter of time before someone reported her. She explained the "phallic implications" of the river in *Heart of Darkness.* She translated the dirty jokes in *Hamlet* into normal English, and did not cover the film projector lens with her hand during the bedroom scene in *Romeo and Juliet.* When they read "Song of Myself," she asked Tom's buddy Kevin to read the passage about the swimmers.

" '. . . Twenty-eight men and all so friendly.' " Kevin read it awkwardly. He was too intent on the enunciation of each word to comprehend what he read, and he failed to understand the giggles in the class. " 'They do not think whom they souse with spray.' "

Mrs. Cankerborg explicated texts in a tone of indisputable authority. "It is generally acknowledged," she said, "that the woman in the passage is a mask or persona that Whitman uses to present his own attraction to the young men described. Many of our most prominent artists have been homosexuals, but what is remarkable about Whitman lies in the direct way he presents his feelings in his poetry. There are numerous examples in his work of homoeroticism." She printed the word on the chalkboard—*homoeroticism*—and the brown-nosing students who took notes dutifully added it to their lecture outline.

After class, the guys teased Kevin ferociously—Are you "so friendly," Kev?—Hey faggot, let me souse you with my spray!—Suck me, dickhead—but Tom kept quiet. He looked down at his copy of *Leaves of Grass,* and it burned in his palm like a dangerous isotope. He rode home alone on his bicycle in fear of Walt Whitman and what Mrs. Cankerborg called his "appreciation of masculine beauty." He sat on the rim of the bathtub and jerked himself off again and again, crying and soused with lust.

In the winter of Tom's sophomore year, Bishop Madsen requested interviews with all the boys in the ward over sixteen to prepare them for their mission call. "I want to give you boys plenty of time to do your spiritual homework," the bishop told Tom as he sat across the desk in the church office. Between Tom and Bishop Madsen's folded gray hands on the desk were two framed photographs: a double profile in golden light of Bishop and Sister Madsen, taken for their fortieth wedding anniversary, and a family portrait with the couple seated in armchairs and their five daughters arranged behind them in a fan of girlhood. The picture was old: the girls had long, flat, straight hair and wore ankle-length long-sleeved dresses in a palette of pastels. When the picture was taken, only one daughter was married; when Tom looked at it, none of the daughters had fewer than three children. "This ward has some of the finest young men in the state, and we want to be sure that everything is in readiness when you are called to the mission field."

Tom listened to the bishop offer a brief prayer asking God to see that Tom was good and true and honest in answering the questions that would be put before him. He blessed Tom in his privileged position as a future missionary for the Church. The bishop asked Tom a few questions about his family life—if everything was okay at home, if he was obedient to his parents, if he had ever done anything wrong that he didn't tell his parents about. Tom wanted to answer truthfully that he had secrets. He held off because he didn't know how to reveal them. But Bishop Madsen's list—a photocopy in an open manila folder, which the bishop would glance at after each of Tom's uninformative responses—spiraled down toward the difficult questions, down toward sex.

"Have you ever touched yourself with a sexual purpose in mind?"

Tom hesitated. He said yes.

"That's a dangerous thing, Tom. It's an act of filthiness that will corrupt if it's not stopped. Like holding a stick of dynamite. Understand?"

He said yes.

"What do you think about when you do this dirty thing?"

He couldn't explain what he thought about. He said he thought about nothing.

"Have you ever kissed a girl, Tom?"

He said yes. He had kissed Jennifer Carlson, a junior varsity cheerleader, after a track meet.

"Have you ever gone too far with a girl? Do you know what too far is?"

He said he wasn't certain.

"Have you ever engaged in tongue-kissing, monkey-bites, necking, or petting?"

He said no.

"Petting is the worst, Tom. There's nothing wrong with a sweet innocent kiss now and then. But these other things are bad news. You will never do them, will you, Tom?"

He said no.

"Do you ever think about girls, Tom? In an indecent way?"

He said that he didn't think that he thought of them that way.

"And boys, Tom. You've never thought about boys in that way, have you?"

He said he didn't think so.

"That doesn't quite satisfy me, Tom. You've never had any sexual feelings for boys, have you? You have friends, don't you, Tom?"

He said yes.

"When you think of your friends, you never feel anything besides a sense of comradeship and brotherhood, do you?"

He said no.

"Do you ever see another man, another boy, and think he's handsome?"

He said sort of, sometimes, maybe.

"You know that this thing we're talking about is one of the greatest abominations, don't you, Tom? The Church is especially concerned about this sin because it can not only destroy the boy it affects but become the ruination of others. You'd better tell me everything you know about this, Tom, and everything you've ever thought about it. This is important, Tom."

He had been saving money for his mission since he was four and his mother gave him a special piggy bank. If he couldn't go because the bishop wouldn't approve him, his parents would be angry. He thought it was better to be honest while there were years left for him to change—even if most of the truth was anxiety and doubts—than to wait and be rejected at the official interview before his mission. Tom told the bishop about the Hand Through the Zipper, about his nightdreams, about watching his teammates, about Mrs. Cankerborg and Walt Whitman. He must have made the small, vague events sound more significant than they were, because Bishop Madsen became grave and ripped a sheet from his appointment pad.

Tom's father went to see the bishop at the Madsen Dairy during his lunch hour. When he came home that night, his father frowned through dinner, then ordered Tom and his sisters upstairs to do their homework. After a silence, Tom heard his mother cry—wailing, up the stairwell.

His mother drove Tom to the family G.P. Tom undressed and sat sideways on the vinyl-topped examination table. The doctor checked his heart and blood pressure, his eyes and weight. The doctor lifted Tom's penis with a gloved hand and studied it from all angles, as if looking for one of the taunting childhood words written there. He cupped Tom's testicles and asked him to cough. The doctor told Tom's mother that he was in fine shape and recommended a psychiatrist if necessary.

The weekly trips to Brigham Young University began. On Friday nights his parents would drive him up to stay with his Aunt Brynda in Provo. His mother and father would sit rigid in the front seat, pointedly avoiding any discussion of their destination. They would leave him at the end of Aunt Brynda's driveway, then turn around at the end of the cul-de-sac to make the four-hour trip home. They would return for him sometime after church on Sunday. For three months they drove at least sixteen hours every weekend for him. So that he could be cured.

Initially, the Saturdays with the psychiatrist at BYU were expended on talk. The doctor took elaborate histories. He wanted to know about Tom's childhood in voluminous detail. The doctor kept hinting that there were secrets in Tom's life to which he had no conscious access. There were hidden memories—repressions—in Tom's brain, which had leached out indirectly, staining and deforming other, more readily accessible thoughts. The doctor implied that Tom's early childhood had been interfered with, and he wanted to find out who had "gotten to" Tom and how. Uncles, cousins, and family friends drifted in and out of the sessions, with a potentially sinister nimbus attached to each name.

During the second month the treatments began. The room looked like one of the practice rooms for the high school band or the impersonal cell used for a police interrogation. Tom changed into a hospital smock and sat in the reclining dentist's chair. The specialist, and often his psychiatrist, sat at a nearby table. An intern daubed the electrodes with a drop of salve and attached them to Tom's penis. They projected slides on a screen for him to examine. Pages of men from *Playgirl* and a pornographic magazine had been photographed—often blown up to focus on the genitals. The specialist studied Tom's penis with intense concentration as Tom watched the slide show. For a long time Tom was too nervous to pay attention. The people in the room were polite to him, but he sensed a barely disguised distaste, as if they doubted that their treatment would succeed against his depravity. He squirmed in the chair. The pictures went around and around and repeated and repeated until some of the characters became familiar: the Blond Guy; the two brunettes, Mr. Cowboy Hat and the Kneeling Man. He listened to the nervous sound of the doctors' breath and the buzz and tick of the carousel slide projector slowly orbiting at the far end of the room.

One of the slide men had reddish-blond hair, and he was turned three-quarters away from the camera to show his backside. The Hand Through the Zipper. When Tom was tired, he thought about the man while looking at the others, and his penis stirred slightly under the wires. An electric shock surged through the electrodes and spiked him with a brief intense pain.

They would shock him intermittently as he watched the slide men parade. They wanted to destroy his perverted sexual proclivities toward men and guide him carefully to a proper attitude. Women, nude and cunningly arranged, began to appear among the slides. Each woman would linger for a long voluptuous moment within the parade of men. He would never be shocked when the women occupied the screen. Eventually there were many more women than men, and the men were invariably accompanied by pain.

When Aunt Brynda picked him up at the campus, she would ask him, "So what did you do today?" Tom would stare at her for a moment, then tell her he was tired and tilt the car seat back with his eyes shut. When he went home on Sunday nights he found that he couldn't speak to his family for several days. He wanted to talk, but he couldn't articulate anything that didn't sound confused and angry. He kept his thoughts from escaping into sound.

Tom went to the psychiatrist's office for the last time the week after the treatment ended. He sat on the soft couch, and the doctor gave him some advice. "We've done a lot for you, young man. I should say you've done a lot for yourself. But you must be vigilant. The best thing for you to do is find yourself a nice girl. Somebody you can take to your heart. Then, after your mission, you should marry, start a family right away, and keep your life on the right track."

Classes ended. Summer started. Tom looked for a nice girl. He went to all the church dances and dated three nights a week. He couldn't look into his mother's face; he found it a struggle to meet the eyes of any woman. He never spoke to his father again beyond the necessities of living in the same house. In the fall his mother heard from the PTA that Mrs. Cankerborg had been asked to teach Remedial Grammar and four periods of Typing I. She moved out of Sterling the next spring.

Tom met KathLeen over pizza in the winter of his senior year and believed he had found the girl he wanted. He was less certain what purpose he wished her to serve. He didn't imagine marriage; he wanted to share with her.

Both he and Kath circled like minor satellites around a core group of friends, boys and girls who hung out together in the cafeteria and over burgers or pizza after games. He had watched her sometimes at lunch hour across the picnic table. She would sit demurely on the bench next to Cynthia Bingham and idly pat her full brown hair, which was fluffed into the Farrah Fawcett flip she hadn't abandoned since sixth grade. She would laugh appreciatively at a joke told by one of the boys and fawn convinc-

ingly over someone's new class ring or Park City ski trip. But he
sensed that, like him, she held something back. When he drove
by her after school, as she sat waiting for the bus on the curb
with her bare knees drawn together under her modest tartan
skirt, he felt a magnetic vibration in the back of his neck different from anything else.

When he finally spoke with her in the padded booth of the
pizza parlor, he discovered that she was not the flavorless, pe-
ripheral girl she pretended to be. She had her own opinions and
her own style. She dismissed Derek Mortensen, a popular boy in
her junior class, as a pea-brained dinosaur, a coelacanth who had
somehow escaped prehistory without evolving. Kath was a person he could talk to, and if he were brave enough to tell her
everything, he felt, she would listen. She wasn't caustic in the
manner of purportedly sophisticated girls like Dana Surovy, former San Franciscan and prima donna of the drama department.
She wasn't studiedly sluttish like Kimberly Nelson or DarCee
Peterson, cocaptains of the varsity cheerleaders. She was active
in the Church, but she wasn't fearsomely devoted like Alison
Blaine, who sang the hymn at every school assembly. There were
places inside her that weren't entirely located in Sterling. She
had a great tensile strength at her core and a high melting point,
unshockable, unbruisable.

Tom sensed her power, but he couldn't reach it. They dated
through the spring but were never alone. She clung to her friends
and bright public places as if he were Death in a Poe story, drawing her away from the ball of life. She was tense, nearly angry,
and, when he touched her, subtly rigid. The effort of forcing
themselves to be a couple left them no energy for joy. He resolved to kiss her, to snap the entropic bands between them, to
stir up her decarbonated sweetness. When he acted on his plan
that night in her backyard, he was startled by his own authority.
He snared her lips with his and massaged them apart with his
tongue. He was not heedless; he was conscious of his calibra-
tions. If he couldn't feel anything, if all the slides and jolts had
failed to alter the subrosa map of his desires, he could assure

himself that no one else would suffer from his numbness; he could overmaster love with the same discipline he had brought to running and divert his wife's eye, forever, from the slight cowlick of insincerity that he might never smooth down.

When Kath pushed him away, he thought she had discovered the calculation in his kiss. He had inadvertently touched the depth in her that he had sought, but, instead of leading to understanding, her depth would work to incite her disgust. He couldn't remain to observe its growth. He ran.

He received the call for his mission, learned the rudiments of Spanish at the Missionary Training Center, was set apart in a temple ceremony, and received his garments. He became Elder Anderson.

On his bicycle, Tom flew through Mexico City days of unease and boredom. He and his partner canvassed regions of the city, visiting families, pressing for conversions, guiding the receptive proselytes along a narrow channel toward baptism. He had his satchel of pamphlets and his memorized spiel in phonetic Spanish. The homes they visited were primarily among the city's equivalent of the middle class. He had gotten whiffs of the true city with its teeming poverty and recognized how near the apex of the pyramid the people he met were poised. In the United States the families would be ordinary, somewhat below the material comfort line, but here they balanced at a vertiginous height above a lake of disconsolate faces.

He was protected from the worst—the hovels and stench of abandoned despair. They all lived together in the mission home, and the city seemed to fester outside the building's perimeter of safety and cleanliness. They proselytized all day and studied scripture at night. It was a sacred summer camp headed by the Mission Leader and his wife. The boys had their uniforms: dark polyester suits, white shirts, and ties. They had curfews and prayer and repeated testimonies that theirs was the one and only True Church. The boys lived with a background noise of tension from the threat, real and imagined, of constant surveillance. They were doing vital work, expanding the boundaries of the

Church, and needed protection from the foaming chaos of the city nipping at their ankles as they rode their bikes up and down the streets with their hearts and mouths stuffed full of Truth. They were not allowed out on their own; they never left their partner's side; they took recreation as a group. Periodically they would fill a bus to sightsee.

Once the group toured the Pyramids of the Sun and Moon. And Tom felt the world fall away. On the rough brown steps, steeply graded toward the home of stellar bodies and infinite space, Tom floated free of the other young men who surrounded him with their regulation hair and earnest smiles. He saw the plumes of the headdress, the gold and bright fabrics. He imagined himself plunging the dagger into the chosen victim. He imagined himself receiving the dagger, with the hands of the acolytes pinning his wrists and ankles while the blade etched a screaming path through his bones and sinew. The flat-nosed, blaze-eyed priest raised the pink orb of his heart aloft, beating free in the sunsplay, in the moonwash. Like the Hand Through the Zipper, the vision terrified and excited him.

After cycling down the narrow streets with their ties flopping over their shoulders, Tom and his partner, Paul Bartsch, stopped to cool down under the shade trees in the center of a plaza. Tom remarked that they were too easy to identify as Mormon missionaries with their white shirts and bookbags and the bike clips on their long pants. Although he didn't say it, Tom was annoyed that he stood out, that he could be identified. Paul replied that their visibility was part of their service to the Church; he was proud to be noticed.

Paul daunted Tom with his devotion. He was a nice, regular guy encased in the impermeable sheen of true belief. Tom felt that if he strived his entire life, he would never be as good, as dedicated, as Paul was during the months he was Tom's partner. Paul had red hair and a broad face dusted with freckles. His thick-muscled arms and chest stretched the top of his garments when he pulled off his dress shirt in their dormitory room. Each night Tom managed to climb into bed first and watch as Paul undressed. After lights out, Tom would study the spotted shadows cast on the ceiling by the high square window, and they would talk about the future. Paul would tell him about his college plans and his girlfriend. Tom didn't have any plans; he didn't have a girlfriend. He told Paul that he wasn't sure he wanted to go to college or get married for a while. But Paul couldn't conceive of a future without school and a wife at its center.

Until Paul fell asleep, Tom counted the spots on the ceiling, which circulated like protozoa under a microscope as the wind stirred the trees outside. He checked Paul's heavy breathing, then opened the door and shifted down the hall to the bathroom. At the training center they had been advised to monitor their partners and fellow missionaries for signs of self-abuse, for overeating, for the use of profanity and other aberrations. He had to be careful; he had taught himself to come quickly and silently. He could not luxuriate in the sensation, but it was something.

They were cycling in the outskirts of the city when Paul drove under the drooping branch of a wax-leafed tree. A fine yellow dust powdered his shirt and the back of his slacks. Paul ignored his dusting until the long pedal home, when his back began to sweat. He itched. In their room, Paul tossed his satchel on the desk and tore at his clothes. He contorted his arms to scratch his back through his garments, and finally stripped them off as well. "Tom, could you scratch there or wipe this stuff off me or something?" Paul pointed to a spot between his shoulderblades.

"If it's a rash, you shouldn't scratch it."

"Come on, Tom. I'm going nuts." Paul sat on the edge of his bed, and Tom stood above him. He scratched the spot cautiously. "Harder." He scratched vigorously. He grabbed his shower towel and wiped at the skin of Paul's back. He settled one hand over the dots and spatters of freckles on Paul's shoulder to hold him steady while he worked. His hand must have remained an instant too long after he finished wiping, because Paul twisted his head to look into his eyes. Tom stared down at the swelling pouch of cloth between Paul's legs. Tom was hard himself.

They would wait until the Mission Leader had paid his nightly visit. Tom would slide into Paul's bed, and they would find each other through the leg holes of their garments. They seldom dared to come outright, to risk noise, to leave stains. They squeezed each other until they were impossibly stiff, impossibly yearning, and they couldn't stop themselves. They never spoke about it. They never touched each other in daylight. Tom ached at the silence between them. He thought he might be in love, but he knew love could not exist in their situation.

As spring approached, imperceptibly in the sticky city, they prepared the Martinez family for baptism. They covered all the lessons with the husband and his wife and their ten-year-old son. Paul became increasingly agitated. He would lose the thread of the lesson, and Tom would need to prompt him or take over entirely. After they asked Señor Martinez if he could accept the teachings of the Church with a pure heart and a clear conscience, Paul whispered to him, "How would we answer that, Elder Anderson?"

After dinner one night, Tom returned to their room to find Paul's bed stripped and his dresser emptied. The Mission Leader called Tom to his office. Tom sat on the padded folding chair while the short, sinewy Mission Leader hunted through a filing cabinet. He was a retired potato farmer from Idaho Falls with six children and seventeen grandchildren, whose pictures filled the wall between the windows. The man stood behind his desk and glared at Tom. "I don't think I need to tell you why you're here."

"No." Tom could guess: they had found out somehow.

"What you did to that boy is unforgivable. He broke down blubbering and told me the whole sick story. And he was one of the nicest boys. One of our best before you got your mitts on him." The Mission Leader looked into a booklet he had unearthed from the file drawer. "Now some of the teachings would say that you should be given a chance to explain yourself and you should be able to repent your sins and suchlike. But you know what, I think you're scum. I don't think there's a whole lot of point going on with this, is there? Your bishop at home can deal with you if he wants to, but I won't waste my breath. If it was up to me, I'd boot you right out into the street. But it ain't up to me entirely, so Sister Skousen and I will drive you to the airport as soon as possible. Till then, you can stay in your room and pray that God will see fit to still reckon you a human being after what you've been up to."

They sent him home to Sterling. He heard that they sent Paul back to Philadelphia, but he was dismissed for health reasons, not immorality. Tom's father spit into a sand-filled ashtray when Tom stepped off the plane in Las Vegas. His mother cried. For months after, his parents were too ashamed to go to church. His father watched baseball, and his mother listened to "The Spoken Word" with the Mormon Tabernacle Choir on the kitchen set while she baked bread. Tom pulled on his jeans, gassed up his truck, and headed into the canyons. He drank a lot of beer; he bought joints from an old classmate in the parking lot at Boonies. He got tanned and drunk and stoned and didn't care.

When he saw Kath hanging out, improbably, with Cynthia Bingham, sporting the unbrushed hair and raccoon eyes of a heavy-metal goddess, he thought, Here's your last chance. It would never happen with anyone else. He didn't expect to be saved, but he hoped he might be happy.

And he was happy. He surrendered himself to the precision of pleasure and never considered whether, below the surface of sensation, he felt anything real. He assumed that life could go on and on and on with Kath—although he made mistakes. There was the black man at the rest stop who tugged Tom hard and put his finger inside him while Tom moaned into the man's mouth over the reek of the chemical toilet. And the night he went home with Lloyd Mortensen, the Biology and Driver Ed. teacher at Mesa Vista. Kath called at noon the next day, and Tom's mother found his bed made and—she later confronted him with the incriminating details—felt his toothbrush and found it dry. But he could give it up, he believed. If not good, he could be, at least, sane.

A father, though, was something that he couldn't be. Not yet.

• • •

Kath looked at Tom across the gulf of smeared plates and empty glasses. "But you are, Tom. We don't have the choice." She wanted to smack him. "Do you want me to feel sorry for you? You make me want to vomit. And it's not because I'm a bigot or I can't understand what you're going through." She looked out the door, where the sky was nudging purple toward dawn. "You're just not a nice person. What, did you think you could just use me for entertainment? What gives you the right to even think that?"

"I'm sorry."

"Please God, don't cry again."

"I won't. I won't." Tom stood. "We'll work this out. I'll call you after I get some sleep. And think. Okay?"

He tried to caress her throat. She flinched. He left, easing the screen door shut behind him.

The last definitive sighting of Tom in Sterling was made at two o'clock that Sunday afternoon by Stacey, the cashier at the drugstore. Tom had stopped to buy a six-pack of Coke and a package of disposable razors. Around lunchtime his mother had heard him yanking his tent out of the hall closet, but that wasn't unusual. When she entered his bedroom in the early evening to put away his laundered socks and underwear, she was surprised to find his bureau drawers cocked open and emptied.

Kath told her parents that she was pregnant and that Tom had fled. She had to tell them because she wouldn't agree to go to Planned Parenthood with Cynthia and "deal with it." Her father wanted to put the police on Tom's trail. To stop him, she screamed across the kitchen and pulled the receiver from his hand by its long yellow cord. She didn't want to find him. She would not force Tom to marry her and make a dull throbbing hell of both their lives. The fact of his leaving was confirmation that Tom was not worth having around. Her father was baffled; he could not comprehend Kath's reasons. Her mother was tart.

She made Kath sit at the table and eat a tuna salad sandwich while she spoke. "If you don't care that your baby will grow up without a father—and I find this notion absurd, but I won't argue it with you—then you must still be practical. Children can't be fed and clothed with love, Kath. Every family needs a provider, and that is the man's job. If you don't want a husband, well, you're disturbed. But not wanting Tom to provide for the baby is criminal."

"I'm not going to ask you for money, if that's what you're worried about. I've got what Grandma left me, and when that runs out I'll get a job."

"You are insane. You are truly, truly deranged. I only hope it's not too late to find him when the tragedy of your situation sinks in for you."

Kath never looked for him, and her parents stopped pressuring her; perhaps they thought that if they stopped shouting at her, she would drop her rebellious stance and see the wisdom of their advice. Or perhaps they hoped that the quiet in the household would allow the attention of Sterling to shift to some other unfortunate family. Kath was glad that they left her alone.

While her stomach swelled over the months into a taut, suppleskinned melon, she kept to herself in the empty corners of her parents' house. At first her family treated her with the untiring concern awarded to delicate invalids, but she couldn't respond appropriately. When her father brought her bowls of fresh raspberries from the yard, or her brother, Carl, offered to run and fetch the magazine she had forgotten in her room, or her sister and cousin sat down next to her on the sofa to talk, she could only stare at them sullenly. She wasn't worthy of their attention; she was a pregnant, husbandless teenager, like the girls she had dismissed as cheap and stupid. Considering the boyfriend she had chosen, she was more idiotic than those girls were. She wanted to be forgotten.

Eventually her father and brother and sister and cousin stopped trying to engage her attention. When they found her in a dark room staring at a lightless TV screen, they would regard her with little more concern than they gave to the house's other fixtures and furnishings. She would sit on the back stoop watching Champion chase an empty milk jug around the yard, and sometimes her father would hand her the garden hose with a nozzle attached to spray the grass or the nearby planting beds. She didn't venture beyond the porch if she could help it. She couldn't cope with the thought that every head which turned to her in Sterling concealed knowledge of the child inside her, as if they could look through her skin.

Yet in the whole town, only her mother regarded her as a project demanding constant attention. She would wait with Kath at the kitchen table to assure herself that Kath didn't skimp on her requisite servings of milk. While she gulped pleasurelessly, her mother would badger her with prenatal advice. "You need to get out more and exercise," she would say. "Don't think your pregnancy will be one long vacation. It's hard work."

Kath knew she was not on vacation. She did little, but she didn't rest. By her fifth month, the days of her Wild Summer were as shriveled as stars, and the presence of God—her testimony to Church and family—which had drawn off into the distance while she was with Tom, swelled with a separate heartbeat in her body. She felt that her Heavenly Father observed her with particular concern, and she worked at being good. But she knew that it would take more energy than she could find in herself to succeed.

In her eighth month she moved down to the sofa bed in the basement. She set up Carl's old bassinet and changing table in the corner in preparation. No one came to visit her; her mother would not allow her friend Cynthia, whose jeans jacket reeked of smoke, into the house. No one suggested a baby shower.

PearLeen stopped by with a present in the week before Kath went into labor: a certificate for baby photos hidden in the tissue of a large department store box. "I'll knit you up something cute when we know whether it's pink yarn time or blue yarn time," she said, then swiped at her eyes with a handkerchief.

"Oh, I'm so sorry for you," she cried. "But I know you'll make the best of it. There'll be a man in your life again before the baby knows the better of it. You'll see."

When Daron was born, he was beautiful. She held his mouth near the hollow of her throat to feel his small, definitive exhalations. She knew what the past year had been for: she had been given someone to hold on to.

She wanted them to be independent—her boy and her—and when Daron had convinced her that he could be content for a few hours in the world beyond the crook of her elbow, she found an afternoon job in an ice cream parlor. Her mother claimed that babysitting was relaxing after enduring Kath's restless roaming through the house with Daron in her arms, and Kath was glad to be free of her mother's constant surveillance.

At the shop, Kath spoke with Merrill Nelson for the first time since the day she had ridden the pony into his backyard. He had come in to buy a mud pie for his mother's birthday. She dripped HAPPY BIRTHDAY CLOVIS in looping chocolate cursive onto the pie, and Merrill tipped her two dollars and invited her to the monthly singles dance at the Stake Center. Kath's mother was ecstatic that Kath had stumbled on a good man from a good family who was willing to take up with her. She bought Kath new shoes and a dress.

Merrill was not the man she would have chosen for herself. He was the photo-negative of Tom: blond, tall, and solid, where Tom was compact and dark-haired. She had loved Tom, and she did not love Merrill. But he charmed her. He took her out to dances and dinner. He crept over in the night to hang rattles and squeak toys from blue ribbons on the tree outside the front window. And he charmed her family. He helped her father rewire the taillights on his camper and took Carl deer-hunting in the mountains. After one dinner at which her mother plied him with pot roast and cherry cobbler, Ardeth tapped a knife handle on the table and said, "Don't you dare lose him."

Kath kept on with Merrill because he offered a kind of salvation. Tom had been full of doubts; he had divided her from the foundations of her life. Merrill was firm. He led her back to her family and faith. Tom had required her strength, but in her friendship with Merrill, he was the one to offer comfort.

He stretched out on the back stoop and read to her from the Bible and the Book of Mormon while she sat in a lawn chair with Daron swathed in a blanket, her eyes welling. Merrill was honest: he told Kath that his family was reluctant for him to date an unwed mother, but he had convinced them how essentially good Kath was in her heart—how it was an honor to give her child a father and raise him right. Because Tom had left her miserably alone, Kath assumed that Merrill was bound to bring her joy.

She refused his first proposal in Cousin Berma's miniature ghost house because she worried that he was making a mistake. He deserved a better wife, and she didn't deserve to be rescued. Her rejection had been definitive. When he continued to stop at the house each night after work to see her, she recognized that he must love her. Or else she had become a dogged crusade for him. Because they both believed their marriage would be her redemption, the distinction between his love and his duty was negligible. He had convinced Kath of his necessity for her future. When he took her to the gully to shoot tin cans, he asked her again. Bullets rang, piercing metal; she accepted.

Kath finishes her coffee, and when the waitress refills her cup she asks to see a menu. The longer Merrill fails to appear, the more apprehensive she feels. She wants to be steely and tough with him; she struggles to believe that he has no power over her, that he cannot hurt her. In getting ready to leave the house, she found herself slipping into a dress and curling her hair. She grew angry that he could still affect her behavior and carefully changed into torn jeans and a tanktop.

While she flips through the laminated pages of the menu, the waitress stands over her, clicking the button on her ballpoint. "Hey there!" the waitress calls. "How's tricks, Skunk?"

Kath looks up as Merrill drops onto the bench across from

her, raises his eyebrows, and smiles. The waitress offers him a menu from the clutch of them pressed under her elbow, but he shakes his head. "What can I get you?" He orders two hamburgers with a double scoop of potato salad and a large milk. While the woman scribbles this on her pad, Kath watches Merrill spread a paper napkin over his lap and stretch his thick arms along the back of the bench.

"And you? Decided yet?" the waitress asks her.

She finds that she is crushing her lips, nervously, between her fingers. She folds her hands together under the table. "No, I think just coffee will be fine. And separate checks, please."

Merrill grins. "I'm buying, Katie-Kate. Why don't you get yourself a nice lunch. The soup's good here. Have you forgotten?"

The waitress stares down at Kath impatiently. "Coffee," Kath says, and watches the woman shift away.

"I'd have never guessed you were so hard, Kath. Have you changed, or did you just put one over on me back then?" He lowers his arms, and the folds of his freshly pressed red T-shirt hide the slight paunch he has developed since she last saw him, close-up, in daylight.

"What do you want?" She wants him to make his point. She feels her new self, her strong self, disappearing.

"What do I want? I want what you do, Katie-Kate. Remember the dream I had? We were supposed to be a forever couple. But it takes two people for those kinds of dreams."

The waitress brings his milk, and he drains the glass. A white drop escapes from the edge of his mouth and dots his T-shirt. "And you don't seem to believe in dreams. You saw the angel, and you know that I was chosen by God for something. But you don't even care. So how can you be the right woman? I asked myself, how can she be?" A cracked egg smile breaks slickly over his face. "So I'm gonna give you what you want, princess. Let's get ourselves divorced."

Daron: Social Studies

One day at Berma's, Skunk found Daron on the back lawn. He sat down in the grass and explained the rewards of the afterlife: men will eventually become like unto God and rule their own planets with their many wives. Afterward, Daron drew a detailed map of heaven in his Sterling notebook, giving everyone their own planet, with God's planet, Kolob, in the center—although he didn't quite know where to put his mother. When he looked at the picture in his Sterling notebook a week or so later, he decided to rip the pages out. There was no room for speculation in his book. As a researcher, it was his duty to stick to the facts.

The WELCOME sign at the outskirts of Sterling claims that the town and its immediate vicinity contain 1,250 inhabitants. When Daron counts the people on both sides of the street—on the sidewalk, in buildings, in cars—while riding slowly down Main, he gets totals of twelve or fifteen, which makes him wonder where all the people are. Because he lives in Las Vegas in a closely-packed apartment complex, because he attends a large elementary school seething with anxious children like kernels in a popcorn popper, because he has visited his mother's casino, where tourists swarm through a maze of lights and bells in a perpetual midnight, he finds Sterling unsettlingly sparse, as if most of the population has been carted into space by UFOs and those left behind drift around forlornly waiting for the others to return.

He recognizes the same faces. In the grocery store with his mom on Wednesday afternoon. At the gas station with his grandfather Thursday morning. At his grandfather's lumberyard. Out for pizza Friday evening. And every face is repeated on Sunday at church.

In his notebook, Daron has written down the names of the people he has met. He studies them closely in their natural surroundings and takes notes. He observes their clothes and habits and speech, and when he is finished he will put them in categories.

PEARLEEN PRATT: His great-aunt has embroidered a handkerchief for each day of the week with a tiny señor and señora—he in a sombrero, she in a mantilla—in various poses next to a cactus and with the day spelled out beneath them (he has sketched a representative example in his notes: TUESDAY, in which the man plays a guitar while the woman swooshes her skirts in a flamenco veronica).

When she met Daron in the grocery store one day, Aunt PearLeen kissed him on the forehead and left a smudge. Oh dear, she said, let me get that. She lifted the TUESDAY handkerchief from her purse, folding and wetting a tip. Wait, it's Monday, isn't it? She slipped the handkerchief back into her purse and licked her thumb to remove the lipstick.

DOUGLAS PRATT: Whenever Daron meets his great-uncle, Uncle Douglas winks and says, One of these days we're gonna get you on the back of the widow-maker, huh, sport?

Uncle Douglas has stolen a body. Rhonda, his mother's cousin, said that he had a dream. In the dream, he got out of bed and crept downstairs. She was there, the skeleton-woman, huddled by the furnace. Her fingerbones were slowly turning a valve to flood the house with gas. Uncle Douglas woke up, in the real world, and loaded the box with the body into the bed of his truck.

JARED AND JASON PRATT: His cousins are ignorant of American culture. For example, neither cousin was able to identify the powers provided by the ten Magus Crystals in the *Steel King* comic series (1: Invisibility, 2: Control of Gravity, 3: Telepathy, 4: Chameleon abilities, 5: Magnetism, 6: Thermal projection, 7: Sonic projection, 8: Necromancy, 9: Prophecy, 10: Synergy). Jason's response was: Who cares?

The cousins do, however, know the name of every hose and valve in the engine of the 1978 Camaro that Jared is rebuilding for when he gets his license next year.

DON MILLER: His grandfather wears one of three baseball caps continuously from the time he leaves the bathroom after his shower in the morning until he sits to watch the evening news at ten o'clock. Throughout the day he absently removes the cap, smooths down his thinning gray hair, and replaces the cap, tugging the bill firmly over his forehead.

JULEE MILLER: His aunt keeps a large black nylon bag with her at all times. In the morning, before she gets ready for the day, she takes all of her hair-care products, her hair dryer, her curling iron, and her cosmetics out of the bag and puts them away in their proper places in the bathroom drawers and cabinets. Then, after breakfast, she returns to the bathroom and puts all her things back in her bag when she leaves the house.

One evening a wasp darted in through the back door while his mother was unloading groceries. It probed the upper corners of the front room with a soft hum, then buzzed the lamp by JuLee's head. She flew to her feet and swatted at it with her *Glamour* magazine. For gross, she said, kill it, kill it! When the wasp rested on the shade, Daron covered it with a plastic cup and slid a *Newsweek* underneath to capture it. He carried the caged wasp through the house and released it on the back stoop. He watched it, a dark spot bobbing in the burgundy blue of the sky, until it dipped behind a blackened hedge. His aunt popped a Dr Pepper at the screen door. You should've killed it, she said. What if it gets in again?

KATHLEEN MILLER: His mom is a different person in Sterling than she is in Las Vegas. She talks less; she smiles less. She prays and goes to church more. She would be a good person to study because Sterling has changed her so much. But he doesn't understand her at all.

ARDETH MILLER: When Daron visits Berma's house, he usually finds his grandmother in the master bedroom. The walls are covered with gold, flocked wallpaper and very old, cheap prints of wildflowers under dusty glass. On the tall dark-wood dresser are two cameo silhouettes of Berma and her sister, Clovis, cut from black paper. In the corner by the window is a washstand with a white ceramic jug and basin. One day his grandmother was folding her clean laundry and putting it back in her suitcase. She asked Daron to tell his mother to send extra towels from home for her to use. Daron asked why she didn't use the towels hanging on the rack of the washstand. I'm not staying here, honey, she said. I'm just visiting.

Often, when he arrives and climbs the stairs to see his grandmother, she draws him behind the half-closed door and tells him that Skunk is waiting to see him. Hush now, she says, and leads him down the stairs. With the stealth of robbers, they creep to the front door or the back to avoid Berma. He wonders what he sees in her movements or hears in her voice that tells hims the visits must be kept secret.

BERMA KIMBALL MORTENSEN: Cousin Berma bakes delicious brownies, crusted with tender brown flakes at the top and detonating with moist, deep, semisweet chocolate in each bite. She fashions marvelous cakes and pies, but, mysteriously, no dish she cooks besides dessert succeeds. Her salads are indifferent; the Jell-O is embedded with raisins and shreds of carrot, like the blocks of amber he has seen in pictures: full of outsized mosquitoes and trilobites. Her main courses are mucky beige bogs. Alarmingly, Cousin Berma offers her recipes to the members of the Relief Society, which threatens to overrun Sterling with the seepage of a thousand chicken casseroles.

When she watched Daron after dinner, Cousin Berma prepared for bed before sitting down to doze by the television. Behind the half-closed bathroom door she removed her floral housecoat and stepped into her pink flannel zipper-front robe. With the cardboard roll held on one finger, she unspooled a length of toilet paper and wrapped her blond hairdo in a loose turban—to keep its shape, she explained. He told her the story of the woman whose beehive concealed a silken nest that later burst into a flood of baby spiders. Cousin Berma touched the white fringe across her forehead with anxiety. She laughed and poked him with the toilet paper tube.

INA KIMBALL: Old people may be different beings entirely. Infants are obsessively absorbed in the act of becoming a person; Aunt Ina is intently focused on ceasing to be. Daron sat at the foot of her bed while Cousin Berma served her dinner. Berma shifted several pillows under Aunt Ina's back to raise her from the cradle of lamb's wool. She filled spoons with broth and pudding from the bowls on the tray in her lap. Although Berma made a conscientious display of moving the liquids from the bowl to Aunt Ina's lips, the contents of the spoon dribbled in feeble streams along the heavy wrinkles bracketing Aunt Ina's chin and were wiped away by the thick towel in Berma's other hand. The meal was imaginary—a duet of mutual comforting. Between Aunt Ina's pretended sips, Berma squeezed her hand and stroked the white hair from her forehead; these caresses were the food to stave Aunt Ina's true hunger, the only hunger she couldn't ignore and didn't want to forget.

Kath: 10

Kath cradles the phone against her shoulder and pulls out another drawer.

Damask napkins. A red-and-white-checkered Italian restaurant tablecloth. Dr. Seuss pillowcases, mismatched. Yellow slatted, sushi-roller placemats. Holly-bordered Christmas table runners. Motley scraps from an unfinished crazy quilt. White lacquered napkin rings—a handmade gift from Aunt PearLeen. Three large boy's T-shirts, in the original plastic, forgotten. Belgian lace wrapped in blue tissue—"Blind nuns sew it all by hand," PearLeen had explained when she brought the present over after her trip to Europe. A lavender tricot nightgown with a grape-cluster appliqué dangling from the bodice by a few threads. A polished rosewood box half filled with silverware service for four and a booklet outlining other utensils available in the "Moonglow" pattern. A cake knife detached from its plastic-tortoiseshell handle.

"Are you sure it's the second drawer down? I can't find it."

Her mother responds impatiently in Kath's ear, "I know I put it there to sew up a corner of the nametag."

Kath stretches the yellow cord farther around the corner to search another built-in drawer down the hall. She digs through old diapers, a Gerber bottle full of diaper pins, her old white suede vest with the silver-tipped tassels on the breasts (from her parents' trip to Tijuana), and an assortment of baby outfits. "I don't see it anywhere, Mom. I'll just wear a T-shirt."

"What color?"

"A pink one."

"Yes, but what shade of pink?"

"I don't know, Mom. Sort of bubblegum, I guess."

"Ours are a dusky rose."

"Mom, it's only for one night."

"And theirs are peach, I believe."

"I'll look for five minutes more. Then I've got to get ready."

"Don't be late."

Kath hangs up the phone and heads directly to the bathroom. She refuses to waste another second hunting for a bowling shirt. Both teams know each other intimately, and it is unlikely that the Super Marketeers will be duped into believing that she is on their team. Her mother's team, the Beauty Roses, who are principally the women on the executive board of the Civic Beautification Committee, are pitted against her Cousin Rhonda's team of waitresses, cooks, and busboys in the quarter finals of the summer tournament. Kath is the only woman her mother could think of to replace RaNae Wilcox, who has been knocked out of the running by a summer flu.

She brushes her hair and applies a rudimentary touchup of lipstick and mascara. She has no time; her mother was on her way to the bowling alley. Kath needs to get her father to drive her, because her car is in the garage with dead solenoids in the starter motor. She knocks on her brother's door and pokes her head around to tell Daron to get his shoes on. And to go to the bathroom—Daron hates public restrooms and becomes absurdly panicky when he is forced to use them.

She plows through the suitcase on her bed for the T-shirt. She hasn't unpacked; she wants to avoid any acknowledgment that she has been in Sterling for three weeks. She hasn't accomplished anything in town, unless she can consider her imminent divorce an achievement.

She pulls on the T-shirt, which, she notices, actually does become a mother-infuriating peach under certain lights, and looks at her father through the kitchen window. He stands in the center of the lawn with his thumb stuffed in the end of the garden hose to shoot water over the zucchini. Madame rushes daringly back and forth under the arc of the spray. "I'm ready."

Her father drops the hose, and a fleck of water taps Madame's back, spurring her to charge around the side of the house. "Did you find it?"

"No. But I think this shirt's okay."

"Uh-oh. Watch out."

"What can she say? I'm doing her a favor as it is." She can't say anything too mean-spirited to him about her mother since she has been assigned the task of bringing them together.

They walk through the house, and she lifts her mother's spare ball and spare shoes. "Daron! Come on!" He appears from the hall with a stack of comics and a video game in his hand. "What're those for? You're supposed to be cheering your mom on to victory."

"Yeah, right." He grins, and she rests her fingers on the hollows behind his ears where she used to rub him to sleep as a toddler. They haven't spent much time together in Sterling, and she misses him; she misses their family of two, their own tiny home in Las Vegas.

· · ·

Her mother stands, pert and petite, outside the lighted door of the bowling alley when they pull into the parking lot, as if her impatience would be transmitted to them more effectively in the open air. Her father parks in a space opposite the door, and Kath leaps out, jerking the ball from the seat beside her. When her mother sees Kath, she taps her finger to her watch, grandly, like a silent-movie duchess. "You're late!" she shouts. When Kath enters the light from the door, her mother glares at her shirt. "And you're not dressed. Well, never mind. Rhonda has started her first frame. And I went ahead and put you second on our roster. I thought we could get you out of the way early."

"Your confidence in me is overwhelming."

"How long has it been since you bowled, honey? I don't think I'm out of line. Hello, Daron." He has come up behind Kath to peer at the huge trophies in the display cases bracketing the entrance. "I hope you'll be rooting for your grandmother." Kath's mother twists one of her earrings, a burgundy button to match the silk trim on the collar and short sleeves of her bowling shirt. "Oh."

Kath follows her mother's gaze over her shoulder. Her father has left the truck and stands in the drive, a few feet from the curb. Her parents haven't seen each other since she arrived; they haven't spoken, except for a few awkward seconds when Kath hasn't been home to answer the phone. From the first day, her father eagerly delegated the housekeeping responsibilities to Kath, and as time has eased them toward a facsimile of routine, he seems to forget the crisis in his home. He never mentions his wife. He has stopped asking the family to pray together for her return.

"You'd better hotfoot it, honey." Her mother pushes her toward the door. "Get those shoes on, and I'll be with you in a minute. You too, Daron. Go on."

Daron lugs the ball case through the swinging glass door, and she follows him into the dim foyer lined with old photos and limp banners. They pass the halfdoor marked Rentals and the snack bar. She hears the conk and clatter of toppling pins. "That way," she says, and guides Daron toward the lanes.

She looks out to the lighted sidewalk, where her father and mother stand close, talking. With his boots in the gutter and her bowling shoes on the curb, they are the same height. Her mother points to the darkening sky toward the end of town, and her father reaches out to cup her elbow and—shocking Kath—gently stroke her upper arm. Her mother leans and plants a quick, tight kiss on his cheek. She turns for the door, and Kath jolts forward into the raucous noise of the alley.

First frame: The shoes don't fit, and the fingerholes in the ball are awkward. Kath consoles herself with these facts when she leaves herself a 7–10 split after her first ball. Her second ball rolls silently between the two pins, unimpeded.

Second frame: She hoists the ball confidently and bowls a spare.

Third frame: She lifts her ball from the rack and glances at the stands, where Daron taps his thumbs on the buttons of his game. Rhonda, after a triumphant turkey in her first three frames, leans on the chair of a dark young man in torn jeans. Kath leaves three pins standing.

Fourth frame: Miraculously, a strike. She pumps her fist into the air. The Beauty Roses applaud.

Fifth frame: She pays for her cockiness when the ball thumps off the lane into the gutter.

Sixth frame: Gutter.

Seventh frame: A failed split.

Eighth frame: A strike!

Ninth frame: Zip.

Tenth frame: Her mother watches her with the weariness of a woman who had expected every child she raised to bowl perfect 300s. She leaves herself another 7–10 split. When she meets her mother's eyes, she sees her father's stroking hand, her mother's kiss. The ball kicks the ten pin across the gap. She makes the spare.

"You bored?" Kath rests her chin on the rail in front of Daron's seat.

"I'm okay."

"I guess the agenda is we all go out for ice cream after."

"Oh."

"Hey, don't sound so enthused." Rhonda motions for Kath to come over to her seat in the row above the Super Marketeers.

"Let's go meet Rhonda's boyfriend."

"Mmmm."

"He must be a great guy. Uncle Doug hates him." Daron looks up from his game and smiles. Without discussing it, she and Daron have agreed implicitly that Uncle Doug is a jovial asshole.

Rhonda and her boyfriend sit side by side in the bolted bucket seats, holding hands. His hair is jet-black; his thick eyebrows meet above his nose; he is fiercely handsome.

Rhonda whistles. "Not bad, Kath. You're no threat to the pros. Hey, you're no threat to the Super Marks, if I say so myself. But not bad."

Rhonda introduces them to Manuel, and when he shakes Kath's hand his grip is firm but sensuously soft, almost a caress. "Good to meet you." His voice is low and sweet.

Rhonda stretches her meshed fingers above her head. "Can I buy you a beer, Kath?"

"They serve beer here now?"

"I don't drink that much," Rhonda says. "But I like to be seen putting away a few brews when the Beauty Roses are around."

Kath remembers her at Boonies and laughs. "You're wicked."

"Just a sweet little Miller Girl." Manuel flips Rhonda's long braid and tickles her cheek with the end. "Cut it out." She punches his arm. "Make yourself useful. Go get the athletes their brews."

"My mom would kill me, Rhonda." Kath pulls a few bills from the pocket of her jeans. "Daron, do you think you could go with Manuel and get us Cokes or lemonades or something?" He shrugs and reluctantly follows Rhonda's boyfriend to the snack bar. "He's hot shit. Gorgeous."

"Yeah."

"Any progress with your parents?" Kath asks, with a hopefulness she doesn't feel.

"Who cares. But, you know, Manuel's transferring to the University of Arizona this fall, and I think I'm going with him."

"That's going to please them royally, Rhonda."

A tall woman, whose huge hairdo folds open from her face like the brown leaves of a book, points to Rhonda to bowl the tiebreaker. "Know what, Kath?" Rhonda bounds down the steps toward the ball return. "I—do—not—give—a—fuck!"

Her mother polishes her ball intently with a square of felt. Kath sits beside her and cranes her neck to the exit to look for Daron. "So." Kath puts her feet up on the empty scoring table chair in front of her. "What did Dad have to say?"

"Who was that with Rhonda?" Her mother pokes the felt into the holes with her pinky.

"I'm sure you can guess."

"I am amazed, frankly, that she would bring him here."

"Aren't Mexicans allowed or something, Mother?"

She frowns. "This will get back to her father."

"She knows that."

"Her father's temper is not something to toy with. He burned down his mother's house for less reason than this."

She mentions Uncle Doug's arsonous rage so blithely that Kath cannot believe she has heard correctly. "You always said it was a Christmas tree!"

Her mother folds the felt and rests it in the bottom of the ball compartment in her bowling bag. "Your father asked me to help him with the twenty-fourth."

"You're going to?"

"He needs me." Her mother suddenly points to the tall brunette who sits marking the score for the Super Marketeers. "That's the one he drives home, by the way. I really can't believe it. Your father can't abide moosey women like that."

Kath doesn't know what to say. Every word her mother speaks stuns her ears like firecrackers in a garbage can. There seem to be no family secrets that her mother would not disclose and no subject she would hesitate to broach. Her mother rises to bowl her round, and Kath twists again to hunt for Daron.

"Excuse me, Mrs. Miller?" Kath looks around to find Daron at her side and Manuel addressing her mother by the ball return. He holds a can of Budweiser in each hand and makes a feeble effort to hide them from her mother behind his back. "There's an important call for you in the rental office."

"Thank you." She studies the electric scoreboard above the lanes as she leaves.

Kath takes a cup of lemonade from Daron and takes Rhonda's beer from Manuel. She sucks at the beer. "Do you know who was calling?"

Manuel shakes his head. "A woman, I think."

Kath watches the door until her mother reappears. Her mother squeezes her earring and fixes her hair where the telephone receiver has mussed it. She glares at Kath's beer. "Put that down." Automatically, Kath hides the can behind the seat. "It was Cousin Berma. Aunt Ina has passed away this evening." Her mother walks out to the lane, bowls a strike to finish her game, then bends to untie her shoes.

Daron: The Dead

On an empty page, Daron writes: Aunt Ina Is Dead.

The words stand alone in the center of the page. Just words. It only takes four to record the event, and they don't tell him anything about what has happened.

He didn't know Aunt Ina that well. When he first met her, she already seemed to belong to another time; in some crucial sense, she had already left her home. His mom said that Aunt Ina had been frail since his mom was a child. It had taken death all these years to decide.

When Jerry the Lizard died, Daron found him curled like a dry-skinned leaf in the corner of his terrarium. His mom lifted the stiff carcass by the tail like a reptile popsicle and rested it in a shoebox. He asked her, Where does he go now?

I don't know, hon, she said, and hugged him. Maybe there are animals in heaven.

But she had misunderstood him. He wanted to know whether they would put Jerry down the toilet or bury him or throw him out in the garbage. He hadn't known then that whatever had been Jerry, whatever had quickened his scaly tail and claws, was gone. He had thought Jerry was still somewhere inside the brittle body.

When he looked at Aunt Ina in her coffin, he didn't have this confusion. He knew that she had left forever, as surely as the woman in Uncle Doug's basement. He knew that she had wanted to go, had wanted to die. At the luncheon at Berma's after the funeral, everyone tried to comfort him; they wanted him to know that she was in heaven now, that she didn't suffer, that she looked down on them with love. But their calming tone was unnecessary. He did not want soothing.

Even his mother did not understand—only Skunk, who stood without speaking on the front porch, then left early, and Berma, who drank lemonade with him from bent-necked straws. They knew that silence was the language of the dead.

Kath: 11

The morning after Aunt Ina's funeral, Kath's father sits at the table after breakfast reading the *Salt Lake Tribune*. He has reached the age when the day's routine includes scanning the obituaries for friends and classmates and customers. "I guess it's true about death striking in threes," he says, and taps his thumb against the newsprint. "First there was Elijah Sorenson, the grocer, then Ina, now here we are again."

"Somebody we know?" Kath asks, but she isn't really interested. She cooked, served, and cleaned up after the funeral luncheon. She feels too drained to confront another tragedy. She gathers plates and carries them to the sink.

"It's To—" His eyes meet hers over the milk jug on the counter; he glances down. "No one you'd know. An old customer."

"Dad," she begins, on a different subject. She has tried to talk to him about her mother all through breakfast, but she can't find a way to start.

After the funeral, her father went out to sign some checks at the lumberyard, and she turned her attention to the laundry, which had grown into large mounds in the hall. As she carried a bundle of towels through the house to the washer, she saw a glint of sun from a car window in the drive. Through the screen door, she saw her mother standing on the front porch with her fingers gripped tightly around the handles of her suitcase. Her mother had avoided Kath's father at the luncheon but had taken Kath aside to say that Berma might be better off alone for a few nights and she might come home. Kath had not expected her to appear unannounced. Kath stood very still, observing her mother as she swayed in her heels, and her mother did not notice her in the shadows of the house. Her mother looked to the side of the door, where a black-and-white cutout of a cow was nailed. THE MILLERS was printed in bold script along the cow's flank. "Oh," her mother said. "No." She turned away from the house. "Not yet."

Kath watched her walk down the steps and over to her car. She waited until her mother drove away before moving off into the house.

Kath wants to tell her father that his wife came home, that she stood within inches of the door. She is certain that if he made some show of love and goodwill, their separation would be over. But her father seems incapable of acting on his own, and she feels too embarrassed to prod him; she cannot point to the success of her own example.

"Something wrong, Kathie?" her father asks. He stands to reach for the bacon plate.

"It's nothing," she says, and reaches for the steel wool to scour the skillet.

Her father carries the crisps of leftover bacon outside to scrape into Madame's bowl, and Kath finishes clearing the table. As she refolds the sections of newspaper her father has left scattered, she scans the narrow obituary columns, full of photos twenty years out-of-date. She finds Ulma Anderson, Tom's grandmother, backlit and glossy, circa 1945. Death number three, she thinks.

At noon she watches Daron saunter down the back road on his way to visit Berma with a clutch of comics and one of his mysterious notebooks. She had told him that Berma might want some time to herself, but when she called ahead, Berma had insisted he was welcome. Her father has driven off to consult with Uncle Doug about a building project, JuLee is at work, and she has the house to herself. She finds an aluminum-frame chaise longue folded up in the toolshed and drags it out to the center of the lawn. She decides she deserves to relax. She has exhausted every vacation, sick, and personal day she has coming, and during her last phone call to the casino her employer was full of vague threats. She wants to enjoy her last few days.

She stretches out in a pair of running shorts and a bikini top borrowed from JuLee's closet. In Las Vegas, tanning is not one of her pastimes, and her pale skin heats quickly under the full sun. She spreads a layer of baby oil on her stomach and legs and sips an iced lemonade. She listens to the pump of the swamp cooler and Madame creeping by the stoop, and thinks that she and Daron spent their happiest hours in Sterling in this yard. After she married Skunk she would come home and sunbathe. When he was old enough, Daron would toddle around the perimeter of the grass in search of bugs. He would sit and watch the black ants stream in regulated lines across the sidewalk. Then he would dip a tiny paper cup into a bucket of water and splash them. The water would flower in brown stains on the cement, the ants would scatter in random tangents, and Daron would scream with laughter. Kath falls asleep on the chaise, remembering the ovals of dirt she would wash from the ball of each small bare foot.

By ten o'clock in the evening her face feels taut and slightly burned. She sits on the couch with a bowl of cereal in her lap, watching the late news. Her father is in bed, Daron is eating ice cream in the kitchen, and her sister is out—with no return foreseen, as usual. It surprises Kath that she is staying in a house full of people yet spends most of her time alone.

The phone rings.

"Would you get that, hon?" she calls.

She hears Daron's voice speaking carefully and politely around the wall. She listens as he sets the phone down on the counter and steps lightly into the front room. "Phone's for you."

"Grandma?"

He shakes his head.

"Who is it?"

"A man."

"A man? Is that the best you can do?"

"He didn't tell me." Daron sits and flips through channels with the remote control.

In the brighter light of the kitchen, Kath picks up the phone.

"Kath, it's you?" a man's voice asks.

"Who's this?"

She breathes in shallow sips through the lengthening pause.

"It's Tom," he says.

"Tom."

"I'm in town. For my grandma's funeral. I was calling because I thought your mom would know your number in Vegas . . . or . . .

Look, can we meet somewhere? I can't do this over the phone."

"Not tonight." Never, she thinks, never. But the years of his absence have toughened her. She should be strong enough to handle him.

"No, not tonight." He sighs. "I've got the funeral tomorrow. But tomorrow afternoon. Say one o'clock by the new post office? The benches outside?"

"All right," she says. Later, in bed, she can't stop counting the falling beads of each second threading toward tomorrow afternoon. She thinks she will never sleep. But she does.

Her mother has decided to take Cousin Berma on a shopping expedition to St. George to distract her, and Daron is going with them. "I'll try to buy him decent socks and underwear. His shorts are *gray,* Kath." She drops Daron off at Berma's house and drives along Main with no plans to fill the time until one. She looks in at the beauty parlor, where her Aunt MargaLee is the owner and beautician emeritus. Her aunt is at home, but Donna Speck, a high school acquaintance from her good-girl years, has a free hour. Kath has her hair cut, shorter yet, and elicits the latest gossip from Donna and JuDee Clayton. Her old friend Cynthia Bingham took her kids and her trailer and moved up to Seattle. Blond, raccoon-eyed DarCee Peterson, former Mesa Vista cheerleader, former BYU cheerleader, former Utah Jazz cheerleader, had a miscarriage in the winter after her third child and is thinking of adopting. As Donna holds the hand mirror for Kath to examine her hair, Kath asks if people talk about her. "Sure, it's a small town, Kath. But it's been how many years? The novelty wears off after a while."

She leaves her car at the beauty parlor and wanders up the street to stop for an ice cream cone to take to the post office. She sees two men reflected in the glass of the hardware store, superimposed on a display of fishing rods and reels: one wearing a gray suit, one in black, waiting at the crosswalk on the opposite corner. By the time she reaches the intersection of Main and

Fortune, the men have crossed. The taller man steps behind the other in single file to pass her on the narrow sidewalk. She notes that they are both handsome and healthy—urban healthy: not ruggedly hale, burly and big-gutted, like ranchers and miners, but machine-toned and aerobically trained. They are too attractive for Sterling—no one with beauty moves into town; no born beauty stays. The dark-haired man stops short near her, and the taller one jerks to a halt behind him, steadying himself with his hands on the other man's shoulders. "Kath."

She feels her spine pulled taut as she looks at Tom. His hair is cut as short as a missionary's but, unlike a missionary's, with longer locks on top brushing across his forehead. He inhabits his charcoal suit and muted-pattern tie with ease, unlike most men in Sterling, who may wears suits on Sunday or workdays but move stiffly in them as if trapped in a prison of papier-mâché. He is neat, ordered, un-Tom-like without his torn jeans and sexy suspect hygiene, but recognizably, undeniably Tom. "Hello."

"I didn't recognize you for a second," he says. "New hairdo and everything."

"It's been a while." Kath shrugs. "I'm sorry to hear about your grandmother."

"Thanks." He stares at Kath intensely, then breaks off sharply, embarrassed. "We just got done at the cemetery. Oh, Kath, this is Artie—Artie Cooper. Artie, this is Kath."

"Hi." The tall man at Tom's side extends his hand and shakes Kath's vigorously. He has an eager, curling grin on a triangular face, a vase blooming at the top with carrot curls. Freckles bunch on his cheeks and the backs of his hands. He wears his black suit with an affable irony, a recognition that conservative black suits are inherently amusing. Standing together on the street, well tailored and relaxed, he and Tom seem to breathe at the same frequency. He is Tom's lover.

"Nice to meet you." She waits for her reaction to strike her like a blow, but if it comes at all, it is muted—a weak shiver of disappointment, nostalgia.

She shifts her feet, and Tom catches her arm, encircling her wrist. "I thought we'd have lunch. Have you eaten?"

"I was going to have ice cream but . . ."

"Let's go to the café." He lowers his voice. "Okay?"

She looks at her watch, although time is not an issue.

"I didn't know you were in Sterling," he says. "I didn't know if we'd get this chance."

She follows them into the café, to a booth in the front window. Artie slides onto one bench and Tom onto the other; she stands awkwardly by the waitress to choose which side to sit on. She scoots in next to Artie; she wants to look at Tom.

When the waitress leaves, Artie opens his menu, then slaps it shut as if reconfirming his familiarity with its contents. "You must be really pissed off at this guy." Artie points at Tom, with the attention of his body turned to Kath.

"Artie." Tom loosens his tie.

"You've been nicer than I would've been in your situation. Better than he deserves."

"Fuck, Artie! You're really getting things off to a good start."

"I'm not angry," she says. Although she is the ostensible subject of their argument, Kath can't shake the sense that she is interrupting them. "Anymore."

"Excuse me. What can I get you?" The waitress returns, balancing three water glasses in her hand. It is the same woman who watched Kath haggle with Merrill over the check.

"We're just being mildly dysfunctional here. Sorry," Artie says. "I'd like the chicken sandwich and fries." While she and Tom order, Artie taps his spoon lightly against the Formica.

"Do you live in town again, Kath?" Tom lifts his water glass, speculatively, without drinking.

"No. I'm here for my mom and dad. They've separated."

"Oh, I'm sorry."

"But they're getting back together. Maybe. I guess."

"Good. Good." He drinks. "And Daron. How's he?"

It unsettles her that Tom even knows Daron's name. "He's fine."

"He's ten now."

"Right," she says.

"God. Ten years," he says. "And how many years have you been in Vegas?"

"Almost six."

Tom looks at Artie; she can't decipher it.

"I didn't think you'd ever show up here again," she says. "Even for a funeral."

"I didn't either. But I loved her. My grandma. And I realized that someday you've got to come back."

The earnest gravity in his voice annoys her. It was too easy for him to leave; it shouldn't be easy for him to return. "You deserted people. That's not a mistake that's easy to forgive."

"It wasn't a mistake, Kath. I had to leave. You know that."

"Why do I know it?"

"You know it. I did it for you as much as for me."

She fights the idea. Tom left her. He abandoned Daron. And she cannot accept his explanation that he acted out of mercy. She was taught that marriage was the inevitable outcome of love and goodwill. She wants to believe that her life has been the exception and the absolutes still hold true. She wants to believe that Tom's excuses make no sense. She sits speechless as the food arrives. She and Tom stare at their plates, unmotivated to pick up their silverware and start. Only Artie eats, looking from one of them to the other, his face volatile with impatient silence.

"We couldn't have married. They told me to. Everyone in the Church always told me to find myself a wife and I'd be fine. But I couldn't put us through that. I'd always be slipping into the bushes. Or maybe I could control myself, but I would have resented you for it. I didn't make a mistake when I left." Relieved of some tension, Tom bumps the butt of his palm against the bottom of the ketchup bottle and slathers his omelette in a red stream. "Other than that—leaving—I did what I could for you. For Daron. You never cashed the checks I sent."

The checks had arrived for the first few years in a birthday card—about two months late, since Tom must have guessed at the date. He sent a larger check each year, but she fished the cards quickly from the mail and tore them up.

"When I heard you got married, I thought you'd rather I just backed off altogether, let him be the father. I didn't forget, though." He cuts into his omelette.

Kath takes a bite from her sandwich but can't locate her appetite.

"I always kept in contact with my sister Caroline. She told me all the news. Her daughter went to the same preschool as Daron, you know, and she sent me the class picture. I picked him out of the group. Made me cry. That was a long time ago."

"Here." She lifts her wallet from her purse and tugs Daron's spring school portrait from the plastic holder. Tom examines it closely, then passes it to Artie. Artie smiles and holds it out to Kath. "No, keep it," she says. Artie returns it to Tom, who rests it against the ketchup bottle in front of his plate.

"For years I thought I would have to be alone. I thought that was the price of it. It was all about giving things up. But Artie . . ." He looks at Artie with such unambiguous love that Kath's stomach wrenches. She wants Tom back; against time, against nature, she wants that look for herself.

"Artie's convinced me I'm wrong. I don't just mean I'm not alone because I'm with him. I'd given up on a lot of things. I was living there in Salt Lake, and I thought I'd never see or speak to anyone I knew ever again. Holidays would come around—Christmas—and I'd want so desperately to be with someone I'd known for longer than six or eight months. It was like I was exiled on an island. I'd chosen to leave, but I felt like I'd been banished. Finally I broke down and wrote to Caroline, but that was it." Tom stops to finish his omelette; his eyes have the glassy, flooded look of held tears.

Artie twirls the frilled toothpicks from his sandwich. "We were thinking of going to Vegas to look for you," he says. "We're not going home till Pioneer Day."

"Looks like you found me." Artie doesn't deserve her bitterness, but what else can they expect from her?

"We saw my mom and dad at the funeral. Didn't talk to them, though. They looked away from us. It felt like a cold wet sheet dragging over me." He picks up Daron's photo and slips it into the pocket of his coat. "What I can thank Artie for is showing me I don't have to go along with it. I mean, because people shut me out and hated me, I closed myself off. But it's not me that's the problem. I can be open. I can have hope. I can love my grandmother. I can come back to Sterling when I want."

"Jeez, don't make it into some life philosophy." Artie shoots a toothpick spear between the lapels of Tom's jacket. "I just told you to lighten up and stop being such a wuss about it."

Tom responds with a sad, slow-rising smile. He squeezes the toothpick in his fist. "I want to see him, Kath."

She flips over the check and tallies her portion. "What do you want me to say?"

"Say yes."

"He doesn't know who you are."

"Look, Kath, I can understand why you wouldn't want him to meet me. But I wouldn't ask if I didn't think it was the right thing. For all of us."

"He's real shy." She is shocked to be on the verge of considering his suggestion.

Tom watches her for signals, for tremors, for storm warnings.

"Artie too?" she asks. It's too late to change her mind, she realizes: she has already conceded.

Tom leans further into the cushion, relieved. "He should meet Artie. If you decide to tell him, then there can't be any more lies."

She exhales loudly and takes out her wallet. It may be time to stop hedging and tell Daron everything. Tom is his father. "I'll talk to him about it. But he's a smart kid. I won't force him. It'll be his decision."

"Okay."

"Okay?" Daron's answer—firm and unhesitating, if not notably enthusiastic—short-circuits Kath entirely. She had expected him to refuse or to hesitate, and she had prepared herself for the odd moment when she would find herself attempting to persuade him. She had brought him out to stroll along the breezy ridge above the pond in the park anticipating protracted, painful talk, but his rapid acquiescence has left her with almost nothing else to say.

"Like you said, if he is my dad, I ought to meet him."

She follows a slanted path on the pondward side of the hill. Daron walks the spine, and their eyes are at the same level. "Are you mad at me?"

"Why?"

"I don't know. Cause I guess you have a right to be." She looks down at her sandals scuffing the patchy grass. "I let you think Merrill was your dad."

"I knew he wasn't."

"I feel like I owe you an explanation. Like you should know more about Tom before you meet him. Why he left."

"Doesn't matter."

She stops and looks over the pond and the road to the houses in Clearidge at the base of the hills. "I just feel so bad, hon. I'm afraid I've failed you. That you should have a real family. That you deserve better than this."

"It's okay, Mom. Really."

She grabs Daron and hugs him. She swings him in the air for the first time in years, and he's much heavier than she imagined. They almost roll into the lake. They sit in the thick grass by the shore. "He has a friend with him. Is it okay if he comes too?"

"I guess so. Yeah."

She rips out clumps of sticky grass and tosses a confetti of blades into the lake. She can no longer tell what Daron is feeling, and she worries about him, alone inside his head.

She arranges for Tom and Artie to visit in the morning, when she knows JuLee and her father will be out of the house. When they arrive, they knock hesitantly on the back door, and she calls to Daron before answering. Out on the stoop, she introduces them to her son: Tom and Artie. She asks Daron in a whisper if he would mind if she ran inside for a second to get everyone something to drink. "Sure, Mom," he says patiently. By the time she has filled the pitcher with ice and lemonade and shifted clean glasses to the wicker tray, they have vanished.

Kath looks out the screen door, but she can't find them. Tom's car remains parked on the back road, but the three of them have disappeared.

Madame sits upright in the backyard with her nose pointed into the sky. She seems to watch the passing of the high, thin cirrus or the tingle of the yellow-green leaves in the morning breeze. Her broad, shaggy back aligns perfectly with the thick trunk of the oak in the corner. Madame poses intently. Kath discovers three pairs of legs sprouting from among the leaves at slightly different altitudes. There are two hairy pairs—one thick and freckled, the other lean and achingly tactile in Kath's memory. The pair encased in slender blue jeans is the one she knows best. She worries absurdly that Daron has left her for a new life in the trees.

When they fall, finally, from the tree and tumble, laughing, in the grass and under the dog's licking tongue, she leaves the house to greet them. Daron scrambles up and runs toward her to reach for the lemonade, with rare half-moon grass stains at his knees. "We're going camping," Daron announces. He sucks at the lemonade. "I mean, can I go?"

"Camping? When?" The thought of Daron alone with these two men terrifies her, but she feels that she must not allow a single doubt to cloud her face. She smiles.

"Today," he says, and tilts the glass back until the ice clicks at his teeth.

"Today?" Her voice cracks with more concern than she intended to display. She wonders what is making her uneasy; she cannot identify it. She believes that Daron should get to know his father, even if Tom is a stranger to them both. But she worries—irrationally, she hopes, but unavoidably—about what might happen to Daron while he is with these two men—these two lovers—how they might change him.

"I know it's short notice, Kath." Tom sits on the stoop and motions Kath to join him. Daron runs off to throw a frisbee with Artie at the end of the yard. "But we thought we could drive over to Zion National Park. Just overnight. We've got a tent."

"Absolutely not." She hears her own mother's intonation, her imperious tone, and she blanches. "It's Pioneer Day tomorrow. The family party." She attempts to justify her refusal by using the holiday as an obstacle. But the party is really beside the point, a weak argument, and she is sure that Tom knows this. "He doesn't know you, Tom. I don't know you either. Anymore."

"I won't hurt him." Tom's voice threatens to quaver, and she vows to herself that she will punch him in the face if he starts to cry.

"I know that."

"You could come too." He sounds suddenly hopeful, as if he hadn't thought of this possibility before.

She remembers the eagerness in Tom's voice when he used to ask her out onto the desert and the thrill his invitations once gave her. Now she recognizes that they will both be relieved when she declines. "I have to get stuff ready for the party."

"But will it be okay if Daron goes? We'll have him back in time. You just say when."

She sets her glass down between her feet on the lower step and rubs the gathered condensation from her hands onto her jeans. "You have to promise me—and I'm within my rights, Tom—you have to promise me you won't hurt him."

"I just said!" His voice rises, and he shifts on the stoop next to her. "Do you really think that of me?"

She doesn't look at him but at Daron, making a wobbly toss with the Frisbee.

"I don't molest kids," Tom says. "You never used to be small-minded."

"That's not what I meant." It wasn't—although the thought had made a queasy dash across her mind. "I just don't want you to give him false hopes that you're going to be there for him. That he can depend on you."

"He *can* depend on me."

"Just don't . . ." She doesn't know how she might finish her thought: Just don't make him love you?

"Okay," Tom says, "okay." He stands and brushes the seat of his shorts.

"Okay." She echoes him. She understands that Tom has won the discussion. She is already planning what she will need to pack for Daron; she is already sending him on his way, alone.

Daron: Tom and Artie and the Gunnery Girls

The buttes and boulders, the pillars and towers of the national park spread across the horizon steeped in endless colors and textures. Often the stone is sanded smooth, as if a sculptor has begun to blast a massive form out of the raw rock; many of the stones have been given names on the ranger map and the placards at scenic turnouts—names that Daron recognizes from Primary class and Skunk's stories, like Kolob and Moroni. The road winds between frozen mounds of pudding in butterscotch, vanilla, and chocolate; the green of pistachio meat and the red of pistachio skins. Around Las Vegas the desert is dead, but here he senses that the sand and the sandstone are ready to burst into molten life. Every overhang and every slope of rubble seethes with arrested motion.

Yet, after sunset, the desert of shapes and colors shuts off rapidly, like the end of a videogame.

After hiking and sightseeing from the car, Daron helps Tom— his father—and Artie lug the gear from the trunk of Artie's overstuffed Nissan to the farthest, quietest site in the campground. While Tom and Artie set up the tent, he digs out the cookware before his father comes to light the fire in the pit. He hunts in the cooler for a Coke. He has been instructed in the art of the cocktail: how to measure out the triple sec and tequila and pour them into the shaker for margaritas, how to proportion the lemon and gin for Tom Collins. He laughs during the bartending because his mom would disapprove. After sunset, Tom feeds sticks into the campfire, and the swelling light throws a luminous circle around them. Their campsite becomes a stage in the darkness of a theater. For the first time, Daron feels uncertain about being in the wilderness with two men he barely knows. So he imagines that they are all actors reading lines in the hush of the night. He thinks of them abstractly, as characters. This makes things easier.

Tom: Daron forgets sometimes that Tom is his father; he is as loose-spirited as the linen shirt he pulled over his tanktop after sundown—with none of Skunk's cloudy earnestness. And without the unspoken threats that sour Skunk's breath when he tells his stories. Daron has a list of qualities that he imagined a father possessed: disciplining, assured, confident, expectant, aloof, disapproving, domineering, jovial, reserved, remote. But he is unable to find any of these in Tom. He had somehow expected Tom to fill automatically the slot in his mind that he had labeled "father." Instead, Tom tossed the canvas rucksack his mother had packed into the back seat and shouted, Let's get outta this town! He jumped in and gunned the engine, pitching them headlong down the empty streets of Sterling.

After driving awhile, Tom pulled off the road, and Daron scrambled with him and Artie up the skirt of rubble below a massive red stone fin. They looked back across the plain, dotted with buttes like stovepipe hats laid out on a bronze table, under endless blue. Climbing down, Daron skidded on the razor-edged rocks and scraped a long tongue of flesh from his shin. Although he didn't want to cry out, he did. Artie zigzagged down the slope and through the scrub to get the first-aid kit. Tom helped him to a plum-red boulder, hot through the seat of his shorts; Tom sat beside him, put his arm around him, and pressed him close. No one but his mom had held him like this. While they waited together, as a pinpoint thread of blood traced a sickle curve around his calf from the bottom of the scrape—for the moment that Tom hugged him, Daron felt that Tom might become his father in the same basic, ineffable way that Kath was his mother. But he didn't entirely trust the sensation; he may never trust any good, solid thing that comes too easily.

Artie: He is already a friend. Daron likes Artie without thinking, as if he has always been around—likes him more than his other friends at home—likes him more than it is sensible to like any adult. Artie ignores the evidence that Daron is a child. He tacitly confirms Daron's suspicion that he thinks too much and sees too clearly to be as young as people say he is. Artie is the greatest authority Daron has met on comics and movies and music. He can not only list the ten powers of the Magus Crystals, he can identify in which issue of *Steel King* they made their first appearance, and, further, provide detailed explanations of the four apocryphal Maya Crystals (1: Mutation, 2: Hallucination, 3: Ectoplasmic projection, 4: Diabolism).

When he took his turn driving, Artie sped along the plateaus, took wide curves in the hills, and sheered close to the perilous drop-offs. He recited the lyrics to pop songs—k.d. lang, Kirsty MacColl, the Pet Shop Boys—in stentorian tones: I was faced with a choice at a difficult age . . .

He twitched the car over the broken yellow line to pass a semi.

. . . would I write a book or should I take to the stage? But in the back of my head . . .

He leaned into the steering wheel and hammered the accelerator as the vast silver wall of the semi trailer slid by the side windows.

. . . I heard distant feet: Che Guevara and Debussy . . .

He flipped on the turn signal and dove in front of the semi before the car could smash into the blunt tan face of an approaching motorhome.

. . . to a disco beat!

Artie is an artist at an ad agency in Salt Lake. He does layouts for print ads and storyboards for television commercials. You never see my stuff, he said. It never escapes the office. At home, he writes and draws an underground comic book: *The Gunnery Girls*. When they stopped for lunch, Artie found a copy in his backpack to give Daron. The front cover had been torn in half and taped together, and Daron asked if he had a slipcase to keep it safe in. Don't worry, Tom said. There's plenty more where that came from. He's got boxes of them all over the house. His father looked to Artie. Should Daron be reading that?

Artie shrugged, and Daron flipped the black-and-white pages greedily in case they decided to take it from him before he was done. He found a few more issues scattered on the floor of the back seat and read these as well.

The Gunnery Girls are four female commandos who rocket across a postapocalyptic desert on a flat-topped sledge with caterpillar treads. The sledge is pointed at the prow and sprouts steering and gun controls shaped like microphone stands with motorcycle handlebar antlers. The Girls stand side by side at the controls in their string bikinis and thick black boots, ready to fire off the Gatling guns mounted on the sides of the sledge. After four issues, the Girls' goal in life is not precisely clear. Their chief rival is Dr. Remy Martín, a psychotic eating-disorder therapist headquartered in the bombed-out LDS Temple, but they spend most of each issue conversing, and digressing, and arguing. The drawings are anarchic and scorch the white paper with an acrid, exciting whiff of danger. Daron wants to pretend that he understands all the jokes and allusions, although he doesn't—not completely.

While Artie pokes at the flames with a blackened stick and Tom stretches out on a saddle blanket, Daron leans against a rock at the edge of the fire. He finishes the fourth issue by the flickering light, then asks, So what happens next? Is this the last issue?

I'm working on a new one, Artie says.

So what happens?

These giant talking beavers have rebuilt Hoover Dam to provide power for the Anthropomorphic Casino.

For what?

Anthropomorphism is when an animal acts like a human being. Like if Tom . . . your dad . . . acted just like he does but was a garden slug.

Thanks, Tom says, and kicks dirt at Artie with the heel of his sneaker.

Artie stands and stares down at Tom. Ask your dad to name the Girls. I'll bet he can't remember.

Sure I can. There's Jazmyn and Jennifer and . . . Simone . . . and . . . Olga? Svetlana? Britt?

Bibi, Daron says. He is pleased that he remembers this fact rather than all the names and dates from Primary.

Told you, Artie says, and kicks Tom's shoulder lightly. I'm gonna take a piss. He slips into the dark.

Daron looks down at the comics cover in his lap, at the illustration of Bibi in her flight attendant uniform surrounded by ravenous robots. He looks up when Tom sits next to him, close enough to brush his shoulder. Tom asks, You having a good time?

Mmm-hmm, Daron mumbles. He hasn't really thought about it.

You and Artie seem to have hit it off, Tom says. He tosses a twig at the red coals of the fire. You understand about me and Artie? Your mom tell you?

Tell me what? He stares intently as the gray stick takes up the licks of flame and burns.

I love Artie very much, Tom says. He's important to me, in a real way.

Tom's voice, his form in the low light, makes Daron feel weird, and he reminds himself that they are only actors speaking lines.

Tom continues, I don't want you to think that I left you and your mother because I didn't like you. That was the problem. I *did* love your mom. Enough not to want to make her unhappy. And we would've been if I'd stayed. Both of us. And you too. I couldn't love your mom the way she deserved. The way I love Artie. And I thought it would be better if you didn't have to grow up with all that tension.

Tom waits for Daron to say something, but he doesn't want to. He watches Artie slip into the light for his sketchpad, then retreat into the tent, and tells himself he doesn't need to be scared.

Tom asks, Has it been hard not having a dad? Was Merrill a good dad?

I was little. I don't remember.

You seen him since you've been home?

Sort of.

Sort of? Has your mom?

No. I don't know. I don't like him.

Tom wraps his arm around his shoulders. I'd like to see you again, he says. You know, more often . . . if your mom agrees, of course. You could come see us in Salt Lake for a long weekend or something.

Okay.

The other thing is . . . um . . . people might say things to you, real nasty things, about me and Artie. People can be such assholes. I want you to know that whatever you hear, you can talk to me about it.

Daron leans forward quickly, and Tom's arm falls away. You're a gay, he says. He doesn't know that this is true until he says it, and even then he is not sure what he means.

Yeah, Tom says. I'm sorry I took so long to find you again.

Tom holds his hands out over the fire, and they both watch the lines of yellow flame between his fingers. Neither speaks until Artie bursts from the tent into the light, holding up a sketch. How about this? Artie shouts.

He holds the sketch up near the light. At the front of the power sledge, between the curvaceous Jennifer and a huge beaver in a hardhat and safety goggles, a boy—Daron—stands defiantly with a serious expression, between a scowl and a bemused smile.

Daron grins. Cool. Can I have it?

Artie tears the page from the pad and gives it to him. He sits on the ground between Daron and Tom and wraps his arms around them both.

Kath: 12

The white dining-room chairs kneel in semicircle on the back lawn, six snowy girls at prayer. Their frosty seats and slatted backs toss sun into Kath's eyes, and they will not stay rooted to the ground. Their legs float along the crest of the blades of blue-grass, ready for rapturous departure. Seeing the chairs outside the house, she finds them alien to the natural world, ethereal. Heaven's chairs. They sing to the dark inside her—"Set down your chair," "Set down your chair"—and she drifts, her eyes focused inward, where the mind projects its illustrations. She falls into the room of her mind. In the somnolent quiet the air is honeyed, slow-dripping from the tongue into the lungs. She sets down her chair and sits.

Madame barks.

Kath shakes herself out into the sunshine and continues un-folding the cloth over the card table. Her mother arrived at the house early in the morning—near sunrise, it seemed to Kath—and Kath has been obeying her commands, dutifully, since breakfast. Her mother intends the party to commemorate her return home; she plans to sleep on the couch until Kath and Daron leave on Monday, then move into Carl's room, and for the next step, "we'll just have to wait and see." Kath doesn't understand why her mother changed her mind about coming home. Perhaps there is an insidious force like gravity leaking from the rolltop desk, the kitchen witch, and the white dining-room chairs, which has roped her mother in; perhaps she has renewed her vows to the house, if not yet to her husband.

Madame yowls and strains at her chain.

With his heavy sack slung across his shoulders, Daron struggles to open the back gate. Tom waves to her over the roof of the car and watches until Daron evades Madame's bouncing paws and reaches Kath's table before he climbs inside and drives off.

"Hi, babe. I started to wonder if you'd make it. Your grandma's fit to be tied."

"Sorry."

"She was worried you wouldn't be here to do the pioneer thing."

"Mom!"

"I told her to get one of your cousins. But she said you'd be disappointed if you didn't get to do it."

"Mom!"

"You get to wear a costume."

"There's my grandson!" Her mother descends from the stoop holding the plastic silverware tray from the kitchen drawer. "I didn't think we would have time to get you fitted." She hands the tray to Kath and helps Daron lift the rucksack from his shoulder. She hands Kath the sack. "Whew! You smell like a pair of sweaty socks. To the showers, young man. Go!" She pats Daron on the back. "Go!" She continues tapping until he hurries to the door.

"I'm going to be busy with Daron for a few moments, Kath. Would you arrange the utensils? And see if we have enough napkins. And you could fill the punch bowl. I usually put one part Hawaiian Punch to one part ginger ale, but you can judge by taste." She stares off toward the Mortensen house across the field. "No, you'd better come do the beard or we might not be ready in time."

Kath trails her mother toward the house. They stop at the patio, where her father sits on a folding chair reading the sports section. Three ice cream makers grind at his knees. "Dear, are you remembering to salt the ice?" He nods without looking up, and they pass by him into the house. "Grab the footstool." As Kath carries the upholstered ottoman from the front room, she hears Daron's voice asking his grandmother if she is home to stay. She finds her mother in the bedroom, unzipping a garment bag from the ZCMI men's department. Daron bends over at the corner of the bed to untie the knots in his thrashed, muddy sneakers. "No, we didn't quarrel, Daron. I just needed to catch my breath. A little vacation. But I'm back now."

Her mother spreads out the black suit on the bedspread and opens the white paper sack from the bottom of the garment bag. The contents of the sack are unshakably clear in Kath's mind: three mimeographed pages stapled in the upper left corner and folded into quarters, a fringe of beard curled like a mouse, a small sticky bottle of spirit gum, and a plastic box of straight pins. "Now go shower. Hurry, hurry, hurry!"

After Daron closes the bathroom door, Kath unwinds the beard on the bedspread. "Why *have* you come back?"

Her mother fusses with the wrinkled suit. "JuLee came to see me the other day. Have you two talked?"

"No, not really. Anything wrong?"

"She wanted me to help her make an appointment with a ladies' doctor. She thinks she's sick."

"What's the matter?"

"This boy of hers has been rough with her."

"God. Who is it?"

"I thought you might know. It's making me quite ill, Kath."

"Is she okay? How bad is it?" Kath feels rebuked for ignoring her sister; she should have made the effort to break through JuLee's moodiness.

"She's going in tomorrow." She fumbles with the clasp of the pin box. "That thing I found in the truck was hers . . . theirs. They . . . did it, there. She admitted that much. It's just replacing one sorrow with another, Kath. And your poor father, he doesn't even know what the problem was." She drapes the pants over her forearm. "Sometimes I think I can again. I say to myself: he's your husband and you love him. But sometimes I just feel cold." She leans against the bathroom door, listening for the sounds of the shower, then knocks. "Daron? I'd like you to try these pants on." The door cracks open, and she pushes the pants inside.

Kath pictures white chairs over endless green. She curls away from the present moment like the tendril of a creeper against a forbidding, searing concrete wall. When she looks out of herself again, she finds her own eyes in the dresser mirror. She begins to see her true age reflected there. She used to think her face looked too young, too mutable, but it has become fixed and determined.

Her mother sorts through Daron's rucksack. She tugs out a piece of paper—a sketch of a boy standing between a creature in a hardhat and glasses and a stripper or showgirl with huge breasts and broad hips. "Look at this. I can't believe you let him go with those men. I told you."

"Tom's his father." When she speaks it her reason sounds inadequate, but it was her mother who had taught her to believe in its sanctity: in the importance of a father, of a family.

"Some father," her mother says and tosses the sketch on the floor.

Daron emerges from the steamy bathroom, bare-chested and slight. He holds the waist of the black pants to keep them in place; his feet are lost in the tunnels of the legs. "Climb on up here." Her mother offers him a clean T-shirt and stands by the footstool with her box of pins. He pushes wet hair from his eye and steps up. She begins by pinning the waistband tight in the back, then kneels to fold up the excess length. "I'll fix these cuffs in a jiff, then you can do his beard. Oh, and you'd better practice your speech." She gives him the pages.

Daron unfolds the sheets and looks up helplessly at Kath. She watches his eyes strain to read the bleary blue type; it is torture for him. In ten years he will either laugh at his command performance or resent it miserably; there is no way to tell which. "Just read it loud and clear," her mother explains with a pin between her lips. "That's all you need to do. Go ahead."

"Welcome! . . ."

"Try it louder, dear."

"Welcome!" Daron reads, with the pages clenched in his fists. "I welcome you, the sons and daughters of the pioneers, on this beautiful twenty-fourth of July. Today is the day to celebrate your brave forefathers who came from far away to begin our state, and I am here to tell you their story.

"My name is Brigham Young. I was the President of the Church of Jesus Christ of Latter-day Saints and the leader of our people at the time our great trek west began. In 1843, our Prophet Joseph Smith was murdered by a mob in Carthage jail. We were living in Navoo, Illinois, and it was clear to everybody that people there did not like us. It was time to leave. In 1846 our first wagons left the city and we began to settle on the west bank of the Missouri at a place we called 'Winter Quarters.' There were twelve to fifteen thousand of us there. The Saints who stayed behind in Navoo were attacked by mobs, and the temple was burned down.

"The next spring it was decided to go west and find a new home for the Church and the Saints. Only a few people had explored the place we were going to. There were no cars in those days, and no railroad to ride on. We rode in wagons pulled by horses. We would line up in single file along the trail, one wagon after another. There were one hundred and forty three men, three women, including my wife, and two children. We had seventy-two wagons, ninety-three horses, fifty-two mules, sixty-six oxen, nineteen cows, and many chickens and dogs and cats.

"We traveled on the north bank of the Platte River. We saw Indians and thousands of buffalo. I celebrated my forty-sixth birthday on the trail. The pictures you see of me today were made when I was an old man, but on this trip I was still youthful and strong. I rode my horse all day and was kept very busy. I had to decide how fast or slow we should travel. I had to choose our campsites, make sure everyone had enough to eat, and make sure that the animals were well taken care of. As President of the Church, it was also my duty to lead the Priesthood and look after the spiritual life of the Saints. Like Moses, who led the children of Israel out of Egypt, I was blessed by God to lead our people to a new Promised Land. By the end of June we had reached the Rocky Mountains."

"Excuse me, hon." Kath's mother rests her hand preemptorily on the mimeograph. "You can do the beard now, Kath."

Stretched out, the beard is a fringe of slightly curled black hair depending from a narrow strip of fabric—a giant false eyelash. The backing is tacky from innumerable applications, and balls of yellow rubber roll under her fingers as she adds a coat of fresh spirit gum. She traces another line of gum around Daron's chin, then presses the beard in place like the strap of a helmet. She grins. Daron glances into the mirror but quickly twists his head away. "Mom! I look like a complete moron!"

Her mother lifts a beaver top hat from a bed of tissue and fits it on his head. "Okay, keep going." Daron sighs.

"On June twenty-seventh, the anniversary of the Prophet's murder four years before, our party crossed the Great Continental Divide. It was a sign of God's good grace. We were following His will in establishing a new Zion.

"In the Rockies we met the trappers and mountain men who told us of the wonders of the canyons and valley which lay before a vast lake of salt water ahead of us. As we traveled through the narrow passes, many of us became sick with mountain fever. I became sick in July and sent parties on ahead. By the twenty-third of July the men had broken the ground for farming.

"My wagon arrived at the mouth of Emigration Canyon on the twenty-fourth. Some of you may have seen the statue of me in the canyon which shows me standing and pointing toward the valley. But the truth is that I was still weak from the fever. I asked Elder Wilford Woodruff to turn my cart around. I looked out at the gently spreading valley below and said, 'This is the place. Drive on.'

"Another five hundred and sixty-six wagons full of Saints arrived by the end of the summer, and the blessings of the new Zion began to grow in Utah. (You may add here an account of any special pioneer or immigrant stories in your own family.) Now I would like to ask one of the Elders present to lead us in a prayer of thanks for the pioneers and the blessings they have brought to our families."

Her mother applauds. "Very nice, Daron. You can skip the part about family stories. Just be sure to introduce your grandfather to do the blessing." Her mother notices the alarm clock on the nightstand. "Oh my, we're running late." She moves to the door, then freezes. "My stars and garters! The sliding ice! We need to get that by five!"

"I'll go." Kath screws the lid on the spirit gum and dumps it in the white sack.

"You'll need to take the truck. I laid out burlap in the back. I was on my way this morning and got sidetracked and clean forgot." Her mother looks at Kath with serious concern. "Now, Kath, don't you go disappearing on us again."

Kath glares back in response until a car door slams in the road. Her mother rushes to the window. "People! They're here already!" Kath has never seen agitation in her mother before. "You'll have to see to them. I've got the ham to check. And the dinner rolls!"

"It's okay, Mom. Dad and I will hold the fort."

Her mother speeds to the kitchen. Kath passes her sister's room; the stereo blares behind the closed door. She should go in, but she won't take the time. She stops at the threshold of her brother's room. Daron kneels against the side of the bed in his Brigham Young costume with his notebook open and a pen in his hand. "Want to come meet some of your relatives?"

"Are you kidding?"

"They haven't seen you for five years. You don't want to be impolite."

"I look fucking stupid, Mom."

"Daron! Watch your tongue! Is that the kind of filthy language Tom's been teaching you?"

"No, Mom," he whines, then shifts to look at her. "Do I have to do this?"

"This is the high point of your grandma's whole year. Just get it over with and you can do whatever you want. Cousin Berma's coming. Jared and Jason."

He groans and returns to his notebook. Kath leaves him to play hostess in the backyard.

Members of the Miller family have a disturbing habit of arriving exactly on time for social events, and Kath is surprised to find many of the guests already at work fulfilling their assignments—erecting extra tables, arranging extra chairs, silverware, plates, dishes for the potluck. Kath greets them as she crosses the lawn to the tablecloth she has never finished unfolding. Her Uncle Stan and his sons and their families. Uncle Cosmo and his new wife—forever "new" despite their ten-year marriage—whose name Kath has never remembered. The twins, Erik and Derek, who are children of one of her cousins—it isn't clear to her which. In the shade of the oak, Aunt MargaLee, the oldest of the Millers, rests in a patio chair. She fans herself with a paper plate, looking frail and overdecorated, her makeup bright and smeared like crayon on crinkled tissue.

She discovers Aunt PearLeen doing her job for her. Her aunt smoothes out the cloth, being careful, as always, of her long coral nails. She beams at Kath in her mauve silk tracksuit. As Aunt PearLeen scoots around the table for a hug, Kath hears the spinning sterling silver spurs—worn "for special times"—hooked to her white suede boots. "Kath. Beautiful day, isn't it?" The frosted leaf in her hair glints in the sun like a chip of mirror.

Kath sees Jared and Jason unload a cooler from their station wagon. "Did Rhonda have to work today?"

"Mmm." Aunt PearLeen lifts the silverware tray and traces her finger along the ridge dividing the compartments.

"Where's Uncle Doug?"

"Oh dear. My Rhonda Lee." She smiles wanly. "I'd better go see to that cooler before the boys spill it all." She presses Kath's arm at the wrist and departs with the silverware.

Kath reassesses the placement of the tables and tablecloths, says hello to assorted cousins, and recalls that she has been assigned the punch bowl. In the kitchen, she hunts around in the overstuffed refrigerator for the bottles of ginger ale. Cousin Berma stands over the sink, her golden beehive made luminous by reflected light from the stainless-steel faucet. She overturns a plate to attempt to unmold an unstable tomato aspic.

"My mom's picked Daron to do the Brigham Young thing this year."

"Oh no. He won't like that one bit, I bet."

"No."

"But he'll be darling at it."

"I'm sure." Kath wishes for some way to prune the family tree—to retain Cousin Berma and discard the rest. The phone rings twice. She moves toward it, but it stops. She lines the ginger ale and the punch cans on the counter and reaches her arm around Cousin Berma. "How're you doing?"

"As I should be, I think. Lonely sometimes. But I'm coping. I'm finally out from under all the leftovers from the funeral. And all those casseroles. That's a relief."

"Good. Good." Kath hugs her, and the aspic quivers in the mold in Berma's hands.

"Kath." Her mother emerges from the living room. "It's Rhonda on the phone."

Rhonda speaks in a murmur when Kath lifts the receiver. "I need your help."

"Sure."

"I need a ride from my house to the gas station."

"Okay. What's up?"

"I'm leaving."

"Leaving?" Kath sees her mother observing the phone call from the bar stools, and she regrets betraying Rhonda with her question.

"Manuel and me are going. I can't take it. I'll tell you when you get here. When can you come?"

She speaks carefully with her mother as her audience. "I'll drop by then on my way to get the ice."

"Ice? All right. But don't drive up to the house. That's why I can't have Manuel come. If Dad saw his truck . . . I'll wait for you on the main road by the mailboxes. Please hurry. Thanks."

When she replaces the phone on its hook, her mother hands her a frosted punch bowl to fill. "Will Rhonda be able to make it to the party?"

"No, she has to work. In fact, she has to work the whole weekend, so I might not get to see her before I leave. I thought I'd stop in on my way to get the ice."

"That's too bad. Here." Her mother reaches into a shopping bag on the floor behind the bar. "It's silly, but give her this. To celebrate. Tell her we're sorry she has to work on the holiday." Her mother hands her the slender cardboard box. Kath hears the metal stems of the sparklers rustling inside.

Memories fly at Kath in unbidden bursts of image and emotion. When Kath saw the smooth black stone with the petrified shell on the windowsill of her and her sister's bedroom—oval, flat on top and bottom, and fitting soundly in the palm—she tasted sorrow before she could explain its source. Merrill had given her a stone like that, and she had warmed it in her fist on the day she married him. She had brought it with her to the tiny room in the wardhouse where she went to adjust her dress before the ceremony. She was going to carry it with her as "something old" in her trousseau, but she couldn't find a place to put it. She had forgotten it until she touched the black palmstone in her sister's room and the rock opened its mouth to speak: "Remember."

Some memories embroider the world of things but never identify themselves—the anger of a loose doorknob, the youthful mother locked in the reflection of cold clouds shifting across a clear window. And others must wait years for their explication. When the road rises to meet a hill, the Pratt house is visible for an instant before the trees and scrub rise to block it from view. In the interval between the house's first appearance and the road's descent to meet it, Kath remembers Aunt PearLeen in her parents' kitchen. An ice cube wrapped in a washcloth soothes the stove burn along the length of her thumb. Kath must have peered in from the hall as a little girl, but she can't place herself in the memory. Her mother holds a letter opener and says softly, "Stay here tonight." Her father is somewhere in the kitchen—or else speaks later to her mother alone. She hears his voice overlaid above her aunt's image. "It's too darn bad. But losing a contract like that, he was bound to take it hard." Kath doesn't remember if her mother responds, but her father's voice rises defensively. "'Course it's not to excuse him. But a man can take only so much of that kind of strain."

Rhonda sits on her duffel bag, shielded from view of the house by the low stone wall that surrounds the Pratt family mailboxes. Her right eye shines lost in an empurpled socket; a spidery cut slices her cheekbone. Kath doesn't need to ask; it is what she expected.

Rhonda opens the passenger door and pushes her duffel in ahead of her. Kath must have grimaced, because Rhonda nods her head. "Belt buckle."

"I can't believe it."

"Can't you? Can't you really?" Rhonda's words come hard, like holes punched in metal.

"Do you think it needs a doctor?"

"So it's only happened a few times. Does that make it okay?"

"No."

"Let's go. Let's go. He's down in the basement, but I don't want to risk it. Don't turn around in the driveway."

Kath reverses along the highway until the shoulder grows wide enough to back into. She flips the front end of the truck around and heads into town.

"It's all because I said I was going to bring Manuel to this fucking party. He went all psycho." Her words come quick but muffled, as if her tongue has swollen to fill her mouth. "I was in the bathroom getting ready, and he came there with this belt. He knew he was going to use it. He said he was going to . . . going to see to it I kept myself clean whether I wanted to or not." She stops, and Kath glances over to see Rhonda gently probing the edges of the welt around her eye.

"He said, 'No spic boy's gonna put his fat black dick in my daughter.' Funny how they pretend not to know these words. From the way they talk you'd think they didn't have pricks under their garments. But he couldn't stop shouting about my boyfriend's fat black dick. So I said, what do you think he's gonna do, flash his cock around at everybody at the party? Then he just started whaling on me with the belt."

"Jesus." She slows the truck as they pull into town.

"Manny's there at the gas station." Rhonda points, then dabs at her face with a tissue. "And my mother. I could see her in the bedroom across the hall. She had all these outfits spread out on the bed to decide on. And when the shouting got loud, she shut the door. She shut the fucking bedroom door." Kath stops at the light across the intersection from the station. "So I'm going, Kath. We're gonna stay with his sister in Phoenix. You were so smart to get out of here. But I'm never coming back."

Manuel leans against the bumper of his mini-pickup at the corner of the gas staion lot, with the hoses for air and water coiled at his feet. He jumps up and opens Rhonda's door. "Motherfucker." He reaches out to touch Rhonda's bruise, but she winces before his fingers reach her face.

"Let's go." She hurries for his truck. He slides the duffel off the seat and follows her.

Kath chases after them. She leans into the open window where Rhonda sits waiting for Manuel to stow her bag. "Good luck. Call me. Oh, here." She yanks the sparkler box from the back pocket of her jeans. "My mom sent you these. I told her you had to work."

"Rhonda! Get out of there! Now!" Uncle Doug has blocked the entrance to the station with his truck. He bounds toward them. Kath snaps back instinctively as Rhonda rolls up her window. Manuel climbs into the truck and locks the door. "Rhonda. Come out, Rhonda." He tugs at the door handle and pounds his fist against the glass. "Be a good girl and get out here."

Rhonda won't look at him; she flips him off, staring through the front windshield.

Uncle Doug walks around to the driver's door. "Don't think you're going anywhere with my girl, son. Open the door." Manuel starts the engine. "I'm gonna put my fist through your face, you little turd." Uncle Doug stands in front of Manuel's truck and pounds the hood.

Kath hears Manuel's voice from a crack of open window. "I don't want to fight you, man. Just get out of the way."

Uncle Doug glares into the cab, then turns to Kath. "And you. You bitch! You corrupter!" She shrinks, expecting his fist, but he runs to his truck. He bends over to lift a bundle out of the bed. He strides forward with it draped in his arms. The dead woman.

His path is strewn with patches of dress, chips of ivory. "You wetbacks. You dirt-eating redskin Indian scum. Who do you think you are? Read the scriptures, boy. You Lamanites are born from shit. Shit! You're the black-assed bastards of Cain. You're dogs! Here's your momma. Your poor dead momma!" He slams the body on the hood. She shatters at last, her ancient ligaments too brittle to survive the impact. Tatters of cloth, bones, and flotsam skin slide into a heap on the ground. He rips a large bone— a femur, a tibia—from the huddle and slams the knobbed end against the windshield until the bone cracks apart.

Uncle Doug jerks back with the woman's dust smudged on his face and neck and hands. He spits the woman from his tongue in strings of gray saliva. He wipes his fingers together savagely. He wails.

Manuel puts the truck in gear and drives slowly over the body. The upturned skull disappears into the shadow between the tires. He turns the truck sharply onto the sidewalk and drives along the storefronts until he can slip onto the road between a lightpole and a fire hydrant. Neither Manuel nor Rhonda looks around as they speed toward the interstate.

Uncle Doug jogs to his truck. He stumbles but rises and hurls himself into the cab. He backs over the pile that was a woman and kicks up dust and crunch and splinters. He roars forward over her, leaving her spread in gray tire tracks on the asphalt. He hammers through the red light after his daughter.

From the bed of her father's truck Kath pulls one of the large burlap potato sacks meant to shield dripping ice. She spreads the mouth of the sack and begins methodically to gather the skeleton.

Her friend from the beauty parlor, Donna Speck, was gassing up the family camper, and she and the station attendant approach Kath with a broom and a dustpan. Silently they help her sweep the woman into the bag.

The young man asks Kath, "Do we call the police?"

"Yeah," she says.

She straightens up and grips the bulky sack. She finds her mother and Aunt PearLeen standing behind her with their shoulders arched together; it surprises her that, even now, her mother and her aunt would find themselves supporting each other. "I mentioned Rhonda's phone call to PearLeen," her mother begins. "No one answered at the house, so we were driving there . . . "

Aunt PearLeen spreads her arms. Her tiny spurs chime— *click-whizz-click-whizz.* "What is it? Where are they? All right, or are they . . . what?"

Although she feels no sympathy, Kath would like to help her aunt, because Kath knows she will suffer and PearLeen's hold on the world is too tight to encompass tragedy. Yet Kath has nothing to offer but a sack swollen with another woman's bones.

Daron: Invisible History

Because the tables were already set and the food was out of its plastic tubs and foil bundles, Daron's relatives stuck around to eat. But as soon as the blue bowls of homemade ice cream were passed around and eaten, everyone left quietly, with no suggestion of ice sliding, fireworks, or other entertainment.

Daron is relieved that he didn't have to give his speech. His grandfather announced that there had been an argument at the gas station, then led a prayer for the people involved as part of his blessing.

His mom and grandmother have not come home, so Daron locks himself in the bathroom to clean the beard from his face with a bottle marked "spirit gum dissolving," and with nail polish remover, and with soap. He emerges with his face stinging and the taste of nasty chemicals on his lips. He stands near his grandfather, napping in the front room, then takes a soda from the fridge and steps into the yard.

Three black garbage sacks bulge by the back fence, but a few scraps of paper have escaped attention. He gathers them up, then sits under the oak on one of the dining-room chairs.

He hears pebbles scatter into the ditch on the far side of the back road and steps over to the gate. Skunk stands in the center of the road with his hands hooked in his back pockets. The shade from the bill of his cap swallows his eyes. Hey, son, how was the party?

Okay, he says. He doesn't want to talk to Skunk here. Except at church, he has never seen him away from Cousin Berma's.

Where's your mom?

Daron doesn't answer, and Skunk shifts a few paces closer to the gate.

I'm not invited to come into your yard, so you'll have to come out here with me.

I can't.

Course you can. Just open the gate, he says. I've got the most important story of all to tell you today.

I can't. Daron shifts a few inches farther back into the yard.

All right then. Skunk leans his hip against the fence. But you listen close.

Skunk tells Daron about Invisible History, written in dream-words, inscribed on clouds and sunshafts, untouchable to the tongue but heavy and potent to the heart and head. Although there is no language for Invisible History—this is why Jesus spoke in parables—Skunk wants Daron to fine-tune his ears and eyes.

He first learned to interpret Invisible History when he was Daron's age. Skunk asks him if he knows the Ninth Article of Faith, and it is one of the three he has memorized.

He will yet reveal, Skunk recites, many great and important things pertaining to the Kingdom of God.

When Skunk studied the Article in Primary, it was revealed to him that the Holy Ghost suffused each limb and leaf with a form visible to very few. Skunk stole away from his parents' house early one morning in the spring and climbed into the hills. In a clearing protected by walls of rock, he found a pool of clear water. Skunk believed that he had found the true source of all waters. He knelt by the pool and prayed.

It was then and there that he saw the angel come to drink. The Being spread his snowy raiments on the bank and dipped his head to the cool water like a beast of the field. His lips kissed the mirror of the pool and sipped of it. Afterward, the angel stood in the air over the pool and reached down to cup some of the water in his palm. He swept toward Skunk, who was frozen to his spot, with his white robes accumulating and evaporating like cloud. The angel drew his finger through the puddle in his palm and anointed Skunk's ears and eyes. "Open thy mouth," the angel commanded. When Skunk obeyed, the angel touched the tip of his tongue. "I am come unto thee," said the angel, "to lift the blinders from thy eyes and pull the stoppers from thy ears that thou might see and hear the glories of Our Father's Kingdom made manifest on earth. I loose the tongue in thy mouth that thou may speaketh unto the heavenly host. There are a great many things that Our Heavenly Father has in mind for thee."

From that time forward, Skunk has seen the angelic host everywhere as they carry out the will of the Father, Son, and Holy Ghost. He has seen them ministering to the sick and old;

when an Elder gives his blessing, an angelic hand is folded through his human one. The angels stir in the church rafters on the updrafts of hymns and watch over the passage of buses on their way to school each day. Skunk has been a party to Invisible History in Sterling; he will be given a role to play in it—after the test, he says.

Your mother knows, Skunk tells Daron. She saw him in the tree, he explains. She might deny it, but she did. The thing is that angels don't speak to women. They may have talked to Jesus' mother, Mary, but that was special. Your mother had to go inside the house before he spoke to me.

Daron asks why this is true, and Skunk gives the answer he always gives: That's the way things are meant to be.

Before he crosses the road back into the fields, Skunk advises Daron to keep the secrets of Invisible History from his mother. It is the duty of men to record this history in the language of masculine silence.

Kath: 13

The car is loaded, except for Daron's box and her cosmetics bag. Kath has sprayed the windows with glass cleaner. With the starter motor fixed, she hopes for a few eventless hours on the road; she has promised Mr. Warren to be home in time to take the night shift at the Bellefleur. Her final duty is to wait for her passengers.

From the stoop she watches Madame pace and pace, impatient, at the limits of her chain. A car has gunned it fast along the back road, and Madame sniffs at the curtain of descending dust. The dog craves the opportunity to tussle with an automobile; Sparks and Panda died from the same desire. Champion died while the rest of the family was on vacation. From a sudden illness, she told them. When her family got home, she said that the vet put Champion down rather than let him suffer. The clinic disposed of the body; she didn't know where. And that, at least, was true. She doesn't know where he is buried.

The first time Merrill proposed, the sun bled sundown savage through the window of Cousin Berma's house. Kath was ashamed, uncertain, and she said no.

The second time Merrill proposed, the dust and heat blared louder than the gun blasts in the gully where he had taken her to shoot. Kath was needy, hopeful, craving affection, and she said yes.

And then what?

She asked herself what came next as she stood in her parents' kitchen rocking Daron in her arms. They would be married; Daron would have a father; she would be made respectable—and then what? She could foresee no new happiness, no break in the clouds of disappointment she was resigned to live under. There were too many pleasures she did not expect to meet again: the joy of freedom, of sex, of limitless choices. But the marriage would put things right for her in the world: her parents would be content, she would no longer need to look for disapproval in people's faces, she would be freed from awkward explanations of Tom's disappearance. Safe haven in Merrill's arms was the most that a woman in her position could expect. Cradling Daron, she prayed quietly to be satisfied with the blessing of Merrill's protection. And then what? If being Merrill's wife was the last choice she would make, the last action she would take, then what? She would raise Merrill's children, wait for the grandchildren; she would be the homemaker, the shelterkeeper; she would even love him—love would come or she would force it. But she couldn't imagine how she would fill the days. Instead, she began to realize, she would need to find some means to escape them.

She held her hand to Daron's heart through the soft cotton blanket. She wanted to remain united with the one thing in her life that wasn't a compromise. But even as she held him with a love so great it could have no outlet, she sensed the dark room growing in her mind where she would pass her time alone.

Two months after his proposal, Kath and Merrill were married in the wardhouse, with a reception afterward in the ward gymnasium. Bishop Madsen counseled them to wait before going through the temple ceremonies; Kath sensed that she would be required to prove her worthiness. Merrill had been disappointed after the interview: their union wouldn't be real, true, celestial, until they were married in the temple—just an earthly shadow. But by the day of the wedding he had regained his enthusiasm: their marriage was a project, and he would strive devoutly to prepare his wife to be sealed to him for time and eternity.

They spent their honeymoon camping at Lake Powell. As a wedding present, his parents had rented them a houseboat. She and Merrill explored the narrow canyons flooded by the Colorado River—stark salmon-stone arteries. She could feel the walls rising, rising to close off the blue slit of heaven. Constriction was everywhere. She was dry as sandstone inside when Merrill entered her. He was tender—a rain-summoned sprig—but she was arid; he toughened to survive. He would slam her hard against the wagonwheel headboard in the tiny cabin, and the boat would pitch. "Will you be able to have another one right away?" he asked her with his hand between her breasts. "I've heard it's best to wait awhile. But you're ready, don't you think?" He had been inside her before the wedding, and he had used a condom, then lectured her on the evils of birth control. He wanted children. He wanted to be a patriarch and unfurl the umbrella of his priesthood over his offspring. At sunrise each morning they knelt on the deck of the houseboat and prayed for his vision.

To love him, to be content, would be to surrender, to drift, to let him steer the boat around her twisting canyons and decide which crevices would be explored and which ignored, to let him fill her up with seed and babies, to let his voice speak through her mouth and his eyes guide her vision. She set down the furniture in the tomb of her mind and—incrementally, so that he wouldn't notice her vacancy—began to shut the door and commence her absentee life.

While they were gone wandering the water, her mother packed her things and her father drove them over to the Nelson house. A flight of redwood steps behind the two-car garage led to a small apartment—light with many windows and warm with tiny rooms. After retrieving her baby from her parents, she watched Merrill carry Daron upstairs in his car seat—he insisted that she wait in the yard—then she clung to his neck as he swept her over the threshold into the house. She leaned against the refrigerator holding Daron as Merrill planted his palms on the formica kitchen counter. He beamed. "You and Daron are home, Katie-Kate. Consider this home."

For four years, Kath considered it. She worked at it like a puzzle that required solving. She kept her senses tuned to the moment when the apartment would become something more than indifferent, slightly alien. She held her breath for the turn of the key that would open wide doors onto a flood of comfort and intimacy. But the apartment's eggshell paint, beige carpeting, and marbled gray Formica wouldn't yield, despite the hours upon days upon years that she lavished on them. She tried to train the rooms—the family room, the kitchen, the bedroom, the bathroom—to break their glacial spirit, to impose herself. But Merrill didn't like decoration—clutter—mess—empty adornments—fanciness. The relentless walls were interrupted by a portrait of Joseph Smith, a portrait of President Kimball (later partnered above the sofa bed by one of President Benson), and photographs of the St. George Temple and the Salt Lake Temple. They were the same artworks, available from catalogues and Deseret Books, exhibited in every home in Sterling. The Salt Lake Temple, granite gray and severe—a cathedral of monochrome Legos topped with spires and the golden Angel Moroni—hung on the wall opposite the bed. The lacquered photograph was mounted on an irregular round of polished driftwood. In the halflight of morning it looked like an amoeba percolating up the wall in a wet stain.

Kath stitched simple samplers—GOD BLESS THIS HOUSE, FAMILIES ARE FOREVER, JESUS LOVES THE LITTLE CHILDREN—that Merrill refused to hang and that she gave away as gifts. She gave COME, COME YE SAINTS to her mother-in-law, Clovis, who placed it behind the door of her sewing room across from her own needlepoint tapestry in seventy-three hues of thread: "The Coming of Christ to America," which took Best of Show at the county fair. "No, that one's my daughter-in-law's," Clovis was anxious to tell guests.

Whenever Kath left the apartment—for an hour at the supermarket in Alma or for the week they spent in Yellowstone—she hoped her return would engulf her in an outpouring of warmth, security, release. What she inevitably felt was familiarity, well recognized but impersonal, the familiarity of shopping carts and gas pumps. She would lean into Merrill's shoulders as he sat at the table after breakfast and suggest how nice it might be to move to a bigger apartment with another room for Daron, one that would be a place of their own, not Merrill's bachelor rooms—"our place." Merrill would reach up to take her hands and squeeze the fingers tight. "It's children that make a house a home."

She had considered this option herself; she had yearned for it. After three miscarriages in two years, her doctor performed a tubal ligation and told Merrill he was lucky to have a wife with her health safely intact. There were options—they could adopt—but Merrill wasn't interested in alternatives. Often he seemed to forget the operation and spoke bitterly, as if she had willfully staunched the flow of her fertility. He stopped making love to her—"What would be the point?"—and slept with the Bible and the Book of Mormon stacked between their pillows: an invisible wall of God's wrath and splendor dividing the bed.

Clovis regularly invited her down to the house, but she felt like an intruder with Merrill's family. His mother would not stop vacuuming or dusting or canning peaches to speak with her. At Sunday dinner with the Nelson family, Merrill would ask various members of the household to look in on Kath while he was out making a run in his truck. She needed—he implied—constant supervision. Kath might escape next door to Aunt Ina and Cousin Berma's house, but it wasn't far enough. She took Daron downtown, or to the park, or to her parents' house to play on the back lawn while she sunbathed and pretended she wasn't married and there were still choices to be made.

Her mother and Merrill confronted her with their disapproval simultaneously, as if they had conferred about her (as they had, Kath later learned, when Merrill visited her mother surreptitiously before his second proposal to ask for advice on how to proceed). While Daron jumped giddily into the aerated diamonds of a garden sprinkler, her mother delivered another of her inexhaustible sermons on child rearing. "A mother's place is with her child, yes. But there's such a thing as overmothering. You mustn't spend every waking hour entertaining the boy or you'll cripple his attention span. He's small for his age, and I would be willing to wager that's because you've quite gone and smothered him. Save some of that attention for your husband, Kath, or otherwise your marriage will founder."

Merrill made the same observation with blunter force. "You're keeping Daron too much to yourself. If he's gonna get a father's influence, I'd better keep him under my thumb on the weekends." On his days at home he would strap Daron into the car seat and drive him into masculine territories—to toddle down the fishing aisle of the hardware store, where he would stick curious, cautious fingers into bins of sinkers and bright lures; to visit Merrill's hunting buddies for conclaves on guns and bows and RVs; to the dusty fields and gullies along the post office road, where Merrill blew holes in tin cans and Daron shrieked with fearful delight at each report.

Kath stayed in the apartment, where there was no one to distract her from its monotony. Her friend Cynthia, who soloed with three kids in a trailer in the old KOA campground, told her she was lucky to get a breather—but what was she going to do with the time? When Merrill was in town she couldn't see the old friends he called dissolutes and deadbeats. When they did sneak a visit, she refused their cigarettes and six-packs, sounding self-righteous and stuffy. Her friends stopped making the effort. She had ample hours to clean the rooms without Merrill and Daron underfoot—and then what? She stirred up cups of Carnation Instant Breakfast Drink, thick, with only half the milk, and sat in the kitchen watching tree shadows pivot from row to row of the vegetable garden as the sun swept west; sat at the simple table in the tomb of her mind; sat in obliteration.

At night Merrill took Daron downstairs with him to watch sports with his father, Joe. At home he would go into the bedroom and shut the door on Kath. He would pray aloud and lapse into the voice of prophecy—keening, murmuring, wailing—unworded, uninterrupted. Every morning after family prayer, Merrill would take Daron's hand and lead him out back—"among the fruits of labor and beasts of the field"—to lay hands on Daron's head and bless him.

And then Kath saw Merrill's angel in the backyard tree. The bounty of its robes against the tapering trunk. The cold coruscation of its light on the circumferences of leaves. Its dark radiance. She was drawn toward it until the tears fell and budded the yellow roses underneath. She shook with its sorrow and fled, while Merrill knelt on the wet grass with his head cocked to its leaf-blown murmurings.

And then what? If she had seen the angel who guided Merrill, how could she dispute her life with him?

Kath's father won a trip to Florida at the lumberyard—Disneyworld and EPCOT—as a commission incentive from a power tool company. Her parents and Carl and JuLee drove to Salt Lake to fly out of the airport there, and Kath agreed to house-sit while they were gone. Merrill didn't seem to mind—he didn't object; he was making long runs into California, Oregon, and Washington, and he was seldom home. On the days he was in town, they slept in her parents' bed, and the king-size mattress allowed Merrill more space to place between them.

In her old home she moved freely again. The apartment had her doubled over in a crouch with her breath rasping hard against the walls of her throat, but now she could stand upright and breathe easily. Her mother had left her several twenties paper-clipped to a long list of housekeeping instructions, and she enjoyed having money that did not depend on Merrill's permission. She bought goodies for herself and Daron—M&Ms, Oreos, cans of squirtable cheese, jumbo pretzels, frozen eggrolls, doughnuts, fudgy brownies, premium ice cream—making certain to eat them and bury the boxes and wrappers in the trash before Merrill came home.

On the final Friday, Rhonda stayed over, and Kath fixed an elaborate dinner: chicken cacciatore and fettuccine with a green salad, garlic bread, and a fresh strawberry pie. They ate and laughed and pulled all the old children's games out of the hall closet; they played Candyland and Chutes and Ladders with Daron, and, after he went to bed, they tackled Concentration, Battleship, and Scrabble. When they climbed into bed together in her parents' room, late in the night, giggling, Kath felt lifted, light.

The windows above the bed were open—it was an unseasonably warm May—and before she fell asleep she heard an engine on the road in front of the house. The rumble faded, and she waited; Merrill had the key to the front door, but he always called if he was coming back early. She wasn't expecting him. She drifted. Champion barked in the backyard, and she opened her eyes to the featureless blank of the ceiling. He barked, and his chain scraped across the sidewalk. She grew sleepy again, listening, and the barking grew fainter and stopped. She slept.

Waking, she hoisted a pair of gray sweatpants under the long T-shirt she had slept in and kicked her feet into a pair of tennis shoes. She looked down at Rhonda, asleep with the spare pillow smashed over her face, and quietly closed the hall door behind her. The late-morning sun stumbled through the new leaves of the trees and sprayed tessellations of light and shadow on the kitchen linoleum—patterns that repeated on the earth below the trunks outside the window, insubstantiating the walls of the house. Her feet might swim through the delicate shift of the mosaic and leave her standing on the back lawn, the house dissolved behind her.

She blinked and yawned to knock the dreamy trance from her head and opened a can of dog food at the counter. She knelt by the back stoop and scraped the greasy, red, rank blob out of the can into Champion's bowl with a butter knife. She dumped the leaves and grass and drowned spiders from his water bowl and refilled it with the hose. "Champion! Breakfast! Breakfast of Champions!" she called, expecting him to come charging around the side of the house, his loose white and caramel hair flowing back from his long face. She listened for the scramble of his claws in the gravel. Nothing.

She stepped around the evergreen shrub at the corner. Between her vantage and the gate to the front she recognized a stack of firewood for the wood stove under a blue tarp, the old shell for her father's truck on its side, an aluminum stepladder flecked with creamy yellow paint from the living room, but no Champion.

His chain stretched in a straight line down the center of the walk. She followed it, link after link, toward the back gate, where it terminated in an empty clasp hook.

She opened the gate and searched along the back road. "Champion!" She held her hand curled to her mouth. "Champion!"

She squinted into bright sun at the new green and old brown and unchangeable gray-blues of the fields, the bulbous dark heads of the few uncut cedars, the slate blue of the Mortensen house far off to the side, the starry field of bits of glass and chips of quartz glinting in the hard-packed drive. An insect noise rustled from the corrugated steel pipe that channeled the irrigation ditch under the road. It was low, dry, insistent. It repeated her name. "Kath? . . . Kath? . . . Kath?"

Merrill sprawled in the dry ditch at the opposite end of the pipe, his shoulders raised against the metal edge, his chin tucked to stare at his stomach. She looked down at him from the road. His clothes were shrouded in dust, with crusty black stains on the knees of his jeans. His scuffed brown work boots flopped laceless on his feet and wagged wide tongues. He patted his hands absently on his chest.

"Merrill? Skunk, are you okay? Are you hurt? Are you drunk?"

"Kath, I heard you." He tilted to stare straight up at her. "Oh, Kath. I did it. I did it, but it didn't work."

She eased down the weedy slope and stood at his feet in the curling flakes of dried mud. "What didn't? What's wrong?"

"I saw him again. His wings spanned the sky. Like cirrus clouds in moonlight. They sliced the heavens in half." He spread his arms until he touched both banks of the ditch. "And when he asked me to do it, I couldn't . . . but I didn't . . . but I did."

"When did you get in? Have you been out here all night?"

"I was on the freeway, Katie. And he was on the horizon. He used the mountains to pillow his feet. He was so huge. And I had to turn the rig around. Had to. Had to."

"Let's go in." He held up his hand to her, and when she took it, he pulled her down onto him. He hugged her fiercely and cried. While he wept and rolled his knuckles against her spine, she stroked his cheeks. She remembered the cold-burning light in the tree.

He held her at the throat. "I'm sorry."

"Sorry for what? What is it?"

He lifted his head from the shade of the pipe, his eyes filled with sun, and his mouth opened to speak. But he shrugged her off his chest and shakily stood. The lapels of his red-and-navy flannel shirt had been tucked across his chest, and they fell open. The silky white of his garments was pocked with russet stains. "Come," he said, and ran without waiting to see if she would. The ditch cut deep into a rise, then curved, and Kath lost sight of him. She didn't want to follow him, but she did.

The ditch ran along the length of the Montgomery orchard, and she stepped over the single strand of barbed wire that marked the perimeter. The close, solid rows of apple trees seemed to bend and snap as she passed them. She searched down each bright yellow corridor between. Shapes of birds, crows or large starlings, stirred in shadow; they crumpled dry leaves and pecked at sticky patches of last year's crop. Some stilled when they sensed her. Others tossed dust with uneasy wings.

A thread of dust hung in one aisle. A larger cloud—expanding—in the next. She jogged up the aisle, and the crackle of twigs under her shoes alerted the birds, which fluttered and skittered, softly cawing, cawing. Through a break in the trees she saw Merrill far ahead in the next corridor, past the dust, clomping, bowlegged by his loose shoes—a shambling man flapping his shirttails.

She jumped over the stump of the missing tree and ran.

Unprepared, she stumbled into the bright eruption of a clearing. The earth had been churned by the treads of picking trucks and tractors, their tracks now petrified. A red stone rose from the center in a fringe of scrub—too immense to be moved. Merrill stood on the flat summit, legs spread and arms crossed. He stared down at his feet.

"Skunk? What are you doing?" Her breath came hard as she circled the stone. The boulder tapered on the far side into a bank of sandy soil. She bent low and chose her footholds carefully until she reached the crest. She stumbled and scraped her knee when she saw.

The hollows on the top of the stone were filled with wet black, shimmered with oily rainbows. Champion's legs were bound with shoelaces—one for the front pair, another for the hind. A black belt cinched hard around his muzzle. His collar lay unbuckled nearby.

"It looks worse than it is. It was quick. I did the rest after. Because He wouldn't say what He wanted. He wouldn't tell me how."

Shiny-faceted flies danced on tufts of stiffened hair. One puncture flayed the ribs behind the front leg. His neck bent far back and was slit with purple lips. Eyes gouged to dark puddles. She wondered which one came first, which blow had been the quick one; the question made her sick. She jumped down and spit bile into the sage.

"God wants to test me. He's chosen me for great things." Merrill's voice fell from the ledge above her. "But He didn't stay my hand, Kath. He didn't stay my hand."

She stepped over tire ruts toward the trees.

"We'll need to get rid of . . . " He didn't finish.

"Don't come to the house. I need to take Rhonda home, then we'll deal with it."

She walked home, fixed breakfast, drove Rhonda across town, and set Daron in front of the television with a stack of coloring books before returning. As she counted the orchard rows to find her way, she prayed that she would find a deserted clearing, with Merrill gone. But he lingered on, squatting at the base of the stone; he squeezed the diamond-grip handle of his hunting knife—a smooth curve backed by broad serrations for sawing hide. She forced the shovel and an old bedsheet into his hands. He dropped the knife and looked at the sheet, then up at her, as if he expected her to fix things for him. He was her husband, but she wouldn't do more. She flew down the gallery of trees, and a winged cacophony screeched her name out of the shade: "kath . . . kath . . . kath . . . kath."

When Madame loses interest in the road, she returns to examine Kath's shoes on the lower step of the stoop. Kath says good-bye and scratches her under the chin, but she can't tell whether Madame realizes that she and Daron are leaving. She kisses the dusty fur between the dog's eyes and shags her ears with both hands. "Be good." She steps in to prod Daron and JuLee to the car.

Her son lies on his uncle's bed, reading a book. "Ready?" she asks from the hall. He hops up and lifts his bag from the floor. "Go say good-bye to Madame. We'll be out in a sec."

She knocks on the bathroom door. "We're ready when you are."

Her sister opens the door, brushing her teeth. "Just a jiff." JuLee spits foaming paste into the sink.

Kath retrieves her bag from the bathroom vanity and carries it into the kitchen. She writes "Have Mom call me" on a Post-it note and sticks it to the phone receiver. Her parents have taken PearLeen to Salt Lake for the arraignment. The police pulled Uncle Douglas over near the Glen Canyon Dam, before he reached Page, Arizona. She doesn't know if he caught up with Rhonda and Manuel, and she hasn't heard from her cousin.

When Kath turned the sack with the body over to the officer, Aunt PearLeen stared vacantly from the bench under the gas station awning. The police questioned everyone at the station; then men from the Park Service arrived with maps and charts and more questions. They didn't explain what the charges against Uncle Douglas would be—theft, destruction of property, assault, desecration—but they made it clear that disturbing gravesites and stealing artifacts would not be ignored. There will be a trial; they might want her to testify.

At the end of the yard, Daron spins the hot-pink frisbee into the air for Madame to chase. She catches it and shakes it in her locked jaws like a living creature that needs to be subdued. But she yields it easily to Daron, who throws it again in the opposite direction. Kath watches and wonders what their trip to Sterling has meant to him. Daron seems happier, as if all the bolts that held him in his compact and quiet shape have been loosed a few turns, but she can't guess why.

"Okay, ready. I'm running late." JuLee stands beside Kath in her supermarket smock. She is cheerful for the first time since they arrived. She has applied a suggestion of salmon to her lips and sprayed and feathered the bangs of her hefty hair.

Kath ignores the temptation to revisit the rooms of her childhood before she leaves. Her relief outweighs nostalgia. Her homesickness is for her apartment, her job, her friends—her real life. She waits by the back gate for JuLee to lock the house. Daron slides into the back seat, slips on the earphones of his stereo, and opens his notebook. She and JuLee get in front, and she drives onto the main road, then onto the freeway toward Alma. "You have a ride home, JuLee?"

"Yeah."

Kath glances at her sister. JuLee's smile has evaporated, and her clear eyes focus on a distant point ahead of the car. Kath hasn't asked what happened with the doctor because she wasn't certain that she was supposed to know about the appointment. The road passes under the shadow of an island cloud, and she reaches for the radio tuner. "Mind if I turn it on?"

"There's something . . ." JuLee looks at Daron, engrossed for the duration of the long ride in his music and literature. "I should tell you."

"What is it?"

"I haven't told Mom or Dad yet, because we have to take care of stuff. But I thought you should know before you go back." JuLee doesn't continue. She opens her purse on her lap and hunts around in it lethargically. "I feel weird about it, Kath. Though he says it will be okay."

"The doctor?" Kath bites her lip, too late to catch herself.

"No, that's not who . . . but yeah, he said I'm fine. But how did you know?"

"Mom told me. I didn't want to say because I thought it might be a secret."

"I told Mom I was sick. But that's not it. I'm pregnant."

No, Kath thinks, no. The news sickens her.

"Sorry I've been such a grouch your whole trip. I was afraid to tell him, and I didn't know what to do. But when I got up the nerve, he was just so happy. It blew me away."

JuLee waits for Kath to respond, but she can't. They drive in silence until Kath exits onto the Alma off-ramp. The supermarket anchors a shopping center at the outskirts of town, and she turns in to the parking lot behind the towering Food King sign.

"I know it's kind of weird, with you being my sister. But we love each other. And he said it would be okay with you."

"With me?"

"We'll get married after your divorce goes through. Merrill and I want to start a home as soon as possible." JuLee opens the door and steps onto the curb in front of the store. JuLee smiles. She believes that her difficult duty is over. She believes that the worst obstacle to her future bliss has been overcome. "I've got to run. Have a good trip. And call tonight so I can tell Mom you got there safe." She knocks on the back window and waves. "Bye, Daron! Bye, Kath!"

"JuLee, you can't," Kath bleats. Her heart pounds, throbbing in her throat and in her head.

"Oh, Kath, don't be a spoilsport. We'll talk later. Bye."

The electronic doors slide apart, and JuLee slips between them. Kath can't raise her hand to wave JuLee back; she can't raise her voice. She wants to call to her sister, to lead her back to the car and drive away with her—away from Sterling, away from Utah, away from the destiny that JuLee has ignorantly chosen. But Kath is guilty: she never warned JuLee about Merrill— she never told anyone. She is an accomplice to their romance. She hates herself for throwing the car in gear and speeding out of the Food King lot, but she knows no words potent enough to stir JuLee to knowledge, no words to smother hope and bring light.

*D*aron:
Fall into Winter

September: School

Summertime ticked away while he was busy with his head bent over his notebooks and comics. Since he and his mom returned from Sterling, he has been thinking about his family. He knows almost the whole story: from his grandmother's first Christmas memory of a doll with porcelain hands to his mom's triumphant tale of coaxing a raise from her boss when she went back to work. There are only little bits left he doesn't understand, but these fragments of unrecovered time are all he can think about. There are holes in his mother's life, and as he pushes back into his own childhood he finds his memories growing sparse and vague—dimly discernible, like the engravings in old books viewed through sheets of protective tissue. He remembers the watertap next to the back stoop of his grandparents' house, and the creaking springs of a foldout bed. He flipped through the pages of his Sterling notebook hunting for the traces of these things, and by the time he looked up, fifth grade had engulfed him.

The best thing about school is that he was chosen—along with his friend Tina Linder, Luisa Rodriguez, and Kimberley Brown—to participate in the new gifted-student program for two hours each morning.

He and the three girls wait in the study room in the library until their instructor arrives—always a few minutes late. From the window he watches Ms. Montez park her car in one of the faculty spaces and stride rapidly around the flagpole to the side door. As she walks she performs an array of other activities, like a one-woman traveling carnival: finding a place for her car keys in her swollen backpack; brushing her short, crumpled hair; juggling a stack of papers, notebooks, books, visual aids, tape recorders, videocassettes, toiletry items, empty fast-food containers, doughnut boxes.

Daron and the girls sometimes sit in the corner beyond the conference table on the burnt-orange industrial carpet and listen to Ms. Montez talk. She told them the name of her black leather boots, Doc Martens, and the meaning of her T-shirt: the insignia of the Alice Hitachis, a women's folk band. She has a story for each of the buttons studding her denim jacket: YOU CAN'T HUG YOUR CHILDREN WITH NUCLEAR ARMS and SILENCIO = MUERTE. She gripes about her trouble with her boyfriend: he thinks she should be less political now that she has stumbled into a good job, that she should focus on her work, but she refuses. Sometimes she encourages the class to talk about themselves and their families, and everyone shifts uncomfortably and looks up at the chalkboard or out the window. Daron wonders if the girls are like him, if they are painfully aware of a damaging shyness in their character. No one ever says much, and Ms. Montez doesn't press for information. She doesn't seem inclined to teach very much; she props a loose fence around the perimeter of a subject and sets them free to wander.

They have studied Shakespeare's The Tempest, and Ms. Montez asked everyone to memorize and recite a passage. He chose Ariel's song:

Full fathom five thy father lies;
Of his bones are coral made;
Those are pearls that were his eyes;
Nothing of him that doth fade
But doth suffer a sea change
Into something rich and strange.
Sea nymphs hourly ring his knell:
Hark! Now I hear them—ding-dong bell.

Then, in watercolors on a large sketchpad, he painted a picture of the spirit Ariel flying over the island.

Ms. Montez asked him why he chose that subject—she is always asking why they do things, as if intuitions and thoughts could be made concrete, then described like furniture or strings of beads. He told her that his stepfather had seen an angel. She said, That's cool, that's cool; and he worked the wet brush across Ariel's blue-and-green outline, melting him into the colors of the sky and sea.

October: In the Mail

Daron keeps his archives under his bed. They are stored in a dinnerplate box of reinforced cardboard from his mom's best set of china. The box sits under the bed frame, in the back corner, protected from discovery during his mom's casual cleaning inspections by the larger, heavier box of comic books.

Daron keeps essential mementos in the box: ticket stubs from his favorite movies, a rubber-banded bundle of Zenith comics trading cards, and a small chunk of fire-red sandstone from his trip with his dad and Artie. However, most of his documents are from the mail.

After his mom has read and rearranged and forgotten the mail for a week or two, Daron gathers the interesting pieces and hides them in his room. At the end of each month he selects the most important exhibits, joins them with a heavy-duty paper clip, and stores them for the future.

He retrieves the last entry for October from the space between the counter and the refrigerator where it has fallen, neglected, and pulls the month's other material from a drawer of his desk to prepare them for the archives. The first document is a post-card of a roadrunner from his mom's cousin Rhonda, who is now living in Phoenix, Arizona. There is a Halloween card from Berma and a letter from his dad with illustrations from Artie: they have invited him to visit in Salt Lake when his mom goes up to testify in his Uncle Doug's trial.

His newest addition is a rectangle of stiff green paper folded in thirds. On the first panel inside, a cartoon couple—a boy and girl with swollen heads and huge eyes—hold hands above a cursive caption: "We Pledge Our Love Forever." On the center panel, in a round window, Aunt JuLee and Skunk pose under a tree; their heads are turned to bathe in each other's gaze. The third panel is engraved with the announcement:

Mr. and Mrs. Donald E. Miller
request your attendance
at the loving union of their daughter
JuLee Nell Miller
and
Merrill Stuart Nelson
son of
Mr. and Mrs. Joseph L. Nelson

The week before his mom had argued for hours on the phone with his grandmother. While he sat with his homework at the kitchen table, his mom stretched the phone cord around the corner into the hall. But he could hear her end of the conversation: It's a huge mistake . . . Yeah, I think I would know best about this

. . . He's not a good man . . . No, I . . . can't say why. But he's not . . . It's not sour grapes . . . Come on . . . Let me talk to her . . . Why won't she? . . . But what is there to be afraid of me for? He's the one to be afraid of . . . Fine then. Good-bye. *Clunk.*

The card was postmarked on the day of the ceremony. To avoid the slight chance we might want to come, his mom said.

Daron slides the announcement under the paper clip. Skunk was his father; now Skunk is his uncle. When he looks at the green paper later, he will try to make sense of this. And he will remember that whenever his mom glanced at the card, she seemed to hold her breath.

November: Cousin Rhonda's Suitcase

Daron wakes to the phone's ring at four in the morning and stands with his cheek to the cool jamb of the door while his mom speaks low in her room across the hall. He drifts sleepily until his mom bursts toward the bathroom with a flurry of nightshirt and robe wings and empty sweatpants. It was Cousin Rhonda, she says when she notices him. In the vanity light, she pulls on sweatpants, sheds the robe, and brushes her hair. She's here, apparently.

Because tomorrow is the weekend, his mom lets him ride with her to the bus station.

Rhonda waits at the curb of the terminal, sitting on a piece of coral pink Samsonite. Daron scrambles through the gap between the front bucket seats while his mom opens the trunk for Rhonda's suitcase. He hears his mom say, Well, welcome to Las Vegas.

Rhonda says nothing and climbs into the front seat. He looks at the back of her head and her braid, which has come unstuck and grown spiky with loose hair. She jerks her head rapidly, sensing him. Oh, hi, Daron, she says. I'm a fugitive.

On the way home, through desolate streets, his mom asks her cousin what happened. But all Rhonda says is, I just left. I just left is all.

In the house, his mom rests the suitcase against the coffee table, and Rhonda slumps on the couch with her jacket around her shoulders. Daron stands by the hall door with one hand on top of the television. His mom says, Go to bed, hon. But she speaks without conviction, and nobody moves.

I guess we all ought to get some sleep, she says in a more determined voice. Do you mind sleeping on the sofa?

Let me get my toothbrush, Rhonda says, then waits, then jumps up to open her suitcase. She spreads the halves in the free space between the edge of the coffee table and the front of the TV stand. Daron and his mom watch her spread the contents across the floor as she searches, like the woman who showed his mom the Christmas Cosmetics Collection. And whatever is inside Rhonda's head opens as well. She talks and talks without prompting. I grabbed what I could. I didn't want to wake him up, she says, and tosses a yellow cable-knit sweater, a plain white T-shirt, and a single blue suede boot on the floor.

His mother's such a bitch. She and Abuelita, his little granny, would drop by the place just to tell me how much they disapproved of us. Rhonda unloads a wad of bras, nylons, and panties wrapped in her Super Marketeers bowling shirt. So we get down there and he expects me to get a full-time job while he's in school. And wash his clothes. And have dinner on the table when he gets home. And I got to thinking Mrs. Ortiz was right. What was I doing all this married shit for? She lifts out a light blue waitress uniform and a portable stereo with headphones. You know, it seemed so great last summer. It seemed like such a big deal. My dad went to jail, and I felt almost obligated to make it work. But I just can't do it. I don't want it anymore.

She finds her toothbrush and holds it up triumphantly. I guess that makes the Miller Girls one for three in the relationship game, unless you've got someone new, that is. His mom shakes her head. I heard about JuLee, Rhonda continues. That must be kind of weird for you, huh? His mom smiles weakly but doesn't speak, and they head for bed. Daron looks at the clock on the microwave. It is 5:32 A.M.

Rhonda sleeps on the front couch until his mom's day off, when Daron rides with them in his mom's car to St. George. They leave Rhonda on the porch of her friend Euba's house. Euba still works at the café, and she is going to help Rhonda get her job back. She isn't home, but Rhonda insists that it is okay for them to leave. Daron turns in his seat to wave, and they leave Rhonda sitting on the steps with her arms folded tight.

His mom fills the gas tank at a full-service island to avoid stepping out of the car into Utah.

December: Deck the Halls

His mom decides to decorate the apartment before they leave for her to testify at Uncle Doug's trial in Salt Lake. She borrows her girlfriend Carole's truck to pick up a tree. Daron thinks about the Christmas Safety Program he watched on the cable public access channel and has doubts about leaving a tree unattended. He stands next to the bed where his mom is seated, pulling on her boots. He asks, Didn't Uncle Doug's house burn down from a Christmas tree? His grandmother had told him the story as a lesson in fire safety before he went camping with his dad and Artie.

Your grandma has more than one story about that fire, she says. She pulls her jeans jacket from a peg on the closet door. But don't be such a worrywart. We're not going to leave it plugged in.

They drive to the dusty lot at the corner of La Morena and

Payntor, and Daron forgets his reservations to concentrate on the tree selection. The perfect tree must be tall enough that, when standing at its base, you cannot see the top. It should smell earthy—of fresh-cut wood and pinesap rising in honeyed dots to the flake-barked surface of the trunk. The needles should be pliant, not brittle; prickly, not limp; and sturdy enough to support thin metal ornament hangers. The limbs should be well proportioned and evenly spaced, without naked spots that open to reveal the tree's structure and its spindly core. The tree may be shaped in a classic witch's hat cone, a wide-bottomed pear, a pine cone, a teardrop, a diminishing stack of evergreen Hershey's kisses, a deeply capped toadstool, or a swollen umbrella, depending on the variety of the pine and the requirements of the room. The tree should stand straight. Never assume that adjustments to the stand will compensate for a crooked trunk. A slight bowlike curve of the tree's spine will resist all attempts at disguise.

Within fenced rows strung with thin cheap strings of multi-colored bulbs, it may be tempting, as it used to be for him, to linger in the aisles of flocked trees. Although the trees are intended to suggest boughs heavy-laden with snow, they look whirled in cotton candy and smell of toasted packing peanuts. They are the trees of another world, bundled in sleet-white coats, constricted. These confectionery conifers are not what you seek. You want a lively tree, respiring with scent. While ecological considerations might lead you to examine the racks of artificial trees, real rough texture and biting perfume provide something irreplaceable.

After two hours of increasingly irritable consideration, Daron and his mom wrestle the chosen tree through the front door and raise it in its stand. A tonic crackle freshens the air, as if positive ions bubble from the tips of the deep green needles. His mom struggles, cursing, pleading, haggling with the snarled strings of lights, while he hides the tree stand beneath a gauzy cotton skirt.

As she wraps the wires around and over and under the

branches, he strings popcorn and listens to a Christmas tape—
Chestnuts roasting . . . later on we'll conspire . . . no crib for his
bed . . . walking in a winter wonderland . . . round yon virgin
mother and child . . . hark! the herald angels sing . . . just like
the ones I used to know—of mellow choruses that cloy his ears
like gulped swallows of snowcone syrup. When the lights fail to
shine out after she plugs them into the extension cord, his mom
shakes the tree as if it were somehow responsible. She spends
an hour yanking the little bulbs in and out of their sockets until
the light, mysteriously, returns.

Daron festoons the branches with popcorn garlands, hangs
red satin balls and crystal icicles, clips quilted elves and Santas,
while his mom ties ribbons around small bundles of gathered
needles. As the last act, his mom, grunting, boosts him into the
air to place the angel at the apex. The family angel is not one of
those little girl spirits in lace and tights with combed yellow
tresses and a tinsel halo-on-a-stick; their angel is not Moroni,
gilded and trumpet-toting; their angel has carved white wings,
a swirling organdy robe, a cherubic androgynous face, and tapered arms reaching out and up.

Daron strides four paces to the opposite side of the room to
judge the completed effect. But when he turns to look, his eyes
shift from the tree to his mom. She faces the dusk in the window.
The lights of the tree are reflected in the darkening glass—only
the lights; the tree dissolves, and the globes glow unsupported
around his mom's silhouette in a firmament of deep green mist.

December: La Casa Pequeña de
Tom y Artie

For the whole trip from Las Vegas up to Salt Lake, Daron
pays attention. When they reach his dad and Artie's house, he

scrutinizes each detail. Later, he diagrams the rooms on a sheet cribbed from Artie's stash of graph paper. If the house disappeared, in a fire or a dream, he could reconstruct its walls from memory.

Viewed from the street, the front of the house that Artie and his father rent on a steep avenue by the University of Utah appears squeezed in a vise by the fatter, broader houses on either side. On the first floor, a tracery of frost hangs on a multipane window next to a door with a holly wreath. Upstairs, two close-set windows stare down beneath the frosted brow of a green tar shingle roof. He steps into the prints of his mom's boots in the feather-snow coating the freshly shoveled walk. While his mom testifies at his uncle's trial, he will visit his father. His mom has not decided where to stay: reservations are available for the witnesses at a hotel, and his father has offered her a bed. We'll see what happens, she said.

In the slim front room a squat Christmas tree—the Christmas shrub, according to Artie—stands between two overstuffed chairs. An intricately patterned rug spreads over the hardwood floor. Bright pillows mound on a futon in the corner across from a television and a stereo system. There is a Chagall poster, floating bride and blue horses, and a torchiere floor lamp. His dad is not yet home from work with dinner, so Artie leads Daron and his mom to the twin chairs and brings hot chocolate. When he leaves to answer the phone, Daron peers around the bulge of the Christmas shrub at his mom. She sips from her mug and watches out the window, the way she came in.

The house narrows further at the center, and an alcove with a shelf is scooped out from the inside wall—the Phone Shrine. Artie stands in the passage and shouts Spanish into the receiver: No, mi nombre es Artie . . . Su hijo no está aquí . . . Nunca . . . Nunca está aquí.

The old woman calls at least once a day and asks, ¿Quién es? She believes her son Carlos lives in the house. His dad had the phone number changed, but she found the new number. She also sends postcards of the Sacred Heart levitating out of the body of

Jesus: My love, my heart, I forgive you, she writes in the message space. His dad and Artie learned Spanish to cope with her. She's benign but crazy, Artie explains. Our ghost. El Fantasma de la Casa Pequeña.

The house expands to its full width at the rear. To one side of the back door is the dining room; to the other side is the kitchen. Instead of a window, the dining area has a wall of translucent glass bricks, which break the outside light in shifted patterns on the tablecloth.

As the wall falls black, his dad arrives with pizzas. Hey, kid, he says with a large smile. He reaches out to hug Daron until his eyes meet Daron's mom's. He hesitates, then goes ahead and crushes Daron to his side. Good to see you.

And hey, Kath, how was your trip? he asks. You still like olives and extra cheese on your pizza?

Still do, she says, and her smile turns in. Daron wonders about all the unrecorded meals they had together.

While Daron wrangles the oily worms of melted mozzarella that dangle from each wedge, his parents joke and deny and remember; he wants them to lose the friction, uncoil the tension, and be happy together. Artie sits quietly, his fingers on the edge of the pizza box, his eyes cast down.

His mom rejects the offered Corona but, after her second slice of pepperoni and black olives, slips over to the refrigerator and helps herself to a bottle. On the freezer next to his watercolor of Ariel, a black magnet holds a picture of a man in torn underwear, ripped from a magazine. His mom quickly drops her eyes.

We debated about taking that down, Artie says. I guess I just forgot.

His dad dumps Parmesan on his pizza and says, You just forgot?

The beer spits and foams as his mom pours it into a glass. She sits down at the table. Why did you come to Salt Lake anyway, Tom? It's not exactly San Francisco.

What do you mean, it's not exactly San Francisco? His dad's voice rises.

You know what she means, Artie says. But, see, Salt Lake was the most cosmopolitan place Tom could imagine. Everything outside Utah was the Outer Darkness.

Artie, his dad starts. But he doesn't finish. Daron can't tell who is angry, whether anything is wrong.

Everyone grows suddenly intent on eating, and, when the food is gone, they study the greasy plates and wadded napkins. His dad begins to speculate about Uncle Doug's trial. I hope he gets more than a crack on the knuckles, he says. His disrespect on top of everything. And the fact that he's completely unrepentant.

Artie laughs into his bottle. Unrepentant? So who made you bishop, Elder Anderson?

His mom carries plates and silverware to the sink. Daron doesn't know what she thinks about testifying. She says nothing. Then she announces that she is too tired to hunt for the hotel.

The stairs begin in the kitchen—from bed to refrigerator in five seconds, Artie says—and fly steeply to a hallway on the second floor. The front of the house is a bedroom, except for a corner square blocked off for a bathroom. The opposite door leads to a study looking behind, over the flat white plain of a one-story house. A desk with a computer and a drafting table buried in Gunnery Girl sketches fill the space under the single window. By the door are bookcases, and a gorilla costume half stuffed into a cardboard box. I did birthday parties in college, Artie explains, a long and surprisingly unfunny story. Exercise equipment occupies the rest of the room. After a long period of shifting boxes and barbells to clear the floor, Artie and his dad drag the futon up the stairs into the study. It is too cold to sleep downstairs.

Daron gets ready for bed in the bathroom across the hall. He slides into pajamas and tugs on thick white socks because a layer of thin, true cold snakes along the bare floor.

His mom, in her monstrous quilted periwinkle robe, crosses the hall to the bedroom to ask for an alarm clock. Around her shoulder and through the half-open door, Daron sees the moon frost through the windows above the large bed. Artie stands at the dresser in his pajama bottoms. His dad presses close behind him, one hand flattened on Artie's stomach, the other curled on his freckled shoulder. His dad pulls away quickly, and Daron and his mom both swallow audible lungfuls of shivery air.

With great alacrity, his dad locates a wind-up clock in the nightstand, and Daron slides under the puffy duvet in the study before his mom can turn around to see him.

As she prepares for court in the morning, his mom packs her suitcase and leaves it in the front room. On the porch, she tugs down Daron's stocking cap and says, What do you think, should we stay in the hotel tonight? I think so.

He answers firmly as he pulls on his gloves. No. Please, Mom?

Okay, she says, we'll see. He watches her go, her narrow heels leaving divots in the fresh veil of snow on the walk.

December: Snow

Flake. Grain. Powder. Filament. Crust. Slush. Daron has played with snow before, in the mountains with his mom. But in his dad and Artie's yard the snow's manifestations surprise him. Lacking scent and silent in its unvariegated white, the landscape needs to be touched to be known. Frozen pellets, small tender peas, roll on the glinting surface—a brittle crystalline, netted over the snowbanks in an ice-moth cocoon. Beneath the brilliant crust lies a layer of snowdust, fine and loose, which sifts through the fingers of his glove and scatters in plumes. The powder hides a dense base of heavy snow that squeaks like styrofoam under his boots.

He leaps from the salt-scarred sidewalk and lands on his back in the drift. He makes a snow angel, flapping his arms and spreading his legs together and apart. Snowdust creeps over the barrier of Artie's green scarf and melts at the nape of his neck. With the snow crushed close, his coat fails to divide his body from the cold; he cannot distinguish the end of his flesh from the beginning of the ice.

The sky above is flat slate, gray mask, and he is floating head first down a dead river. He shuts his eyes and the river narrows to the width of his shoulders; canyon walls rise red, bathed by the bloodlight of his eyelids. The cold sleeps in him. The cold tells him to rest. To stop. The cold against him—the cold against him sharpens into memory.

He lies inside the yellow house; he sees the sky—bright—out of its smudged windows.

Daron thrashes to his feet out of the snow.

The angel's outline blurs—

Memory

I can tell you, but I cannot act.
From where I sit, time is finished, and the past is always.
What was said, what was done, this I can illuminate.
But do not ask for explanation; do not ask for intercession.
I will tell you, but I cannot judge.

The ice. It was the twenty-fourth of July, and Daron was four, and the ice was slick and cold when he pressed his palm to the dripping sides. The blocks were stacked in a tall cube as high as Daron's head. The sides glimmered out from beneath a shawl of rough-edged burlap in the light from the open door; there were suggestions of reflections and a play of delicate rainbows.

Skunk scuffed circles in the thick dust with his boots and wiped at the tears and clear snot that had collected on his upper lip. "It's the time I told you about." Skunk tapped his chest with his open palm. "God's here. Right in here, today." He scooped his hands under Daron's arms and raised him on top of the blocks.

He pressed Daron down with a hand at his throat. "Lie still now."
The burlap was wet, and then it was chilling. When Skunk
moved his hand away to pull a card of twine from his pocket,
Daron struggled to sit up. "It's too cold."

"Do it." Skunk pushed his shoulders down. "I don't want to
bind you before the blessing. But I will if you don't stay still."
Daron stiffened his arms and legs and tilted his head to watch
Skunk go outside and shut the door. He didn't sit up again, but
he arched his back until the ice touched only the heels of his feet
and his shoulderblades. He couldn't stay like that forever, and in
the dark the ice wasn't like glass, it wasn't like building blocks,
it was only cold.

Kath fingered the fossils basking with a dull sheen in the sun of
the windowsill. Three nickel-sized trilobites clustered on a flat
gray rock. Others, freed from stone, encircled the rock like
lumpy checkers. Merrill had discovered them while hunting in
the desert up north. Their ridged and rumpled bodies, segmented
in three and pressed into a somehow oval, somehow triangular
coin, once splayed along the water bottom in profusions. Utah
had been submerged in a sea—Lake Bonneville—seething with
activity like a vast purse seine. But the water had whorled away,
leaving the concentrated residue of the Great Salt Lake as a puddle in an empty tub. To the north, the high deserts were full of
shell shards, trilobites, and slabs incised with skeletal fish.

When Merrill brought the fossils home, fresh from baking on
his dashboard, and dropped them hot into Daron's hands, he told
her son that the earth was four thousand years old. He had found
the water creatures left high and dry on the desert floor—an un-
mistakable sign that the earth had been drowned in a great flood.
Kath had watched her son with the round stones filling his
palms, and she asked Merrill if it wasn't true that the dinosaurs
lived millions of years ago. He glared at her and told her to study
the Bible; the life spans of the prophets since Adam had been
recorded and calculations could be made. He told Daron that the

scientists were wrong about the dinosaurs. They might have drowned in the flood. Or else their bones came on meteors from space and weren't born of the earth.

Kath shifted her eyes down from the fossils to the half-peeled cucumbers on the counter. She needed to finish the salad before leaving to help her mother with the Pioneer Day party. She lifted the knife distractedly. It was easier to think of the million lost years than of the morning now passing, impossible to think of the future.

She had gotten up early to cook for the party before breakfast, and Merrill arrived from a run in his truck. She heard his boots drop behind her to the kitchen linoleum. He stood in his stocking feet and shivered with his hands hooked under his armpits, although the morning was already hot. He stared at her—ecstatic or terrified—until she asked what was the matter.

"He stopped the truck. I swear to you, He killed the engine." Merrill flung his arms out. "He said I was to be tested again."

Kath didn't want to hear. She said, "You'll need to get the ice." They had bought the sliding blocks yesterday and stored them out in Berma's old house to keep them cool.

"Let me tell you what happened."

"I need to get over to Mom's soon."

"You need to hear me out. You're my wife."

"I don't—"

"You saw Him. We are wed in this. You are wed to my duty, Kath."

"No." She *did not* hear the angel's voice. She *did not* kill Champion. She hurried to the bathroom and locked the door; she flicked on the little radio and turned on both taps in the shower full blast.

Kath was devoted to her husband—she had vowed to care for his home under the guidance of his priesthood—but when she looked at Merrill she felt the angel burning and saw Champion's broken eyes. She would never love him again. Merrill pressured her toward a temple marriage; the bishop had decided they were ready. Sealed to Merrill, she would live with him forever in the celestial kingdom; he would take other celestial wives, they would become her sisters, and she would serve with them under his leadership on the planets he would be given to rule. The earth's span was brief at four thousand years, but she would be wed to Merrill forever among the unbroken crystals of the cosmos.

It filled her with horror, and if she refused to listen it was because she was afraid she would believe him. She had seen the angel, and if it could speak, it would say nothing human; she didn't want to hear. If Merrill had lied about its voice, she hated Merrill. If Merrill hadn't lied, she hated Merrill and she hated God.

The water thumped against her face and neck. She allowed the shower stream into her mouth to fill the basin of her tongue and overflow the curled rim of her lip and spread across her chin to join the water rushing over and between her breasts. She breathed some in and coughed, steadying herself with a hand on the tile wall. She washed her hair, squeezing the soap in fiercely until she winced at the tugged follicles. She stood before the vanity, wiped the steam from the mirror, and did her face and hair. When she emerged from the humid bathroom into the dry heat of the apartment, she saw that Merrill and Daron had gone.

On the kitchen table, Merrill had fixed the stem of a yellow rose in a seltzer water bottle. The heavy bud bent the stalk, nearly bloomed, the petal-tips already winding back. For Kath, the rose was as sharp and meaningful as a knife. She couldn't scream. She must wait on the will of the angel and do nothing. She pulled at the belt of her robe, cinching, tighter, until the air in her body had nowhere else to go and she did scream. But quietly. Kath considered her tight, controlled shriek—how it didn't escape the apartment, how it didn't leave the kitchen, how it was just loud enough, and fearsome enough, to fill her own head.

First Merrill blessed the twine. Withdrawn to a place apart, he knelt on the hill across the gully from the yellow house, near the twisted trunk of a cedar. He prayed that the bonds he would fashion from the twine would serve Heavenly Father's purpose.

Next he blessed the knife. He caressed the hilt and shaft with consecrated oil. "In the name of Jesus Christ and by the authority of the priesthood I hold, I bless this knife and offer it unto you, Lord. I pray that this blade will be adequate to serve you."

Then he clenched his fists around the knife hilt and closed his eyes. He prayed, tightly and densely, his thoughts spinning fast and curling in around the bright core of his knowledge of his special place in God's heart. He waited to feel the adrenaline of the Flight—of the Angel of the Lord soaring over the little house.

The dog her parents had bought to replace Champion was too new to have a name. She was called "the puppy" or "little widget," which was Kath's father's name for small children and babies. The puppy was a single shaggy black earmuff scooting footlessly through the long grass of her parents' backyard. Kath watched the puppy move, then returned her attention to her mother.

Her mother worked at the tough plastic wrap on a package of paper plates. "Would you do the tablecloths? When did you say Skunk and Daron were coming?"

"Soon."

"They went for the ice?" The plastic wrap yielded at last, and paper UFOs soared onto the lawn.

"Yes." Kath bent low to gather the plates. The puppy scrambled over one of them, leaving miniature muddy prints, and clamped small jaws on the rim of another. Kath wanted to believe that they would arrive soon, that the truck would soon pull up with strings of icy wetness dripping from the sides of the tailgate, that Daron would lower himself from the passenger side and come running to hug his grandmother and play with the dog. She didn't want to focus on it; she didn't want to answer questions. Her role was silence. She could console herself that she had acted correctly if she didn't have to consider it. Couldn't she? She twisted her tongue between her teeth and gnashed it. Hard.

She gave a little cry. The puppy stopped dragging the plate toward her water bowl and lifted her head.

"Is something wrong?"

Kath knelt on the grass and shook her head. "I believe in God. The goodness of God."

Her mother peered down at her quizzically over the tower of plates and the edge of the card table. "Of course you do, Kath-Leen."

"If he . . . if God . . . asked you to give up something, someone, would you do it even if . . . if you had to surrender what you loved?"

"God would never ask something like that. What is it, honey? What's wrong?"

"I can't. I can't." Kath wanted to tell her mother, but her mouth had only these two words, beating like a metronome. "I can't. I can't. I can't. I can't."

"Are you sick?" Her mother walked around the table and touched her fingers to Kath's forehead. "Let's go inside."

"I can't." She shook her head and shrugged off her mother's hands. She tore the waist of her dress on the chainlink in her haste to open the rear gate.

Daron had been lying on the ice with his arms tucked underneath him, and when he lifted his hand to wipe his runny nose, the restricted blood roared through the freed veins, throbbing. It was too dark to see his hand in the smudged light, but it felt larger than a baseball mitt. He slammed the cold, wet fingers against his side, and they were numb, dumb leather. His mother would know what to do—puncture it like a balloon, douse it in water, squeeze it into a mitten—but she wasn't there. Skunk had told him to wait. Skunk had told him that he should pray to Heavenly Father for guidance. Daron tried to shake the dead hand off his wrist until the hand began to wake, fizzing like soda under the skin.

. . .

Kath discovered Merrill before she began to search for him. She
had parked the car out of sight below the curve on the post office road and jogged up the center of the graded dirt. She saw
the roof of Cousin Berma's old house rise above the cedars in the
gully, and as she ran to the overgrown path leading up to the
front door, she spotted Merrill on the opposite rise. His back was
turned, his spine rigid; he faced the sun. From a slightly different angle at the base of the hill she saw the large blade in his
hands. She caught herself turning in, blanking out her senses,
closing the door. But she had to stay in the world, because she
had to know.

She stepped carefully—swift and soundless—in the loose
earth of the gully until she had a clear view. Merrill was alone
on the rise. Daron must be waiting inside the house with the old
air and the same dust Merrill had brushed aside when he proposed to her. She ran up the hill across from Merrill, forgetting
quiet, hoping only for speed.

A thick stick fixed the hoop and clasp of the padlock, and she
wiggled it out, scraping her fingers on the splintered wood of the
door frame. She kicked at the warped door until it swung in.

Daron was on the ice. He didn't look up when she came in. He
didn't move. He shivered.

"It's Mom," she whispered, and he shifted his head. "Come
on, baby. Let's go."

"Skunk said to lie down. He said I had to."

"No you don't. Come on." She lifted him from the ice and carried him, cradled, out of the house. She started down the road
toward the car. When she glanced up, Merrill no longer knelt on
the rise. He had disappeared into the gully on his way to the
house. There was no time to reach the car. He couldn't be allowed to see them; she couldn't leave if he saw them. His voice
would freeze her. His eyes would capture her. He would catch
them.

She climbed into the scrub and trees on the far side of the
road. As Daron nestled in the crook of her arms, she felt the chill
damp of his clothes, his skin mottled and coolly thick. She had

no free hand to reach for balance as the ground sloped sharply before her, and she climbed cautiously. Loose stone scraped down on other rocks below. She rested an instant. She couldn't turn to look for Merrill and risk losing her balance, but she held her breath to listen. She was being too noisy.

She crested the ridge, and Daron grew instantly heavy. Her arms threatened to spasm with paralysis. She lowered him to his feet before she dropped him. Below them the ravine broke the land. On one wall of the ravine the white, hard-packed earth of the trail she had ridden with Honey the Pony seared its winding scar into the deep purple-brown of the slope. She scooted Daron up into a piggyback, coiled her arms tight around his thighs, and raced down to the nearest bend of the trail, zigzagging to keep her balance. Kath sensed how exposed they must seem from the vantage of the ridge, how vulnerable, although nothing stirred but tiny bug-catching birds and nervous brown lizards.

At the head of the trail she threw her weight to slide the rusty bolt of the ranch gate while Daron stared down the length of the fence at the parallel strands of barbed wire. Kath hurried Daron gently with a hand at his shoulder as they jogged toward the buildings ahead. They rushed between the two large horse stables, and Kath felt safer, as if she had entered a real world unvisited by specters of Wrath and Prophecy.

Mr. DeSoto stood at the washstand outside the second stable, unwrapping a new bar of Lava soap with hands stroked and dashed in brown saddle polish. He saw them and smiled. But his smile fell away in stages. It may have been her face that alerted him—an unsuppressible twinge of fear around her eyes—or else it was Daron's feet. She followed Mr. DeSoto's gaze to discover her son's small, pale feet, shoeless and scored with countless tiny scratches. She hadn't noticed; if she had, she would have spared him from walking. She cursed herself for another failure of attention and will.

On the screened DeSoto porch, she drank a pitcher of lemonade and told Mr. DeSoto the story. She told him about Merrill's plans, about Champion, about the house and the knife. She told him everything but the one thing: the angel.

Mr. DeSoto was furious and shouted down Mormon insanity and supernatural bullshit. He shouted for his wife to bring the phone, and she yelled back, "Hold your horses!" Kath saw Mrs. DeSoto with Daron through the window into the house. She had planted Daron on the dining table and dug at the sliver-filled pads of his feet with tweezers. Daron lay stoic with his foot raised in Mrs. DeSoto's hand, clenching his jaw. Kath never wanted to see her son lie immobile and silent again.

Kath pleaded against the police, and not just because she feared that they would judge her stupid and neglectful. She worried about the angel: what if its pronouncements were true? As easy as it seemed on the DeSoto porch to drain belief from her head and dismiss the Light in the garden, what if she had earned the angel's wrath?

She and Daron needed to leave Sterling as quickly as possible. Even if the police were called, there would be a period before Merrill was apprehended in which they would not be safe. And after he was caught? What had he actually done? How long could he be locked away from them? She convinced Mr. DeSoto—and Mrs. DeSoto, who finished with Daron and came to stand with phone in hand at the screen door—that it was best for Daron and her to disappear. She was certain that Merrill would not hunt for them. She didn't know the nature of her certainty, but it was deep and honest. They would flee and find shelter in another place.

Mr. DeSoto nodded grudgingly. He opened the ranch cash box and handed over five hundred-dollar bills. He made Kath promise that she would use the money to buy distance; if she wouldn't call the police, she must move far from Sterling and never return—that was his requirement for silence.

Mrs. DeSoto loaded a grocery sack with any food from her kitchen that was immediately edible—potato chips, carrots, cookies, apples. She rode with her husband to the post office road and drove their Lincoln back. Mr. DeSoto returned with

Kath's car; he hadn't seen any activity behind the Nelson house.
Mr. and Mrs. DeSoto escorted Kath and Daron out of Sterling.
At the on-ramp of the interstate, Mr. DeSoto accelerated and
pulled up beside Kath; they stopped in tandem for a moment.
Mrs. DeSoto rolled down the electric window and called to
Kath, "About your family . . . ?"

"No!" Kath shouted. "Don't say anything!"

"But you have to tell them."

"I'll call them," she promised.

Merrill stood under a tree in the corner of his parents' yard and
stuck the tip of his hunting knife into the gray bark, then jerked
the knife sideways with a crack to the bark. He did it repeatedly,
carefully, systematically, as if he were trying to strip the tree
bare. Or he expected to find something underneath, something
he had been looking for. When he stopped, his face was wet with
tears. He threw the knife toward the lawn, and the blade sank
with a deep thud into the wet sod. He began to stomp on the
rosebushes under the tree, breaking the stalks and grinding the
yellow heads of the flowers into the earth.

In early evening Kath and Daron entered the lobby of the Bellefleur. They were tired and sticky from the hot car, and the cool
air inside the hotel gave Kath shivers. For a moment the interior
was impenetrably dark—her first experience with the uncer-
tainty of time in Las Vegas hotels. She led Daron over to the desk
and asked for a room. The man, in a crisp blue suit, was doubtful but found them a single with a cancellation. She was shocked
at the price; the five bills in her pocket would not last. She had
chosen the Bellefleur on a whim, because it was new, because
she had seen a billboard, but they would find a cheaper place.

Kath ducked into a dim alcove full of telephones and dialed
her mother. She heard the tension in her mother's voice as she
answered the phone, and also the distant sound of dishes rattling.

Kath told her mother that she had left Sterling, that she had to leave, that she couldn't say why or tell where she was. Her mother said, "I see," then fell silent. Kath tried to apologize until she realized that her mother had hung up.

Daron waited at his mother's side, facing the opposite direction, toward the beeping, jingling, flashing depths of the casino. He was comforted by the people milling among the warm lights and the ringing machines.

In later months he would wake up in the night and cry until his mother bundled him into the car to see the lights and people and he could finally sleep with the sounds and colors draining pleasantly from his ears and eyes.

While driving from their new apartment to the job she found at the Bellefleur Casino, Kath would sometimes glance nervously into the cabs of semis. She did not expect him to come for them, but they might meet accidentally. It was her dependence on good fortune that frightened her most.

What Daron remembers is the ice. The ice and its numbness.

But Kath remembers every detail. The events line themselves up in her mind like a formation of orderly crystals, like the light spotting the leaves of the tree.

*K*ath:
Winter into Spring

December: Place Settings

The angel is askew.

Kath's eyes are drawn up as she rushes across the room.

Or maybe it's the tree.

Kath slides a dining-room chair over to adjust the figurine, but she can't reach it while balancing in her heels. And she doesn't have much time before everyone returns from their impromptu caroling. She wants her home to be crisp, ordered, beautiful. But she supposes nothing can be perfect.

She steps off the chair carefully, pressing her tight skirt decorously to her knees even though there is no one in the house to see it rise. She grabs the place cards from the top of the refrigerator and approaches the laden table. She worries that they will think the cards are silly and old-fashioned, but she has never hosted a real Christmas dinner before, and she wants it to be flawless.

She decided to invite Tom and Artie for the holidays while folding clothes in Daron's room. She had thought of calling them, then paused in an ache of indecision. A year before, she never would have considered spending the holidays with Daron's father and his lover. She realized that she had passed beyond some boundary where the counseling voice of her church and her family grew mute and could offer no guidance. She possessed only her own limited wisdom and believed that her son deserved to celebrate one Christmas with people who were something like family while he was still near childhood. When she asked Daron if he liked the idea, he looked up from his book to the window and said, Sure, with perfect disinterest. But she sensed he was pleased.

Tom and Artie were thrilled, and by the time she bought the groceries the party had grown to seven—the most people they have ever had in their house at one time. It is the first time she has used the leaves for her table.

As she sorts the cards in her hand, she tries to remember the etiquette for table seating. She knows it should be boy-girl, boy-girl, but the other rules remain obscure. She decides that it is her prerogative as hostess to place the cards according to her whim.

She seats herself at the head of the oval nearest the kitchen.

On the plate to her right she props Daron's card.

As if she were following the injunctions of a mysterious alchemical formula, she has bought every item on Daron's Christmas list—which he had organized according to priority, including size, quantity, price, and suggested place of purchase. She sought out the right kind of marker, the proper notebooks, the correct anthology of classical mythology, the essential selection among the three listed video games. On her own initiative, she added some needed school clothes, socks, and underwear. When she looked at the pile of gifts on her bed before wrapping them, they seemed distressingly unfestive and decidedly unchildlike. She ran to the store and purchased a stuffed panda just to comfort herself.

Daron had insisted: No Santa this year, okay, Mom? And so the little tags all read: Love, Mom. When he sat under the tree and opened the gifts in the morning, he stacked the boxes neatly, said: Thanks a lot, Mom, and carried them—the panda on top— into his room. Along with a pile of books and tapes, Tom and Artie had brought Daron a hand-carved wooden circus set with wagons and a ring and beautiful miniature clowns and animals. Daron smiled with delight despite himself, and for a moment Kath grew intensely jealous. She felt like the curmudgeon who had killed Daron's childhood.

Next to Daron she places Rhonda.

She arrived on the bus from St. George two days ago with the same piece of battered pink Samsonite she had hijacked from Manuel's mother the month before. Rhonda's talk steamed the windows of the car as they drove to the apartment. So, she said, my mother thinks that of course I'll come home for Christmas since my father's gone, but she just doesn't seem to get it that I've got this gripe with her as well. Although I was . . . I am an idiot. I just can't make it on these waitress wages living on my own. I'm looking forward to going to school and taking out lots of loans I can't pay back.

Kath listens to her complaints, but she hears the brightness in Rhonda's voice; she is still young enough to iron out the creases in her spirit without a trace.

She seats Artie beside Rhonda.

When they first met, she had made a concerted effort not to like Artie because—even if she could not accuse him in any rational way of "stealing" her old boyfriend from her—Artie represented the reality of Tom's detachment from her life; he was part of the alien world that had swallowed Tom. Her coolness toward him was also because Artie so easily melted Daron's reserve that she often felt cast off into the periphery of her son's life. She had been so eager to dismiss him that his bizarre, tenacious charms caught her constantly off guard. He would enter a conversation from the sidelines with a comment that made her laugh, often carving through the bullshit she and Tom had been tossing back and forth. She realized that his teasing cleared the air and made it possible for her and Tom to find new ground. For Daron's sake. She feels retroactively grateful.

Artie had arrived the day before, banging loudly on the front door with a six-pack cooler in his hand. Hurry! Where's your kitchen, he shouted. We brought snowballs. He quickly loaded foil bundles into their freezer while Daron attempted to peel back the wrappings. Artie whisked the ball away. No peeking.

Later, while Daron watched the Grinch on television with Tom, Artie sat over a beer in the kitchen. She looked up from slapping stuffing into the cavity of the turkey, and he said, All right, I wasn't taking chances on melting. Half of them are mashed potatoes.

Somewhat reluctantly, she puts Tom across the bottom of the table from Artie.

It seems to spoil her boy-girl arrangement, and it violates another rule about not putting couples together. But she can't think of them as lovers for very long without distress.

Tom took her aside on his first day in Las Vegas, into her bedroom, latching the door behind him. Kath, he said. They stood by the dresser. She looked at him and felt the familiar catch in her breath. She sat on the bed to regain her distance. Kath, I just want you to know how much I appreciate it—your asking us here. It's one of the nicest things anyone's done for me in a long time. Tom's eyes glistened and filled. He looked up and away, tapping his fingers on the dresser. Sorry, he said.

Kath was irritated that he could cry so easily, with no fear of appearing pathetic. She examined her lap silently and began to see that she was envious. Tom's tears were too quick, perhaps too easy, but he could reach them. His emotions were accessible like oils daubed on a palette, and Kath had her balance, the reserve she had acquired from the room in her mind. I'm glad you guys could come, she said. Daron's in hog heaven.

She had assumed without considering it that Tom would carve the turkey, but she isn't sure if this is wise. To offer Tom the host's role, to make him the man of the house, might be a surrender to the past. However, it is too late to reorganize the table; she decides to stop worrying.

She seats her friend Carole at Tom's right.

She knows that this position will please Carole, who has been flirting futilely with Tom since she arrived after breakfast in the morning. Kath explained the situation to her, but Carole seems oblivious.

While they opened presents, Carole sat on the floor at Tom's knee and fondly conveyed Tom's packages from under the tree into his lap. Afterward, she responded to his simple question about her job with her Legend of Las Vegas routine. Kath has heard Carole unearth this story for men at the hotel where they work, but the only man who seems to have fallen for it was her ex-boyfriend John. He was always encouraging Carole to resume her "career."

Carole explained, So I came to Las Vegas as a dancer, but they still had all those old-fashioned shows—no real dancing, just feathers and tits, excuse me, Daron. And I wasn't what they called statuesque enough. So I had to dance cabaret in one of the smaller rooms for Rex Coogan, Alex Dean—real lounge lizards. So I realized that I wasn't making any more money than the cocktail waitresses and—she raised her voice—*and* I didn't get tips. So I gave it up. Now, Rex Coogan tried to talk me into sticking with dancing, but hey, I don't like to be poor. After twenty-five, that whole starving-artist thing gets really unappealing.

Artie coaxed Carole into demonstrating how a showgirl would stride in her heels while carrying a basket of Pepperidge Farm cheese and sausage. She tottered among the shreds of gift wrap and discarded ribbon, smiling down at Tom at every opportunity. Rhonda shot Kath incredulous looks, and Kath felt so embarrassed for her friend that she retreated to the kitchen to wash the dishes.

As they prepared to go caroling, Carole kept clutching at Tom's elbow, giggling over naughty stories about Charo with Siegfried and Roy, and Kath could only speculate that Carole had gotten Tom's name confused.

At the last place setting, to the left of her spot at the head of the table, she propped the card for Artie's brother, Zach.

Zach lived in Los Angeles, and, for reasons Kath didn't know, he was no more welcome at his parents' house than his brother was. He usually spent Christmas with Artie and Tom, and Artie asked her if Zach could join them. She had felt uneasy about sharing Christmas with a stranger, but she is glad that she relented. A shiver of mischievous pleasure shoots through her at the thought of seating him next to her. Carole has squandered her time on Tom and will miss her chance with Zach.

He had spent the day apologizing. He had loaded two sacks of gifts to take to the airport with him but forgot them in the trunk of his car. He hoped that she wouldn't find him ungracious for arriving empty-handed. When Carole began her showgirl demonstration, Zach slipped into the kitchen after Kath to help. She lingered with him by the breakfast bar, talking, studying his face. Zach is dark, and his features are sharp; he is unlike his brother Artie with his fair, freckled redness. If it weren't impertinent, Kath would have asked if they shared the same set of parents.

After she pulled a hot stack of her good china from the washer, Kath stretched up over Zach's head to put them in the cupboard. Her mouth drifted close to the curl of his ear, and she was tempted to take a small nip at his earlobe. She shook her head, laughing, instead and wouldn't tell him what was funny as she stepped back in the kitchen.

Zach had asked to stay and help while the others went out, but she had insisted that he go with them. She needed the time to think. It has taken her all day to realize that she is "getting along" with a man, but she forgives herself for her rustiness.

She hears the carolers at the door, laughing through "Jingle Bells," and hurries into the kitchen to check on the turkey. They all rush in, pull off their jackets, and pile them on her bed. While everyone argues about who gets to use the bathroom first, Zach enters the kitchen with his fingers tucked into his armpits. He asks, Is it always this cold here this time of year?

You Californians are spoiled, she says. She hands him a pair of oven mitts. Here, put these on and help me get the turkey out. While he bends down to lift the pan from the rack, she leans close, then notices Daron in the doorway. His eyes seem to judge the shrinking distance between where she and Zach are standing.

December: La Belle et la Bête

Kath and Zach find their assigned seats at the employee dinner and wait for their cocktails to arrive. Zach is staying at the Bellefleur (despite her warning that it is expensive), and he agreed to accompany her to the New Year's party.

The Bellefleur qualifies as a French hotel under the same rules of suspended belief that identify Caesar's as a Roman palace. A three-tiered paddleboat sits trapped in the indoor French Quarter courtyard. The paddlewheel churns water in a coin-stuffed fountain, slot machines clang, and waitresses in pirate-wench costumes serve hamburgers at "Pegleg Fred's" on the boat's top tier. Floor after floor of wrought-iron railings look down onto the boat between the plastic fronds of the palms. Far above, painted stars and a slice of pensive moon shine down from the black ceiling.

There are several bars, restaurants, and other eateries on the lower levels of the courtyard: the Black Bottom Jazz Bar, the Bourbon Street Buffet, and Samantha's Kitchen, a café decorated with biscuit tins and pickaninny rag dolls in a rainbow selection of skin tones. But the employee party has taken over the hotel's prestige restaurant, La Bellefleur. The restaurant is at the top of the building, floors above the painted sky of the courtyard. The inspiration for La Bellefleur's design was the Jean Cocteau version of *Beauty and the Beast* (the only subtitled movie on public television that Kath has been able to sit through). Tables fill the dining hall of a haunted French château. White marble arms reach from sconces on the wall to hold brass torches and soft globe lights. Tall windows look down onto the night in Las Vegas; their sheer curtains billow on an imperceptible breeze. On one wall, flames lick ceaselessly at simulated logs in a huge stone fireplace. Hooded caryatids hold up the mantel shelf, and their eyes follow the guests who walk past. Kath feels adrift at the hotel without the usual pressures and responsibilities. Tom and Artie are staying with Daron, so she has nothing tangible to fret about. From her end of a table for sixteen, she contemplates her place in this fairy tale, the story of appearances, mistaken and genuine.

If she were the heroine of the evening, her tale would have begun this afternoon. Daron and Artie and Tom had convinced Kath to stand on the ottoman and spin around in her new dress while they applauded approvingly. The dress was a Christmas present from Daron (he and Tom picked it out at the Nordstrom's in Salt Lake), and, while it was much too expensive, it is extremely pretty, tasteful and simple. The indigo cloth is shot through with metallic red threads. She is pleased that the people from work can see her in something attractive and not in the cream-and-blue uniform she wears every day at the Bellefleur. But, in honesty, she must admit that the care she took in dressing was less for the benefit of her fellow employees than for inspection by Zachary Cooper.

She studies him while he taps his tongue to his upper teeth. Long pauses punctuate every exchange in their conversation. His eyes drop to search for confirmation of his thoughts among the dishes, glasses, saltcellars, and place cards occupying the tablecloth. The ovals of candle flame in their slender glass chimneys catch in his gold-flecked irises with the wet shine of stones in a creekbed. He parts his full lips before speaking, and she feels the wet ridges of his teeth with an imaginary tongue. The fantasy embarrasses her—perhaps she is attracted to Zach for his connection to Tom (although this makes no sense), or as an antidote to Merrill (but she never thinks of him except to worry about JuLee). Perhaps the thrill only seems frivolous because she has forgotten to leave a space for desire in her life.

She watches Zach gamely eat a hard breadstick with butter. He has avoided all the courses, but, aside from mentioning his vegetarianism, he has been too polite—or too bored—to make another comment about it.

They had been discussing money. Kath wondered how he could afford the hotel, his casually expensive clothes, his year-old Volkswagen. When they met in the lobby, he gave her a present: a charm on a gold chain—a cross with a hoop above the bar at the top. An ankh, he said. It's the Egyptian symbol for life. But it's not some California bullshit. I just like the way it looks. It's to make up for Christmas. Kath lifts the smooth ankh from the hollow of her throat with a fingernail and lets it fall back with a soft pat. She asks, Would I know anything you've written?

Zach composes music for television; he is an artist, one of the rare similarities with his brother. It's all been local stuff mainly, he says. He touches tongue to teeth again, then produces a soft baritone: "Safe and smart, Prompt and kind, You can trust us,

We don't mind, We're Great Pacific Bank, And we care." They gave me the lyrics, he says. I just did the tune.

Sounds good, she says. I mean the music. You have a nice voice. She fingers the ankh.

Zach has an artistic family. His mother sang in a Lutheran choir; his father is an architect. He speaks of them with affection and credits them with inspiring the music inside him. But when he attempts to explain why he didn't go home to Salt Lake for Christmas—after a silence prolonged beyond his previous record—his words are confused and caustic. They're like chairs, he says, with the stuffing pulled out. You can't sit on them anymore. I was a bad kid. Drugs, petty thefts, ditching school all the time. And they don't forgive. Now Artie was the angel. But he got it on with guys, and that was it for him. Outta there! They've still got our sister. Monica's home for the holidays. She was the middle kid, so she slipped through. What were you?

The oldest, Kath says. But she doesn't want to discuss her family. She concentrates on dessert, and soon everyone sings "Auld Lang Syne," although it is December twenty-ninth.

In the elevator, she thanks Zach for escorting her and enduring the dreadful vegetable plate. I'm well acquainted with steamed broccoli, he says. As she prepares to say good-bye and cross the lobby to her car, Zach invites her to his room. Casino sounds ring over the iron rail on the top floor of the courtyard as she follows him into the dark.

He has condoms in the nightstand drawer. They had a machine in the locker room downstairs, he says. And I thought I might as well in case . . . He rises up on his knees between Kath's legs to unroll it, on the bed where she has been kissing him, half-dressed, his hand under her bra, brushing nipples, her tongue satisfying its curiosity about his teeth. She wonders if he was certain he would need the condoms—with her—or with someone. She begins to tell him that pregnancy is not an issue—there is no chance—then she realizes that pregnancy is not the only problem. And she feels scared, and foolish, and dangerously desperate—until he returns to cover her with his weight and his kisses.

You need to call home, Zach says later, and reaches across Kath to place the receiver in her hands. After she dials the number, she hears Artie's sleepy voice and doesn't know what to say; she breathes. Her indigo dress stretches uninhabited but somehow alive on the other bed, and the red threads spark in the light from the nightstand.

Me, Zach says, gimme. He takes the phone and leans into Kath, his free hand cuddling her stomach. Hey, bro, he says. Can you stay with Daron for the night? I don't think KathLeen should drive home. Too much champagne.

She wonders why drinking is a more acceptable, more innocent, excuse than love. She has not been drinking—but the bed disincorporates into clouds beneath her, and she is falling, up from soft depths, up into Zach's arms.

March: The Machine

Kath strives consciously and carefully not to act as if Daron were a small, inscrutable, alien genius entrusted to her care, but she sometimes finds herself baffled. According to tests and the opinions of his teachers, Daron is exceptional; he is adept in most subjects, brilliant in some, but he cannot be relied on to remember a phone message. When she came home from work and asked if anyone had called, Daron would usually lift his face from his comic and stare at her blankly. She left a pen and paper by the phone, but he never used them.

In February Kath drove to a bargain electronics store and bought an answering machine. She stared into the daunting complexities of the instruction booklet until Daron plugged the box into the phone and demonstrated how to record an outgoing message. Since setting the system in motion, he has ignored the telephone entirely, as if the device no longer exists in his conception of the cosmos. When she returns from her shift, the red light always blinks at her in expectation.

Beep—KathLeen, it's your mother. It's not important. You don't need to call me back. But, KathLeen, can you afford this machine? Weren't you saving money for a car?
Beep—It's your mother again. I got to worrying where Daron was. Shouldn't he be home now? It's awfully late.
Beep—Daron? Hello? Can you hear this? This is your grandmother. If you can hear this, please answer the phone. We're very worried about you here. Dear, why aren't you home? (Daron was home, but the volume was off—at least, this is what he claimed.)

Beep—Kath, it's Zach Cooper. It's . . . um . . . Friday, at nine-thirty Pacific Time—are you on Pacific Time?—anyway, what I want to say I can't say in a message. I'll call back. (Kath called him when she got home from work—woke him up—and he told her in a thick voice that he felt enraptured by her, that her image rustled ghostlike through his thoughts. She offered him silence; she didn't believe him. Even if she had spent many more than two nights with him, she would not trust his love; she does not trust love.)

Beep—Hi Kath, Rhonda. I just called to see what was up. I've got my new phone number now. It's . . . Shit, I can't find the paper. I'll call back. Oh, I got into the U of U for the fall. About to start my financial-aid shit. I'm sooo poor! Send firewood! Just kidding, I'm doing okay. Mom makes me casseroles and leaves them in the windowsill. Well, it's Mom or the Casserole Fairy. Well, I'd rather spend the money talking to you in person so I'll say good-bye. Good—

Beep—Hi, it's Zach. I'm coming up this weekend. Don't say no. (Daron stayed—under protest—with Carole and her new boyfriend. He drank part of Carole's beer and watched a monster truck contest on cable, then stayed up until four, after they went to bed, watching a three-hour French film. Kath fixed dinner and invited Zach to bed. And it was wondrous.)

Beep—It's your grandmother, Daron. Don't pretend you're not home. Your mother's explained all about this machine to me, and I know you can hear me, so answer the phone or—*Screeech*—

Beep—Hello, Kath. It's Tom. I just wanted to confirm stuff for the Easter break. Artie can drive down and get Daron on Thursday. Unless maybe we could put him on a bus. Give me a call. It'll be fine.

Beep—KathLeen, it's your mother. I'm at the hospital, and this is just a quick call to tell you JuLee's gone into the operating room. The doctors decided to do a Caesarean, but there shouldn't be any other problems. I'll call you when I have news. *Beep*—This is your mother. It's a boy. Seven pounds three ounces. JuLee is doing fine. She's in recovery. And your father and I are going down to see the baby in the window. *Beep*—Where are you? They're naming your little nephew Joseph Heber, after Merrill's father and grandfather. The baby's just adorable. I will call you in the morning.

Beep—Hi, Mom. Happy Easter! I know it's late, but we just got back from dinner. And I went with Artie to this huge comics store. It was way cool; they had all these back issues and stuff. I miss you. We're going to see this all-volunteer *Messiah* tomorrow for Easter. It sounds kind of boring, but Dad says I'll like it.

So anyway, I'll call and tell you. (Kath sat up to reach for the phone, but Zach's fingers were braided in the strap of her nightgown, and she fell back into the crook of his arm; the hair on his chest tingled on her shoulder. She heard her son speak in the next room, but she didn't answer. The maternal bond was disentangling, falling into a looser weave. She was happy. Daron was happy. But they were separate joys—far apart. She regretted sending Daron off by himself. She questioned her motivation: with Daron gone, Zach could stay over. And she feared that she had sacrificed her son for the sake of her love or lust—or whatever it was she had—for Zach. She cried—softly, to preserve Zach in his unstirring sleep.)

May: A Visitor

With her head buried under the sink, Kath doesn't hear the doorbell. She clears out the glass and plastic she has saved for recycling and sorts it into trash bags. Because she is working the evening shift and Daron is at school, she has the afternoon to herself. She went back to sleep after seeing Daron off, and when she woke up the second time and opened the drapes to the warm sun, it seemed like a good day for spring cleaning. She threw out her old cosmetics, the piles of magazines under the end table, and a dozen cheap wire hangers from the dry cleaner. Then she started on the kitchen.

When she pulls her head out to find a place in the sacks for the cache of green plastic mineral water bottles, she jumps at the loud, smashing thumps against the outside door. She finds her mother peering in the open front window with her mouth cupped to the screen. She shouts, Kath! Are you there? I can't see with this glare—What? Her mother looks down and screams, Oh!

I'm here, Mom, I'm here. Kath switches the deadbolt, and her mother steps out of the sand under the window onto the porch.

Her mother pants and kicks at the air with her open-toed sandals. Mom, what's wrong? What are you doing here?

A lizard, she puffs. I was looking in the window for you, and a lizard crawled over my shoe. She hands Kath her purse and a stack of *Ensign,* the LDS Church magazine. She stands on the carpet just inside the door, pulls off her sandals, and shakes them out over the threshold. Are you getting enough sleep, KathLeen? You look tired.

Why are you here? Did you . . . . ? Kath wants to ask if she has left her father again but doesn't dare.

These are all gritty. I'll just leave them out here. Her mother lines her sandals up neatly to the side of the door. She takes her things from Kath and walks to the couch on the squared-off toes of her nylons. That's a nice lamp. Is it new?

Mom.

It's nothing, Kath. Her mother sits on the couch and arranges the magazines on her lap. Carl's coming in from his mission today, and you know how I hate waiting at airports. And all those slot machines ringing! I have a headache just thinking about it. I had your father drop me off. I don't want to interrupt you; just carry on with what you're doing. I'll sit and catch up on my reading.

Mom!

Please, KathLeen, don't be so dramatic. This is just why I didn't call ahead. I didn't know whether I wanted to risk having you ruffle my feathers. Things have settled down at home, and it always seems that the sparks get to flying again when we're together.

Kath ignores the implication that she is the source of every family crisis; she will not argue with her mother. She lets her silence convey her irritation, although her mother is oblivious.

Kath isn't close to her brother. In the few letters he sent her during his mission, Carl exulted in his baptismal success stories and encouraged Kath to attend the Church more often. But the concern he expressed was conjectural. A current of embarrassed resentment at his intractable, lost sister cut through the letters as if this imperfection in his family were a blight on his service to God. Kath doesn't resent her brother's attitude—she wouldn't want his meticulous life—but it hurts and puzzles her that she was excluded from his homecoming. She wonders why. Because Uncle Doug received two years in prison? Because JuLee is married to Merrill instead of her? Because the Church has lost its grip on her? Kath doesn't know.

She looks down at her mother and adjusts the Alice band holding her hair back. Her mother is still breathing heavily from her scare with the lizard. She asks, Would you get me some water?

Kath edges her way through the clutter to the sink and fills a glass. When she returns to the front room, her mother is reading "A Message from Our Prophet" in the *Ensign*. She has dyed her gray hair black and is a different woman—younger, and even more composed and precise. Her mother looks up and follows the path of Kath's eyes. I did it last week, she says. I told Donna I was ready for a change, and she certainly gave me one.

Kath sits in the armchair across from the couch. Her mother looks at the rag and can of polish on the coffee table. You can keep on with your cleaning, she says. I don't mind.

I need a break anyway. Kath picks a dustball from the knee of her jeans and expects her mother to return to the Words of the Prophet. Instead, she describes Carl's college plans and how she has spruced up his room for his arrival. I'll move into JuLee's old bed now, she explains, although the mattress isn't as good.

Kath can't ask her why she isn't sleeping with her father. Instead, she decides to tell her about Zach, but the weight of her mother's imminent disapproval smothers her words. She doesn't speak.

Oh, her mother says with strained matter-of-factness, and the baby. Little Joey is doing fine. Baby Blue, we call him, because we've never seen him when he's not wearing something the same sky-blue shade as his eyes. Of course, we don't see much of him these days. Merrill likes JuLee to keep pretty much at home, as it should be for a new mother and her baby. And I suppose she doesn't need the commotion of us bustling in and out of there every five minutes.

JuLee's life is a subject that Kath has despaired of discussing with her mother. She had been unable to convince her mother to worry. Responsibility for JuLee's well-being has been lifted from her parents' house and placed in Merrill's hands as if, at her wedding, all of JuLee's worries were sponged away. But her mother tenses her lips with dissatisfaction at her own explanation of JuLee's household, and Kath sees that it is worth risking her mother's aggravation to pursue the subject. What she cannot tell her mother heightens the need to stress what she can. Look out for JuLee, Mom. For her sake, keep your eyes open.

See, KathLeen. Her mother closes her magazine and folds her arms across her waist. Here's an example of your mean-spiritedness. You've had these empty words ever since you left Merrill, but you just might consider that the fault in your marriage was with yourself—not him. A woman has never had a better provider. JuLee counts herself lucky.

All I'm saying is watch out for her. I think Merrill is . . . Merrill could be dangerous.

Why, Kath? Why? You say these things, and you've never given anyone any reason to believe you.

Kath wants to speak, to tell her; a hot point burns into the soft tissue under her tongue. But the silent years rise up to accuse her, memories melt into fear, and she cannot speak. To speak is to break the angel's seal upon her lips. To speak is to deny God's messenger, to deny the teachings of her Church, to deny life's plan, and she is not ready, not strong enough. She picks at the nubby fabric on the chair arm.

Because there's nothing to tell, is there, Kath? I think you're just a bitter woman, without a husband and without God.

And what about you? Kath mutters into her lap.

Her mother glares at her. She scoots to the edge of the couch to stand.

No, wait. I'm sorry, Mom, Kath says. She looks at the carpet between her shoes. I'm sorry.

You should be, her mother says, and unfolds the magazine to resume her pantomime of reading.

Summer, Again

Daron: 1

The white tufts billow slow down the sidewalk until they cross a slab wet from sprinklers and stick. All the puddles down Daron's side of the street are bearded with fringes of feathers. As he walks home to his father and Artie's house from the university, he treads straight through the water, and feathers adhere to the edges of his wet rubber soles, grafting tiny wings to his canvas deck shoes. He searches the passing yards for exploded pillows or molting birds, but sees only more feathers caught on blades of grass and blown into the cracks and corners of the houses.

For most of the two weeks he has been in Salt Lake to attend the Explore! program at the university, he has walked to class and back on a different route, and the street seems unfamiliar to him. When Daron spots the house, he runs to unlock the door and rushes in to the Phone Shrine to check the answering machine for messages from his father or Artie. He peers at the steady red light and, disappointed, cuts through the kitchen to the stairs to put his backpack away in his room.

The note from his father on the refrigerator says "Make a salad," and after he changes his clothes, he pulls a variety of vegetables in plastic bags from the crisper drawer and chops them into a bowl. He notices the difference between his behavior at home and in his father's house: if he were home, his mother would need to cajole him over the phone and probably browbeat him in person before he would take the time to make a salad. But in the crowded kitchen at the rear of La Casa Pequeña, he is willing to perform the task promptly. He cannot explain his attitude unless it stems from the novelty of living away from home or from his desire not to disappoint Tom and Artie. He wants them to view him as fully capable and independent; he never worries about what his mother thinks.

When he finishes the salad, he fits the bowl into the stuffed refrigerator and pours a root beer. He carries it out the front door and sits down on the stoop to read a photocopied packet about dinosaurs for tomorrow's class, resting his bare feet tenderly on the hot cement steps. "No one knows what color the dinosaurs were," he reads, and lifts his eyes from the page to picture pterodactyls as vibrant as butterflies.

Artie arrives home first, at the back door, with a pizza box; the men have an unquenchable appetite for pizza, but Daron has gotten bored with it. He fixes a peanut butter and jam sandwich and eats it before his father gets home. When his father steps through the front door, Artie pushes the papers and folders in Tom's hand onto the lap of the couch and hugs him, grunting—"Unnh." They kiss lightly on the lips, and for the first time, his father does not search warily over Artie's shoulder to discover if they have attracted Daron's attention.

His father encouraged Daron repeatedly to come to him with his confusions and concerns, but for Daron the situation seems simple: his father and Artie love each other, and their bond is real despite people's disapproval (his grandmother's, for one). He doesn't try to understand them in any bigger way; he doesn't know what he feels about queers. Boys at school called him names—faggot and queer—because he is small and quiet and the sole boy in his gifted class, and it hurt. He looked up "homosexuality" in reference books in the city library to discover whether it is hereditary (opinions were inconclusive, but tended to be doubtful). He doesn't use these names for his father and Artie, although Artie's QUEER AND PROUD button puzzles him, and he senses that, someday soon, he will need to figure things out.

At the table, they praise Daron's salad and divvy up the pizza. Daron begins the ritual of describing his day in detail—during the two weeks, he has watched rehearsals of a student production of *Androcles and the Lion,* studied the red shift and the cosmology of the universe, and, today, learned the classical principles of painting. Artie sits on the tall, red, ladder-backed chair that would normally stand ornamentally in a corner of the front room. Accommodations have been made—mismatching chairs, transforming a study, clearing out closet space—to squeeze Daron into the two-person household. They drink their usual beverages: his father swallows beer from a can, Artie rises and returns throughout every meal to polish off three or four glasses of tap water, while Daron works at a large, iced tumbler of lemonade. His father brings a can of grated Parmesan to the table to shake onto his slices, but Artie pulls the cheese and toppings in an oily slab from every other piece he eats (Artie worries about his weight).

Daron finishes his account of the triangulation of figures while he peels and eats the individual slices of pepperoni from his second piece of pizza—with his father on piece number three and Artie reaching the outer crust of his first denuded slice (piece number two). While Artie speculates about the Gunnery Girls and their place in art history, his father studies Daron seriously. "So anyway," he says, as if he has been speaking all along, "we've been talking about it and I think we can do it financially. God knows I owe it to you and your mom after all those years I did nothing for you. It would be a big deal, and we haven't worked out all the logistics yet, like maybe we'd find somewhere that was cheaper but bigger and—"

"Tom." Artie reaches out and butts the heel of his palm into Tom's shoulder. "Get to the point."

His father shoots an irritated glance at Artie, but before he can speak, the phone rings down the hall. Daron squeaks his chair from the table and jogs to get it. It is his mother. "Oh, hi, Mom."

"Hi, babe, what are you doing?"

"Just eating some pizza."

"I won't interrupt your dinner then. I just called to say I'm still in Las Vegas, 'cause I just found out I have to work tomorrow and Saturday. But I called your grandma, and if your father still wants to bring you down to Sterling tomorrow night, she said it's fine if you stay there a couple days. Would you tell your dad that, and he can call me if there's any problems."

"Okay."

"That'll get you halfway home. Then I'll drive up to Sterling on Sunday and be there by . . . " Her voice drifts away into the invisible room where she is calling, "Could you hand me that paper?" Daron hears Zach's voice, a low timbre in the throat of the telephone, then his mother returns. "I'm on the late shift, but I can be there by afternoon. So I'll see you then. Love you. Is everything okay?"

"Yeah, it's fine." He doesn't feel like talking and says goodbye quickly. As he returns the receiver to the Shrine, he watches the sunset burnish the windows of the house across the street. His mother told him that Zach would be staying with her in Las Vegas for a week, but the sound of Zach's voice in his house, in his absence, upsets him. Daron seldom considers that his mother's life continues when they are apart; if he imagines her at all, he pictures her sitting statically in some gray limbo, waiting for him to return. Zach's visit disturbs him not because he fears that a boyfriend will steal his mother's heart but because he must acknowledge that his mother talks, eats, thinks, and feels without him. He walks back to the table, obscurely angry.

He tells Tom and Artie that his mother won't be able to meet them in Sterling but he can stay at his grandparents' until Sunday. "I couldn't go Saturday," his father says, "but Artie could take you then if you'd rather."

"That's okay." He looks forward to spending Saturday with Cousin Berma, eating brownies, being spoiled.

Artie sticks the rest of the pizza in the microwave to reheat it, and his father explains the proposal, which Daron failed to understand before the phone rang. There is a very good private school in Salt Lake with some of its classes taught on the university campus. Jared Heflin, one of the supervisors of the Explore! class, called his father at work to say that he was very impressed with Daron's potential and that he thought he could get Daron into the private program in the fall if they wanted. Artie and his father seem thrilled with the idea: he could live with them during the school year, they would find a bigger place, money wouldn't be a problem. To please them, Daron wants to say, Sure, Yes, but he has learned to be cautious. His mother had been reluctant about the Explore! program and had tried to convince him that they could find something as worthwhile at home. She hadn't forbidden him to come, but it had made her uneasy. He knows that she will hate his father's new idea; she will not agree to it without a fight. And Daron doesn't know if he would want to be away from home so long. He tells Tom and Artie that he needs to think about it.

The next morning after roll call, the supervisors escort the class to the Natural History Museum. Daron stands with the class in a room of fossils—bones and plaster casts under anesthetizing layers of glass. A broad, flat panel of stone fills one wall; it is indented with the tracks of saurians, dead for infinity. While the professor explains how the shape, depth, and intermittent pattern of the footprints allow scientists to gauge the dinosaur's weight and balance and center of gravity in order to gain a picture of the creature's movement across the once-soft, ancient mud, Daron tries to imagine the color of its absent hide. There is no answer. He feels that any understanding he possesses will always be matched by the ungrasped, the unseen.

Kath: Kiss

Kath stands before the bathroom mirror and pops the cap from her lipstick. She has ten minutes to fix her lips, eyes, and hair before leaving for the casino. She has been alone for an hour since Zach left for California, and she is half glad to work, to get out of the vacant apartment. She needs to prepare for a weekend of stress and exhaustion. Jane Smirney is in the hospital with a kidney stone, and Kath is covering her Friday evening and Saturday graveyard shifts at the cashier window. On Sunday she is driving to Sterling to pick up Daron. She twists up the stick of color and studies her lips in the mirror. They have tingled since Zach kissed her good-bye, and she wonders if his kisses have actually changed their texture, robbed them of natural defenses, or if her lips are just remembering.

PRACTICE: JuLee sat with her legs pulled up on the coral pink shag of the toilet seat cover; she was in elementary school and had no opinion and very little interest in the subject of boys. Rhonda stood on the lavender plastic electric scale and scrunched her face with displeasure at the red numbers throbbing between her flaking silver toenails; Rhonda's attraction to junior high boys was preparatory, a dry run, a fire drill—not the real thing at all. Kath leaned against the marbleized pink Formica surrounding the sink; she was the only one who felt a physical tug of yearning at the turns of the conversation.

The three Miller Girls had gathered secretly in Aunt PearLeen's palatial bathroom to discuss the techniques of the kiss. Aunt PearLeen and Uncle Doug had separate bathrooms at opposite ends of the master suite. Aunt PearLeen's bath was vast, with a walk-in closet and a separate vanity table with a stool like a giant pink powder puff. Pinks and purples were everywhere, like a room from the Barbie Dream House expanded to human dimensions. With the door to the bedroom closed, they felt they were in an alternative, entirely feminine world. Here, surrounded by mirrors and transparent canisters of golfball-size bath soaps, they explored the mysteries of lip on lip. If she were asked for an honest opinion, JuLee would admit that she found the idea of pressing her mouth against a boy's—any boy's—disgusting and incomprehensible, but it made her feel sophisticated and adult to be included in the group; she kept silent. Rhonda was more cooperative.

Rhonda's curiosity focused on the mechanics: whether the lips were kept loose or puckered, whether saliva was exchanged, whether people's noses interfered, whether it was necessary to hold one's breath, and, most particularly, what it felt like. Rhonda had smuggled in her old life-size Barbie hair and makeup head, which stared—forgotten now—from the vanity. Kath had tied back the hair into a severe ponytail and painted on a mustache and bushy eyebrows with eyeliner. But the mouth was far too small and a brutal, hard plastic. Although she had never been kissed and did not yet spend her after-school hours spying on track and field practice from the bleachers, Kath knew what to expect from a boy's lips. They would be pliant but muscular, softly silky but tactilely alive. And they would be parted slightly to reveal a hint of white tooth and warm tongue underneath. Barbie, with her thin rigid grimace, could not provide a proper model.

The alternative she conceived was to use Rhonda's lips for the demonstration. When Kath suggested it, JuLee said, Eeeuuw, in the long whine of a kettle coming to boil. That's gross, she said. That's not nice. She hugged her knees closer on the toilet lid. No, Rhonda said, nice girls don't kiss. Rhonda smiled. She hoisted her butt onto the counter by the sink and exercised her mouth in preparation—stretching and compressing her lips. Kath was wearing a thick layer of Aunt PearLeen's Frosted Cherry lipstick to leave the proper smooch marks on Barbie, and she considerately blotted the excess with a folded sheet of toilet paper. She instructed Rhonda with an assumed (and imaginary) authority: tilt your head a little—no, the other way; close your eyes; okay, now don't pucker but keep your lips still; open them just a little; too much; okay, now let's say it's the end of the second date and this is the first kiss.

It was the first kiss. Kath moved closer, careful not to touch Rhonda with any part of her body, careful to align her head with a tilt opposite to Rhonda's own. She realized, as Rhonda's lips were in proximity, that she was acting the boy's part in this kiss— she had always assumed that the boy would steer himself toward her like a fighter plane while she waited, lips upraised, for the bomb to descend—and she doubted she would learn how a real kiss felt. Her lips glanced across Rhonda's, brushing membrane, and Rhonda's breath was hot with chocolate from the bag of chips she had been eating in the kitchen. Kath pressed with greater force, rolling Rhonda's lips under her own with a film of oil from the lipstick, and she felt her lips melting horribly—wonderfully—into Rhonda's until Rhonda giggled and opened her eyes and pulled back, wiping a slick of Frosted Cherry with the knuckle of her thumb. Kath was shocked; she had forgotten the game. She laughed to hide the confusion, but already, after the kiss, she knew that her dry, prolonged, nonsensual adolescence was over.

SERIOUS: When her father told the story of taking her mother to the Halloween dance, Kath wondered why he said their kiss in the dark of the spook alley was serious. For her, kisses were joyful and arousing; she had begun to seek them out from boys at school, and they never failed to spark her with excitement.

One night early in the Wild Summer with Tom—before sex and Tom's tears began—she returned at sunrise, exhilarated, to her parents' house after a night drive in Tom's pickup. As she nudged the bathroom screen from its track, she noticed the camper and truck parked on the cement slab at the side of the house. She was surprised that her father was home; he had put his gun out by the kitchen door in the morning and left to go hunting after work. She climbed through the window, lowered herself gently to the rim of the tub, and replaced the screen. She slipped down the hall with noiseless confidence. Her nightly disappearance had become routine, and she no longer expected to encounter anyone awake in the familiar dark. She was startled by a dim light from the kitchen, which crossed the hall threshold and left a faint yellow square on the opposite wall. Touching the wood trim around the doorway, she paused in shadow before cutting through the light. Her parents stood near the sink, illuminated by the bulb in the range hood. He was dressed in a green plaid shirt and overalls with his cap pulled low on his brow. She had tugged on her robe, unzipped, with her feet bare and white and plump on the linoleum. He bent his head down with one ear curled toward his shoulder. She raised her hand to the exposed curve of his neck but failed to rest it there. Don, she said in a whisper, it will be all right. It will be all right. She kissed him on the cheek.

Kath remembers this kiss as viscerally as one of her own. Her mother's lips, greased with a moisturizing ointment, brushed against coarse stubble in the slack skin beneath his cheekbone. The kiss was intended to reassure her father, to bolster him against his mute anguish. But Kath knew that her mother had no illusions that the kiss would succeed. As Kath dived past the light toward the safety of her bedroom, her mother stepped away, and Kath saw the dab of ointment that marked her father's cheek with cold solemnity.

WILD: The sky was a deep dish of baked-enamel indigo with hard stars beaded on the gloss. The corrugated truckbed poked its ridges at her shoulderblades, and Tom's rolled-up Levi's jacket scratched at her neck as she watched the early dark deepen. Tom slid down from the open tailgate to take a piss, and she heard the six-pack of Stroh's pour from him and patter on the dry ground somewhere to the left. It embarrassed and excited her to hear it, and she concentrated on the sharp sure line of the belt of Orion. They had pulled far off the road, and the desert spread around the truck—unseen beyond the walls of the bed. She floated; she felt the sky surround her.

Tom bounded into the bed; his boots drummed metal, and the truck bounced on its shocks. He knelt at her side, and she reached out for his bare shoulders. She asked, Aren't you cold? He grunted and nuzzled her neck—You'll keep me warm. Tom's kisses were indecorous, impolite, unhinged. She imagined a palette of flavors: sour of puckers; sweet of wet, open lips; saline of tongue; and bitter suction. His tonguetip grazed the rim of her jaw, batted the silver hoop in her earlobe, and slipped inside her ear. He ate her cheek in tiny bites and swallowed her lips; she clenched her hands and weighted them against his back. His tongue, undulant, muscled everywhere: under her lips across the face of her teeth, into the slick tender pools under her tongue—tickling the frenum, then venturing out to flick into stunned nostrils, lapping and lathering until her face was damp and quivering with chill between his hot breaths. His tongue played with hers—his mouth plastered across her mouth—as he unzipped her jeans and slithered fingers down. She watched the dark shape of Tom's head fill the night; his eyes always sealed when he caressed her. Open your eyes, she thought. It was too dark to see, but she wanted him to look for her. Unable to speak, she repeated, Open your eyes, open your eyes.

MARITAL: Merrill prayed in earnest with his voice rising in and out of intelligibility, his head bowed, and his hands spread in a butterfly—thumbs touching—from hip to hip across her pelvic girdle. She reclined at the edge of the bed in her robe while he knelt on the floor between her dangling legs. And we thank You,

Heavenly Father, Merrill said, for the procreative organs which allow us to be fruitful and multiply. We thank You for the pure desires of the married state which . . .

She stared at the light fixture over the bed: a star flattened against the cottage cheese spackle, made of complicated milky, bubbly glass. She was grateful to Merrill—Daron had a father; she had a husband. God had given her this grace; she did not deserve it, and she would not forget it. She followed a spider's glinting thread from one point of the unlit star to the corner above the nightstand. She listened for Daron's rasping breath—he had a bad cold—from the sofa bed in the front room, around and beyond Merrill's blessing. The refrigerator rumbled to life.

In the name of Jesus Christ, he said, amen. He lifted his hands, and one side of her robe slid open. Cool air bathed her leg. She lifted her head to discover if Merrill was finished and she could get up. She saw her thigh, gray and sodden heavy in the blue light from the bathroom. Merrill bent to kiss the flesh, then raised his head, unsmiling. He stood and unzipped his jeans. Get into bed, Kath, he said. She dropped her robe to the floor and peeled back the covers, exposing a pattern of seashells in the drowned sea of the sheets.

PERFECT: She digs the applicator brush into the nearly empty tube and wishes she had saved her old mascaras when she cleaned the bathroom. As she leans over the sink to study her lashes, she wonders if Daron and Tom are on the freeway to Sterling. Her mother sounded strained and weary on the phone, and she hopes it will be okay for Daron to be there.

He kisses her lightly at the nape of her neck. She spins and drops the mascara. The door was unlocked, he says. Zach stands in the doorway with his bag slung over one arm. I was cruising down the freeway, he says, almost to Whiskey Pete's. Then I thought, How can I leave this woman? So I'm going to stay until Sunday. Assuming, I mean, that's okay with you?

She nods, and nods, and glances over the edge of the vanity for the lost mascara brush—but forget it. She lunges for his lips.

Daron: 2

Berma lays out her spread for double solitaire, snapping each card from the deck into successive piles on the red plastic table-cloth. "Do you remember this room?" she asks. Daron stops shuffling to examine the gray Formica counter in the kitchen; nothing stirs. For him, the whole apartment is an anonymous motel room where Berma's few possessions sit isolated like showroom exhibits. He has been told that he lived in the apartment for several years, but the rooms left no impression. "I was too little, I guess," he says.

The apartment—with its whiteness, and grayness, and stark light from fixtures on the ceiling—has become Berma's home. Aunt Ina named her son-in-law, Joe Nelson, executor of her estate, and Joe and Clovis thought that the place next door had too many rooms for one old lady to knock around in. Joe shifted Berma's things to the apartment over the Nelson garage, and the newlyweds, Aunt JuLee and Skunk—and now Baby Joey, Baby Blue—moved into Aunt Ina's house. It seems unjust to Daron, but Berma shows no signs of sorrow or rancor, although she has made no effort to decorate her new rooms.

Berma had baked brownies in anticipation of his arrival, and when his Uncle Carl drove him over around noon, she was waiting in front of the garage, delighted to see him. She is the only person in Sterling who hasn't treated him as an interruption in their routine.

When Artie parked the car at the back gate of his grandparents' house, it was nearly midnight, and the porch light over the stoop spread feebly across the yard. Madame barked, bounding at the end of her chain, as his father lifted his luggage from the hatchback. A hand shifted the curtain in the window near the door, then vanished. His father grabbed the suitcases and walked with him to the back stoop, dodging Madame's scrabbling claws and swooshing feather-duster tail. They found his grandmother waiting, peeking from a narrow opening in the door. She opened it further to acknowledge them, but she didn't speak; she would not allow even the slightest pleasantry to slip from herself to his father. The silence infected Tom; he hugged Daron to his side and squeezed his shoulder, wordlessly, before jogging down the walk to the car to begin their long trip back to Salt Lake. His grandmother pulled the larger of the cases through the door. He followed her into the kitchen with the other.

"You're late," she said. She slipped her hands into the pockets of her bathrobe and looked at the clock on the stove. "If they knew they wouldn't get here until the middle of the night, I don't know why they didn't just tell me so I wouldn't fret. Do you need something to eat?"

He was hungry—vaguely—but he shook his head.

"Then let's get you to bed." She dragged the suitcase behind her past the door to the front room, where a television mumbled at low volume. "Daron's here." She spoke to the dark head resting on the arm of the couch. The head twisted its face toward the door and said, "Hey," before returning its attention to the talk show. Daron had met his Uncle Carl briefly once before, when he came to Las Vegas for a scouting event, and, like JuLee, Carl made him feel both freakish and invisible.

His grandmother flicked on the hall light. "I'm sorry your grandpa isn't here to greet you. He keeps his gun out all the time now, and there's no telling when he's going to head out. I expect he'll be back tomorrow afternoon."

His grandfather, when he was home, slept in the master bedroom; his grandmother had settled into his mother's old room. They had set up a cot for him under Uncle Carl's window. He had napped during the unexciting ride through the center of Utah;

he wasn't tired, but, after he tugged on his pajamas and brushed his teeth, his grandmother told him good night and shut off the lights in the bedroom and the hall. From the edge of the cot he reached down to black shapes on the floor, for the suitcase and the pocket with his personal stereo. He slipped the band of the speakers over his head and drifted into the wash of the music. When he woke up the cassette had ended, but he heard a thick, wet rhythm in the darkness. In the bed, his uncle panted to the creak of the box springs.

Daron rolled over to face the wall, lit by partial moonlight seeping down from the folds of the curtain. The stereo slipped from the blanket and clattered.

"Daron," his uncle whispered, "I'm sorry. I'm sorry. I thought you were asleep. I'm sorry." Fully awake, Daron rolled onto his back. He heard Carl shift on the mattress. When Carl rose from the bed, Daron saw his back and buttocks, blue and dim in the middle of the room. His uncle pulled his sweatpants up from his knees and quietly opened the door to the hall. Daron listened for the toilet flush and pretended to sleep. He lay very still when Carl returned to his bed.

At breakfast with his grandmother, Daron asked to be taken to visit Berma. He had never made a request or a demand in his grandparents' house. When he had visited with his mother, he read his books and listened to music and remained as unobtrusive as possible. But, on his own, he felt trapped and spoke up to rescue himself. His grandmother responded with a surprised "Oh. Yes. Of course."

Uncle Carl drove Daron over on his way to the wardhouse for basketball practice. Carl didn't speak until Daron got out of the car at the Nelsons'. "Call when you want to come home. See ya." When Daron slammed the door, his uncle plunged the car into reverse and sped out of the driveway, ignoring Berma, who waved to him from the front of the garage.

She hugged Daron to her side when he reached the garage. "Hello to you too, Carl." She grinned and led Daron around the walk to the rear. "Has your uncle been moody? Some of them get like that. They get back from their missions, and they don't feel special anymore. Their families don't treat them any different, don't see that they've changed, grown up."

"I don't think he likes me. You're the only one who cares."

"Oh, hush," she said.

Daron wins the second round of solitaire and gathers his cards together while Berma gets up to switch on the radio. For Christmas the Nelson family gave her a massive boom box with numerous silver knobs, buttons, and slides; it reminds Daron of the front grille of a car, with speakers instead of headlights. The equipment is more than adequate to provide Berma with her daily dose of talk radio. The voices thunder and bounce around the apartment until Berma adjusts the volume.

". . . 'at's right, Lyle. I should never argue with the man who has his finger on the off button—ha, ha—Hello, America! I'm Dr. Sheila Maytag, it's Saturday afternoon, and I'm here to answer your questions. Before I take your calls, I'd like to address something I'm hearing a lot about lately. When people talk about breast surgery . . ."

"What would you like to do today?" Berma carries the crumb-speckled brownie tray, the sandwich plates, and the milk glasses to the sink. As she rinses the dishes under the tap, the sun from the window catches in her hair. Last summer her hair had looked like spun golden sugar, but her new, tighter curls are crisp redwood shavings. She looks both younger and older. Without the dazzle of her beehive to distract him, he notices the liver spots, unmoved by the clear water cascading over the backs of her hands.

He doesn't know what he wants to do; he is disappointed that she asked the question and interrupted the quiet excitement of their lunch together. He waits for her to make a suggestion. "What we ought to do is take you next door to see your cousin. It would be a shame if you didn't get to see Baby Blue while he's still so small and darling."

"Does he really wear blue all the time?" The idea of the visit does not appeal to him at all.

"Yes—well, every time I've seen him. Your aunt loves to dress him up and show him off like he was a perfect little dolly." Berma turns from the sink with a look of concern and corrects herself. "I don't mean to say JuLee's not a good mother. She's just in a swoon about how adorable Joey is. And Merrill, the way he dotes on that child! Two Sundays back I stopped over in the yard when they got back from church. JuLee had the baby in a basket sleeper, and we were just talking about this and that when we noticed the doves—two of them—white doves on the picnic table, right near the basket. You don't see doves in Sterling. And Merrill was in high heaven. He said, You saw that! He brought the doves down to him! My son brought the doves right down from the sky. Merrill was so happy. He treasures that boy. You can't help but love a little baby."

"How come you didn't have kids?"

A hole opens out in their conversation, and in the hollow Berma stares into the backyard, searching. His question sinks deeper than he intended; he feels rude and stupid; he wants to withdraw his words from the air. "I believe God makes everybody the way they are for a reason, Daron. Since I wasn't blessed with children, it must be that I was put here for something else." He wants to ask what reason, but he doesn't. "We should get going," she says brightly. "Only I hope it will be okay. JuLee's been feeling a bit poorly lately, and Merrill hasn't wanted her rest interrupted. I know for a fact she hasn't been out of the house in over a week. I've kept an eye out for her. I'm an old snoop." Berma laughs. "Let me put on my shoes."

He waits in the kitchen until Berma returns in her tennis shoes. She fixes a platter of brownies, frosted sugar cookies, and round butter cookies smothered in powdered sugar, then covers them with a tent of foil. "Let's go."

He follows her down the steep flight of stairs onto the deep, lush lawn. At the end of the yard, before the dusty mounds of the gully, a vegetable garden edged with flower beds bakes green in the bright sun. A bed of yellow roses circles a tree in the corner; the dark bushes are dense with buds as large as Christmas bulbs and blown flowers like piles of lemon confetti cupped in invisible palms. He wonders if these are the bushes that caused his mother's aversion to roses. On Valentine's Day, Zach Cooper sent a her a dozen roses of mixed red and yellow. She took them to their neighbor Mrs. Killan, who nestled them in the crook of her elbow like Miss America while holding her dog Bashful to her chest with her hands. Mrs. Killan was thrilled but puzzled; his mother explained, "It's the thought. I love the thought behind them. But I don't want to look at them. I just don't like them." The Nelson garden is a profusion of roses, and he guesses that she wants to forget them but can't.

Berma's sister, Clovis, stands at the sliding glass door of the downstairs house with the phone cradled against her shoulder as they walk the length of the yard. She waves at them; he waves back and hopes that they won't need to visit the Nelsons as well. As they near the ditch, the grass thins, and a path of overtrampling is discernible, leading to the plank over the irrigation ditch. He watches Berma cross the drooping board before attempting it himself. He looks down into the ditch lined with wet gray mud. The ditch bends around the rear of Aunt Ina's old yard in one direction and in the other disappears into a corrugated tin pipe that snakes under the asphalt. Farther off, he can see the furrow reappear at the perimeter of a gray-green apple orchard on the other side of the road.

The splintered plank shudders under him with each step, and he bounces off the far end with a boost of energy. Halfway to the back door of the neatly painted white house, Berma looks around for him, and he runs to catch up with her. A swamp cooler mounted in one of the upstairs windows chugs quietly; the pale green garden hose, which hangs from the cooler to provide water, drips from its coupling onto the patio slab. The curtains are drawn in all the windows of the house; in the kitchen, the sill shelves of small houseplants are isolated from the inside by a dropped roller blind. In the room at the head of the stairs where

Aunt Ina had dozed in her bed, a pattern of blue and green clowns glimmers reversed through the fabric of the unlined curtains.

"Hey! Where are you going!"

Berma jolts at the fierce shout, and a few cookies slide from the platter, trailing plumes of powdered sugar. Skunk rises from a hole in the lawn at the corner of the house with a pipe wrench slung in his hand. He jogs toward them in a heavy shuffle. "You can't visit. Not today, Berma." He dumps the wrench on the picnic table and stands between Berma and the door. Daron stops farther back, at the corner of the patio.

"Is JuLee still under the weather? I'm sorry. I just wanted Daron to see his cousin."

"Daron?" Skunk notices him for the first time. Skunk holds his forearm level with his forehead to shield his eyes from the sun. "What a blessing." He strides past Berma, and his dripping workboots leave horseshoes of mud on the slab. "How long are you home for, son?" He extends his arm to shake Daron's hand.

Daron jerks back; his feet drag on the close-clipped grass. He doesn't want to be touched. "I'm not home," he says. He stalks away, over the ditch, and sits at the top of Berma's stairs.

He watches Berma leave the platter on the table and creep over the quivering plank. Skunk stares at Daron across the ditch, with his thumbs hooked in the pockets of his jeans.

Kath: Angels

Kath is sleeping. She drifts off after the graveyard shift, after setting an early alarm. She stirs when the heavy Sunday paper hits the front door with a definite thud, then subsides. She dreams—something about cars, something about windows. She feels Zach's hand come to rest on her stomach—his thumb curling into her navel—then her body forgets the heaviness, forgets his hand is different from her. She is sleeping.

Angels eat clouds for breakfast. They swim in the ether. They guard the pearly gates. They dance on the head of a pin (or do so hypothetically, incalculably). They are infinitesimal. They embrace the earth with milky arms from horizon to horizon—from sundown to sunrise. They have glistening raiments. They have golden locks. They have downy wings. They ride in silver chariots. They are wheels within wheels. They are the spirits of dead children. They are older than time. They are not human. They are not made in God's image. They are reflections of God—refractions of His Will. They are Love. They are Truth. They are Fate. They are Calls to Action. They are sunbeams. They are falling stars. They are nine orders: angels, archangels, principalities, powers, virtues, dominions, thrones, cherubim, and seraphim (Kath memorized these from a dictionary as a child.) They are harbingers—glistening and whispering in the night. They are messengers—radiant with light, opening and opening like a new sun, like a new day.

When an infant sleeps, with his cheek nestled in his hands, his parents mutter, What an angel. When a mother asks her son to perform some small task, she says, Be an angel. When a lover presses her lover's chest to her own, she shouts, You are my angel!

Morning sprays pick-up sticks on the floor from the half-closed blinds. Zach is stroking her thigh, cupping and releasing her breasts, smoothing her arms, knuckle-brushing her neck. Mmmmmm, she says. Mmmmmm, like a sleepy kitten. She reaches for the clock to read its numbers, but Zach snatches her hand from the air and lands it at her side. He dips into the golden mound of jewelry on the nightstand and uncoils a shivering chain. The ankh flies, with round hollow head and outstretched arms, on a shaft of errant sun escaping around the blinds—angel on a string. The angel soars, then rests his cold golden body in the soft between her breasts. He spirals down to her open mouth, lighting on her lips, then dips in to be wetted. Zach closes his mouth over hers, and the angel frisks between their tongues.

When she was very young, she sat in her mother's lap in the wardhouse basement to watch a movie. The projector said *br-r-r-r-r-r-r-r*, the pictures flew over her head on a flickering beam, the cinderblock room was cool; she lulled, she lolled her head, and, near sleep, she saw the angels on the screen. They wore long, reflective robes full of drapes and folds—like the ceramic angel wired to the rafters of the Christmas manger. But they were children. They cried and wrung their fists against their eyes. They huddled in the mists of the preexistence. If their parents didn't want them, they would never be born. Her mother was pregnant—if they were both very still, Kath could feel the infant-motion in her mother's lap—and she prayed that one of the sad, sad angels would come to earth and roost inside her.

The angel tugs from her mouth and glistens wet in midair. He skates over her stomach, tickling, raking his path into gooseflesh. He dives into her navel, buries himself in slack chain, then slithers below through curling snares of hair. Zach presses his thumb to guide the angel gently in. She expects it to hurt her; it doesn't.

When Merrill first told her, she was quietly skeptical. When she thought of them—angels—she imagined them elaborately costumed and coiffed, radiating a delicate amber aura in the sky over ancient Israel; or hovering cool and white among the deep green leaves of Joseph Smith's forest grove. Merrill reminded her of the precedents for southern Utah. In the St. George temple, President Heber J. Grant had received a visit from the spirits of the Founding Fathers—George Washington among them—who revealed to him the divine inspiration of the American Constitution. On the map of the spirit, Sterling was equal to any place on earth. And Merrill believed he was as worthy as any man—more worthy than most. He had been chosen. He didn't describe the angel; she didn't ask. Its visits left her apprehensive; after Merrill spoke with it, he would toss all night in the bed and wake her and Daron at dawn to pray and pray at white heat.

Before she saw it in the tree, she smelled it. She was scouring burnt stew from a crockpot with a steel wool pad, and the scent arrested all motion in her body. The fragrance was citrus—not lemon, not orange—a cutting acidic perfume. What's that? she asked. Merrill sat before a spread of newspapers on the table, cleaning his rifles. Hmmm? He glanced up, irritated at the interruption, and his eyes fixed out the open door. It's Him, he said. He ran down to the lawn. She followed. It was all presence, without form; it had no face. It was all brightness, without light—white fire at the bottom of a lake. She expected the tree to burn and the leaves to shrivel into soot. But twigs and branches spread out, untouched, around it. She watched it cry, and its tears were hard, luminous diamonds that fell and sparked among the yellow roses. If it was any single thing, it was immense sorrow, unquenchable anguish. Merrill knelt and wailed in the wet grass. She ran inside, away from its pain. Often, she wants to delete the memory. She erases details: its scent, its lack of color, its tears—everything can be negated but its effect. And if it changed her, she cannot deny it.

The alarm buzzes, and Zach stretches to punch the off button. Damn, he says. Can I steal some more time from you? Zach eases the chain, and the angel swims free, bathed in her. Zach tastes the angel at his lips.

Daron: 3

Daron turned down the offer to go to church—at first politely, then with a definite refusal. He remembered the dreadful Sister Sillitoe and the fragments of the Articles of Faith that he can't erase from his head.

His grandmother responded with exasperation: "You are getting out of hand, young man. I don't know what your mother's going to do with you."

When he wakes up Sunday morning and wanders into the kitchen, his grandmother is gathering the breakfast dishes. His uncle and grandfather have left for their priesthood meeting, and she is hurrying to get ready for Sunday school. He might never see his grandfather at all; aside from his breakfast plate, the chief evidence of his return from the mountains is the corner of the camper visible through the window, and his rifle, gear bag, and hunting boots standing on a rectangle of newspaper by the back door. His grandmother doesn't seem angry at her husband's long absence; instead, she rushes to get to the wardhouse in time to walk into the meeting room with him. Yet they don't sleep in the same room, and Daron senses some make-believe at work.

"So, what *are* you going to do with your day?" she asks as she slips a slate-gray jacket over a fuchsia silk blouse.

Daron remilks his bowl of cornflakes. "Go to Berma's maybe. I don't know."

"You'll have to walk then. There won't be anyone around to chauffeur you today." She says good-bye and leaves for the garage, but returns to add an instruction: "If you go out, anywhere but in the yard, lock the door."

When she leaves, and the car has disappeared down the road, and Madame has stopped barking, the house is becalmed. He puts his dishes in the dishwasher and goes out onto the lawn to play with Madame, but she has stretched to sleep in the shade, her spine lodged against the cool foundation of the house. He grows bored sitting on the stoop examining the processions of ants on the sidewalk. The books he brought are difficult and too serious (most of them were bought with his father and Artie, and he didn't want to disappoint them by seeming lightweight). He fiddles with the remote control of the television for a few minutes, then decides to walk to Berma's.

He considers the advantages of traveling incognito along the post office road, which curves by the blackened chimney of the leveled Traveler's Haven lodge and into the hills. But Main Street is equally deserted with everyone at the wardhouse, and the chance of encountering anyone he would have to talk to is relatively small.

He locks the door and addresses Madame's sleeping face to

say that he is leaving. He walks along the hard-packed dirt behind the house until it joins the paved drive, then along the road until it feeds into Main Street. He never strays from the asphalt, except for twice when a car approaches and he continues forward on the shoulder. Small brown birds peck at the uneven border of grass; larger birds sit in clusters of three and four on the overarching arms of the streetlights. He stares into the dark windows of the shops, and dares to cross against the light at the three major intersections. He sees a young man washing his car in a tanktop and cutoffs, and sidesteps a little girl squatting over her toy xylophone on the sidewalk. No one else appears on the street. The doors of the garage at the Nelson house lie open, and the stalls are empty. He bends to watch giant bumblebees dock like heavy zeppelins in the hearts of the daisies at the side of the garage.

When he climbs the stairs, Berma's door is open. He steps into the sudden shade prepared to shout hello and sees her bent down to pull on her shoes. She looks up and smiles. "Oh, Daron, you're just in time. I'm just on my way next door. I saw Merrill pull out in his truck early this morning. And I'm sure your aunt would be happy for the company."

Daron kneels on the kitchen floor and pulls at the sticky bits of weed caught in the mesh of his shoelaces, which had dragged along, untied, through the dirt.

"We won't stay long. Just peek our heads in and see if she needs anything."

Even if the truck has reached the California state line, he doesn't want to go back to Skunk's house, but he can't think of an excuse to stay behind. He is certain that Berma thought he was rude to run from Skunk's handshake, and he doesn't want her to think he has gotten out of hand.

He acquiesces and waits for Berma on the landing outside the open door. A hot gust stirs the trees and lifts dust from the hilltops. Berma rummages in a pocket of her purse and extracts a silky scarf with gold paisley worms backed by dusty rose. She folds the scarf into a triangle and ties it loosely over her hair before descending the stairs. They walk side by side across the lawn; then Daron rushes ahead to the plank. The ditch is alive with opaque brown water; it sucks and gurgles between the narrow banks, then hisses into the pipe under the road. As he hunts for a stick to drop into the flow, Berma passes him and cautiously teeters over the board. He rests a possible twig on the grass for later use and catches up with her at Skunk's back door.

Berma knocks and knocks again. She cranes her head to look up the face of the house; the scarf slips back from her tight shining curls. "JuLee! Hello? JuLee?" she calls. But downstairs the shutters are closed; upstairs the windows are shut and the curtains seamlessly sealed. The fan churns in the swamp cooler, and threads of water snake along the hanging hose and patter on the patio, wet brown from white dust.

Daron tries the knob, and it turns in his hand. "It's open."

Berma steps onto the coiled hemp mat before the door. "Should we? I don't see why not." She flashes out of the sun into the dark house. He hears a metallic clank above, but when he looks, the second-story windows reveal nothing, and sun bakes on the shingles of the sloped roof.

Inside, before his eyes adjust, detail vanishes into slumped shapes, gradations of brown shadow. On the kitchen counter, light from the door ignites the crumpled foil on yesterday's platter of cookies; his vision circles around the sheet of flame. Berma navigates the familiar house—her house—instinctively attuned to the delicate shifts of direction and balance necessary to slip through the dark rooms unhindered. Daron trails after, his senses heightened to avoid the trip of a floor runner underfoot, the sharp bump of a table edge. "JuLee? JuLee, are you upstairs? It's Cousin Berma. I've brought Daron to see you." Berma pauses at the foot of the stairs with her hand on the polished railing. Yellow light, indirect and attenuated, bends down the stairwell and mists her upturned face. "Let's go up."

All the doors on the second floor are shut tight except for one at the end of the hall; yellow slivers from the open crack. Berma pushes; the crack becomes a gap. Daron tenses behind her, expecting the light to rush like a flood surge after the long darkness. He sees his aunt curled on the bed in the bright circle of the nightstand lamp.

JuLee lies on her left side, above the patchwork quilt, with her legs tucked to her chest inside the circle of her arms. She wears a peach tricot nightgown, under it a pair of faded jeans, over it a man's black-and-red-checked robe. Her eyes are open, but they stare unfocused at the wall.

"We just stopped in to see how you were feeling. Are you all right, dear?"

"Fine."

Berma hesitates before entering the room. "Is it the flu, do you think? Can I get you anything?"

"No." JuLee frees a hand from the embrace of her knees and rubs her nose. "How did you get in? Where's Merrill?"

"Where? Didn't he leave in his truck this morning?"

"He left?"

"Yes, I think so, dear. Didn't he tell you?"

"No."

Berma looks up from the back of JuLee's head with a flustered glance at Daron. He remains in the hall, in the half-light. Chill air rolls out of the room from the cooler behind the curtained window; he folds his bare arms over his chest.

"Have you put Joey down for his nap?"

"What?"

"The baby, is he sleeping?"

"Mmm."

"Do you mind if we look in? We won't wake him. I'd like Daron to see his cousin."

"Oh."

"You're sure there's nothing I can do for you, honey? Did you see the brownies I brought for you yesterday?"

"Where?"

"In the kitchen."

"Oh, I don't go downstairs anymore." Her voice grows small, like a heartbeat echoing from the chambers of a seashell. She tightens her hold on her knees, hiding her legs in the tent of the robe.

"We'll just take a quick look." Berma reaches down to touch JuLee lightly on the shoulder. As she meets Daron in the hall, Berma pulls off her headscarf, which has slipped to encircle her neck. "Oh dear," she murmurs to herself, or to Daron; he can't be sure.

The green and blue clowns smile and wave on the walls and curtains when Berma opens the nursery door. Because the drapes are thin, the room is filled with gauzy, expectant light. Aunt Ina's narrow bed and its companion have been replaced by a bassinet under the window and by a rocking chair. The changing table that stored Aunt Ina's things nestles in the corner. Berma turns around to whisper, "It looks like a nursery again."

From his vantage in an empty stretch of the hall, Daron can see JuLee stretch her legs and roll onto her back in one room, and he can see Berma tiptoe to the bassinet with her scarf draped over her fingers in the other. Both scenes make him uncomfortable. He leans back to scrape his fingertips on the sandpaper surface of the old wallpaper. JuLee sits on the edge of the bed with her head slung forward as if her vertebrae have snapped. Berma lifts the hem of a quilted powder-blue coverlet from inside the cradle. Daron listens: he hears the cooler in the bedroom, the refrigerator downstairs. JuLee pounds loose fists rhythmically against the bedspread between her thighs. "Fuckfuckfuckfuckfuck . . . ," she mutters without inflection. Berma moves away from the bassinet, incrementally, like a film reversing one frame at a time. She sits heavily in the rocker, and it swings under her, scooping her feet off the floor. "Oh my!" She gasps and looks out into the hall. "Daron."

He rushes in to help her but skids on a pile of wet brown on the rag rug. He thinks of reeking foul diapers and reaches up to squeeze his nose shut. Blades of grass and tiny pebbles are smeared on the sole of his sneaker.

"The mud." JuLee fills the door; her hands grasp the doorjamb on either side of her head. "Sorry. Merrill was in here with his boots on. He'd been fixing the plumbing."

"JuLee . . . " The scarf trembles in Berma's palm as if a mouse wriggles in a trap of cloth.

Daron faces the bassinet. The baby's chin points up. His eyelids furrow, retracted, over white eyes. His tongue swells from thin lips like a black slug. His cheeks are mottled—baby pink and eggplant dark and pus yellow. Above the rumpled coverlet, his hands curl on the chest of his blue terry romper.

"He wanted to put my baby in the ground last night. But I wouldn't hear Joey cry if he was way out there."

Berma leans forward in the chair but cannot escape the backward rocking. "We've got to . . . you poor girl."

JuLee grabs Daron by the shoulders; her fingers dig deep into muscle. "It should have been you. He told me that. He told me it should have been you." She pushes him until his hips brush the bassinet. "Cousin Berma says you want to see. Do you want to see?" JuLee reaches around him into the bed, and he struggles to free his body from the fierce vise of her arms. She hooks two fingers under the neck of the loose romper and peels it gently off the baby's shoulders and down. Instead of a chest—soft and round with small pink nipples—there is a hole, immense and crusted black. Daron screams; he hears his short howl rise from a distance as if a proxy screams for him. He kicks JuLee viciously in the shins until she relents and frees him. He runs, half-falling, to the door. "I wash and wash and wash him. And it just keeps . . . what's the word . . . seeping? Seeping. Seeping, seeping, seeping."

Berma recovers herself and scoots slowly from the rocker seat. "Daron, I think you should wait for me outside." But he doesn't need encouragement. He flies through the dark, down stairs, around corners, rattling cups in the china hutch; he gropes for the doorknob and leaps out, scraping and tumbling into the grass beyond the patio.

He hears a crash and looks up in time to see the rod and the clown-spotted curtains tumble from the window. His aunt's pale, rather pudgy, dimpled hands claw under the sash and thrust the window up. "Fucker. Fuckhead. Fucker. Fucker. Fuck." She speaks in a loud, neutral voice—each word like a square of machine-drilled metal falling into a bin. "Fuck. Fuck. Fucker. Fuck." He hears Berma's voice in a low rumble underneath.

JuLee rests a blue bundle on the window ledge, then shoves it over. He jumps up to catch it—if it's the baby—but he cannot reach it in time. The bundle touches down softly on the concrete. He digs his hand into the pile of clothing: blue rompers, blue bubbles, navy-blue pajamas, whisper-blue nightgowns. "He wants 'em out, I'll put 'em out." JuLee pushes the mouth of the diaper pail into the opening. Berma's hands grasp her elbows, but his aunt shrugs and bats them away. The contents of the pail drift down in a slow fall. More baby clothes. He lifts one with dark spots on the front and back. The stains grow in succession. A final nightgown drops, blackened and stiff. JuLee reaches inside to tug out tightly stuffed sheets, splattered, sodden, with blood. She hurls them in a wad over Daron's head. In a fury, drawers of booties, diapers, and baby blankets pour from the window.

Then nothing. The window empties. JuLee cries, out of sight, a punctuation to Berma's soothing coo.

Daron looks around at the summer Sunday. The same unused streets and the shells of houses. The same scarves of dust hanging over the hills, where the breeze has raised, then abandoned them. Fat bees combing the hibiscus stamens. Flies proclaiming their screed of slow buzzing. The irrigation water rippling with a raw scent of earth and manure. It is hot and will be hotter—the day's peak is ahead—and distant objects seem to waver under screens of mirage. Nothing has changed; nothing is the same.

He sorts the clothing into two piles: the soiled and the clean, the innocent and the guilty. The police—there will be police, he is certain—will view the spatters and stains as evidence. They will squeeze liquid into petri dishes; they will finger the holes in the sheets. With his foot, he slides the marked pile into the protective shade of the house; it leaves a faint, blackened-red streak on the cement.

Berma leans from the window next to the cooler in JuLee's bedroom. "Daron, I think you should wait at my place. I've got her settled in and—"

"What happened?"

"She . . . she couldn't tell me. That's why she was upset. I asked her, and she . . . So I think you should wait at home. I'll come along soon, when we . . . when I figure out what to do." Berma jerks her head inside and slams down the sash.

Daron gathers the other clothes and searches for a clean place to put them. He walks toward the chairswing, then changes his mind and carries the pile in his arms to the bridge. He stares into the empty necks and flattened sleeves of the rompers. They were washed and folded, readied for a lost time, a lost world. He shudders.

He squats at the center of the plank and raises a pale blue nightgown trimmed with silk bows. He drops it. The nightgown rides the flow, twisting, sinking as it disappears along the ditch. He drops a bonnet. Then stockings. He releases Joey's things, one piece at a time, to float in the brown murk and stands to watch the procession slip into the tunnel. When he sets the plastic soles of the last pair of booties on the surface, he whispers, "At least you're not in the ground. Good-bye, Baby Blue." The booties rush off and flip over. The knit tops soak with scum, but the white plastic shines in the sun. Daron jumps off the plank and follows them along the Nelson side of the ditch, where Berma's flower beds will not get in his way. He races the booties to the roadside, where they are swallowed by the dark. Crossing the asphalt, he climbs onto the protruding pipe to watch the shrinking oval soles as they trace watery curves toward the stand of distant trees.

Daron: 4

For a long time, as Daron sits on the corrugated pipe incising the water's surface with the heels of his sneakers, he expects to hear approaching sirens. One car passes while he waits; he feels the vibration in his thighs, and pebbles tap against his back as the station wagon roars by. But he sees no lights or the high-speed flash of black-and-white vehicles on the road from town. It is still morning; Sacrament Meeting has not let out; Sterling is resting. He wonders what Berma has done, whether JuLee has told her what happened, whether she has called anyone. But as he watches the submerged tips of overhanging grass extend, then snap back against the current, he forgets.

He needs to tell his mother about the school in Salt Lake; he wants to go, and he hopes she will understand. His thoughts drift from the baby upstairs until he catches himself, chastised. He doesn't want to ignore and forget.

A heavy thud reverberates from the direction of the house, and Daron climbs to his feet on the crumbling edge of the asphalt. He scans the curtained windows, but they reject his attention along with the sun. He runs across the front lawn to the wooden porch steps and climbs them on their extreme edge to avoid the sagging, creaking center. Sliding beneath the screen, he opens the door. "Berma? Are you okay?" His low voice disappears into the hall; there is no answer. His eyes adjust to the dark; he sees the metal fingerplate on the swinging kitchen door. But he cannot move forward into the house. Mixed with the ticking pendulum of the hall clock, he hears a thin, irregular squeak. He looks behind him at the dry grass and the old stumps of the elms that once lined the road. He knows he shouldn't be in the house; he should have left when Berma asked. He jumps from the end of the porch and dashes around the side.

He skirts the bank of the ditch and lands both feet on the plank bridge before he dares to look back. On the patio next to the picnic table, Skunk lies curled around a canvas backpack printed with summer camouflage. The skin of both his arms is scraped in little smudges to reveal fiercer blood-dotted pink beneath. A black bruise swells his forehead. Chalky dust shrouds his jeans and T-shirt. He is motionless.

Daron starts carefully across the bridge. "I fell off the roof. We were up there behind the chimney, watching you. The angel and me. But I fell." Daron continues moving. "Hey, Daron, can you help me up?"

Daron doesn't turn. He plants one foot in the Nelsons' lush grass.

The bridge shudders like an elastic, and Skunk flies forward. He snags his fingers into the collar of Daron's shirt. Falling, Daron tenses, but there is no impact. Brown water churns over his head; he chokes and closes his eyes. He struggles to breathe, to lift his head higher than his knees, while Skunk's hands fish for him, nibbling at his clothes. Skunk finds a hold under Daron's arm and hauls him to the surface. He gasps and coughs water, then thrashes against Skunk's stomach, kicking wildly. "Go easy, son. I just fell off a roof, remember."

Skunk wades into the canal with one arm hooked around Daron's shoulder and the other crooked between Daron's legs. Mud stings in Daron's eyes as he tries to scratch Skunk's face. His hands claw air. Skunk twists Daron's body and hurls him onto the lawn.

He clutches at the sod with his face buried in the damp. Water spurts from his nose when he coughs; water seeps from his hair and down his cheeks to drip from his lips. He arches his neck to locate the flight of steps to Berma's rooms. He can run for it. He scrambles, his legs disobeying, his sneakers squishing and slipping on the matted slick of grass.

Skunk tackles him, dragging him down to earth again. His cheeks compress under the crush of Skunk's chest and release a spray of spittle or blood. He moans. "Stop! Stop!"

"You gotta be quiet, son. I got a gag for you here." Skunk pins Daron's arms behind his back and pulls down the backpack he has somehow, sometime, thrown over his shoulder. "But we've got to walk a piece, and I don't want you to get short of breath." Skunk hunts inside the pack for a frayed shoelace and ties Daron's wrists behind him. Daron's ear presses hard to the ground, and he hears the deep racing of his heart.

Skunk scoops Daron up by the armpits and sets him on his feet. "Let us go now into the hills." Skunk gathers his backpack and wraps his arm around Daron's shoulders. "Can you walk okay, son?"

Daron jerks his head to stare beyond the ditch at the house. "No looking back now. Be brave. Come on." When Skunk strides forward, Daron braces his heels. Skunk catches him as he stumbles. "You take a wrong step and you're gonna fall flat on your face."

At the edge of the vegetable garden a dirt trail begins in a broad swath of red dust then narrows quickly into a furrow, the width of two boots. It meanders along the ridge of the hill, cutting a deep channel where the rains have followed its path down the slope, and disappearing where the powdery topsoil has blown clear of the hard russet bedrock underneath. The trail ends on the bank of the gully in curls of dried mud like flakes of lavender-gray soap. It picks up again, less certainly, on the opposite hill to wind through dense scrub and cedars.

When Skunk and Daron climb out of the gully, Berma's little yellow house is visible ahead for the first time since they left the backyard. "Do you remember when we made this walk together before, son?"

Daron shuffles the stones under his shoes. His fear has melted—though it lurks, cold and solid, deeper in—and has been replaced by rage. He offers Skunk his insolent silence.

"I was sure then and I'm sure now that we can do this together. We'll show Heavenly Father that we have the resolve. We are blessed with His providence, Daron. He told me to move the truck and hide on the roof. I guess he even made Berma into an old busybody so that she would bring you to me. God has given me more chances to prove my worth than I deserve. And I've wrung my heart into a lump, a lump of gratitude, for Him. I've lacked in faith. I've made false sacrifices. My own son." Skunk's voice withers to a tenuous whine, and his sobs ripple out of him, shaking Daron. Skunk pulls the tail of his white T-shirt from his jeans to wipe his nose and eyes; he adds smears of wet and blood to the mud-specked cloth.

"He took Joey to show me that I must obey the letter of His words and not presume to understand their spirit. That's been my mistake. The angel always—always—said it was you. Your mother and you. But I cheated God, and He made me give Him Joey. And that's why we've got to be extra good today, to at least show that it's all had some meaning— Ahhh." Skunk stops in the round shade of a thickly needled cedar and grabs at the side of his shirt. "Mmm. Think I cracked a rib when I fell off the roof. God's making it hard for us, son, but we've got to be grateful. Grateful I fell off when I did. Grateful He made Cousin Berma bring us together. Let's pray for a minute." Skunk pushes Daron to his knees and clamps one hand over his skull. "Father in Heaven . . ."

The hot breeze shaving over the summit of the hill dries the water on Daron's face and neck, then begins to dry and crack the residue of mud. His skin tightens and itches. He looks along the flattening, straightening path to the abandoned house. The paint has peeled and hangs from the clapboards in long strips that wave and wobble in the gusts like pennants. Last Wednesday in class he had learned about erosion. Given time, the wind and rain will scour all trace of yellow from the wood.

Kath: Backwards

She fists the car keys and spins around her mother's kitchen like the frantic ballerina in a jewelry box. The pig with the tow-

els. The witch on the fridge. The skillet in the sink. The doughnuts on the counter. The Sunday comics spread under her father's rifle and hunting gear on the floor by the door. The long
yellow tail of the phone. Pig. Witch. Skillet. Doughnuts. Comics.
Her eyes settle there. She is laden with guilt and love. She stops
to wind time backwards onto its reel, to search the day for sense
and reason—

Six. In the morning, before she eases from the bed to the shower,
she nestles into Zach's embrace for one more kiss. Zach seals his
mouth to hers with a feather's weight, a filament's stroke.

Five. Outside her apartment, Zach throws her suitcase into the
back of the car and kisses her good-bye. He slams her door while
she buckles the seat belt. She smiles out at him as he stands in
his tanktop and sweatpants with his bare feet hanging over the
curb. He mouths words: I LOVE YOU. She rolls down the window because she wants him to say it again—What? You know
what, he says. Have a good trip. He reaches out to her window
and holds his fingers to the glass as the car slips out from under
them.

Four. On her way from Las Vegas, she stops in at Willard's Café,
and as she waits near the cash register, the lights flicker and dim
before regaining their original glare. Looks like the wind's in the
lines again, the hostess says with flat disinterest. I'll just sit at
the counter, Kath says. Menu? The hostess brandishes a sheet of
laminated plastic. Just coffee. Kath parallels her steps along the
opposite side of the bar. Have a seat then, and I'll get her for you.
She swoops through the swinging door into the kitchen. Rhonda
emerges almost immediately. She reaches over the counter to hug
Kath, then pours the coffee. When she bends over to find a
spoon, Kath notices that her hair is red. Your hair, Kath says.

Yeah, what about it? She growls—then giggles. Cut it. Dyed it. Restyled it. I'm moving to Salt Lake in a month, and I want to leave as much of the old Rhonda behind as possible. Looks good, Kath says, looks real good.

After coffee, Rhonda walks her out to the car. Whenever the breeze picks up, she grasps unconsciously for her stiff cap. As Kath unlocks the door, a dust devil skitters around the café parking lot behind Rhonda, collecting paper cups and toothpicks in its squat centrifuge like a model hurricane. Have you heard from Manuel? Rhonda holds down her apron and her cap, with her white shoes pressed close together. I don't want to, she says. She leans into the open window after Kath climbs behind the wheel. But you're lucky, Kath. You deserve good things for a change.

Three. She arrives home in Sterling and parks behind her father's pickup on the back road, then wrestles her suitcase from the back seat. She scrapes along the corridor between the weedy fence and the side of the truck toward the gate. Is that my eldest? Is that my Kath? The engine block speaks from the shade of its open hood. She creeps around to the front of the truck and finds the toes of her father's boots sticking up from the dust under the bumper. Hey Dad. What's up? He shimmies his shoulders into the light and loses his baseball cap as his head drags on the ground. Just changing the oil. Didn't want to spill it on the driveway. He reaches for his cap, then notices his glistening black fingers. He holds his hands out in useless talons. He has left the border between aging and old; he is old and vulnerable. So, she asks, how are things . . . you know, since I was here last . . . how have things been going? He looks away from her, squinting into the bright fields across the road. We're hanging in there, Kath. Hanging on. She nods, crushed by the sadness he will never express and cannot release. Know what, he says, haven't even seen your son yet. Got back late with the camper, then Carl and I went to church before he got up. Is he in the house? she asks. Don't think so, he says. Bring him out if you find him.

• • •

Two. She opens the gate to her parents' backyard. A wet half-moon curves on the sidewalk from the sprinkler attached to the hose. She considers leaping over the sparkling strings of water, but she might not manage it with the suitcase. She carefully sidesteps the spray. Madame rushes forward, barking madly and kicking up crystal beads from the wet grass, and Kath rushes up the back steps before the dog can swipe wet flanks against her jeans. She peers into the dark of the house. Hello? She hears rubber soles padding quickly toward her. Kath? Kath, is Daron with you? She says no, and opens the screen. Her mother emerges dim and gray from the hall. I thought you might have picked him up on your way.

Kath latches the screen door carefully behind her to prevent Madame from nudging it open with her nose and romping through the house with her muddy feet. Her mother leans from the hall; she looks winded and ashen, as if she has run from a distance and the blood has drained from her face. Daron walked to Cousin Berma's while we were at church, she says, but now Berma's on the phone saying she doesn't know where he is. I sent Carl out in the car.

I'm sure it's nothing, her mother says. Daron was supposed to wait for Berma in the apartment. But he didn't answer when she called from JuLee's, and he wasn't there when she walked over. He's probably on his way home right now. Kath leaves her suitcase by the table, drops her keys and purse on the counter, and walks around the bar for a drink of water. She asks, is something up with JuLee? Her mother leaves the threshold of the hall and follows her into the kitchen. She doesn't answer, and after Kath fills a glass at the sink, she meets her mother's red-rimmed eyes. Oh Kath, she says. It's awful.

Kath asks, what is? She sets the water glass on the counter, prepared to hear her mother's interpretation of what Cousin Berma said. They found Joey, her mother says. He's dead. Horrible. She covers her mouth, bending at the waist. Her mother says she can't understand how it happened. They love that child, she says. Her mother rests her hand on Kath's shoulder. She whispers, You don't think there could be trouble with Daron? Kath says nothing, shuts her eyes, and breathes deep.

One. She hears her voice etch the air as she tells her mother to call the police. She is furious with Berma for waiting after she found Daron was missing. She shouts, There's no time! Her mother leaves the kitchen to call on the bedroom phone.

Zero. Kath shakes off her distraction and rushes for the kitchen door, for the car, but she can't stop remembering the morning with Zach, that moment, that kiss, when she could live her life on the surface of her lips.

Daron: 5

Skunk stuffs the balled-up gym sock deep into Daron's mouth and fixes its place with another shoelace tied around his head. He has pushed together the upturned crates in a low dais and arranged Daron on top with his legs trussed ankle-to-ankle, his arms bound behind him. Daron's finger fits into the cracks where the crates meet under his back, and he traces the cross at the intersection of four crates compulsively. He stares up at the warped ceiling, knitted with cobwebs, and at a round hole—a porthole—gleaming with brilliant blue sky. His jaw aches from the sock; a thread dangles into the opening of his throat and gags him, tickling.

He thinks it might be better to be sleeping or lost in thought-less fear. But he thinks on and on and on. He will not escape on his own. If Berma comes out to find him, he doesn't know what she could do. She might come too late. When he pictures Berma swinging open the loose hinges of the door, he cannot imagine himself inside. Inside, Baby Blue lies stilled in his bassinet. Inside, Aunt Ina's head dents her pillow, gaunt and spectral. Inside, the ancient woman in his uncle's basement curls her pitted skull to her knees.

While Skunk roots in his pack on the floor, Daron traces the grooves: up-down, left-right; up-down, left-right; up, left, down, right. The mummy woman might have been young when she died from fever or disease. She might have been hidden in the rock for centuries. Or for much less time. She might have been a fur trader's squaw, bought with pelts, shot through the head when she grew tiresome, and stuffed out of sight. Daron traces the splintering edges. Don't let me die, he thinks. Please don't let me die. Please. He fires his pleas up the hole to the sky like the thought balloons in comics, not knowing whether there is a god to hear them, not knowing whether telepathy exists, not knowing any certainty except that these prayers are the only messages he can send.

"I will not hurt you," Skunk says. He flips the cap on a squirt-can of lighter fluid and aims the stream at the floor around the crates. "The angel will come unto me and take the knife from my hand—you must trust in God's power, Daron—and then I'll free your bonds." Daron watches the fluid spray from the can and spread its acrid sting through the air. "They won't understand my actions in this world, son. See, there's nothing I could say about Joey to worldly people. My exaltation will not come in this world. I'm being called on to glory in the celestial kingdom. My duties are there. So when the angel comes, I'll be the ram. I'll go." Skunk squirts the rest of the can onto the piles of dried leaves and scraps of paper blown into corners. "If I could spare you this hurt, son, I would. But Abraham couldn't switch his old gray chest for Isaac's, and I can't either. It's not our covenant."

Skunk throws the empty can with a clang into the alcove of the kitchen. He kneels by Daron's head and wipes dried blood and dust from his hands with a square of flannel. He unsheathes his hunting knife. "In the name of Jesus Christ and by the power of the priesthood I hold, I bless this blade. May this knife serve You, Lord, and may I be strong and pure enough to carry out Your will." Skunk squeezes both fists around the handle and steadies the shaft above Daron. "Heavenly Father, I offer this boy—my first, my spiritual son—unto You."

The point pricks flesh in the hollow of Daron's throat. He rolls his eyes to avoid looking at the shaft glinting from the sun in its blue portal.

K a t h : Forward

Kath throws the car into gear, squeals the tires and sprays gravel as she pulls out from behind the truck. She shouts, Gotta go! when her father calls out from the side of the road. (You have no time. You are late. You are years too late.)

She races onto the main driveway, turns left on Main Street, honks at the motor home creeping into town ahead. Honk. Honk. Honk. Flooring the accelerator, she flips across the double yellow line into the left lane. She ignores the shudder of the little Toyota motor as she slams the car back to the right in front of the motor home. The pens and maps and snack wrappers slide along the dashboard and scatter to the floor. (Bastard. Bastard. You led Merrill to your sister. You fed him Daron and JuLee and Joey. Fed him is the right word. He is a cannibal. But you are guilty. You have allowed yourself to forget.)

She swerves left—signals, too late—in front of the red Volkswagen, which screeches its brakes—onto the post office road. The construction paper butterflies taped to the windows of the Slumber Bee Day Care Center flash colors for an instant in the corner of her eye. She takes the first long curve, hugs the inner edge of the road, grinds the gravel. (You are guilty. You could have stopped him. You could have ended him. And what stopped you? The angel? Then the angel is a sign of cowardice. Fuck the angel. No excuse.)

She banks to either side of the road, left or right, whichever is faster. (Don't think about the speed. Don't worry that you are not in control.) She jerks the wheel to the right to avoid smashing into Mr. DeSoto and his grandson on horseback. (Don't look at their fear, the surprise in their eyes.) She floors it. (It's no excuse. You are guilty. Daron. Oh please, Daron, no. You bastard. Fucker. Fucker. Fuck.)

She searches for the house, small, yellow, on a rise. (That hill—no, that one.) She hits the brakes and holds her breath as she heaves forward into the strap of the seat belt. Before she gets out of the car, she reaches back between the bucket seats, searching with her fingers. (Fucker. Cannibal. He doesn't have a soul. He won't be forgiven. You won't let him be forgiven. You won't give him the chance. Daron, please be alive, please be, please.)

Daron: 6

This is the edge.

Daron dies. The pain tears itself apart like a sheet of ripped cotton—instantly absent; for pain is life—and under the pain—under it all along—is the bright white. White, intense, unvaried eternity. And there are no bodies, no sighs, no scent of gas or roses. There are no robes, and there are no rivers, and there are no scales to weigh the beating of a billion silenced hearts.

Or Daron doesn't die. An angel, a thought in the shape of an angel, turns the knife in Skunk's hand. The blade drops to the ground. The blade severs Skunk's aorta. And Daron's breath is his first breath. The minutes start at zero.

And, on the edge, Daron remembers the ice. He will never be warm. The ice will melt inside him always, dripping down his veins like the bloodrush in the arm pinned under his waist. He closes his eyes because he can no longer stand to watch the future sway, giddy, on the edge of the knife.

He hears Skunk jump to his feet. His boots stamp over the floorboards. The knife falls—hilt down—onto the crate at Daron's side. "Kath!" Skunk shouts out the door. "It's happened! The angel called out, and I turned my head, and you were coming up the path. Don't you see? It's over. Thank you, God. No, Kath, it's over!"

By wriggling his shoulders and tilting his head, Daron can see Skunk framed in bright sun just outside the door. Skunk holds his hands out, his palms up. "It's over."

The noise, in the tiny room, is absurdly loud—thunder in a bucket—and, as the report dies from the air, it continues to sting Daron's ears. Fragments of Skunk keep flying—blood drops, knots of skin, burnt cloth—in a swarm of flesh, while his body blows back to crash against the floor. His arms squiggle senselessly over his head through a fan of blood as bright as spray paint on the dusty boards. From the top of his chest to his hips, Skunk has been mauled, chewed-over, chain sawed; the soaked tatters of his shirt mingle interchangeably with shreds of flayed skin. As his body stills, the rising blood is thick, nearly black— the sign of a gut shot; Skunk taught Daron the tracker's blood signs on Cousin Berma's porch last summer. In the emptied doorway, his mother stands holding his grandfather's rifle with its barrel drooping to the ground.

"Daron?" She squints into the house, a few feet away from the door. Her eyes avoid looking down at Skunk. Daron can't shout back, but he pounds his heels against the crate.

She throws the gun aside and comes for him. She steps around the bulk of Skunk, skidding on crimson. "Baby. Oh God, baby."

She pulls the shoelace over his head—snagging his ears—and rips the wet sock from his mouth. He coughs, and she cradles his head.

When she finishes untying Skunk's knots and he is free, she hugs him tightly. He closes his eyes and imagines that they are already somewhere else. His mother takes his hand. "Let's go." But he shrugs away and fishes his fingers into Skunk's backpack. He knows she will not be free to leave. Skunk was unarmed, he did not threaten her, and she killed him. They need to complete Skunk's plan. He finds the book of kitchen matches and begins to strike them and throw them around the floor and onto the crates. The room fills with yellow; yellow reflects on the wet floorboards. He tosses the matchbox into the flames. "Okay." He jumps out, over the hulk in the threshold, into the sand. His mother shifts Skunk's legs inside and closes the door. "Okay," she says. He tells her, "Take the gun."

They run along the path to the road together. He hobbles, thinking that the laces have put his feet to sleep, until he tumbles over in pain. He sits in the weeds and carefully rolls up the mud-crusted leg of his jeans to see the blood; a small piece of shot must have pierced his calf. But his mother isn't looking. She has turned to watch the yellow walls as fire takes them, and the black smoke, which curls up from under the eaves. "Look, look." She locks her fingers behind her head. Out of the cloud of black smoke, from the open circle in the roof, a pillar of gray—near white—streams up. When the pillar meets the gusting breeze, the gray bends and spreads, like a great bird tugging its long tail from the hole in Berma's house. His mother sinks to her knees in the center of the path and sweeps a circle through the dust around her as she weeps.

Daron: 7

They hear others approach: sirens and the crunch of tires in one direction—voices and boots scuffing loose stones in the other. They bury the rifle in the loose sandy soil under a clump of sage. His mother scrapes a trench with the gun barrel while he scoops dust from the shallow hole with a flat rock. The air is sticky with the oil of melting tar shingles, and, for a moment, they are protected in an alcove, a cul-de-sac, of smoke and gust-born debris. His mother fits the gun in, and they kick soil and rocks over the gray metal and burnished wood. When the smoke thins and Uncle Carl climbs from the gully, his mother squeezes Daron to her side.

Carl inches uncertainly into the smoke with his eyes lowered to pick out the path in the dirt. When he looks up and sees them, he stops short; he asks if they are okay. His mother nods, slowly, and Carl stuffs his hands in the pocket of his jeans. He doesn't ask what happened; he doesn't meet their eyes again, as if a scrim of smoke still obscures his vision. Daron senses a different pall surrounding them; they are descending—new-formed—from another world and have not yet touched earth.

More people arrive: Joe Nelson, some of his daughters, Mr. DeSoto and his grandson, then Daron's grandfather and grandmother. They all stand a few feet behind Carl. For the moment, he and his mother are untouchable. The shades of men—firemen, policemen—shift behind them to the house, leaving them unnoticed in the smoke. Then Berma comes, puffing, up the hill from the gully. She steps around his grandmother on the hillside and reaches out to embrace them, crushing him even more tightly to his mother. "Thank God," she says. "Thank you, God."

As if under a broken spell, the others surge forward before Berma lets him go. They all want to touch them, to bring them at last to ground. His grandmother hugs him and kisses him—repeatedly—on the forehead; she chips away flakes of dry mud from his cheeks with her fingernails. His grandfather pats his shoulder. Mr. DeSoto tousles his hair. And they all ask questions. His mother doesn't answer them. Her eyes drift slightly aside of whichever face addresses her; she hums low in response. Daron tells them that Skunk took him to the yellow house, tied him up, then untied him and threw him out the door before throwing the match. His grandfather leads him down the path to an RV trailer parked beyond the fire trucks on the post office road. His leg has begun to throb and his sock squishes with blood inside his sneakers, but he cannot cry out or let the pain show on his face because the gun never fired; he has no wound. His grandfather sits with him in the trailer's kitchenette—his mother is taken into the bedroom—and someone brings him lemonade. They offer him oxygen, but he shakes his head. He tells his story again to a policeman.

He glances anxiously along the narrow hall to the closed bedroom door; he hopes his mother will remember not to contradict his story. Once, while he describes the shoelace around his wrists, he hears his mother call, "Daron! Where's Daron?" The door opens a few inches, and his grandmother peers out. "He's fine. He's with your father and Sergeant Myers," she says, shutting the door. Outside, an ambulance parks with its rear doors open to the trail; two men in white smocks unroll a black zippered bag onto a stretcher and carry it up the hill.

His mother hugs him close in the police car on the way to the hospital in Alma. "I shouldn't have let you come here. I shouldn't have let you leave me."

"It's okay, Mom. It's not your fault." She rubs his cheek until it becomes sticky and hot. He wants to sit up and push across the seat to a cooler space by the window, but he knows that any movement apart would upset her, and he doesn't dare. His grandfather, in front with the officer, looks at them unreadably through the ventilated glass.

In the emergency room, they are separated again for examinations, and as he follows the nurse down the corridor, he expects his mother to break from her doctor's guiding arm and come flying to his side. He turns, but she has vanished behind one of the tan doors. The nurse leads him into a white cubicle and asks him to sit on the flat, cold examination table; he feels drained, limp, as if the room's colorless paint and chrome were themselves anesthetic. The nurse tries to help him with his shoes, but he insists on untying them himself. When she lifts her hands out of his way, there are red spots on her fingers. He searches for signs of shock or disapproval in her face, but she offers no reaction. She works every day in a place of bloodied, ruptured bodies, and she couldn't know that his wound is meant to be secret; his leg holds no surprises for her. She asks him to lie down. Before he finishes adjusting the dense foam pillow under his head, the nurse has sliced into his jeans with heavy shears.

With great difficulty, he attempts to devise an explanation for the gunshot, but nothing seems feasible; his ideas are too baroque for credibility—because truth can be complex, but lies must be simple. The doctor storms in, with a clipboard, grinning, and quickly examines the wound. The nurse dabs at his leg with a sponge while the doctor sorts through a pan of instruments. As the doctor steadies his leg and yanks, the pain is suddenly intense. "Look at the size of this splinter, kiddo. Bigger than your leg almost." He holds up a diamond chip of blood-soaked wood at the end of long, narrow tweezers. "Looks like a three stitch job. You up for it?"

Daron nods, so relieved that the thought of stitches holds no fear; he must have scraped his leg against the crates or the plank bridge. He closes his eyes to the queasy, blinkless light from the ceiling panels; he unclenches his fists.

In another room, he rests on a cot in order to convince the doctor that he shows no signs of smoke inhalation or heat prostration or whatever unnamed malady they might suspect. His grandfather shifts his vigilance nervously from his room to his mother's down the hall. With his cap pulled low, he sits by

Daron's cot, reading a *Field and Stream,* when Carl and his grandmother appear in the corridor. Their eyes dart back to a paramedic pushing a wheeled cart on which JuLee lies immobile, strapped under a sheet. In the house she was wild; in the hall she is a tranquilized zoo animal, cloudy-eyed and listless. His grandfather rises and blocks Daron's view through the doorway; he whispers something, and his grandmother replies, "No, she was sleeping, but they thought it would be better if she came here for observation. How are they?" His grandfather mumbles something else. "We'll get her settled, then Carl can drive you all home."

Daron's mother props a pillow under his foot, then squeezes into the free space at the far end of the couch. He settles his head against the cushioned arm at his end to watch *Jason and the Argonauts* on the television in the opposite corner of the room. The picture window above the set is filled with sunburn sky, and the red deepens perceptibly as he studies it. He wishes his mother could relax; the muscles of her jaw tense rhythmically and her palms rub slowly over the jeans stretched on her thighs. It depresses him to see her distracted and fragile. He can't pay attention to the movie, he can't disappear into routine, until she rests.

His grandfather rattles through the kitchen, fixing eggs for dinner; Uncle Carl pushes a mower over the front lawn. When he rolls into the vicinity of the open window screens, Daron hears the slicing hiss of the blades. The whirring stops as Poseidon holds a passage open for the *Argo* between the clashing rocks, and Daron assumes that Carl has moved on to another part of the yard. But Carl stalks quickly through the front room into the kitchen. "The police are coming," he says beneath the slap of Poseidon's great fishy tail. Daron lifts his head to look down at his mother, but she is lost in the television—or inside her head.

Car doors slam in the driveway, and his grandfather shuffles around the couch with his hands in a dishtowel. "Kath," he says.

Her eyes are fixed.

"Kath," he says again, more harshly, and drops the towel. "The police are here."

"What for?" Daron asks. "What's wrong?" He asks, but he knows.

"We all heard the shot, Kath. And there's my gun missing. But after Daron said what he said, we all agreed not to say anything. Thought we could put an end to it." He takes her hand cautiously and helps her from the couch. "I guess Joe couldn't convince Clovis, though. Merrill is her son."

The doorbell rings; a bloated fly bumps its head against the TV screen, against the blue Aegean sky.

Kath: Ladies

Breakfast, ladies. Line up.

Hustle your butts, ladies.

Lights out, ladies. Good night.

Kath knows that the guards—Janice and Deanna and the part-time one with the spidery, broken veins on her white arms—do not use the word politely. They do not use it to restore and maintain anyone's dignity. They use it to demonstrate that they have no illusions about the character of their charges; the unsaid halves of damning phrases linger in the air: —of the evening, —of ill repute. Sluts. Whores. Bitches. Damaged goods.

However, the female guards, in their black polyester pants and regimental blouses, are more considerate than the male guards at the door to the exercise yard. To them Kath is one of the girls, barely capable of independent thought. Don't slip, girls, it's wet out. Okay, girls, put your toys down and get back to the lockup. Move it, girls.

Janice, at least, will speak to her without a tone of officious frostiness creeping into her voice. Each night she stands in the door of the rec room, and Kath pauses to talk to her. Janice fingers the surface of her dark brown hair, teased into a dome like a motorcycle helmet or a female Elvis pompadour, and idly rolls her minimal lipstick around her lips. Yeah, I read about it all in the paper, she says. It's a real shame. I'm not saying you should've done what you did. I can see your point, though.

Kath might inform her that she had no point. She never made a decision; she acted. But it isn't worth the effort to explain. Since that day, she has told the story and told the story and retold the story until the events have solidified into a minor drama, an anecdote, a fairy tale. She catches herself recounting the details by rote. To Janice's experienced ears, she simply sounds hardened—another one of the ladies on the ward.

Kath would like to believe that in some deep essence, at some moral molecular level, she is a good woman. She acted out of love, and she does not regret it, although its frightens her to acknowledge her lack of repentance. She killed, and lied, allowed her son to lie, and she is only sorry that afterward she lost her resolve and tried to hide what she had done. She might easily have said that she fired in self-defense; she might have curled Merrill's hand around the knife—another lie, but closer to the truth. Her lawyer encourages her to avoid remorse. She says, You did what any mother would have done.

Tom found Erika Carlson through mutual friends, and while Kath cannot judge whether she is a good lawyer or a bad one, she is impressive. When Erika visited before the arraignment, she arrived with a huge brown oxford box from which she extracted pens, a legal pad, a tape recorder, and a thermos of herbal tea. She is six feet tall, with shoulder-length hair like highly polished copper. When she talks, she plays with three strands of turquoise beads at her throat—even over the phone Kath hears them clicking. She speaks in the measured tones of an actress, carving each syllable into individual shape. At the first meeting she explained her plans for the case, and Kath was willing to believe that she could do everything she said; Kath would be home soon.

Erika called later to explain why the judge had set the bail impossibly high. In his chambers, he informed Erika that Kath had violated two commandments: thou shalt not kill and thou shalt honor thy husband; women like her should not be free to walk the streets, he announced. Erika had explained the exceptional nature of Kath's case to him: Merrill was her ex-husband, he was a killer, Kath and her son were in immediate danger; Kath had clearly acted in defense of her child, and any court would see that. But, she told Kath, Judge Granger is a chauvinist bastard. And this is Utah, after all.

She met with Erika Carlson in a featureless room occupied by a table and two chairs—exactly like the room in her mind. She became queasy after they locked the door and she sat in the stillness waiting for Erika to appear—queasy with the sense that her life had been leading up to her presence in this room. And now it no longer comforts her to retreat to the room in her mind, with its simple table and simple chairs. It has become a fragment of prison lodged inside her head.

She wonders what she is made of now.

While Kath waits her turn at the phone, she looks into the study room next door. It is a slow time. Dinner is over, and most of the women are in the rec room, watching television. A few women slump in the padded chairs under the windows, reading thick paperback best-sellers, and Rella has spread her sticker books out on one of the tables at the back. Rella is the only lady of the ward who talks to Kath.

One night Kath had watched Rella with her books, fascinated by her self-absorption. When Rella noticed Kath, she waved her over to view her collection. Her friends and family send stickers in the mail, and Rella carefully files them in their appropriate places. The red book is organized according to subject: teddy bears, flowers, unicorns. The smaller blue book is divided into sections for individual artists and companies: "Peanuts," Boyntons, Mrs. Grossmans—distinctions Kath would not have conceived. Rella slips the stickers into transparent plastic pouches like photographs or rare stamps. Rather than peeling away the backing, she trims the waxy, excess paper from the edges of each with embroidery scissors. She allowed Kath to help cut out one of the figures, although she insisted on completing the sticker's more intricate outlines herself.

Cinderella Vane Dobson is nineteen. She was caught holding the door at an electronics store while her boyfriend loaded boxes of VCRs into the back of his van. Earlier, she spent a lot of time in juvenile detention for shoplifting. Rella's mother is black; she isn't sure about her father. Her skin has the tone and shine of toffee, and her hair twists into blunt dreads like the stubs of fat cigars. She graduated from high school; she was a B student—a fact she is especially proud of because she was also raising two children: a boy, three, and a girl, eighteen months. Her mother looks after them. Her mother wants to be declared the children's legal guardian because she believes Rella is hopelessly irresponsible. But Rella refuses to give up her children without a fight.

Kath struggles not to think of JuLee when she talks to Rella; they are the same age, and they both seem to float in their own distant orbit—jaded and innocent. JuLee remains in the hospital, and Kath sent her a letter. From one institution to another. JuLee hasn't answered.

Kath waves from the study-room door, and Rella calls her over. Kath checks the availability of the phone again before she enters and sits across the table. Rella holds out a long strip of stickers. Look, she says, Daffy Duck.

Great, Kath says. She watches Rella study the tiny pictures for a moment in taut silence; her son is the only other person she knows who has such intensity of concentration. I've been meaning to ask you, what was your mother thinking when she picked your name?

What? Rella responds blankly. She snips carefully around individual tail feathers.

I mean Cinderella is kind of unusual.

And what about you, Kath*Leen,* she says, still cutting. What happened when they named you, girl? Did the shift key get stuck on that hospital typewriter?

I didn't mean to criticize. Kath is less chastened than curious to learn how Rella knew her name. She asks, How did you know how it was spelled?

Saw it somewhere. In your file.

You saw my file?

Sure.

Kath doesn't ask when and where she saw her file; she accepts that she has no secrets left. I'd better go make my call, she says.

The phone is unoccupied, but as she digs her phone card from her pocket, she glances anxiously along the hall to make certain none of her intimidating cellmates is preparing to muscle in front of her.

She leaves a brief, cheery message on Zach's answering machine. He wanted to fly in to be closer to her, but she insisted he stay in California. She must be released from her old life before she can see him again. She hangs up, then dials her parents' number and waits without breathing until Daron answers the phone.

It's Mom, she says. How are you doing?

I'm okay, he says. After a pause, he asks, How are you?

I'm fine. She strives to sound carefree; she will spare Daron from further pain if she can. It's boring, but the food is better than you'd think. Better than school lunch.

That's not hard. His voice sounds young and small.

Tell me what you did today. What's going on?

Berma's moving back to her old house. She and her sister got in a fight about it, but Berma wouldn't back down.

Good for her, she says, and leans against the slick, cool wall. What else is up?

Daron talks about visiting JuLee, and buying comic books, and talking to his father, and while his voice fills her head, she forgets. She forgets the painted cinderblock and one-way glass. She forgets Merrill, and Merrill's body, and the smoke.

While Daron is telling her something about his summer school in Salt Lake, Kath interrupts him. I care about you very much, baby. You know that.

He doesn't speak. Perhaps she frightens him with the fierceness of her devotion, but she cannot tolerate his silence. You know that, don't you?

Sure, he says slowly. I love you, Mom.

It is what she hoped to hear, and it is too much. She reels with longing for her son. I love you too, honey. I'll be home soon, I promise.

I miss you.

Me too, she says, then says good-bye, and feels her heartbeats rebound against the walls of the empty corridor.

Her love opens cracks, and when she stretches against the wall in her cot after lights out, Kath feels the weight of her days revisit her. Her happy childhood marred by streaks of anxiety and disappointment. Her Wild Summer with Tom swathed in a nimbus of confusion and fractured light. Her marriage to Merrill soaked in a ten-year crimson stain. And through layers of years like a hole stabbed through successive folds of heavy fabric, the angel unsheaths its wings. And whose angel was it? Merrill was convinced that the angel spoke in a secret tongue for him alone, that the angel was a telephone from God's breath to his ear. But the angel might have been her own testament. When it cried yellow roses, it might have come from the future with tomorrow's sorrow stinging its eyes. The pain she felt that night in the garden has found its source in her at last, in the ache of love and loss.

But from the burning house, from Merrill's bubbling flesh, from an integument of flame, the angel wrenched itself; and she watched it soar, free of the earth, free of its duty as witness, free to find its home far from the intoxication of human love and the wounds of human misery.

• • •

Daron: 8

Daron slumps in the back seat with his head wedged between the cushion of the bench seat and the padded wall by the window. In his skewed position, the lap belt digs into his stomach and the shoulder harness saws at his neck, but he feels too inert to sit upright. He is hot and sticky; the sun blares fierce into the passenger side of the car. The other half of the seat looks temptingly shaded and cool, but a move would require shifting the three-layer birthday cake, which Aunt PearLeen has elaborately packaged to take to the prison for Uncle Doug. Daron can't find the energy for the maneuver. If he did change places with cake, Aunt PearLeen would fret about melted frosting for the rest of the trip.

Daron is used to riding in compact, utilitarian Japanese cars or scruffy pickups with Indian blanket seat covers and cracked dashboards. Aunt PearLeen's Cadillac is the largest, most luxuriant car he has ever sat in—a vast rectangular space that he imagines as a houseboat floating on a lake or a cabin strapped to the underside of a dirigible.

Although his grandmother sits behind the steering wheel, Aunt PearLeen twitches and flutters, working invisible pedals with her feet, and staring with fixity at the road ahead. She will take the car to the supermarket but would never consider driving on the freeway for hundreds of miles. Uncle Doug does the distance driving, and he was not an option for this journey. Daron's grandfather was not an option either, because someone needs to stay home in case they decide to release JuLee from the hospital, and his grandmother has made it her personal duty to accompany Daron to visit his mother.

He had been told that his mother would be in jail overnight. Then she was transferred north for obscure, jurisdictional reasons, and he was told she would be free in a week. When he spoke to his mother's lawyer on the telephone, and she told him brightly that she was working night and day on the case and his mother would be home in a matter of days, Daron did not allow himself to depend on the news, to rejoice.

He knows that when she does get out, she will likely not be allowed to leave the state, which probably means they will be moving back to Sterling. He dreads it. A school bus leaves Sterling at seven in the morning on a forty-five-minute drive, with stops in two other towns, to the middle school in Alma. There is no gifted program, no Tammy Montez in Doc Martens.

When he mentioned his apprehension to his grandmother she said, "It's a good school. Your mom and your aunt and uncle went there." When he mentioned it to Berma she said, "You poor dear," and hugged him. He never told his mother about the school in Salt Lake, and now he can't. When he speaks to his father and Artie, they are careful not to mention it, not to burden him, and he doesn't know if the deadline has passed, if their plan is still an option.

In a furtive fantasy, he dreams that he and his mother will move to Salt Lake, next door to Tom and Artie, and he will go to the private school, and his mother's case will be dismissed, and he will have three parents and be happy. But he doubts his dreams and denies himself the pleasure of greater speculation. He feels vaguely ashamed for thinking ahead at all; he can't consider the reality of his future until the present becomes reasonable and recognizable again.

For some time he hasn't paid attention to the conversation across the front seat. His grandmother has wandered from arrangements for the Sterling fall flower show to possible topics for Relief Society classes and back again, with Aunt PearLeen unable to concentrate from the stress of her autonomic driving. But when his great-aunt speaks out sharply, Daron turns to her, away from the spare dryness of the heart of Utah hurtling by the windows.

"Why did you pick me, his sister, to be the first person you tell?"

"Someone has to be the first."

"If you want to know what I think, I think you're a fool. How are you going to pay your way in the world?"

"There will be half of the retirement plan, and I can work. I worked for my father."

"You worked for your father for two years, and that was part time, and you set your own hours. And that was thirty-five years ago."

"I'll manage. I think it's important not to be false about these things, about marriage, about love."

"Then why did you wait so long?"

"It's not an easy thing. I don't deny that. Last summer I almost did it . . . but I'm even more certain about it now. It's best for him too, you know, although he might not see it yet."

"I don't see how you can just shrug off a marriage like that. Will you stop going to church?"

"I don't believe I have done anything wrong, PearLeen. There are worse things than separation or divorce. I can't count the number of times you've worn your sunglasses in church or kept your coat on and your hands hidden in your pockets. Do you think God approves of what Doug does to you?"

PearLeen stops driving and stares out the passenger window. "Oh look, is that a new shopping center up there on the hill? I don't remember that being here." Aunt PearLeen pulls one of her embroidered handkerchiefs from her purse and folds down the mirror on the back of the sun guard. She pats around her eyes with a tip of cloth. "So, you'll ask him to leave?"

"He can have the house. Perhaps Kath and I can find something together."

Daron weighs this idea. He loves his grandmother, he supposes, but he can't tell her the things he tells Berma, or his father and Artie, or his mother. But if it means they could live in Salt Lake, if they could live anywhere but Sterling, he would gladly accept it.

There are things he won't tell anyone. He hasn't told anyone
about the nightmares. When he wakes in the dark, he covers his
mouth and hopes he hasn't shouted in the night. In the dream, they
lower the baby in a shoebox into the ditch, and the box rocks from
side to side as it plunges down the canal. He can't tell whether the
water is choppy or the baby is struggling to open the lid, and he
wants someone to stop it, to fish the box out and check. But they
are all walking toward the house; they have all gone inside.

He tells himself that the nightmares will disappear. He con-
vinces himself not to worry because they are just his mind's way
of settling his fears. Then he recognizes that every sensation he
will ever have will come with a similar explanation attached, like
a washing-instruction tag. Each intense, unique emotion will be
accompanied by the deflating knowledge that this feeling is a
part of life, understandable, and temporary. It hurts him to think
that his life may not allow him any permanence.

His leg itches around the stitches—which he assumes is a
good sign of life in the skin. He crosses his ankle over his knee
and rolls up his pants. He peels back the strip of surgical tape
and lifts the cotton gauze. The wound is healing, but he hopes
that there will be a small scar left behind as a memory.

When they pass the state penitentiary at the Point of the Mountain, PearLeen waves at Uncle Doug, hidden somewhere among
the low ugly buildings and miles of wire fence. His grandmother
keeps driving another fifteen or twenty miles north into the heart
of Salt Lake City. As they ride across town on a broad street
packed with urban traffic, Daron arranges his stereo headphones, his book, and his notepad in his sack. He looks ahead
through the windshield and asks, "Did you get reservations at a
hotel somewhere?"

"Downtown," his grandmother replies. "I'd like to walk
around the temple grounds this afternoon. Would that be all
right, PearLeen?"

Aunt PearLeen nods, engrossed in maneuvering her phantom car through the heavy traffic.

They pass downtown and continue east into the foothills, toward the university. His grandmother scans a fragment of pen scrawl on the flap of a pink envelope. The streets become familiar. He asks, "Where are we going?"

"I think you should stay with your father. Until your mother can take care of you. I think it's only right."

"But . . . " He is speechlessly surprised, delighted but shocked. His grandmother has never disguised her disapproval.

"I know you're aware, Daron, that I didn't believe this before . . . but the situation is different now."

As the Cadillac strains up the tree-lined avenue, he spots La Casa Pequeña, with its windows and door making a face above a collar of blooming flower beds, and he shouts for his grandmother to stop. They park on the street, and he gathers his gear. His grandmother hoists the suitcases from the trunk, and they walk together over the grassy divider onto the front walk. Aunt PearLeen stands by the car with both hands folded over the clasp of her purse; she looks determinedly away from the house, down the sidewalk.

Artie answers his grandmother's knock in a T-shirt and cutoffs. He beams behind the grid of the screen door and shouts over his shoulder, "It's Daron!"

His father dashes, shirtless, the length of the house, throws his arms around Artie, and looks over his shoulder. When Tom sees Daron's grandmother, he quickly drops his hands from Artie, out of sight. "Mrs. Miller," he says. "Please come in." Artie opens the screen.

"We're late at the hotel. Our reservations." She positions the suitcase with finality on the porch. "I'll call you later about picking Daron up for the visit," she concludes in her clipped, all-business voice.

The air tightens, shrink-wrapped, around them, and when the phone rings in its shrine, Daron is eager to escape and answer it.

"I'll get it!" he shouts, and nudges past his father and Artie in the doorway.

When he answers, the woman asks, "Is this four-four-six . . . Daron, is that you?"

"Yeah," he replies uncertainly.

"Hey, baby, it's your mom." His mother gulps excited air. "I've got great news, Daron. They're letting me out."

"When?" he asks, his skin full of pins. In the Chagall poster on the wall ahead, the bride floats, bent like a boomerang, up into swirling air.

"Tomorrow, I think. Would you tell everyone? I have to call my lawyer back right away, then I'll call tonight with the details. Love you." Her voice clicks off in his ear.

His mother's call disorients him. He knows that by the time he reaches the front door to convey the news, he will be elated. But as he steps around pillows and newspaper spread on the floor of the room, he feels his thoughts in transition: his old life with his mother in Las Vegas seems long ago, and his new life with her in a different home waits beyond the door, beyond the afternoon, yet to begin.

He looks through the screen at Artie and Tom, who have moved outside, and at his grandmother, who is halfway down the walk. He calls her back and steps out to the porch as she returns to stand beneath him. He repeats what his mother said. "Terrific!" Artie shouts, and his father hugs Daron close.

His grandmother squeezes his arm, then turns without speaking, and Daron waits with the men, prepared to watch her to stride away toward Aunt PearLeen, who has returned to sit in the car, her face averted. But his grandmother lingers with her head lowered toward the border of California poppies, intensely orange. "Be good to my grandson." She doesn't meet his father's eyes, but when she says it, she smiles.